The man was a bad sport and a poor loser, but she hadn't expected this...

The swift beat of the pounding hooves tore through the crowd, the yells of the men in the stands drowning out the screams of the jockeys and mounts. Horses pushed at each other, nipped at flanks.

Positions were changed, challenges faced. The cries of the onlookers rose in a fevered pitch, but the riders heard nothing. They felt the wind whipping at their clothing, their skin. They felt the challenge of the next turn, the demand of the other racers. To do their best, to win, to show a good sport, and to succeed. Most of all—to ride.

The last turn reared close ahead. Master Greg needed no encouragement to take it. He flew ahead, well-groomed hooves throwing dirt and dust onto the riders behind him.

Reed pushed his stallion into the roan's wide and muscular flank. Reed's horse stumbled, but regained his footing. Reed forced the pressure onto the young jockey.

A.H. was trapped against the rail, his riding boots doing nothing to protect the delicate skin of his knee as it ground against the rough wood. His only option would be to slow. Not for him, but for his mount who had to have taken some damage.

A.H. ripped at the reins, forcing Master Greg to slow. He came in third, behind Reed and a white mare named Glory. Coming to a stop away from the others A.H. jumped from the saddle and almost fell. Small hands went to a blood-red knee.

Alex Hollister was always one step ahead of the rumor mongers. As the reclusive A.H., she was a successful horse breeder, an unbeatable jockey, and a savvy businessman. As the fair Alexis, she was a demure and proper lady. Her life was exactly how she wanted it, and her plans were finally ready to be enacted. Everything was running smoothly until her temper landed her in a marriage with a man who didn't want her, a man who could ruin everything she had worked so hard to achieve.

Marcus Clifton wanted nothing more than to outlive the falsehoods that had ruined his family's reputation. He had worked hard to get back into the good graces of the elite and had even arranged a marriage that would make the past rumors disappear altogether. He thought he finally had everything that was important to him. Then his cozy and disciplined life came to a crashing halt when an act of uncontrolled temper ended in a marriage with a woman who could destroy it all.

pense, a number of clever surprises, and marvelous characters you won't easily forget, *The Infamous A. H.* should hold a place of honor on any bookshelf. ~ *Regan Murphy, The Review Team of Taylor Jones & Regan Murphy*

Author's Note

The Year 1800

Political

Napoleon establishes himself as First Consul in the Tuileries. In 1799, he pushed for peace, but when England and Austria rejected his proposal, he took his army across the still-snow-covered Alps to attack Austria's forces in Italy. On June 14, 1800, he defeated them at the Battle of Marengo.

The French Army defeats the Turks at Heliopolis and advances on Cairo; defeats Austrians at Biberach, Hochstadt, and Hohenlinden; and advances on Vienna.

The US federal offices are moved from Philadelphia to Washington, DC.

Thomas Jefferson wins the US Presidential Election.

Religious

Cardinal Barnaba Chiaramonti is elected as Pope Pius VII.

Science and Medicine

William Herschel discovers the existence of infrared solar rays.

Royal College of Surgeons was founded in London.

Allessandro Volta produces electricity from a cell—first battery of zinc and copper plates.

Technology and Growth

Eli Whitney makes muskets with interchangeable parts.

Everyday Life and Advancement

Letter Post is introduced in Berlin.

Robert Owen (1771-1853) takes over New Lanark Mills and starts social Reform.

Bill Richmond (1763-1829), a former slave, becomes one of the first popular boxers.

The Arts/Music
Boieldieu LeCalife de Bagdad, opera, Paris

Cherubini Les Deux Journees (The water carrier), opera, Paris

Nicola Piccini, Italian composer, Gluck's rival in Paris, dies.

The Arts/Theater
Thomas Morton's *Speed the Plough* comedy in which Mrs. Grunby appears.

The Arts/Literature
Maria Edgeworth's *Castle Rocrent*, Gothic Novel

Jean Paul's *Titan*, German Novel

The Infamous A. H.

Dawn Chandler

A Black Opal Books Publication

GENRE: HISTORICAL ROMANCE/ROMANTIC SUSPENSE/REGENCY
ROMANCE

THE INFAMOUS A. H.
Copyright © 2017 by Dawn Chandler
Cover Design by Dawn Chandler
All cover art copyright © 2017
All Rights Reserved
Print ISBN: 978-1-626948-37-2

First Publication: DECEMBER 2017

Published by Black Opal Books http://www.blackopalbooks.com

DEDICATION

To all the fathers who love, and support, their children.

Whether you are dad through blood, marriage,
or otherwise, you deserve much appreciation.
And to those dads who didn't have to be,
you deserve the world.

For my dad. Thank you for always being there for me. Thank you for
helping to turn me into the person that I am.

For my papa. Thank you for stepping up to be
the father that I needed.
You both will always be loved and greatly missed.

Chapter 1

Paddington, England, fourteen miles from London, March 1800:

I am betrothed."

Alex Hollister nearly swallowed her tongue. She gazed up the stairs and tried to make sense of the conversation going on above her, but she could only make out half the words. It was hard to hear around the heart pounding in her ears.

She didn't want to believe she had heard him correctly. But there her brother was, clapping Marc on his wide back in congratulations, making denial impossible.

She stared at the tear-clouded shape of Jeremy's lifelong friend, Lord Marcus Reyes Clifton, the next Duke of Paddington. He was taller than her brother by several inches, and he was also the most handsome man she had ever seen.

His wide set shoulders and blond, wind-blown curls gave him a dangerous look that had always sent shivers down her spine.

She had spent so much time with him while growing up that she no longer needed to see his face to picture his dark green eyes and wicked grin. In fact, all she had to do anymore was close her eyes.

Their families had lived beside each other since long before their births were even a thought. Generations upon generations had passed down the beloved friendships. For Alex, growing up together had strengthened the relationship until it was now an extended family. She found she could not bear the thought of another woman intruding into their lives.

Marc's sisters had argued for years that Alex felt more for Marc than mere friendship, but she had always denied it, honestly believing they were wrong. Now she realized it was she who had been wrong. Now that it was too late.

She blinked back tears and was forced to admit, to herself if no one else, that it had always been too late for her and Marc.

Marc had never wanted her in that way, and she had deluded herself into thinking she didn't care. She knew without a doubt she was too stubborn and too outspoken for a man like Marc—a man whose biggest concern was what society expected. A tear broke free and trickled its way down her cheek, but she could not draw forth enough energy to lift her hand and wipe it away.

"She and her family will arrive soon to meet everyone properly and spend the night."

As Marc's soft words settled upon her, Alex could not stop a sob from escaping. She saw both men's heads turn toward her, but she could not get her eyes to focus through the stinging tears.

Marc took a step toward her, his eyes filled with pity. "Hell, baby I was going to tell you."

Her mouth opened, but the air seemed sucked from her lungs. How could he? Baby? *Baby*—how could he still call her that? He had called her that forever, but she wasn't a baby, not anymore.

She struggled for the strength to tell him she was a woman, to tell him she loved him and that he couldn't marry someone else. To tell him all the things she had denied all this time. She struggled to get the words to come, but all that came were tears and frustration. She turned and fled.

Blurry furniture sprang up in front of her and seemed to grasp at her skirts as she swerved past them. In her rush to be free, she slammed her fingers into the polished oak entrance door eliciting a grunt of shock.

She ignored the splintering pain, threw open the door, and ran. The safety and comfort of the thick woods that surrounded the property were her goal. The thick trunks and branches were her salvation, holding peace and freedom, just as they had ever since she was old enough to walk alone. The sweet, comforting aromas wafting from the multitude of flowers growing throughout the trees told her she was close.

Daring a glance over her shoulder, she saw the blurred images of the two men chasing her. Marc was a few steps ahead of her brother, and they were gaining on her. She ignored the deep ache in her side and fought for more speed. She had to reach the trees before they caught her.

Marc watched with a growing knot in his stomach as Alex drew closer to the tree line. He pushed himself harder, sweat starting to bead on his forehead. He knew that if they didn't catch her before she made the tree line, she would be lost to them. Jeremy's labored breathing came in deep, harsh gasps competing with his own as they tore across the sprawling lawns.

He hated that she had found out about the betrothal this way. He berated himself for not speaking with her sooner. He had meant to, but their relationship as of late had been strained. He had not known how to approach her. Now all he could think of was the pain in her pale blue eyes.

He cursed as she disappeared into the shadows. His only chance now was if her grief and tears slowed her. He cursed again, knowing the chances of that were slim. A few moments later, both men plunged into the chilled darkness of the woods.

Marc glanced at Jeremy and gave a quick nod. Jeremy returned the nod and disappeared down the well-worn path. This was not the first time they had chased the little imp into these woods. There was no need to waste time with speech. Both knew what needed to be done.

As Jeremy's booted footsteps faded down the path, Marc turned to his task. He knew their chances of finding her now were slim, but he could not give up. With a bitter grunt, he plunged deeper into the trees.

Worry gnawed at him as he combed the underbrush. "Damn," he whispered under his breath. Barbed wisps of self-deprecating guilt dug into his skin and pricked his conscious. Her tear-streaked face teased him from the shadowy realm of twisted branches and dancing leaves. "Hell and Damnation." His quiet curse echoed back to him in bitter mockery.

He hated to hurt Alex. She was like a sister to him, always had been. She had been born in the same room, the same day, and just hours before his little sister Ashlee. The girls were born and raised like twins, with two mothers, two fathers, and two sets of families to keep them safe. As a surprise pregnancy for both women, the families had doted on the girls, spoiling them.

Alex had never taken to the pampering the way that Ashlee had. No, Alex always wanted to be off on her own. He grunted, realizing that nothing had changed in all the years that had passed. Alex was still independent and bull headed.

Branches snagged his clothing and slapped against his face as he pressed deeper into the trees. A soft rustling to his left brought him to a sudden stop. He cocked his head and listened, uncertain if he had imagined the soft noise.

He closed his eyes and drew in a deep breath. He held it and concentrated. The wind danced across the leaves. They sighed and rustled in the cool breeze. Birds chirped accusingly at him as they flitted from branch to branch. He could even hear small animals scurrying in the dead leaves that littered the forest floor, but what he could not hear was the noise that had brought him up short.

The air in his lungs turned to fire and heat began to spread up his throat as the breath fought for release. He ignored the feeling, struggling for a few more seconds, just enough time to hear—upon a soft breeze came the unmistakable sounds of tears—soft, delicate sounds that knocked the breath from him.

He found her, hugging her knees, rocking back and forth, and lost to the world. He touched her trembling shoulder. "Baby, come, let me help you."

She jerked away from his touch.

Guilt swallowed him. "Baby, please."

She stiffened but made no answer. Unsure of what to do next he touched her arm.

She leapt to her feet. "Do not touch me," she hissed.

He opened his mouth, but before he could get a word out, she flung herself at him. Her fists pummeled the hard planes of his stomach and chest.

He grasped for her hands and missed. She was not hurting him, at least not physically. It was deep in his chest that he felt the blows. His heart ached at every swing and every tear.

A deep sob escaped her. "How could you do this to me? I—I—" The tears were coming harder, the blows weakening.

He finally caught hold of her wrists and forced them behind her. Her back arched and her breasts pressed against him. She slumped, her head falling against his thudding heart, her tears slowing to ragged hiccups. Thinking she was calming, he began to relax his grip. "Baby, listen—"

She exploded into a hell cat. He was caught off guard by her aggressive outburst. She twisted to get her hands free. Her breasts rubbed hard against his chest. The soft cotton of her flowery daydress snagged on the buttons of his tailcoat, and the bodice slid down her shoulders to reveal pale, delicate skin. She jerked and twisted, tugged and kicked. The dress lost more ground. He tried to keep his mind on the hellcat within the circle of his arms. He tried, unsuccessfully, to ignore the ever growing expanse of smooth tempting skin.

"Stop fighting." His voice came out in a strangled gasp. "You are going—"

One soft rose-pink nipple escaped, showing through her almost translucent chemise. Marc's breath ceased, his heart lurched to a shaky stop and then exploded through the gates like a race horse hell bent on coming in first.

He struggled to regain control of not only her, but of himself. He tried, but could not pull his eyes from her exposed breasts. The rounded tops, covered in silky batiste, beckoned his hands and his mouth. He fought the urge to sample them and cursed himself. What the hell was he thinking?

When had she developed so well, and where had he been when it had happened? He drew her tighter against his chest in a desperate attempt to hide her tempting flesh. Her small, yet beautifully formed breasts seemed to scorch through his clothing. When had she stopped being a girl and become a woman?

He was surprised when her struggles stopped. Even more so by the feel of her soft trembling lips under his own, his tongue pushing against them, demanding entry.

He couldn't remember getting there. He had, though, because there he stood, bent before her, the smells of lilacs and roses invading his senses, kissing her with a passion and desperation he had never felt before.

Her response was immediate and warm. She twisted her hands and slipped them from his distracted grasp. Reality forced its way through the fogs of passion. He reluctantly slowed his kisses. Their lips parted as he fought through the fogs of passion that had addled his mind.

Alex slipped her arms around his neck, drawing him back. Her hands timidly caressed his neck, her warm uncertain fingers pulled him even closer. He forced the kiss deeper.

He slid one hand down her thin waist and found the gentle swell of her bottom. He lifted her, settling her against his arousal. His kisses became forceful and fevered. His erection pressed hard against his breeches insisting on release. Marc tried to ignore it, tried for some semblance of control, but as Alex's tongue, hesitant and tentative, grazed his, the fogs of passion engulfed him. He gave in to the desire of her inviting flesh. His free hand searched out her breast, the soft chemise cool against his fingers, the hardened nipple like a stone beneath his palm.

He pulled her closer and reveled in the lithe way she moved against him. He broke the kiss and smiled as she strained to regain his lips. He trailed kissed down her chin, across her jaw and gently bit at her ear. She dropped her head back and let out a low groan that reverberated through every fiber of his already painful lust. He kissed and nipped at her neck until her breathing was labored and she clung to him. He dropped his head and was only a breath away from the tops of her beautiful breasts when Jeremy's deep call echoed through the trees.

Marc let out a curse, pulled back, and stared down at her up-turned face. "Baby?"

Eyes so blue they were almost clear were darkened with passion. "Huh?"

Her brow furrowed and, as the soft smile slipped from her kiss-swollen lips and clarity brightened her eyes, he knew her brother's voice had soaked into her drugged thoughts.

She gave a shaky laugh and joy lit her face. "I think we had best say you never found me." With that, she was gone, and he turned on shaky legs to face his friend, his heart heavy with remorse.

"There you are. Did you not find her?" Jeremy's face was tight with concern for his stubborn sibling, but it was obvious that he had not heard what had almost happened.

Marc took a deep breath, but where relief should have been, there was a cold spasm of guilt. "No, I thought I heard her, but if I did, she was gone before I got to her." He could not meet Jeremy's eyes. The lie stung his lips, but Alex was right. They could not admit he had been alone with her in the woods.

It would be devastating to both their reputations, both already in a fragile state.

Alex, the society darling that she was, had too many disappearances the previous season and rumors were starting to swirl. Her reputation was already tottering dangerously on the precipice and would not take much to push it from rumor to downright scandal.

Marc's reputation was on the cusp of being perfect. His reputation meant everything to him, to his life and his plans. He would not let anything jeopardize all that he had worked so hard to accomplish.

He just wished she had not looked so happy—so hopeful as she had run from him. What if she thought he meant to break the betrothal? He did not want to hurt her again, and he hadn't meant to lead her on. He had lost control, something he rarely did. He could not fathom how he had messed up so badly, not this close to having his life together.

"Well, perhaps she is already back at the house," Jeremy said.

Marc grunted. "Hopefully. For, if not, we will not find her now."

Jeremy peered into the trees that surrounded them. He shook his head, looking around before speaking. "Do you plan to announce your betrothal at the party tomorrow?"

"No, it is the girls' night. Besides she wants one more season as a single woman. We will announce it at the end of this season and marry at the beginning of nex—"

There was a sharp gasp from above, and both heads jerked up at the muttered word that sounded suspiciously like, "Bastard." The branches shook in violent objection, chastising the intruders.

"Lord, she was right above us." Jeremy stared up at the leaves drifting lazily toward them, but all was now quiet. Even the birds were silent as if in deference to her pain. "Bloody hell, we just made it worse."

Marc held his tongue. At least if she had gone back thinking he was not going to marry she would be safe at home. Now he wondered how long she would hide out here. If the past was any indication, it could be many hours, but she was always home by dark. *Though*, he thought, with one more look into the dense branches above him, *this is no ordinary situation.*

Alex maneuvered the thick tree tops, moving in near silence from branch to branch putting as much room between her and Marc as possible. The forest had grown together throughout the years, top branches and limbs had long since intertwined to make a thick canopy. It was usually an easy task to move from tree to tree and, even if in spots she had to make a short leap, it had never been a problem. Her tears were slowing her, but anger kept them at bay, and she managed not to slip and crash to the ground.

Alex released a breath of relief when her favorite spot came into view. With trembling muscles, she slid onto the well-worn branch and lay back in the elbow of a limb. It cradled her in a familiar embrace.

Closing her eyes, she drew comfort from the cool, time-worn branch. She shuddered at what had almost happened. Marc was an honorable man, and if he had sullied her, she had no doubt that he would have married her. While she was glad nothing had happened, nothing that would have left Marc stuck in a marriage he did not want, she was also stung by regret.

A tear slid down her cheek. She opened her eyes and looked through the veil of leaves. From her secluded spot, she could watch, unseen, the front doors, as well as the servant entrance, allowing her to keep an eye on everyone who came and went from the manor. It was one of the reasons this was her favorite spot.

She took up a sailor's spy glass, given to her several birthdays ago by a close friend, and peered through it.

Marc and Jeremy trudged across the lawn, every so often looking back over their shoulders as they made their way to the house.

Sunlight shone through a break in the canopy. It danced through her hair and caressed her sweat dampened skin. She tilted her face, closed her eyes, and basked in its warmth. A soft, cool breeze stroked her skin. The collision of warmth and chill sent a shiver tingling down her body leaving gooseflesh in its wake.

Confusion invaded her peace, pricking at her like the thorns of a berry bush. She sighed and tried to understand why Marc had kissed her. He had, for the most part, ignored her since last season, since that dreadful night with Danton.

Although, she remembered, for a moment at least, *I had thought he was going to kiss me that night.* She scowled at his retreating back and wondered again how she had misunderstood that night so much.

She could still see the anger that had clouded his face and regretted the deep rift that had developed between them.

She took a deep breath and could almost smell the sweet roses as she pictured Danton dragging her from the dance floor and into the darkness of the garden. She wrinkled her nose at the memory of Danton's sour breath overpowering the sweet call of the flowers when he had dropped his liquor-tinged lips toward her. She shivered, thinking of the way his cold lips had slithered across her cheek like wriggling worms.

She had felt a moment of fear, and then Marc was there, his fist connecting with Danton. Dark blood had trickled from Danton's split lip, but he was on the ground for less than a heartbeat before he jumped back to his feet and disappeared into the darkness with a snarled, "You both will regret this."

Alex had felt a wild exhilaration at being rescued by Marc, could still almost taste the excitement she had felt at the prospect of being alone with him in the forbidden darkness of the garden.

Then it had all gone wrong, and she still could not figure out why. She had turned to thank him, and his anger froze her heart.

What kind of a stupid child was she, did she not have any brains floating around in her head, did she want to be thought of as a loose girl, did she want to shame her parents, did she not know this was dangerous…

On and on he had accosted her with questions until she could take no more.

She shook her head in confusion as Marc and Jeremy closed in on the house. One minute, Marc had been yelling at her and the next she was in his arms, a strange heat cocooning her in a dizzying warmth that made thoughts difficult. He had stared at her lips in a strange way that had sent chills down her spine. Somewhere in her imagination, she had pictured him leaning down and kissing her, but his dark curses had quickly jerked her from that delusion. He released her. She had stumbled, her body drawn forward, as he pulled back. Then, without a word, he had walked away, disappearing into the darkness and leaving her feeling empty and confused.

The same way she felt now.

Since that day he had been distant and cold. A vast difference from the way he had been while she was growing up. She had tagged along after Jeremy and Marc all her life, and her heart cried out for the loss of their easy going friendship. She dragged Ashlee along as often as she could, but Ashlee had better things to do, like the piano forte or needlepoint, things Alex found mundane and boring. So more often than not it was just the three of them. They had laughed and joked with her, treating her like she was a friend and not just a young and annoying child.

Alex scrubbed her eyes, now tender and raw. How had things gotten so out of control between the two of them? Tears flowed for both the loss of that wondrous past and for the uncertainty of the future to come.

She slumped against the tree limb and tried to gain at least a semblance of control. Alex brought the glass to her eye once more gazing toward the manor. She knew she would have to face him, but as the carriage of "that woman" pulled up, Alex found she could not.

Her first thought was of going on to the Cliftons', but that would be the first place they would look. It always was. The stables, she thought, a crooked smile stealing across her lips. It would be uncomfortable, but it was a much better option than sleeping the night away in the tree.

Her parents would be beside themselves and, for that, she was sorry, but she could not face him. Not and keep her sanity. She had never stayed out the entire night, but she couldn't bear to face his new betrothed alone. She would wait until morning when Amber and Ashlee would arrive.

She could return then when she had her friends beside her for support. Then maybe she could face Marc and his bride-to-be.

The dark maroon carriage drew to a stop in front of the manor. A footman rushed to open the door, followed at a dignified pace by Marc, Jeremy, and both sets of parents.

Through the wavering view of long glass, Alex watched a short fat man step from the fancy carriage, its thick burgundy-and-gold interior offensive in its gaudiness even from her vantage point. The man, easily recognizable to her, was slovenly beneath his fashionable attire. His thick sausage fingers, double chin, and rounded stomach made him look years older than his actual fifty-six years.

His dark blond hair of youth had lightened till it was almost white, graying around the temples, and his blue eyes were nearly lost in wrinkles. Lord Samuel Rutmeyer, the Duke of Myerdome, was an arrogant bastard if Alex had ever met one.

She had first met him, his wife, and his eldest daughter last season. She had not liked any of them one bit. Samuel was overbearing and loud and responsible for the scandal that had touched the Clifton family so long ago. The scandal that had nearly ruined them.

Next, came the female version of Rutmeyer, his wife, Lady Beatrice. She may have been attractive in her own way twenty years ago, but the life of luxury that many of the ton cling to is not kind to the body or the mind. Her ample bosom swung low over her massive stomach as gravity took its toll on the heavy mounds. Her pale blonde hair, elegantly coiled and piled tall upon her head, was her best feature—if one could ignore the bitter woman that was beneath it. Scowls and frowns had wrinkled her face prematurely, and she seemed to have frozen in an unhappy countenance.

Well, if they were the parents, then she knew who Marc was waiting to greet. Alex scowled. The next two passengers swept from the carriage like queens who could not be bothered by the peasants they were about to greet. The two girls, Caroline and Krystal Rutmeyer, who Alex only knew through reputation, held their heads high, noses in the air. The twins were both petite blondes of fourteen and already had a snobbish cast to their lovely features.

They looked, as Alex would guess, their mother had looked in her prime. Small boned and delicate, their big blue eyes and long waves of golden hair would soon turn many a man's head and purse. Long thin necks pivoted as they took in the scenery, looks of disgust crossing each face. Their gowns, held high away from the dirt, were of exquisite silks and imported laces. Each was a pale peach which made their already pale complexions almost white, as was the fashion. Much in contrast to the dark sun-kissed skin of Alex, who could not imagine a life spent anywhere but outdoors.

Marc stepped forward after a polite and acceptable bow, to greet the next to emerge from the plush velvet interior. The four matched steeds, white as new snow and just as fickle, threw their heads in impatience, pawing at the ground, awaiting the departure of their last passenger.

The horses behind, pulling the wagon of servants and the ones behind it piled high with luggage answered with neighs of restlessness.

Alex knew these magnificent-looking creatures were never allowed to gallop and perform to the best of their quality. No, always on a short rein, they were much like her father and mother wanted her.

A dainty hand emerged from the carriage. Marc reached for it with a gentlemanly bow. The woman who stepped forward was a mirror image of the younger girls, except where their manners and posture spoke of arrogance and pride, hers pushed it further.

She looked in distaste at the dusty courtyard, as if she considered how the hard-packed drive would soil her dainty slippers. She looked down her nose, even at those society thought her equals. Alex knew for a fact that Janice believed she had no equals.

Marc stood with his hand held patiently out to her while she paused, as if to consider remaining in the carriage. Finally, she lay her gloved hand in his and allowed him to assist her. Alex should have expected no less.

Marcus Reyes Clifton was total society. What he did was governed by the rules and strictures set forth. He had spoken many times of his hopes for the future. Hopes that his father's shipping business would flourish under his hands, and so far it had.

Alex thought back to the joy Marc had barely been able to conceal on the day, six years ago, when his father had allowed him to reopen the company. He had slowly brought it back to life and forced people to see beyond their mistrust. She was still frustrated by his refusal to physically see to the ships or any of the cargo, but he was adamant. He had people for that. His solicitor, for one, and the second, well…

She grinned, despite herself. He was totally unaware of the second.

The grin slipped away as she thought of the upcoming marriage. Whether she was to be his bride or not, she still wished him to be happy. He had worked too hard to be otherwise, and it pained her frayed heart to think he was not marrying for love, but for society.

Alex still had to fight anger every time she thought of their scandal and the Rutmeyers' part in it. Ten years ago Lord Samuel Rutmeyer, in a fit of rage, had accused the Duke of Paddington of being a French spy. It was said he used his shipping contacts to pass information onto the enemy. There was nothing that could be proved, and no charges were ever brought, but it had damaged the business.

The malicious rumor had spread through the ton like wildfire, inflamed further by Marc's father, Maxwell, and his unfashionable activities. Maxwell Clifton had always been the one to oversee his interests, never trusting another to do as good a job as he would himself. That menial labor in itself was enough to rouse the good members of the ton to suspicion. No self-respecting member of society would "work." Alex snorted as anger tickled at her.

With the added accusations, the duke and his family had avoided London for many years, even shutting down the company. It had not helped their standing, only added fuel to the fire. With their absence, tongues wagged about the cause of it. Some saying it had to be true or they never hide in "The Country." The last two words were always said with disgust. While country homes were becoming fashionable, one would never stay in one during the season.

Yet, over the last five years, they had moved back into society and were just beginning to out-live the rumors that still floated around. This marriage between the two feuding families would make great strides in regaining all the deserved status.

Movement from the house drew her attention and, as Alex watched the group disappear into the house, she wondered who had convinced the Rutmeyer family to stoop to this marriage. Was it because Janice Rutmeyer was infatuated with Marc and had insisted, or was it something else? Knowing she was acting out of jealousy did not dissuade Alex. She needed to know the reasons for the upcoming nuptials. It had to be more than feelings, or Lady Janice would not want to wait for so long. Even if it was considered acceptable, it was not common practice.

Asking directly of anyone involved would bring no answers. They would think her imprudent to even ask. They would not stoop to that kind of gossip, especially with her. No, they tried to keep anything unpleasant from her.

It was as if they expected her to remain in a bubble, never allowed to know the injustices of the cold world. She, herself, thought the opposite. Everyone should know the troubles of others. It made one more compassionate, more human.

No, they would not tell her what she wanted to know, but she knew who would, and she would be seeing him the day after tomorrow.

Chapter 2

One glance out the large drawing room window showed night quickly approaching. The brilliant clashes of color betrayed the battle that raged as day stood its ground. Thomas Hollister knew it was only a matter of time before the darkness would prevail.

The sun, however, seemed reluctant to disappear behind the tall grove of trees that stood barrier around the manor. It clung to the branches and raced across the grass before stealing through the open window.

The rebellious light flitted around delicate Wedgwood pottery. Its eager fingers explored the tall Chippendale chest. The high polished wood glowed with a life of its own under the warm caress.

Thomas tried to push away the tight convulsions that gripped his stomach and concentrated instead on the faded colors of the sunset. His gaze touched on the glimmer of light and followed its path across the room. It gleamed off well-polished silver candelabras and delicate trinkets. It fell upon furniture that, in his opinion, was elegant, but lost beneath heaps of feminine masses of useless fluff. The satin chaise and beautiful needlepoint chairs were swathed in bright laces, suffocating pillows, and fringed frill. He cringed. This was a woman's room, all the way from the thick floral rugs to the fringed and frilly curtains. It was a room he thoroughly hated, but his wife loved. Which meant he was stuck with it.

Being in this room was bad enough, he thought with a grimace. Forced to share it with Lord Rutmeyer and his entire family made it almost unbearable. The subtle aroma of sweat slithered across the room and choked him. He barely withheld a shudder.

The beauty of the sunset was lost as he followed the aroma. Samuel Rutmeyer caught his gaze and gave a bored look. Thomas smiled wanly and continued his perusal of the stifling room.

Samuel's two youngest sat perched on the settee, hands folded perfectly in their laps as they seemed to practice their smiles and eyelash batting. Janice, Marc's soon-to-be bride, tapped her foot from her position beside the small cold fireplace. Impatience showed clearly on her face.

Thomas closed his eyes and turned away from their guests. He took a shallow breath. *Patience*, he told himself. His stomach clenched in protest. Patience had never been one of his strongest attributes. He knew it was more respectable for the Rutmeyers to remain here as opposed to staying with Marc and the Clifton family, but that didn't mean he liked it.

He sighed deeply and opened his eyes. His breath caught, and all the annoyances of his day slipped away. The vision before him put any sunset to shame.

Pristine white silk fluttered around brilliant emerald eyes. Soft lines lay nearly hidden in their corners, but he knew they were there. All he had to do was make her laugh. A chill raced up his spine in anticipation of that smile.

The sunlight played in her perfectly coiled hair and caressed her smooth alabaster skin. Thomas felt his pulse quicken. After thirty-four years of marriage, she still made his heart race and his loins tighten.

Catherine Hollister pressed the rose embroidered handkerchief to her eyes and sighed dramatically. He knew she was struggling to find tears, tears that were not coming. She portrayed the distraught mother who thought of nothing but her daughter's safety. But it was an act. He knew she was fighting anger at their wayward daughter, not worry.

Catherine twined the handkerchief around her fingers, just enough to look the part, but not enough to be improper. If he wasn't so aggravated with Alex, he would have to smile.

"Where could she be?" Catherine continued. "It really is not like my Alexis to be this late."

Thomas barely held back a disagreeing grunt.

Catherine sighed and dabbed at her dry eyes. He knew his beautiful wife well and knew she was picturing throttling Alex. He could see it in her stance, hear it in the soft twinge of her voice.

He understood her frustration, but he didn't understand why she had expected anything less from the little chit. All last season, Alex had done these little disappearing acts. But she would always show up with some respectable explanation.

This time, of course, there was no chance of Alex concocting a plausible story. Not when the messenger had announced, unfortunately in front of the Rutmeyer family, that Alex was not at the Cliftons' residence. There was no other home within walking distance, and all the carriages were in the stables.

Lady Beatrice stepped forward and laid gloved fingers on Catherine's arm. She gave a small pat. "How long has your daughter been gone, my lady?"

At Beatrice's condescending tone, Catherine's eyes squinted and her nose wrinkled.

Thomas shook his head in irritation. He was worried about Alex, as he always was when she disappeared. But anger overpowered that concern. Angry that she was once more tormenting her mother.

"How long?" Catherine sniffled and patted her eyes. "She has been gone all day. No one has seen her since breakfast. I just do not know what to do." She put on a convincing show of grief, so much so that Lady Beatrice patted her hands in sympathy.

Thomas shook his head. Anger and irritation swirled within him. He might just take a switch to her little hide when she reappeared. He grunted quietly at the thought, even as he admitted that it would never happen.

He looked across the room and was pondering just how he could make his escape when Marc and Jeremy caught his eye. They stood apart from the group, eyes twitching guiltily and looking as if they were ready to make their own escapes.

A quick look behind him showed the guests still fawning over his deceptive wife. He turned, and, with a feigned calm, walked toward the boys.

"All right, what do you two know?" He kept his voice low and his tone firm.

With anxious glances, Marc and Jeremy turned to face him. "Pardon me, father—"

"Pardon denied, Jeremy," Thomas interrupted, ever mindful of the gaggle of guests behind him. His son seemed nervous, but Marc...Marc appeared to be completely shaken and could barely keep eye contact. Thomas had the creeping suspicion that he was struggling with a difficult decision—or perhaps a secret. "You especially, Lord Clifton, look extremely guilty." No answer. "Marcus?"

Marc took a deep breath and tried to ignore the panic that boiled within him. His conscious pricked him, and a nervous tension twisted his stomach. He should have been thinking of Alex being missing.

He should have been struggling with the fact that he knew where she was. Instead what had entrapped his mind was how her soft and supple body had moved against his. The sweet honey of her lips still lingered on his own. The soft aroma of lilac and rose that had encased her warm flesh teased his memory. He had been standing there fighting the guilt and desire that swamped his senses. He took a shaky breath.

"Sorry, my lord." The words cracked, and Marc wanted to disappear into the billowing curtain behind him. It had been meant as a question. A denial of knowledge. Instead, it came out as a plea of forgiveness for a crime he could not even mention doing.

"Sorry for what, Marcus?" Thomas's brows rose, and anger tinged his features. Marc shuddered. Lying to Alex's father was the last thing he wanted to do. He opened his mouth, not sure of what he intended to say. Suddenly the anger was gone from Thomas's face, and a dawning light sparked in his eyes. He nodded knowingly. "Where is she?"

Marc shook his head and tried to lie. He opened his mouth once more, but no words came. Though he could not seem to work his lips, his eyes, to his horror, were functioning just fine. They were drawn, unassisted, to the thick grove of trees.

A sharp laugh startled Marc before he had a chance to get control of his roving gaze. He looked back at Thomas, but Thomas was no longer looking at him. His gaze had followed Marc's, and he was now staring straight at the woods.

Thomas shook his head with another laugh. "The trees, of course." He kept his voice low, mindful of prying ears behind them. "My little wood sprite. At least she's all right."

"You have to do something."

Marc jumped at Lady Catherine's quiet hiss at his shoulder. He glanced over her head to the Rutmeyers who were looking more and more perturbed by this unexpected excitement.

Marc understood Catherine perfectly when she said "do something." Not something to find Alex. They all knew Alex was fine. No, "do something" meant something to keep it from becoming a scandal. Marc knew she wanted her husband to protect her and her reputation.

Marc wanted that as well. He had worked too hard on his reputation to let Alex ruin his chances at happiness now. Everything was finally coming together—from his family's business to his personal life and all the way to his upcoming betrothal. His reputation, and his standing and that of his family, would be restored.

"She is fine in the trees, my love. Alexis will come out before dark, she always does."

Marc let the soothing words wash over him and watched as Thomas tried to calm the distraught woman.

"It will all be fine," Thomas reiterated.

She just shook her head.

"Is everything all right?" Lord Rutmeyer stated. "I am sure she will be fine." He added without pause, not seeming to care what the answers may be. "Perhaps we should consider starting dinner."

"You are right, Papa, the food will begin to get cold," Lady Janice said snidely. "It would be rude to wait any longer."

Her jab left Marc's jaw clenching, but he managed to keep his silence.

"She will return shortly to eat. She must be hungry by now." Jeremy's quiet words made sense, but Marc knew better. He knew she had a cache of food out there somewhere, and he also knew that Jeremy was aware of it as well.

"Indeed." Jeremy's father clapped a wide hand on his shoulders. "Let us go to the dining hall, dinner will be served shortly."

Thomas crossed the room to Lady Rutmeyer and extended his arm. "My lady." He gave a shallow bow and escorted her out of the room. Jeremy escorted Caroline and Krystal, one short twin on each elbow.

Marc bowed low to his future bride and held out his arm.

She sniffed indignantly and, barely touching his arm with her white gloved fingers, accepted his escort. Marc felt his irritation slipping further into anger and took a deep breath to calm his boiling emotions.

In the large and elegant dining room, Marc allowed Janice's weak grip to slip from his arm. He watched for an exasperated minute as she fled to her family's side before he turned and strode to the open French doors.

He looked across the wide expanse of green lawn and tried to catch a glimpse of Alex. He sent up a quick prayer that she would stride through the door. He took a deep breath and turned back to the assembling company. This night was going from bad to worse, and he could think of no way to fix it.

The cool evening air blew gently against his back. He could feel the teasing fingers tousle his hair. He took a deep breath and tried to calm his fraying nerves, but tension clenched his stomach. He was sure he was not going to partake of dinner tonight.

He watched his family, both his by blood and by choice, mingle with the family of his betrothed as they awaited the bell that would announce the meal. The fact that the Rutmeyers didn't like the Hollister family was more than just a little apparent. They nearly snarled as they forced pleasant comments and gentle compliments on the room and the home.

"It will soon be too cold to have the doors open while we eat, right, my boy?"

Thomas smiled as Marc turned his attention to him. Marc was concerned by the edginess in his stance, the tension in Thomas's movements.

"That it is, Lord Hollister." Marc returned the smile and turned his attention back to the tree line.

A body suddenly pushed into Marc, throwing him off balance. He placed a hand on a soft and narrow waist to steady himself. He took a deep breath and looked down into Janice's face.

"Are you looking for Alexis?" Her voice was high, tight, and seemed strained. "I am sure she is fine. She must have a favorite spot she goes. Or someone she likes to visit."

Confusion tugged at Marc. He could not decide why Lady Janice would care one way or the other about Alex. It was well known throughout the ton that the two disliked each other. He shook his head. That was an understatement, he thought, considering the last season of conflicts between the two.

He looked down at her, at the impatience on her face, and realized just what her issue was. She wanted the attention, always did, and it was not going to happen until the little twit came home.

Marcus opened his mouth to respond when Janice's words hit him. A favorite spot. Yes, she had a favorite spot, and he knew where it was. Right behind him. Careful not to arouse suspicion he scanned the woods but could see nothing.

His hand automatically fell from the small waist it held. Indeed, had done so with not so much as a thought from him. Anger and irritation swirled within him. He refused to allow Alex to affect him in such a manner. He pulled Janice close to him. He would show Alex who was in charge. That girl would not govern his actions.

Marc cringed and let his arm drop away from her thin waist. Janice snorted lightly and looked at him in confusion. He looked at her apologetically. How was he to explain that Alex made him do it? Ridiculous.

"Shall we take to the table—" Thomas's words were cut short by a sharp rap on the dining room doors. "Come."

The doors swung silently open. Robert Dunmore, Alex's driver and personal servant, stepped slowly into the room. "My lords and ladies, I apologize for the interruption. A message came from the Pettlenoster Manor." With a low bow, he deposited his message into Thomas's hand and silently slipped from the room.

"My dear." Thomas glanced at his wife and smiled. It felt

strained on his lips, and he could only hope it did not look as false as it felt. "It appears that there was a mix up at the Pettlenosters'. They apologize profusely, but we can rest assured that Alexis is safe and sound with them."

Marc grunted and shook his head. He glanced back at the trees and then at her father. Thomas looked back with the same confusion that Marc felt. How had she reached the Pettlenosters' so quickly, and without taking a horse or carriage?

The night came slowly and dinner passed in a subdued manner. Marc struggled through the quiet meal and longed for the sweet escape that sleep would bring. He was exhausted and was sure it had nothing to do with the long run he had performed in his mad dash to catch Alex. When he was finally able to excuse himself, he went straight for his bed, but the escape that he had anticipated did not come.

He tossed beneath his covers long after everyone else had retired. Finally giving up, he quickly dressed and peered from his bed chamber door. No one walked the halls.

Quietly slipping through the darkness of the halls, he made his way to the servant's entrance. Marc stepped into the cool night air and leaned sluggishly against the heavy door.

His thoughts swirled and rolled within him, his head throbbing, as he tried to gain control. He closed his eyes and allowed the quiet sounds of the night to wash over him. The chirping of bugs in the well-groomed grass, the swoosh of wings from unseen birds fluttering in the bushes and trees, and the far hoot of the owls from the forest as they went about their nightly hunt.

None of these things, things that would normally relax him, did anything to calm his fretting nerves. His thoughts raced, crashing into one another and creating havoc within him. Alex was at the eye of the storm that had created a massive headache.

How had he lost control so quickly with her? He'd asked himself this about a hundred times since he had followed Jeremy out of the woods earlier that morning. He had decided on the only sensible reason that could have caused it. He had not been with a woman in nearly a year.

Marc thought back to that night ten months ago. He had gone to his mistress with anger and confusion in his heart. A confrontation with Alex had left him reeling. The little chit had scampered off into the garden with Danton, and he had barely been in time to save her hide and her reputation. He still fumed thinking about it.

Marc had stripped off his clothing the moment his mistress's door had shut, and he had ordered her into her bed, even though he had quickly realized he was not interested in her. He was not interested in anything except ridding himself of the image of Alex's tears when he had yelled and shaken her. Brandy and rum had not helped. Unbridled sex was his next best idea.

Throwing himself onto the soft luxurious mattress he waited for her to join him. But she had not. She stood beside the bed, looking at him with sadness and worry. Malacinda St. Johns had told him how sorry she was, that she would leave as soon as he wanted her to, but she could no longer be his mistress.

Why? That had been his only response. He could not remember being overly upset with her. Confused, but not angry. He had waited patiently, lying naked on the bed, as she had explained that a friend of hers was in love with him. She felt she was betraying her friend every time he came to her.

He had only nodded. How could one argue with that? So he had not even tried. He could clearly see the surprise on her face when he told her to stay until he found someone to replace her. He had thought it would not take long. He was never one to wait long in between trips to his mistress. That had been ten months ago.

It was not hard on him most of the time. He had not seen a woman that he was interested in taking once let alone setting up in the house. He did miss Malacinda, but more for her laughter and playfulness than for the sex. Those were the things that had attracted him to her in the first place, the reason he had offered her his protection.

He looked out across the moonlit expanse of grass and sighed. A thin cloud darkened the sky, he glanced up. He had been to see Malacinda on occasion since that night, mostly to see how she was and to play chess. He had been surprised when she had the game board set up.

She had been a horrid player before. Now she was quite good. She said a friend had been teaching her. He had laughed, telling her that a high society woman would never stoop to such a game, she was lucky her friends were not of the ton or she would be bored out of her mind with them. Her deep laugh had sent a confused shiver across him, or perhaps it had been the knowing look in her eye.

"Those are the reasons to prefer a mistress over a wife," he told the fluttering shadow of a small bird that whizzed past his nose. His thoughts settled on his upcoming betrothal, and he thought, not for the first time, that he could not imagine what he would do once he was settled down with Janice.

He sighed, his head throbbed. He would have to replace Malacinda, or he would not be able to bear the coming years.

He had no intention of giving up his pleasures after his marriage. Wives, even the good ones, were not playful and relaxed and these were not things he was willing to give up. Not and keep his sanity. Women of the ton were always too worried about what society would think of them. But a mistress. She had no such reservations. They could joke and laugh and play.

His thoughts slipped back to Alex. She was nothing like the other members of the ton. He groaned inwardly and shook his head in exasperation. Even with Malacinda, he had not lost his head the way he had in the woods with Alex. He sighed heavily. The pain in his head began to spread down his neck and shoulders. They tightened, feeling as if smoldering embers were deeply embedded within them.

He wondered again how Alex had managed to get to the Pettlenosters' so quickly and shook his head. Trying to figure out what that girl was doing would only serve to drive him farther into his painful misery.

❧❦❧

Alex snuggled deeper into the rough, but warm, woolen blankets on Robert's cot. Safe in the stables, sleep had found her quickly, and she was deep in dreams.

Marc once again held her to the ground, kissing her and touching her, until she thought she would burst. His hands grasped her in desperate passion. His lips branded her as his own as they trailed down her throat.

Her breath came in heavy rasps as Alex tossed in her sleep. Marc's deep rumbling voice whispered against her overheated skin. "I love you." Alex jolted awake. Disoriented she pulled the blanket to her chin and stared blankly at the ceiling.

"My lady." A sharp cry escaped her at the soft words, and she jerked the blanket up over her head.

"I am sorry to startle you, my lady." She heard the concerned tone in Robert's voice. "Are you all right?"

She took a deep breath and pulled the covers down to her nose. She peeked at him over the blanket that smelled of horseflesh and straw. She inhaled deeply, the aroma soothing her frayed nerves. She closed her eyes and took a long slow breath.

"The message arrived at the Pettlenosters' last night without issue," Robert said in a hushed tone.

Good, she thought. At least her alibi would hold up if questioned. She nodded and opened her eyes.

Robert dipped his head in a deep respectful bow and held his hand out to her. She stared at it not wanting to face her day. She wanted desperately to pull the blanket back over head and wait till the bad dreams of reality ended and the sweet ones of Marc returned.

Robert cleared his throat and twitched his fingers at her in encouragement. "I have informed your father that I am to retrieve you, my lady. If you would be so kind as to hop into the carriage, we shall drive around for an appropriate amount of time for you to change and to, at least, give the appearance that I have indeed done what I said I was doing."

She could not hide in the stable for the rest of her life, no matter how much she may desire to do just that. With a groan, she pushed away the itchy blanket and allowed him to pull her to her feet.

She sucked in a sharp breath as her bared feet connected with the cold stable floor. Spring was well on its way, but the warmth of summer was still months away. Trepidation clung to her as she made her way from the stable. Concern ate at her as it always did when she was trying to get away with a lie. Peering out the stable door, she relaxed slightly. Robert had positioned the carriage perfectly, and her movements would be concealed from the manor.

Once in the carriage, she took several deep breaths, but as she slipped into the extra dress and shoes she always kept in the carriage, for just such an occasion, her heart began to hammer painfully. No matter how she tried to calm herself, she felt control slipping farther away. By the time they had returned to the manor, her breathing was sharp and labored. Tonight was going to be nightmare, she could just feel it.

Peering out the window, she saw the carriage of her reinforcements. Their conveyance was not far in front of her. Her horses whinnied, and the reinforcements' steeds tossed their heads and returned their call.

She released a breath that she had not realized she had been holding and felt tears tickle her eyes. She struggled to keep them contained, but one broke free and slid down her cheek, leaving a warm salty trail.

"Bloody Hell," she cursed and kicked the seat before her.

Dwelling on things she could not change would get her nowhere. She pushed her thoughts of Marc to the back of her mind and concentrated instead on her father. Her father was going to be angry, and she was not looking forward to facing him, but it kept her mind off of the pain that swirled in her heart.

She took a deep, shaky breath. This one helped no more than the thousands it felt like she had already taken.

Her father would not show his anger, at least not outwardly. She supposed it would better if he did. She closed her eyes and leaned against the rocking carriage seat. His anger she could handle, the disappointment she wasn't sure she could deal with.

The carriage jolted to a stop, her head bouncing off the seat. She clenched her eyes tighter and wanted nothing more than to hit the roof and tell Robert to keep driving, but she knew it was a useless wish.

Robert pulled the door open, and she glanced at him. He smiled widely and held out his hand. "No matter what happens, I am here for you," he whispered.

With a deep breath, she laid her gloved fingers across his palm and slipped to the dusty courtyard. Nodding gently to her driver and dear friend, she forced a calm smile onto her trembling lips and turned toward the manor. It took all the courage she had to mount the steps, open the door, and face her family.

She pasted an innocent expression on her face—at least she hoped it said innocence—and forced her feet to move her forward. All attention was on her.

Her gaze fell upon Marc, his wife-to-be holding possessively to his sleeve, and her heart lurched into her throat. For a panicked second, she thought she would lose the fruit and toast Robert had forced upon her for breakfast.

Marc watched her smile slip and felt his heat slip with it. Lord and Lady Clifton stood shaking their heads, with a mixture of anger and disappointment.

Marc's sisters Amber and Ashlee had gathered their long flowing skirts before them in trembling hands, looking as if they may both burst into overzealous tears.

Amber's husband Lord Blakley Fortshaw, the Marquis of Gravenhill ever since his father's death when Blake was only ten, looked from Marc to Alex. His dark skin, bronzed from days on horseback, sparkled with the health of youth. At thirty, he was only a year younger than Jeremy and two younger than Marc. He was tall and dark, his black hair and dark brown eyes lent him a dangerous look, but it was an illusion that was broken by the grin that twitched at the corner of his lips.

Blake grinned and gave a wink. "Gone all night? And with the Pettlenosters? My dear heart, that is just awful."

Amber hit her husband's shoulder, apparently angered by the amused sarcasm. "That is not funny."

Lady Amber Fortshaw looked much like her father. She was tall with dark brown hair falling in soft waves instead of tight curls as her younger sister. Her deep brown eyes were set beneath a high smooth brow and her chin was set stubbornly. Ashlee was different, she took after their mother. Blonde with the grass green eyes and the petite build of Lady Alma. Dainty and soft, not wanting much more than what society expected of a woman. Ashlee and Alma spent most of the time doing knitting or drinking tea.

Marc looked from his two sisters to Alex. She was nothing like either of them. But then again, he thought with an inward sigh, she was like no woman he had ever known.

Alex walked directly into the lion's den, and Marc was impressed with the calm that lay across her facade. She stopped in front of her parents. Instead of looking scared, she smiled widely.

Catherine scowled in return. "We were worried about you. You should know better than to leave without letting us know where you are going."

Marc had seen these arguments enough to recognize the beginnings of a bad one and, with the Rutmeyers present, this was the worst time for a bad one.

Thomas grasped each woman's arm and cleared his throat loudly. Two identical heads turned to cock the same questioning red brow at him. They looked so alike, even with the age difference. One was definitely older, with subtle wrinkles and a touch of gray at the temples of her deep red hair, but, even in movements, were a mirror of each other. The pout of the lips, the flip of the hair all the same.

That is was only a physical likeness, Marc knew only too well. That point drove home as Thomas's sweet-mannered wife came to rein, while the other paid no heed whatsoever.

"I am eighteen, Mama, and more than old enough to make my own decisions." She winced as Thomas pulled her arm, his fingers digging into her soft flesh. "You do not say a word when Jeremy stays out all night, not even when he was my age."

The fingers dug deeper, small white crescents circled his fingertips. Alex grimaced. She began to struggle, yanking her arm to no avail.

Marc glanced down at Janice. Her face showed devious joy at this spectacle. The rest of the Rutmeyer clan seemed to mirror her enthusiasm at Alex's scandalous behavior.

"Stop. Stop." Thomas pulled her toward him. A small yelp of pain erupted from her, and her struggles stopped. Thomas pulled her close. "Look behind me."

Marc had to strain to hear Thomas's whisper. Alex did as she was bade. Her eyes narrowed at Lady Janice, who still wore her smug grin.

"Do you really want to discuss this now?"

She looked up at her father. Her pale blue eyes were like ice chips and just as cold at the moment. The eyes were the only difference between her mother and her. They did not match Lady Catherine's warm emerald green ones, nor did they match the soft brown ones of her father.

"Do you?" he repeated.

"No, Papa." Her spine rigid, she allowed him to turn her toward the group. Her long braid swung well past her rounded bottom. Marc jerked his eyes away from that tempting sight.

Thomas gripped her slender waist in an apparent reminder to behave. He smiled at his guests. "You remember Lord and Lady Rutmeyer, my dear."

Alex gave a half curtsy. "I am much pleased to see you again, your graces." Sarcasm dripped from her tongue as she said all the right words.

Marc watched Thomas twist her long braid around his fingers, tightening until she could do nothing but stand erect. "And of course you remember Lady Janice."

"Vividly."

Thomas gave a slight tug, forcing Alex's head to bob and her brow to furrow with discomfort.

Marc shook his head. He had never understood her stubbornness. If she would just behave, things would go a lot better for her. But then he had given her this advice all her life.

"These are my youngest daughters. Ladies Caroline and Krystal Rutmeyer." The duke spoke with the arrogance of breeding and surety of his place in society. He knew his rank and status and made sure everyone else did as well.

"A pleasure to meet you. I have heard much about you both. I am sure everything that was said falls a cry short of doing you justice." Another tug on the braid.

Marc had no doubt that she would force her father to give a good yank. She didn't care about her reputation or theirs. She thought she could do anything she wanted, but reputations had been destroyed by merely a mention from the Duke of Myerdome. Marc prayed she would keep silent but knew it was futile.

He knew the kind of stories that went around about the twins—arrogant, spoiled, selfish, conniving, back-stabbing. The list went on and in the same vein. He agreed with Alex. He thought the stories fell short of the actual malice they possessed. He just wasn't stupid enough to say it to their faces.

"Lady Alexis, right?' Janice smiled sweetly at the shorter Alex. "I do not know that I recognize you. Were you out last season or is this to be your first?"

Alex's smile was cold. "I was dressed slightly different."

Marc remembered the nearly virginal gowns she had worn last season. They were designed to be in fashion, but the high necklines, much out of fashion, had left her looking much the prude. She was not dressed much different today.

Janice looked her up and down slowly, appraisingly. "I do not think I saw you last season."

Marc knew very well Janice remembered Alex. He drew his hands into fists and took a deep breath. Janice was just baiting her, and he could see dreadful results. He forced himself to keep quiet, determined to stay out of their fight.

Alex had not missed any balls or parties last season. All the members of society threw several gatherings. She always made a point of going to each member's parties, even if she didn't stay throughout the entire affair. All except one family. The Rutmeyers had sponsored four—two balls and two dinner parties—last season. Alex had blatantly missed all four. There was no way Janice did not know exactly who she was.

To make the direct cut worse, Alex had ensured everyone noticed her absence. It was already speculated upon as to whether or not the Lady Alex would indeed snub them so publicly once again. Marc had already heard rumors that it had hit the betting books at Almack's, though he was afraid to see if it were true.

Janice suddenly gave a wide smile. "I know what it is. You did not attend very many parties and balls. Did you not get invitations?"

"Invitations, why yes, indeed, I did, and I attended all the *important* ones—"

Thomas gave that inevitable yank, causing a yelp from Alex, even as the words were still coming from her unruly mouth.

Lady Janice's beautiful face dropped. Catherine stood, holding her dainty fingers to her mouth. Beatrice looked about to faint, and the pompous duke sputtered and growled as his face got redder, the veins pulsing in his forehead.

Before things could get completely out of hand, Amber stepped forward and delicately extracted the long red braid from Thomas's gripping fingers. Amber smiled up at the tall, regal, and enraged earl.

"My lord, allow me to escort Lady Alexis up the stairs. I will help her get prepared for tonight."

"Yes, you go ahead and do that." Thomas's voice was tight with anger.

Marc watched the three girls mount the steps and make their escapes.

Ashlee and Alex, arm in arm, followed Amber up the stairs. Shaking his head, Thomas asked for all to retire to the salon for tea and cakes.

e∂e∂

The three friends fell into a comfortable conversation as Alex sank back into the large copper tub. The warm oil scented water did little to soothe her frayed nerves.

Amber sat on a chair facing the tub and shook her head. "So, does this have anything to do with an upcoming betrothal?" Amber, who was older by only eight years, had always acted more of a mother type to the two girls. Alex respected her opinion and cringed at the thought of telling her what had happened.

"The parents did not seem to know, but Marc and Jeremy looked like they knew something," Ashlee said.

Alex glanced at Ashlee. For as close of friends as they were Alex had to admit that they were almost exact opposites.

Ashlee was a society flirt. She loved the glamor and pageantry that went along with every ball and foray. Her gowns, hats, and gloves were always at the peak of fashion. She never failed to don her umbrella to maintain the pallor that the haughty ton reveled in.

Alex, in contrast, was an adventurer. Her sun-kissed skin spoke of a great amount of time out of doors. She cared little for society or fashion, though she did her best to keep up appearances for the sake of her family.

When Alex didn't answer either of them, Amber cleared her throat. "Well?"

Alex leaned farther back into the warm water and took a deep breath. "I did overhear Marc telling Jeremy of their plans to wed. I understand why this is so important to Marc. If he can put aside the last of the rumors by marrying the daughter of the man who had started them, people will begin to forget. Society is fickle, seeing only what they want." She took another deep breath. "I was more surprised by my reaction to it. I hate to admit you both were right, but…" Alex let her words trail off as the tears threatened. To keep her friends from seeing them, she slid beneath the water.

She emerged and grasped the lilac and rose scented soap. Lathering her long fiery tresses, she tried to smile. "I love him, and now it is worse." Her voice was a tight whisper, pain and betrayal lacing her words.

Amber stood. Two long strides brought her to the tub. She pushed away Alex's trembling hands and finished rinsing away the sweet smelling lather. "How is it worse?"

"He kissed me." Alex's voice was a tight whisper. She was surprised that she had even managed to get the words out.

"He *what*?" Both voices echoed at each side of her head.

"He found me out in the trees. He knows all my hiding places." She swirled her rapidly wrinkling fingers through the chilling water. The soft floral bouquet was finally beginning to relax her, or perhaps it was just being able to talk with her friends. "I began hitting him and screaming at him." Alex gazed shyly at Marc's two siblings then gave a nervous laugh. Sinking back up to her chin, she let her eyes drift shut. "Even though I enjoyed it, I am sure he did it just to shut me up."

Ashlee laughed. "That could be true. When your temper gets going, nothing short of drastic measures can stop it."

Alex twisted her hair through her fingers and laughed. "I know. Sometimes I can get a touch carried away."

"A touch?" The question from Rebecca St. Talves, her young day maid, made Alex jump. The girls were sent into hysterics at this query.

Rebecca approached with extra towels and a wide smile. "The guests should be arriving soon, let's get you dressed." Alex watched as her friends left the room, still entrapped by giggles.

Lost in thought, Alex allowed Rebecca to dry and style her hair. She barely noticed when Rebecca stepped away to get her gown.

Marc's reaction to her in the trees still baffled Alex. He had acted interested and, although her maidenhead was still intact and the first man to kiss her was Marc, she was far from "innocent." The company she kept was loud, boisterous, and, when well into their cups, quite graphic.

Between that and chasing around after Marc and Jeremy, she had learned a lot. More than an unmarried girl should know, more than most married women knew.

She looked objectively at all that had happened and came to one definite conclusion. Marcus Clifton was interested in, at the very least, her body. *His mind may be set on Lady Janice, who would hopefully be as big around as her mother someday soon,* Alex thought with malice, *but his body was perhaps more easily side-tracked.*

She looked down at the high-necked, pale green gown that Rebecca presented. It was very prim and proper, as was the long braid that hung over one shoulder. Both had been chosen, as they were every day, for comfort. Alex smiled. "I have a different idea with my hair."

Rebecca looked at her questioningly.

Marc was stubborn and pigheaded, and she knew he would marry Lady Janice, no matter what. So, while she may not be able to change his mind, she had a good idea that she may be able to torture him. With the Devil's own smile, she told Rebecca what she had in mind.

Chapter 3

Amber rushed down the stairs, looking quite devious. Marc, as well as everyone close to her, knew that look meant she was up to something. Or at the very least knew what she considered to be a juicy secret.

With the two birthday girls still upstairs, Marc could not help but wonder if it involved them.

"You know something. What are you up to, my lady?" Blake smiled at the woman who had stolen his heart fifteen years before. They were childhood sweethearts and, to Marc's dismay, that love still made them act like children on many occasions.

"I am up to nothing—not I," she whispered. "It is not me, but yes, I do know something. Wait just a moment, and you shall see."

"Oh, my."

The gasp came from Lady Catherine, and every head swung to the long staircase.

Descending slowly, every eye upon them, was a beautiful pair. Ashlee, always at the peak of fashion, was swathed in a pale yellow gown, high-waisted, and with just a respectable amount of skin showing above the square neckline. Its ruffled sleeves stopped just above her snow white gloves. The blonde curls were coiled on her head with a small amount of lace holding the mass together. She was impeccable as usual.

Everyone had expected this, but Alex was the one who had stopped the room. Marc took not one, but two involuntary steps forward. His eyes never leaving the proud Alex.

He gazed at the vision on the stairs, her gloved hand trailing the highly polished banister, bringing images of her fingers trailing his hot skin. Where had the little girl gone who had annoyed him so much as she was growing up? He had wondered the same thing the day before, but now it was all he could think.

Just yesterday, an ill-behaved little hoyden had raced into the woods, dressed in her usual soft, comfortable day dress. Standing now at the foot of the stairs, awaiting her father's escort, was a lady.

Her grace and poise spoke of good breeding and a gentle rearing. The pale blue silk of her gown shimmered under the flickering lights of the chandelier and his breath caught in his suddenly parched throat.

Her lace trimmed neckline fell well below what he thought was acceptable. He felt an unaccountable irritation that everyone could see her bared cleavage.

The small puffed sleeves were swept low, leaving the pale, delicate skin of her shoulders bare. Her hair, usually just left in a long braid, was swept up off her long and graceful neck. Marc could feel the pulse of it beneath his lips as if he still kissed her there.

Her long, fiery red tresses shone like diamonds in the sun, the light reflecting off the streaks of blonde highlights. Wrapped several times it was piled high with a disarray of curls left to trail her high cheek bones and perfect ears. One long strand disappeared into the cleft that was tormenting Marc into arousal right there in the middle of the dance floor. For a moment all he could picture was throwing her to the floor, taking her on the high polished marble, and not caring who might witness it.

Head high, shoulders back, Alex gently glided across the room, nodding to people she knew as she went. The gown's full skirt brushed against her father's legs as he took her to the middle of the dance floor, to start off the occasion. Nothing in her movements belied the child from before, the child who had not cared about society nor its rules or her reputation. That had all changed.

At least Marc thought it had.

He could not see the mischievous glimmer of triumph in her eyes as she joyfully watched his jaw go slack and shock register on his handsome face. He may not want her beside him for a wife, but it was obvious as his eyes darkened with the same passion she had seen in the seclusion of the trees that he still wanted her beneath him as a woman.

This ball was the last of the large country affairs before the London season resumed in two weeks after parliament's Easter recess. It was a massive birthday ball for the two girls who had turned eighteen that very morning. The first four dances would be private, only two couples on the floor at a time. First would be father and daughter.

As the two men took their youngest children out onto the large smooth floor, the band struck up the first notes of the allemande. The six servants, all dressed in severe black, who took up the instruments, were the envy of the ton. They played so often that was all they did anymore, even working for other lords and ladies during the season, at a hefty price for those who could procure them for their event.

The Hollister family loved to dance, and all had learned at a young age. The music flowed over the masses of people who had come to celebrate. The light from hundreds of candles wavered over flowing satin and glittery silks. All attention was on the couples, the movements were smooth, beautiful, and full of sweet innocence as Alexis Rose and Ashlee looked up at their proud fathers.

Alex stepped close to her father and was surprised when he took her hand and pulled her closer.

"You are beautiful, and I am so very proud of you."

He let her spin away but did not release her hand and pulled her close once again, not following the steps of the dance. Alex smiled widely and giggled when he kissed the tip of her nose before spinning her away once again.

Beaming deliriously, Alex allowed him to capture her full attention. She knew Marc's eyes were following her. She could feel them like a caress. She was excited to know her plan was working, but the look in the deep brown eyes of the man holding her stole her breath away.

As they spun into the final turn, she smiled sweetly up at him. His eyes were full of laughter and love. His pride meant the world to her, and she would take it as she could get it—because soon that pride would be put to the test. She felt her smile falter at the thought but pushed the unpleasantness away. She was determined to hold onto their happiness as long as she possibly could.

Thomas and Maxwell exchanged girls in a whirl of silks and flying skirts, and the dancing continued. Maxwell proclaimed the same pride her father had. It was more than she had hoped for, and she put aside the guilt that it was all an act. An act that might fall apart at any moment.

The next dance went to the brothers, and as Jeremy bowed to his only sister, he grinned. "You look very beautiful. Very elegant and sophisticated. No one would know you as anything but the social elite. I hope this is a good sign of things to come this season."

A brazen grin and wagged eyebrows were her only response. His grin fell. Alex enjoyed the dance, but she could hardly wait for the song to end. When the last spin finally arrived, she tried to walk away, but Jeremy pulled her against him. Her back rested briefly against his muscled stomach, and he whispered into her ear. "What are you up to, sister dear?"

She looked over her shoulder at him and grinned. "Nothing you are going to like, I assure you."

Alex ignored the look of surprise on Jeremy's face and slid regally from his hands and into Marc's.

With the ice firmly back in her eyes, she strove to be the proper lady. One that Marc would consider good enough for his status and the family reputation he was rebuilding. All just to torment him. She knew a marriage to him was impossible. She could never maintain the facade, but by the dark scowl on his usually chipper visage, it was working.

Marc kept himself erect and properly aloof as the music began to play. That lasted less than a dozen steps into the rhythmic dance. He twirled her, and they stepped together.

"You should be ashamed wearing something so indecent." *And delectable*, he thought with a grimace as heat shot renewed vigor to his groin. He had been fighting his lust and the memory of her supple skin below his exploring hands and mouth since seeing her on the stairs, and he had been dreading and anticipating this dance.

"I am not indecent. I am well within society standards. How dare you say such dribble to me, *my lord?*"

The high-status title, a title of honor and respect came from her mouth like a dirty word. She had never called him anything but Marc in her life. The title surprised and hurt him.

He spun her away, pulled her back, and they stepped together.

"My neckline is higher than that of your betrothed. Why do you not tell her she should be ashamed, *my lord.* Your betrothed—"

"I do not give a bloody damn about Lady Rutmeyer or what she wears." Her eyes widened in shock and Marc wanted to kick himself. He had not meant it to come out, truth or not. "I am more concerned about your reputation because you are important to m—my family. I think of you as I do Ashlee, a little sister."

At least he'd always felt that way before. How had that changed? Now all he wanted to feel were those amazing breasts in his fingers once more.

"A sister?? Like Ashlee?" Her annoyed voice mercifully broke into his reverie before he acted on his urge to pull her close and kiss her. "I will have to ask Ashlee because I am sure she never mentioned you kissing her like that. I think I would remember if she had." Her anger was apparent as she forced the steps of the dance. The first three dances she had performed with elegant grace and, in the space of one turn, Marc crumbled her resolve and turned her into a blundering fool.

He twirled her away. Frustration mounted as the steps of the dance kept interrupting the conversation, and the closeness of the onlookers made it impossible to say the things he would like to say to her.

"I have never kissed Ashlee like I did you." He had lost control of his lust, and the painful throbbing was making an edge to his temper as well as his voice. He tried to keep an eye on her face, but he was so much taller than she, every time he glanced down, he could see nothing but the perfectly rounded tops of milky white skin pouring over the top of her gown.

"Then how can you say you think of me as a sister? Would you do that to a—"

"Stop." He spun her into him, but instead of spinning her away he tightened his grip on her. He didn't think he could take much more. There were at least fifty guests circling the dance floor, the lights from the massive chandelier glowed off the extravagant jewels around the lady's necks and the men's lapels. Marc hardly noticed any of it, just the aggravating morsel in his arms.

"Next time you dress, remember how short you are. From up here, I can almost see the color of your slippers." His eyes widened as she began to struggle in his grasp.

"They are blue *my lord,* as are my chemise and stockings."

As she tried to break his hold, Marc yanked her forcibly into his embrace. Held painfully tight her body molded with his, her breasts pressing into him as he began the next turn in the allemande. "Did you expect to leave me out here on the dance floor all by myself?"

Conversation was impossible as Marc finally released her and resumed the dance, spinning them well faster than acceptable until Alex began to smile. They had danced like this for hours as Jeremy and Marc taught the two girls every dance. Thinking it too tame to dance with their own brothers the girls had felt wicked when they had traded. Alex still felt the same way.

Lost to pleasant memories of her past and the excitement of being in Marc's arms, Alex forgot everything else. She forgot the families and the guests, but most important she forgot the hateful bride-to-be. Once more, they were fluid as they always had been. How she wished they could always be.

On the sidelines, Lady Janice seethed with an unaccustomed jealousy as comments about the couple abounded.

"Oh, what passion they have, someday soon they will see it."

"I am sure there will be a wedding announcement for them this season."

"How can they continue to deny their feelings?"

Janice Rutmeyer tried to ignore them, refused to believe the uncivilized hoyden who had hit her last season was any competition for her. No, that just was not possible.

She felt the first tendrils of doubt when Alex, unrestrained laughter trickling forth and enveloping all who watched, pulled her hand free to clasp both behind Marc's neck. Marc grasped her waist pulling her even closer.

Lady Janice was trembling with rage as she watched them when they finally released the inappropriate hold and resumed the dance, they flowed as one. Step after perfected step. Turn after seductive turn, they moved. The world had ceased to exist for them, and everyone watching knew the only two fools who didn't see their love for each other were the two dancing.

What bothered Janice the most were the onlookers. No one seemed the least bit concerned. They watched Jeremy and Ashlee as much as the other, as they twirled comfortably around the large hall. It was scandalous the way she laughed, the smile on his full lips, and the way they clung in desperation each time the dance brought them close. Marc and Alex's world revolved around the music, each lost to the other's gaze and movements.

Janice snarled in exasperation when it took them a moment or two to realize the music had stopped. She forced herself to remain calm and aloof. She wasn't sure why she was jealous. She did not want this marriage anyway. It was her father's plan and, glancing at Marc, she was not sure she could go through with it.

Marc, disappointed to have the dance end, pulled Alex's small and delicate hand into the crook of his arm. He did not take his eyes off her face as he led her slowly toward the three awaiting families.

Marc felt a tinge of regret as Alex's smile dropped to a painful scowl. Following her gaze, he found his betrothed looking upset, to say the least. Everything about her spoke of anger, but she kept herself in tight, socially acceptable control.

The slumping of Alex's petite shoulders went far to dash cold water on his remaining lust. He could still feel it thrumming just below the surface every time he glanced at her, but at least he thought he could manage not to embarrass anyone. Mainly himself.

Handing Alex over to her mother, Marc bowed over Janice's hand. He had every intention of escorting her to the dance floor, yet his feet refused to move, his innards curling as the Earl of Staten made a beeline for Alex.

Lord Oliver Danton had watched the last dance with growing

malice. Danton knew he was a fine-cut man, tall and wide through the shoulders. Women had always admired his smoky gray eyes, and he was at a loss to understand why women seemed to be more interested in the boring Marcus Clifton.

Danton had known Marc since they were children. In fact, Marc, Jeremy, Blake, and Danton had attended Eton together. They had all been friends until then—until the three boys had learned he had raped a young woman. Danton had never understood why they had been so upset. He still did not. After all, she was only a commoner.

Danton had been beaten and shunned. It was their punishment, as opposed to the scandal that going public with the information would have brought upon his family.

Since then, there had been little contact between the men until last season. Danton had only thought to steal a kiss from the crass Alex. Only a kiss, for there were better fish to be caught than the prudishly dressed hoyden, in her high-necked dark dresses and plain hairstyles.

Marc had stopped him and, if they had not been in the garden of Lord and Lady Malahir's masquerade ball, he was sure he would have gotten another beating. Marc had been livid, so livid he was nearly purple. Danton realized as he approached Alex that Marc's expression was much the same now as it had been that night.

Revenge would be sweet, and that was all he had thought he wanted. But watching the well-formed bosom heaving in laughter before the dance had ended, he had more than vengeance on his mind. Lust rushed his senses, and he pasted a smile on his lips. Pushing his way through the horde of guests, he never took his eyes off his prey.

Danton bowed low in front of Alex and smiled. "My lady, it is good to see you again, may I have this dance?"

Marc stiffened. Danton saw it and rejoiced. Something had happened between them in that garden after Danton had made his escape. He knew it, and he was not the only one. Everyone had seen the changes in the two of them.

Lady Janice pulled on Marc's arm and nearly whined. "My lord, the set is going to start." She nearly pulled him to the floor as Alex pressed her hand into Lord Danton's offered arm.

Alex smiled up at Danton with as much courtesy as she could muster for the monster. A muscle in his square jaw jumped erratically. She had never trusted him. The few times she had encountered him growing up had told her all she needed to know about the arrogant man. She also knew why Marc, Blake, and especially her brother, had steered her clear of him. Her uptight brother would be shocked to his very toes to know she was privy to the details of the rape. *Well*, she thought, her smile widening, *he would be shocked with a lot of the things she knew and did.*

Marc caught and held her eyes, his face a mask of fury and warning. Alex's eyes were reluctantly drawn away from his as the steps of the dance took her attention.

"My dear lady. I must say you look enchanting." Danton pulled her close, molding her body into his.

Narrowing her eyes, she looked up into his smiling face. "Let me loose, my lord. This is far from acceptable."

He just laughed, pulling her snugly against his aching loins. "I do not recall seeing your last *partner* getting the cold shoulder from you. You seemed quite content in his arms."

"That was a different dance, and what I did with my last *partner*—" She gave the word the same derogatory tone that he had, pleased when his eyes widened at her sensual innuendo. "—is none of your concern. Nor does it bear any relevance to our dance." She struggled to put distance between them. To return to the no-touch dance steps required for the cotillion.

"Cease the struggles, else you will make a spectacle of yourself, my lady."

Her struggles stopped. Trying to portray the proper lady image for as long as possible, Alex didn't want to cause a scene.

"Good girl, you would not want to create a scandal. I can assure you, I can make a grander scene than you could ever dream of. I am better at this than you." He pulled her flush against him and took her into a turn that matched the other dancers, even though the others were touching nothing but fingertips. He caught the deadly look in Lord Clifton's eyes as Marc danced beside them.

With a smile, he held Marc's gaze and dropped a small bite onto Alex's bare shoulder. Pain suddenly exploded, as Alex, still mindful of the guests, pulled her knee sharply into his hardened groin. Stars burst behind his closed lids, deep in his brain.

His arousal painfully disappeared, even before he hit the hard wood flooring.

He barely registered the gasps of shock from around him. He saw Marc release the stunned Janice through a dingy cloud of immense agony and flashing lights.

With a fast spin and a cry of concern, Alex flipped the hem of her dress over him blocking his groping hands from view. She quickly knelt beside him. "Oh My Lord, are you all right? What happened?"

In a soft whisper, she added. "I would let go of that if I were you, else everyone will know why you fell."

Marc was the first to reach them. "Very amusing," Marc whispered to Alex as he none-to-gently pulled Danton to his feet. He wasn't sure he liked Alex to be herself, but he realized why he didn't like the demure lady she had been pretending to be all night. It was the suspense, the anticipation, the worried knot that had grown in his insides that awaited...well, awaited the true chit to show herself. Like now.

All attention was on them as Marc, accompanied now by Jeremy, Blake, Thomas, and Maxwell led the limping Lord Danton to the library. He was sure all five men had seen him nip at her shoulder. He knew they were all aware of his actions at Eton, and as they drew close to the library, Danton wondered if he would walk out of it on his own.

Lady Janice joined the onlookers while Alex trailed behind the men, wringing her hands and loudly asking, in a concerned voice, if perhaps a doctor should not be summoned. Much to Danton's chagrin Dr. Philip Monroe stepped forward.

The doctor grasped Alex's hand and pulled her to a stop before she could follow them into the library. "Oh, Dr. Monroe. Thank goodness you are here. Is he going to be all right?"

Danton could hear the laughter beneath the false concern, but the short, fat Dr. Monroe patted her hand to console her.

"My dear girl, he will be just fine. You wait out here, and I will check on him. Can I convince you to wait with you mother? No? At least do not come in."

Inside the dim lit room, Danton sprawled in the large, overstuffed leather reading chair. His hands in tight fists in his lap, his knuckles white, his fingers tingling from pain.

"Are you ill, my lord? What can I do for you?" Dr. Monroe asked, concern tinging his voice.

"Nothing." It still hurt to breathe and, while this was not the first time he had been hit in such a personal area, it was the first time he had been aroused when it happened. "Believe me, there is nothing you can do for me. I—I have an old injury. A riding accident. Sometimes it still bothers me."

"A muscle in your thigh?"

Danton cringed. For the doctor to ask meant he, as well as many others, had seen where his hands had flown, despite Alex's valiant efforts to cover him.

"Yes, in my thigh. I am even now feeling better." Danton took a deep breath to see if he had told the truth, and the pain was indeed less.

"If you decide you need me, let me know. I will let everyone know you are going to be fine."

Danton wanted to ask him to stay, but he knew that would only postpone the inevitable. It would also look suspicious to the doctor and look as if he were a coward to the men waiting for a chance to be alone with him.

The doctor pulled the library door shut behind him. The light clicking of the latch vibrated through Danton like a shot. Thomas took only three strides to cross the wide room.

He leaned down, a hand on each arm of Danton's chair, gripping until his knuckles turned white. With his nose nearly touching Danton's, he spoke with a deep, rumbling growl. "If you ever disrespect my daughter again, you will think what she did to you was a caress. Do I make myself perfectly clear?"

Danton could hardly control the tremor that ran through him. "Perfectly clear, my lord."

While the younger men, he knew would give him a good thrashing, the Earl of Grunby would call him out. He could not win in a duel with him. Thomas's excellence with saber, pistols, and fisticuffs was as well-known as his temper. He was as unstable as his daughter and much more dangerous.

"Good, I shall consider it a personal favor if you were to stay away from my daughter. Can you do that?"

"I shall endeavor to treat her with the utmost respect." *I shall, however, find a time when I will finish our dance*, he thought but was smart enough not to add. He had no intention of staying away, but as long as her father was so protective, Danton would treat her like fine glass, at least as long as there were witnesses. If he could get her alone…well, then he would treat her like the backwoods hoyden she was.

When the men, none looking happy, emerged from the room, Alex rushed to them. A smile strained at the corners of her luscious lips. "My lord, is everything all right?" She ran her hand across his chest in what he knew the bystanders thought was a show of concern. "Dr. Monroe said you had an old riding injury. Does it hurt?"

"That, my dear, is a stupid question."

Her icy gaze held his. She leaned into him, her words coming in a soft whisper. "Perhaps you will think of that next time you challenge me as to who is better."

"Very funny." He was only too aware of her five large protectors right behind him. "You should not have done that. It was not in the least what a proper young lady should indulge in. It could tarnish your reputation."

Alex fought not to smile. She could not give the other guests any more to gossip about than she already had. "Oh, I doubt that, my lord. My reputation is never in jeopardy."

At least not quite yet, she thought, and by the time she decided the time was right and everyone found out the truth, she would have the reputation she needed to help her business. Kneeing Lord Danton would only serve the tough image she would later need. No matter what the doctor said, everyone would still gossip as to the truth and sometimes gossip was better than the truth, if you used it wisely. Her lips twitched. She would see to it that this little bit of scandal made the rounds.

She watched Danton pass a meaningful glance at the men behind him. Their faces were still flushed with anger. "I have wondered about that since last season." His voice was just loud enough to be overheard by the closest of the guests. "With all the scandals and mysteries that seemed to linger around you and with all the unexplained disappearances, how is it that your reputation is still so upstanding?"

She gasped and grasped her chest as if overcome. Her voice was a bare whisper. "My Lord Danton, there are certain things I have learned over the years. One of which is the ton only care about appearances." She gave a slight curtsy, ruffling the end of her long skirt as she did. Her voice rose gently, the guests leaned forward to hear her better. "I never had any unexplained absences last season. There was always someone who had seen me where it was acceptable for me to be."

He leered at her, the pain had given way to the thick anger of knowing everyone had witnessed her unmanning him. No matter the damn story he had concocted. "That does not, my lady, mean you were there." His voice trembled a little louder than she would have liked.

Her eyes flew open in feigned shock, her hands trembled, and she managed a soft sway. "Are you accusing the good members of the elite of lying? How imprudent." Her voice was the dignified squeal of outrage, but merriment rejoiced within her.

He quickly looked around. The members of the elite stared at him with growing rancor. "I would do no such thing." He stepped close, lowering his voice. "Not without proof and I will get proof, my lady." He turned and stalked off in a huff.

She wanted to laugh. Not deigning to even look at Marc, nor her brother, whose faces were livid, she turned her charm onto her father. "Would you dance with me, Papa?"

Lord Thomas, the great Earl of Grunby known far and wide for his uncompromising stature and dangerous disposition, melted before the young woman who had ensnared him heart and soul from the moment she had been born.

With a twinkle in his eye, he led her to the floor. He could not fault her temper or her stubbornness. He may not be the man who planted her seed, but he was indeed the influence of her personality. He had been told a multitude of times that his daughter may be the mirror of Catherine, but she was the reflection of him.

Alex looked up to him as he positioned her for the beginning of the dance. "Sorry, Papa." She dropped her gaze to the floor.

He shook his head with a smile. He placed a finger under her chin and forced her to look at him. "My lovely girl. You are like a small version of me. I see it every time your temper flares and your pride swells." *And it makes me proud and sad at the same time*, he thought but did not add.

Lord Thomas feared for her future. She did not seem to realize that his stricture to the regulations of the ton was not for his benefit. They were for her and Jeremy's.

Keeping with society, Thomas was assuring his children's future standings. His son looked toward the future. Jeremy followed the rules, and Thomas was unconcerned for Jeremy's children.

Alex, on the other hand, was not in the least concerned with herself or the children she would one day have.

"I just wish you would think more of your reputation, your life, and your future. I just wish…" Trailing off, he shook his head.

Disappointment twinged at Alex. He thought she did nothing to look to her future, caring nothing for success in life or the respect of others.

He was wrong. It just wasn't a future he would hope for her.

Alex knew her children, if there ever were any, would benefit from the contacts she had made, as well as the business she was starting. Her horses were the top of the racing scene. Much sought after, although no one knew it was her they dealt with, she was ready. Her horses had grown in number as well as her stash of money in her alias's name. A.H. was the name on her account, as well as how she signed any contracts for the illusive jockey.

She was proud of her success, and she strove for more. She also wanted the respect of others. She just knew the ones who were important to get respect from. Her family, her friends, her business partners, and those she cared for. The rest of the ton...well, they were just self-centered and arrogant fools, and she had better things to concern herself with than them.

"Papa, you make it sound a bad thing to take after you. 'Tis not, I assure you. I may be a girl by accident of birth, but the one I most strive to emulate is you. If only you would let me, you would be proud of all I can accomplish."

The music began to float quietly through the room. The dancers bowed to each other, and the music began to build.

"I just want what is best for you."

The dancers began to move, and conversation was lost, leaving Alex to her troubling thoughts. She had tried to talk to her father about her future. They had discussions of her going into business on two different occasions, never getting to the type of business she wanted to start. It had been when she was younger, and he had loudly put a stop to her nonsense. That she would even suggest a thing like that would devastate her standing. He would not allow that.

Alex thought about his words until the music ended. She leaned into him as he led her off the floor.

He could feel the delicate fingers trembling as she gripped his arm. "Papa, perhaps you can someday want what will make me happy. Happiness should be of more worth than what others think of me."

She slipped from his arms before he could respond, his jaw slack at the pain her statement had caused. All through the remainder of the ball, he stood beside his beautiful wife, watching the girl he had raised. He could not remember when she had become a woman, but there she was. Alex did not miss one minuet, one country dance, or one Pavane. Nor did she miss any of the multitude of other dance songs that played. The only dance she sat out was an allemande. Thomas thought it strange that Marc as well sat out the two allemandes played. He only took his betrothed once to the floor, dancing mostly with others as she did.

Thomas smiled when he noticed Marc's attention, whether he danced or watched, was never but a moment away from Alex.

Chapter 4

Alex tore down the hall, her slippered feet barely making a sound on the freshly scrubbed floors. Excitement thrummed through her veins, her heart pounded. The London season was almost upon her, and she could not wait.

Without slowing, she burst through the library door. The heavy oak slammed into the wall and left the books trembling upon their shelves. Jeremy glanced up from his seat behind the large desk. The early morning light shone brightly off what little could be seen of the high-polished mahogany. Most of the beautiful desk was covered by a strew of paperwork and open ledgers. He looked at her calmly, a small smile playing on the corners of his lips.

Alex slid to a rough stop before him. Her feet catching on the massive rug that adorned the room. She grasped the desk for balance, her stomach lurched, and she had a moment of fear, sure she would topple over onto his paperwork.

Her brother threw his hands dramatically into the air. "So much for the elegant lady of last night." He peered around her and squinted into the hallway. "Where did you hide her?"

She grinned widely and glanced down at her comfortable day dress. It's soft blue rose pattern made her eyes sparkle.

He pushed the ledger away from him with a massive sigh. Then he grinned widely at her. "What happened to the beautiful gown I bought you? You could not, at least, wear something like that, little girl?"

She let the old nickname slide over her without a comment. "I could." She pictured the dress he had proudly presented for her birthday. He had thought he had made the perfect find, and in her opinion, he had. It suited her. It was made of a pale cream satin, not overly fancy but with a kind of grace about it. The delicate lace that adorned it had been exquisitely soft beneath her palms.

"I plan to wear it to the first ball of the season." She smiled down at him. With a pat on his hand, she planted herself on the edge of his desk. "I told you I love it. It is absolutely perfect. I just do not want to mess it up before then. Besides—" She pulled the top of her gown slightly away from her and allowed it to fall back, "—there are certain advantages to having a loose and comfortable neckline." Ignoring his look of shock, she continued. "Now, where is Papa?'

"Standing here trying to decide what advantages there are to your dress."

His voice was tempered with shock and the beginnings of worry. She cringed and glanced at Jeremy. "Thanks a lot," she mouthed. He grinned.

She slid from the desk and turned to face her father. Off to the left of the room stood not only her father, but Marc as well. Her heart thudded painfully.

Marc's face flushed as their eyes met. She could not seem to get command of her tongue. No matter how she tried, it lay like a stone, dead in her mouth. He finally broke the gaze and with a reddening face stared at the floor.

Without him staring at her, she found it easier to concentrate, easier to breathe. Taking control of her traitorous body, she turned her attention to her father. "There are plenty of advantages." Her voice was shaken at first, but she recovered quickly. "But until you spend a day in a dress that has five hundred buttons too small to see—let alone fasten—a stay that binds you, and so many layers of lacy under-*fluffs* that you swelter even before the first dance, I refuse to discuss any merits of my wardrobe with you."

He laughed, the sound a short, relieved snort. "That is what your mother tells me when I bring home some new style I have seen." With a hearty laugh, Thomas clapped Marc stoutly on the back. "But I can think of better advantages than that, eh, my boy?"

Marc's face took on a sudden pallor, and Alex felt a grin tickle her lips. Thomas looked closely at Marc's pale complexion, and Alex thought of a way to torment both men. *Just a little torturous fun*, she thought. She had to bite the inside of her lip to keep from laughing.

She forced the smile from her lips and planted on a scowl. She quickly stepped toward her father and slapped him across the arm.

He spun around to her. "What? You're getting pretty strong there for a girl."

"I cannot believe you could speak of...of...such things in front of me." The sudden look of uncertainty on his face threatened her composure. She held the scowl, but just barely.

"What things?" His eyes narrowed suspiciously. "How do you know of such things?"

She took a guilty moment to remember two days before and the heaving pleasure she had enjoyed at Marc's warm lips. She had to force her mind back to the present before her imagination got the better of her.

Now unsure of how to, delicately, tell her father what she had seen him do, she hesitated. Marc seemed to struggle for breath, the color drained from his face and she knew that he too was thinking about their time in the woods.

To encourage this line of thinking, she struggled with herself, taking deep breaths and long moments to continue. Marc began to fidget with his cravat and nervously shifted from one foot to the other. He seemed to look at everything in the room, except her.

"Well? I am waiting." Thomas's tight, yet loud voice said clearly it had better be good and quick at that.

"Lady Bickerbee's tea party last season."

Marc finally looked at her, his face a mask of confusion that slipped quickly into relief. Her father, on the other hand, paled.

Thomas could feel the color drain from his face as memories of that night overtook him. He had complained that his beautiful wife was not properly dressed, but none of the other women seemed to notice as several of them were wearing day dresses to the simple garden party. He discovered that afternoon that her state of attire was perfect. He enjoyed himself fully with her in the massive and secluded Bickerbee gardens.

"You were in the g—garden?" he stuttered in horror at the thought that his innocent little girl had perhaps witnessed them.

"Papa, you know how I love the gardens, especially there." Her smile did nothing to calm his thudding heart.

"I shall remember that when I choose my hiding spot. I forget you are not a child anymore." It always amazed him how she had grown. His mind still wanted to picture her as the small child running and jumping into his arms. Her next words reminded him fully that she was no longer that young girl.

"Choosing your hiding *spots*—" She put heavy emphasis on the plural. "—better is probably a good idea."

Thomas looked at his son, who stared at him in open-mouthed surprise. He could hear the shuffling of Marc beside him but dared not look at him. "Spots?" There was no stutter this time, but he cringed at the high-pitched word that escaped him.

"Yes, and, even when I was a child, I knew alcoves did not groan and pant. I knew hall tapestries did not shake and shudder, and I knew mother did not scream in pleasure from finding a jar of peaches in the pantry." Her face was bright red by the time she had finished her speech, but her voice did not waver, and she did not drop her gaze.

"Look, I—that is—" Thomas's felt his face tighten in horror, and hot embarrassment swallowed him.

Alex waved off his words. "What I knew most and still know to this day." She laid her cool hand on his arm and gave him a look of love that stole his breath. "What I know, is that you are very much in love with my mother, and that she is very lucky to have such a wonderful man as you to stand beside her all these years. As am I."

Tears caught in his throat as he pulled her tightly against him. It scared him how much he loved her. If one day she found out he was not truly her father, she would hate him for lying, and she would love him no more. When that day came, he knew it would kill him. Fear clogged his throat at the very thought of losing her.

Thomas inhaled deeply. The soft floral scent of her perfume enveloped him. He reluctantly released her. She looked up with devotion and mischief in her eyes. A look that always made him nervous. He narrowed his eyes. "What do you want?"

"Nothing big. I just came to ask if I can go on to London early with Ashlee. She is going to stay the two weeks before the beginning of the season with Aunt Levita."

She smiled at him, her eyes wide. He wondered if that was supposed to be her innocent look. If so, she needed to work on it.

"Alexis, you know how I feel about that woman," With a look of apology directed at Marc, he added, "No offense, my boy."

"None taken. My father's sister is quite eccentric." Marc gave a soft laugh. "I know. I love her dearly, but even before she began to lose her memory, she was a bit daft. Always been."

Thomas thought of the petite little woman. She had the strength of a work horse when she was angry. Her green eyes were faded and her hair gray, but she loved the girls. No matter how bad her memory was, she always seemed to know them.

"I know how you feel, Papa, but you also know we are safe there. With as many servants as she has, nothing could possibly happen to us." Alex's smile widened and he was sure it was meant to calm his fears. It did no such thing. "I will be perfectly safe and guarded." She patted his arm and gave a quick nod of her head as if the subject were already settled.

He glanced at Jeremy and then at Marc before shaking his head in defeat. With an exasperated sigh he said, "I suppose it will be fine, my girl." He was rewarded as she flew into his arms.

She wrapped her arms around his neck and, with her feet off the floor, she hung in his embrace.

He hugged her tightly and found himself unable to release her. She was growing up too fast, and life had a nasty habit of not letting one get used to the changes.

Alex wanted to stay buried in his arms forever, but her heart thudded with excitement. She placed a quick kiss on his cheek and slipped from his arms and raced from the room. She had forced herself not to look in Marc's direction as she went. She had barely looked his way while in the library and had spoken to him not at all.

Ignoring him was part of the plan. Advice that she had received on how to get a man's attention. She grinned as she pulled the door shut behind her. Marc would be livid if he knew his mistress was the one who had been the source of this sage advice. Indeed, if he knew they were friends at all.

Alex had to know if the plan was working, but the words she heard as she paused to press her ear to the door did nothing to comfort her.

After she left, Thomas watched Marc intensely. "What do you think Marcus, my boy, our little girl has become quite the woman, has she not?"

Marc took a deep breath. "She is still an undisciplined hoyden, my lord."

"Yes, but you have to admit she will make some lucky man a very good wife." His eyes never left Marc's reddening face, judging every reaction, every expression, with a deadly seriousness.

"Yes, for the right man," Marc said, then looked surprised that the words had come out of his mouth. He closed his eyes momentarily and then looked apologetic.

"And just what kind of man would be the right man?" At Marc's silence, he probed him. "Well, out with it, tell me what you think?"

Marc looked at Jeremy, but from the look on his son's face, Thomas knew he was not about to add in his opinion. Jeremy just shook his head and grinned.

Marc sighed and turned his attention back to Thomas, glancing at the door, as if to judge his escape and then finally began speaking. "I think the right man would be one who wanted to constantly worry about where his wife was, what she would say next, who she would insult, what she was doing, who would take a knee to the groin, and when her temper would once again override her good sense. If she has any." He sighed and shook his head. "It is difficult to tell since her temper seems riled almost always these days."

Thomas felt a knowing smile begin to spread across his lips. He was beginning to think the rumors were true. At the end of last season, as well as last night, the popular consensus was that Marc and Alex had fallen for one another.

Everyone saw the passion, but the changing relationship was causing strain between them. He knew it was mostly because of Marc's dreams of restoring his family's status and reputation. Marc did not think Alex was good for that future. Thomas could not be angry at this, as he was not sure he disagreed.

Jeremy stood and stretched his back. It popped audibly. "Alex is only out of sorts around you Marc...well, mostly just around you. She does have a temper to rival even yours, Father. Though, I do agree." He grinned. "Her husband, if she ever gets one, is in for one shock after another."

Marc remembered these words a week later, when, on his way to London, he stopped at Aunt Levita's to check on the girls. "What do you mean they are not here?" He was dumbfounded, though he was not sure why he was. With a resigned sigh, he continued. "They are supposed to be here?" Gregory, his aunt's groom and driver for the last ten years, just shrugged and looked apologetic. "Where are they?"

The man, who looked much younger than his twenty-six years, just shook his head, brown curls bobbing and swaying with a life of their own. He shrugged his wide shoulders and shook his head, again sending his curls into a distracting dance. Gregory stood stiff and kept his gaze on Marc's cravat. "I do not know my lord. They have been gone since this morning."

"You are the man who would drive them. Unless you are telling me she drove herself, and I know she cannot do that." How could this get any worse? Marc never should have come to check on her. What he had been thinking, he didn't know.

He had told himself the entire way to London that he was concerned for his sister and her safety. That story had become harder to tell himself the closer he had gotten. Now it failed to comfort him at all. He had wanted to see Alex. Not that he wanted to see her, he told himself. He just needed to make sure that she was not up to too much mischief.

"My lord, I do not drive Lady Alex anywhere." Gregory's voice pulled him from his spiraling thoughts. "Robert does."

Marc just shook his head. He knew that. It bothered him, but he still knew it. The two had been inseparable since she was thirteen years old. That her father allowed her to use him as a personal servant, while the family had to hire another groom, was something else that annoyed Marc.

It was unseemly, and her father, who was usually strict when it came to things like that, had relented when she had thrown a tantrum.

He could not fathom why a child would need a personal servant, a man no less, at their beck and call. Waving away the stuttering Gregory, Marc stomped back toward his own carriage. He had to stop thinking of the damn little chit. She was going to drive him crazy if he allowed his concern for her to take over his life.

He was going to go on to Whites and forget about her. With that decided, he pounded on the top of the carriage. Lying back in the soft leather seat, he thought of the gaming tables that were calling his name.

Marc, to his horror, was unable to even make it back the three miles to London. He thumped on the carriage roof and told the startled driver to turn around. He would just wait until they returned. They could not be much longer if they had left that morning. He, as a concerned brother, was required to see that his sister was all right.

He needed to make sure the arrogant Alex was not being too much of an ill influence on the sweet Ashlee. He could care less what Alex did, as long as his sister was all right. And the fact that someone had let a rumor slip that Alex had a lover…well, that had nothing to do with him being here in the least.

Levita was ecstatic to see him and enjoyed the two days that he visited, though she could not tell him where the girls had gone to, nor even if they were there. The servants knew nothing either. The ladies had not mentioned where they were going nor when they were going to get back. He had believed them at first, but as the two days passed, he learned the servants were loyal to Alex more than to his sister or even his aunt. They would lie for her. This he knew instinctively, and it bothered him.

ꙮꙮꙮ

Alex raised a hand to shade her eyes against the bright afternoon sun. Her thick leather work gloves dangled from her loose grip, throwing cool shadows across her face. The heavy gloves would make her hands sweat, but they were an unfortunate necessity. They were not a comfort item, nor a fashion statement, but they would keep her hands safe and protected. She did not want to wear them. She wanted to feel the leather and horse flesh beneath her palms, but it would not do for her to show up at tea with the calloused and cracked hands of a worker.

She sighed and closed her eyes. A soft breeze cooled her skin, and she let a smile play across her lips. She pressed the heel of her hands into her lower back and stretched. She opened her eyes and looked out across a healthy green pasture.

She rested one booted foot upon the lowest rail of the well-maintained log fence. The leg of her breeches pulled tight across her thigh and bottom, making her feel slightly indecent, but nothing like it had the first time she had donned a pair. She slapped her riding crop distractedly against her boot and looked out across the field of roving horses.

The property belonged to Lord Edward Barlow, but the horses were hers. The pasture stood seven miles from Levita's home and six miles from London. It made for the perfect spot to keep her horses and her carriages. The wide sprawling grounds, with their low rolling hills, made it the perfect place to train, and the thick grove of trees that surrounded it kept her safe from prying eyes.

"Are you ready, my lady?"

She turned toward the quiet voice, her smile spreading to a wide grin. Standing beside her small carriage was a short, yet well-built groom, his hand held out waiting to assist Ashlee to the ground.

Robert Dunmore, her private driver, was one of only two men who were privy to all her secrets. Her father had hired Robert on the faked advice from Lord Blackmore. He had never personally asked Blackmore if he had sent the young man, for which Alex was grateful, but not surprised. Blackmore was a high brow of society, but he was not the most affable of people. It was the main reason he had been chosen for her ruse.

Robert took Ashlee's white gloved hand and assisted her to the ground. Guilt pricked at Alex for lying to her father about Robert, but she knew he would never have hired him if he had known the recommendation had actually come from Lord Edward Barlow.

Robert, his brown eyes shining with his usual good humor, followed closely behind Ashlee. With a sigh of contentment, Alex watched them make their way to her. Though he technically worked for her father, he was her driver and personal assistant, and she was grateful she had convinced him to come work for her.

She waved and started toward them. She greeted Ashlee with a hug and took her by the arm. As they walked, she quickly told Robert which horses she wanted to work for the day. She nodded approvingly as he rushed off to get them saddled and ready for her.

"Come, my dear, let us get you a place in the shade to watch. I want to run a couple horses, get them ready for the races next week." She was anxious about the first race, but she was nervous as well. She always was, but this season was different. This time fear tingled deep within her.

She led Ashlee to a large oak tree whose ancient and gnarled branches threw a massive shadow on the cool grass below. As she helped her to the ground beneath it, Alex realized just how grateful she was that she could share this part of her life with her friend. The fact that Alex was a jockey was only known to a few people.

Edward knew. He helped her with the races and let her use his lands to pasture, stall, and train her horses. At least until the time came that she could purchase her own.

Ashlee knew of the races, but nothing of Alex's other little side ventures. Alex watched Ashlee settle her skirts around her and frowned. It would be nice when all her secrets could be opened to her family. Lying to them left her stomach in knots.

Raymond Dunmore, Robert's brother, also knew about the racing. He was hired by Alex when she was fourteen, because even though she had known she wanted to raise horses, she had known very little about them. He was an excellent trainer and groom. His job was to care for the horses and train them. And her, she thought with a grin.

"Let Robert know if you need anything," she told Ashlee, who leaned back against the wide trunk. When her friend nodded, Alex turned away.

She turned back to the large corral and pasture and waited for Robert to finish readying the horses. She looked over her stock, pride warming her. There were over a hundred head of horses milling around the tall green grass.

Her mind drifted back to that first purchase. She had been fourteen, but even then she had been sure of where her future lay. She had approached her father about her business idea. She would raise, breed, and race horses. They were in her blood.

Her father had only stared at her as if she had grown two heads.

The fact that her father had outright refused to hear her out did nothing to dissuade her. She ran her first race at fifteen and was proud of the fact that she had become the top racer in the last three years. All behind the guise of the infamous jockey A.H. She grinned.

The horses were all of excellent bloodlines and all worth a small fortune in their own right. Not long now, and she would let the world know exactly what she was capable of. By the end of this season, the last race, in fact, she planned to deviate from her routine.

Normally she disappeared right after her last run, leaving Raymond to collect the winnings and make arrangements for the next race. And, of course, leaving everyone to gossip about who this mysterious racer really was. This time, though, she would stay at the end of the race.

She planned to expose herself for who and what she really was. She was terrified of how her family would take the news, but excitement drove that fear away until it was just a tickle in the back of her mind.

"Horses are ready, my lady." She glanced up into Robert's smiling face. He nodded to the horses and leaned against the corral fence. This season, Raymond had been training him to be a jockey. They would be her second and third jockeys, leaving her able to enter her horses into more of the runs each race, a goal she had been working toward for two years.

She had been trying to convince Raymond to become her second for years, but he had been unsure, saying he could train them, but he wasn't a jockey. She was relieved she had finally convinced them both.

As it stood at present, she could only race every other race, but with the addition of the two brothers, her horses could run them all.

As Alex began to warm up a tall roan stallion named Master Greg, she thought about all the people who knew her little secrets. It was a growing list, and that made her nervous.

The idea that so many people, who knew one secret or another, had the potential to reveal her burned at the back of her mind constantly. She did not believe it would ever be intentional, but accidents happened, and people's tongues slipped.

Master Greg pulled at the reins and yanked her back into the present. She smiled down at the top of his head and loosened her grip on the reins. He took only a moment to realize he had his head and tore across the pasture. Smells of grass wafted up at her from beneath his pounding hooves.

She watched his muscles ripple and closed her eyes. The air whipped past her, blowing the sweat from her brow and reminding her of why she loved this life.

She made one more pass before bringing the lanky horse to a stop by the stalls. She glanced at Robert. He was already most of the way across the field to her. He would cool the horses and get them unsaddled as she finished with each one.

She allowed him to help her down and mounted the next horse,

Marylee, a large bay mare, without awaiting his assistance. She watched him as he led the stallion away. Other than Robert, there were only two people who knew everything she was involved in. Andrew March, her solicitor, and Tess Richards, the mammoth of a man she had hired as personal guard and driver for A.H. Tess would take over as her driver and bodyguard when the brothers became full-time jockeys, and her secrets were revealed. Nudging the mare in the side, she realized just how much she was looking forward to the truth being out.

She walked the mare to warm her up, but the horse pulled at the reins, impatient to be off. Alex gave her attention to the mare and let the troubles of the future fade away. She forced the mare to walk until she was certain her muscles were warmed and her breathing even. She then gave her her head, and the mare took it, running faster and faster until the wind tore through her mane and Alex's clothing.

Alex laughed, taking the mare into the turns faster and tighter than she had the day before. She decided then that Marylee was going to be in the first race this season.

She took two more passes before the horse began to slow, her breath heaving almost as raggedly as the mare's. Alex reluctantly turned the horse back toward the stables. She loved being out here. It was the one place she truly felt free. Leaning her head back, she let the cool breeze sooth her sweat-laden face and neck.

"That was amazing."

She looked over at Ashlee who had left her shady position and now leaned across the top of the fence. Her face glowed, and her eyes sparkled with excitement.

Her gaze slipped from Ashlee to the man who now stood beside her.

Alex smiled at him and waved heartily. Raymond looked a lot like his brother, and they both had the same easy going temperament when it came to dealing with not only horses but people as well.

Alex leapt from the horse and threw the reins toward Robert. She raced across the grass and nearly jumped the fence in her excitement. She pulled Ashlee into a tight embrace and spun her around.

Laughter erupted from Ashlee as Alex finally released her. "Does that mean you have decided? She is going to be in the races?" Her voice was breathless.

"Yes, the first race, and we will hope she doesn't spook too badly." Alex didn't believe she would, but with new horses, it was never guaranteed with the excitement of the crowd and the noise of the bystanders and the other racers.

"If I know you, there is no way she will spook, she will do wonderful."

Alex turned toward the voice, a smile touching her lips. She shook her head at the blond-haired man who approached. Edward Barlow was the same age as her mother, forty-seven. They had grown up together. They had been close friends when they were younger, but things had changed over the years.

Edward was so tall that his head almost grazed the branches of the large elm. He was a stern and rugged-looking man. His square jaw and thin lips gave him a sinister appearance. He was not a handsome man, by any society standards, but he had a grace and poise that only added to his mystique. His distinguished looks and straightforward attitude made him irresistible to the ladies, even those of the snotty ton.

He broke into a grin, and she knew why the ladies found him so charming. His ice blue eyes twinkled. He opened his arms to her, and she threw herself into them. Her excitement made her forget all propriety, though out here in the middle of nowhere with no one to see her, she didn't have much propriety to start with.

He tightened his grip, pulled her off the ground, and enveloped her completely in his embrace. The warm aroma of roses and lilacs teased him. He gave one more tight squeeze before dropping her to the ground. Her laugh was contagious, and he felt his grin widen.

"You always have more faith in me than you should." She looked back at Ashlee with a soft smile. "Go rest in the shade." She gestured for Robert and Raymond to remain with her. They took their spots obediently. "Edward, can I talk to you privately for a moment?" She kept her words soft, quiet.

"Certainly, Rose." He answered in the same hushed tone and held out his arm. Alexis Rose, the daughter he wished he could admit to having, smiled up at him. She slipped her glove from her hand and slid her sweat pruned fingers into the crook of his arm. He smiled. "How have things been going?"

Edward took note of the big man who shadowed their every move. Tess stayed far enough back to allow privacy, but close enough to prevent anything from happening to her. Edward also knew he could still hear them. He had asked her once how she had come by the big man, but it had been one of the few things she didn't tell him. At least he thought it was. He watched her sometimes and wondered if perhaps she had more going on than even he knew about.

"Things are going fine." Her voice was calm, but he thought he could hear a tremor running beneath. "Things are like they always are, and the horses are coming along splendidly." She glanced back, past the trailing Tess, and to the three people beneath the large tree's canopy. They were out of hearing range of Ashlee, Robert, and Raymond.

She looked back at him and he knew he had been right about the tremor. He could nearly see her thrumming with what could be excitement, but he was unsure if it was good or bad until she nearly yanked him to a stop.

"I want some information." The calm, see-you-at-tea voice was replaced with what sounded to him like desperation, not excitement.

"Anything I can tell you I will, you know that."

From their vantage point on the small hill they could look over the entire acreage he allowed her to use. He watched her horses roam and waited patiently for her to ask her questions. She took a deep breath. He looked back at her, and she seemed to garner her thoughts.

She leaned closer to him. "I know that Marc is marrying Janice and I understand why he is." She took another deep breath. He felt the warmth across his cheek as she exhaled close to him. She dropped her voice to a bare whisper. "What I want to know is why she is. She doesn't seem the type to go crazy with lust and desire. I cannot see her as the one who is pushing this marriage." She shrugged. "Though I believe she does want him, if for nothing else than just so no one else can have him."

He had heard stories of Marc over the years from her, and he could tell she was fascinated with him, if not already in love. He had seen a lot of her over the years. Her nurse, Rhona Lotios, brought her to him whenever Catherine and Thomas were out of town. Which, lucky for him, was often. They were always on one trip or another, leaving her in Rhona's care for weeks at a time.

He was never in doubt that she was well loved, but he enjoyed his time with her.

As she had gotten older, she had found her own ways to see him, asking outright to have one of his men pick her up. He had sent Robert and ending up losing both brothers to her in the end. He never told her he was her father but made sure she knew he loved her just the same.

"Lord Rutmeyer is in debt. He gambles heavily and is being pushed hard to pay those debts." He cocked his head with a grin. "Do you want me to stop pushing?"

Her head jerked up at him in surprise. "You carry his markers?"

She should not have been shocked, but she was.

"He has amassed a large amount through the house account with me for the horse races as well. He has never been allowed in the back room because I do not trust him, but he is at the main tables most nights."

The back room was a private area in Rose Hall. There were better quality drinks as well as whores at the disposal of the men. It was a distinct group of trusted men that were allowed back there, ones who could keep a secret. Men who would never say they saw Alexis Rose gambling alongside them.

"From what I hear of his bride-to-be, she was reluctant. Lady Janice is like an iceberg. Cold and forbidding." He gave a small laugh. "I hate to think of the wedding night, the poor girl will probably just swoon away." His voice became serious. "Do you want me to back off?"

"Rutmeyer is blackmailing him. He has no money to pay a dowry, but he is getting money from Marc instead." She shook her head in disgust. "Get your money if you can, but it will be a while before they marry. From what I hear, she wants to wait."

"Yes, for as long as she can postpone it." He wrapped an arm around her shoulders and led her back toward her waiting friends. "What can I do to help you get ready for the races, or anything else?"

"Just keep me posted. I am still looking for a couple of great stallions. There is one I am admiring at Tattersall's," she let her voice drop to a whisper as they approached the large oak tree, "but if anyone comes though the Hall with any they might like to lose. I will see that they do."

Edward nodded and turned his attention to the small group under the tree. He held his hand out to Ashlee with a soft smile. She took it with a shy grin of her own. "My lord, it is nice to see you again," she said.

"Lady Ashlee. It is always a pleasure to see you." He dropped a kiss onto her gloved hand and bowed low before turning back to Alex. "I will let you go. I have things I need to see to." He gave another bow and disappeared around the carriages.

"Let's get back to the manor, grab some lunch, and then sleep for half the day." Alex smiled as Robert laughingly agreed.

Back at the manor, a messenger from Lady Abigail Torrens awaited them. Marlon Dessau, a short, bald Frenchman, never without a smile, greeted them with an exuberance Alex had yet to encounter from anyone else. Having spent a lot of time at the Torrens residence over the last season, Alex had grown to care for the older man, who, at sixty, was still spry as a goat, taking on all kinds of assignments from Lady Abigail or her husband Lord James Torrens.

Wrapping her arms around the gaunt shoulders of her elderly friend, she led him to the steps just to have him pull out of her embrace. "Don't have no time for pleasantries, mademoiselle, Lady Abigail has just had her babies. I was coming to find you, having heard you were here. She had twins and could use some help. Lord James is out of town on business, a messenger was sent, but it may be four days before his return." His words came in a rush and ended in a breathless wheeze.

Lady Abigail had not been due for at least several more weeks, but Lady Alex was still irritated that James would leave town so close to the due date. It was never a precise date, everyone, even a first time dad, should know that. "We will meet you there."

As Marlon steered the surrey back the way he had come, Ashlee smiled at her friend. "Alex, I think I will wait down here for you to change."

"No, I am anxious to see the babies. There is clothing in the carriage, I can use it." She laughed as Ashlee looked at her in shock.

"Why do you have extra clothing?"

"Sometimes things are needed," was all Alex said.

Robert rushed them to London while Alex slipped into more appropriate attire in the rocking carriage.

Once at the Torrens's London townhouse, Alex was shocked to see Abigail walking toward the front door to meet them, a newborn in each arm. "Should you be up so soon?" Alex asked. Each girl took a sleeping infant as Marlon scolded Julie, Abigail's young day maid, for allowing her up.

"Oh, now stop you three. The doctor said it was fine if I was up, for just a short time. There is nothing wrong with a little exercise to loosen up the muscles. Come, let us lay these boys down and sit for a while. Are you able to stay and visit?"

Lady Abigail was a tall and bulky woman. Her long black hair was elegant, her dark blue eyes betraying nothing of just giving birth late the night before. She was not a beauty, but her husband loved her with a passion and devotion that always stole the breath of any lucky enough to see them together.

"Yes, we will be here, at least until your husband returns. We will gladly play with the babies and forward our friendship."

The Torrens family was always on the outskirts of society, yet Alex, Ashlee, and Amber had gladly made themselves available to her, glad to have made the acquaintance of another young woman.

At twenty, she had married older than her peers, thinking no one would ever look at her as a future wife. Not until James had come from Ireland, moving here after inheriting a great uncle's home and lands. He was the second child and was more than willing to move to England for the chance at owning the massive estates. As well as the distinguished title of Viscount Torrens. Though Alex knew, without a doubt, that the title and the land had nothing to do with why he had married her.

Over the next two days, the girls laughed and talked. Spoiling the boys who looked just like their father, with their bright red hair and deep green eyes. They both had his loud and boisterous temperament as well. When one would sleep the other would wake, keeping the girls occupied at all times.

James, with his infectious joy, as well as his unabashed regret over missing the birth of his sons, had quickly made Alex forget her anger with him. He had made it in two days, where no one had thought he would make it in four. Leaving the messenger behind, leaving his carriage to catch up, he had changed horses several times, riding throughout the day and night to reach her. He took her into his embrace and kissed her deeply, even before seeing the babies.

Hugging the happy couple tightly, both Alex and Ashlee met Robert to return to Aunt Levita's. Arriving only an hour after the enraged Marc had left, they were greeted by servants from all areas of the house.

Alex smiled as she listened to news of his arrival. The fact he had stayed for two nights tickled her to no end.

Chapter 5

Alex's two weeks of blissful freedom seemed to be gone in the blink of an eye. One moment she was astride the back of her stallion, wind in her hair, and exhilaration thrumming through her, and, less than a heartbeat later, she was trussed up in a fashionable gown at Hollister House, her family's London townhouse. Her hair was bound so tightly on the top of her head she thought she would scream and, now, the only thing thrumming through her was boredom.

She looked down at the pile of invitations that lay strewn across the top of her dressing table. She cringed at the thought of all the engagements she must attend. She sighed deeply. She wanted to be back in the saddle with the soft musky scent of horse flesh wafting up at her instead of the cloying smells of powders and rouge.

She took a deep breath. The constraints of her gown gouged and prodded into her aching ribs. She missed the comfort and freedom of her breeches. She missed her boots. She missed her braid, and she missed her life. Her true life.

This life was so much different. So unlike what she wanted. The rush, the parties, the swarms of people were in vast contrast to the quiet rushing of the wind and the heavy thudding of hooves on the soft dewed grass of the morning.

She shuddered and glanced into the mirror at the fake doll that stared back at her. A doll all dressed up for the night to come, the first social gathering of the season. She forced a breath through the ever-tightening gown, but she could already feel the stifling air of the ballroom overwhelming her lungs.

She could already feel the mass of overly warm bodies, the push and shove of society, both in the figurative and the literal sense. She tugged at the bodice of her gown, trying desperately to draw in a breath.

She closed her eyes and, ignoring a shudder, she forced her mind to calm. She took several deep breaths and tried to bring forth some-thing, anything, besides her own worries.

An image made its way through the panicked fog that had envel-oped her. A memory that reminded her she was not the only one anx-ious about the upcoming season. She could clearly see Ashlee flitting around the drawing room that morning, fidgeting with everything she could reach.

Alex took another deep breath and let the memory sweep her away.

"Ashlee, calm down it is only going to be the Pettlenosters. You have known Lord and Lady Ferdinand since you were six. They are nearly family." Alex had tried to calm her but to no avail.

"Oh, Alex, it is not just tonight. It is the entire season." Ashlee had suddenly spun toward Alex and dropped into a chair with a lack of propriety that had surprised Alex. Ashlee was never one to be anything less than the perfect lady.

"Ashlee—"

"What if I do not find a husband again this season?" Ashlee had blurted out, tears shining brightly in her eyes. "I am almost an old maid."

Alex had barely restrained a grin before it could escape and upset her friend even further. "Ashlee, you are only eighteen. You are also bright and beautiful, and any man would be crazy to pass up the op-portunity to have you. You can do this, so just calm down."

Those had been her encouraging words to calm her friend just that morning. Now Alex tried to remind herself of the same thing as she sat, unprepared for the nervousness that surrounded her. She glanced up at her solemn reflection gowned in a pale cream muslin. It was the gown Jeremy had bestowed upon her for her birthday. She had been right, the gown fitted her perfectly, both in style and color-ing. It was beautiful. Alex sighed. A beautiful lie.

She closed her eyes, but Marc's image invaded the darkness, slipping beneath her defenses. She shook her head, unsuccessfully trying to dislodge him. She could still not believe he was getting married to that woman.

She could not face Lady Janice, and she could not continue to pretend that Marc meant nothing to her. She took a deep breath and reminded herself once more of her earlier words to Ashlee, '*Calm down you can do this.*'

She looked at her reflection, but no encouragement shown back at her in those pained blue eyes. "I cannot do this," she whispered to the mirror.

"Cannot do what, my dear?"

Alex spun around to face her father's smiling face.

"You look beautiful. Jeremy made a good choice." The light cream dress, instead of paling her skin as it would have a woman of the expected pallor, accented her, making her appear a healthy bronze.

"I was just thinking of growing up. Things are changing so fast. We were so lucky with Blake, you know. What if Amber had fallen in love with someone from far away? And Ashlee, she seems to have her sights set on Lord Moore. Philip lives in Northampton." She could hear the desperate whine in her own voice, but could not seem to still the tremors that raced through her. "What if she marries him? How can she be so far away?"

He smiled and held his arms out to her. She rose from the chair and walked into his embrace, wrapping her arms around his waist and clinging tight. "My dear, Northampton is only a few hours away from us. It will not be that bad."

He pulled her roughly against him. He understood how she was feeling. He feared she would move away as well. Perhaps, he thought, that was why he was hoping to see something between her and Marc.

"I know. I just hate to think of everything that is changing. Everyone marrying and leaving. I want it to stay the same, and now with Marc and his brilliant ideas. Janice hates this family." She shuddered and buried herself deeper into his chest. "If they marry, how can I endure her living in the house I was half raised in, so close it makes me ill?" The last words were lost in a broken sob.

Thomas dropped a kiss on the top of his daughter's brilliant red tresses, her head still buried in his chest for comfort. He was sure there was more to it than Janice disliking the Hollister family. He wisely didn't ask, for fear of making it worse.

He was sure he was right. There was something going on between Marc and Alex, something neither wanted to admit. *Even to themselves, more than likely*, he thought wryly. Hopefully, she would come to him when she thought it time.

He realized with a guilty start that he was unsure she would come to him, and his heart ached at the realization. He had a habit, not a good one either, of losing his temper when she approached him. It was only because he loved her, and because she usually wanted to do something stupid—something detrimental to all he had strived to accomplish, not for himself but for her, for his grandchildren.

He knew she hated being "reined in," as she put it. He prayed one day she would understand why he had done all he had.

Understand why she was rarely allowed to ride, only with his supervision, and always at a tame walk on those rare occasions. He had tried to explain to her again and again, it was to protect her from injury, as well as to let all of the ton know she was a proper young lady. He knew she didn't agree, nor did she believe his concerns were valid. Understand why she was never allowed to learn French, as she had begged him to do when she was only five, and many times since. He had told her many a time that it was because of the rumors of Lord Clifton being a French spy. If she didn't even know the language, there could never be any rumors. He shook his head at the memory, she didn't agree with that either.

And her ideas of a high-born lady going into business…well, it should have been apparent why that was unacceptable, but he had still had to explain and explain the reasons he would not even entertain such nonsense.

He forced his mind back to the present, to the current problem. He looked down at the top of her head. Right now the only important thing to worry about was her unhappiness today. Tomorrow would come, no matter the concerns of the moment, but it was useless to fret over the unknown. "Do not think of it now. For now, just know we have one more season before anyone will marry and before things will change. Take this season and enjoy it. Pretend everything will be fine and know I will always be here for you."

Alex tightened her grip and prayed that was true. "I love you, Papa." She looked up at him and added, "I hope you will always know that."

He kissed her gently on the tip of her upturned nose and turned her toward the door.

A few moments later, as her father escorted her down the stairs, she felt her heart sink. The Clifton family had just been announced, which normally signaled them ready to depart. Unfortunately, the Rutmeyers were announced along with them. Alex gave an undignified snort. "How am I supposed to pretend anything is the same when things have already changed so dreadfully? It is bad enough he must marry, but did he have to pick such a snooty bride."

She bit out the words almost silently. Her father gave a quick squeeze to the hand that clung to his sleeve and a gentle tug, leading her toward their new guests.

The Clifton and Hollister family always went together to gatherings while in London. If the occasion was closer to Hollister House, they would all meet there. If it was closer to the Cliftons' townhouse, then they would leave from there. It was how it always was and how Alex would prefer it always stay.

Now there was an addition of three people. Lord and Lady Rutmeyer and Lady Janice stood in the center of the group, Janice with her fingers laid limply across the arm of a stiff-spined Marcus.

"There you two are. We have guests." Her mother's voice was pleasant and welcoming, but her eyes betrayed a deep concern. Lady Catherine shot a warning look at her daughter.

Alex had a bad feeling all would not go well. She took a deep breath and forced a smile, though it reached nothing but her lips. "Lord and Lady Rutmeyer, this is a surprise." She tried to match her mother's well-bred demeanor, though she was certain she fell a far cry from the mark. "Will you be following us over, your graces?" She glanced at her mother and was happy to see the worry lines smooth on her face.

"We will ride with you," Lord Samuel said stiffly. This was clearly not his idea.

"Of course, your grace," Thomas said with a light tone and a gracious smile, but Alex felt the muscles of his arm jump beneath her hand. "The girls are just slight things, I am sure they can make room without a problem, and you are more than welcome to ride with us."

Alex fought against nervous tremors and tightened her grip on his arm. He leaned his head close, his words just for her. "Easy, please, just let us get through this night. It has to get better."

Stiffening against him, her head proudly raised and ice in her eyes, she smiled at the assembly. Alex knew whose idea this had to be. She could see the smugness on Lady Janice's face. She also knew what Janice was trying to accomplish. Alex had heard the rumors swirling through the ton of an impending relationship between Marc and herself and had no doubt Janice had heard them as well.

It was clear Janice wanted to make a statement to the gossips, that the relationship between Alex and Marc was not as stable as they believed. What Janice didn't seem to understand was that gossip, any gossip, was better if it was juicy, and Marc showing up with both women would only add fuel to the fire. Alex didn't want any more gossip, but the ton seeing Marc and Samuel Rutmeyer arrive together would be good for appearances, and that was good for Marc. Alex could live with that.

The seating arrangement of the ladies carriage was quickly determined, with Alex going out of her way to sit as far from the two new passengers as possible. She would do her best to keep her scandals to a minimum, at least for now. She would follow the same rules that she had the season before—the less of a stir she made now, the easier it would be for her to slip away later.

With only one rotund woman, and six dainty figures the seating was easily workable. The lady's arranged themselves quickly and the carriage, despite Alex's unease, was comfortable.

The same could not be said for the men. The carriages held a roomy seating for six, but with five tall, wide shouldered men and one short fat man, it was cramped, tight, and unbearable. They had only a short way to go, but Marc thought the distance forever as Lord Samuel began to squirm next to him.

"So tell me, my boy, do you attend the races often?" Samuel asked, his voice raspy and out of breath from the exertion of entering the carriage.

"Yes, your grace. We try to watch them all." Marc moved slightly, twisting his wide shoulders in a vain effort to make more room. The heat inside was increasing to unthinkable degrees. He could feel the sweat begin to trickle down his neck.

"I have enjoyed the days myself," Samuel said.

Marc knew Samuel enjoyed himself fully. Always betting heavily, and not with luck nor skill. His gambling debts were accumulating beyond his capacity to repay. It was said he owed big money to someone, but beyond useless gossip Marc had not been able to find out to whom he owed the money.

"Which horses do you see as good runners this season?" Samuel asked.

"As far as horses, I could not say to any in particular. I bet the ones I think look good at the moment." Marc answered. He shifted uncomfortably, sure of what was to come, the inevitable question.

"Do you know anything about this A.H. fellow?" Samuel asked, his gaze intent on Marc's face.

Marc barely held in a groan. It was a common question and one he was tired of hearing. Marc had to admit that more often than not he did place his bet on the horses that A.H. rode. The damned jockey was as secretive as the owner and trainer of the horses he rode. The ton was constantly raving about the mystery, bets were placed in all the betting books as to the identity of owner, trainer, and jockey. He never stayed after the races. The jockey was rushed into an all-black carriage before anyone had a chance to see him up close.

Apparently having waited long enough for an answer, Rutmeyer wriggled and pulled Marc from his musings. "It is said that you bet consistently for him. That you know him?"

Marc took a slow breath to keep control of his growing irritation. "I bet on more than just him. There are other horses that I like as well. And no, I do not know him. I have met him as much as anyone else. Why would you think I know him, your grace?" He had heard the rumor as well, never knowing where it had started nor why.

"I have not noticed it personally, but I was told that before every race he looks over the crowd until he sees you." Samuel twisted to look fully at him, his elbow jabbed painfully into Marc's side, though he did not readjust or even seem to take note of Marc's uncomfortable position. His chunky thighs pressed Marc's into the hard side paneling of the jolting carriage.

"I could not say." Marc fought for breath, praying that they arrive quickly. "I sit with a large group when I go. It is possible that he looks for someone else."

"Yes, indeed. I suggested that myself, but it is said that when you are alone, it is the same." He nodded decisively as if he had been the one to witness the occurrence. "Are you sure you do not know him? You do not know the horses he will run or how they are faring?"

Marc shook his head and understanding dawned. Rutmeyer was fishing for betting information. Marc should have realized what he was after. "If I know him, or more importantly, if he knows me, I could not say. I do not remember ever seeing him, except on horseback." He paused, but Lord Rutmeyer stared intently at him, as if daring him to remember some minute detail.

Marc shrugged, the best he could wedged between the large persistent man and the carriage wall. "If I did know him, I would do my best not to ask about horses, which would be unethical. I would never use a friendship in that way." He felt some satisfaction watching the hopeful gleam in his soon-to-be father-in-law's eyes fade. "I bet purely on the horses that are running, but, yes, I do bet heavily on him. He does not win every time, but if you can read the horses as well as the riders, then you can make good judgments. When I do not believe he will win, I bet others. Unfortunately, even then, I may choose wrong."

"What do you think of him? He is a secretive little man, is he not?" Lord Maxwell asked.

Marc closed his eyes in aggravation. He had been hoping for a quick end to this tormented conversation. It seemed lately everyone he met wanted to know about his relationship with the jockey.

"Yes, my lord, he is." Marc let out a grunt of pain as Lord Rutmeyer twisted toward the man across from him. "Do you know anything about him, Clifton?"

"I know rumors. It is said he works for Lord Barlow, but Barlow denies it," Maxwell said.

"Of course he denies it. If he thinks it is not your concern, he has severely tight lips. He is as secretive as that damn jockey." Thomas could hear the anger in his own voice and hoped no one else could hear it. Even after eighteen years, the sting of his wife's betrayal—of what Edward had taken from him—still overcame him.

"Indeed. He has always kept his own council." Maxwell, who had been out of the country with Thomas when Catherine had become pregnant, knew of Alex's true parentage. "Although I am inclined to believe him. He will tell you outright, it is none of your concern if he thinks it is not, whether true or not. Lord Farthing asked if he had a gambling house, which he does, Edward told him it was none of his business and walked away. Lady Johnston asked if he had a shipping business, which he does not, and he told her the same thing."

"Yes, I have found that if he gives you an answer, it is the truth," Thomas admitted grudgingly. He had learned that the painful way when he had confronted him. Barlow, thinking Thomas had the right to know, had answered every question he had asked. Even those he didn't want the answers to.

The worst part was Thomas couldn't bring himself to hate the man. He had known Barlow had been in love with Catherine since they were kids together. Edward had even admitted to remorse over the mistake and gave his word it had only happened once and never again. Thomas had no doubts that he told the truth.

"It has been said it is A.H. who owns his own horses, just trying to come up with enough money to start up his own business, to buy land. If it is true, he will have some of the finest stock around. I envy some of those horses. Would like to get my hands on some of them." Jeremy grinned. "Ridiculous, someone of no status?" Rutmeyer laughed, his girth nearly shaking the entire conveyance. "Where could he come up with either the money or the horses to begin such an endeavor?"

Marc sucked in a deep breath to respond, but the door was pulled open from beside him, nearly spilling him out onto the hard-packed drive. He cursed himself. Lost in irritation, he had not even noticed the carriage pulling to a stop.

It took all he had not to leap from the carriage and run. With effort, he stepped down with a grace and poise he didn't feel, took a deep breath, and stretched his shoulders. Looking toward the carriage that followed, he prayed Alex would mind her manners tonight.

He had seen the effort it had taken her to remain civilized even before they had left, and it did not bode well for the rest of the evening, but he was holding out hope.

The doorman announced them, rounds of pleasantries came and went without incident, and Marc allowed himself to relax. Perhaps he shouldn't be so hard on Alex. She smiled and conversed smoothly. It appeared she was trying to change.

The notes of an allemande drifted across the ball room, Marc turned with a smile to Janice. He had promised to dance the allemande with her, and only with her. It had been the only way to calm her anger after the scandalous, as she put it, way he had danced it with Alex.

Janice inclined her head, and he took a step toward her. He stopped dead, his jaw slack with surprise as a smiling and happy-looking Alex wrapped her arm around that of his betrothed.

"Of course, Lady Janice, I would love to get something refreshing to drink with you."

Marc was close enough to see the shock register on Janice's face. He could tell she wanted to protest, but with everyone watching, she could hardly say she had asked no such thing. Confusion swirled through Marc as he watched the horrid play unfolding before him.

Janice twisted her arm and pulled, but Alex held strong. Janice whispered. "I think from the smell of your breath you have already been well refreshed. Brandy?" Janice wrinkled her nose. "Vulgar drink."

"Yes, indeed it is. Shall we?" With that, Alex tugged Janice away from Marc, giving only a brief, satisfied smirk at his angry face. His fists clenched at his side.

Alex felt an excited ripple of triumph tickle across her. She knew she should be good. She had planned to be good. But the snide and snotty look on Janice's face had been more than she could take.

At the long refreshment table, Alex took two filled glasses of punch, handing one to an obviously angry Janice.

"What is the meaning of this?" Janice kept a pleasant smile on her lips, but the words dripped with disdain.

"I just wanted a chance to talk to you. I think we did not get off to a good start last season, and I would like to start over. As a woman who does not plan to marry any time soon, we will be neighbors and, as my father and my brother are friends with Marc, then we will more than likely see each other often." Alex cringed at the thought.

Through the proper smile, Janice snorted derisively. "Once we are married, his ties with your family will cease to exist."

Her hateful words, as well as the pain that tore through Alex at the thought of losing part of her family drove her to speak out of anger. "I do think that with—" She leaned close to Janice, her voice a slurred whisper that she was unable to curb. "—with Marc spending so much time with his mistresses, that you will be in need of a friend."

Satisfaction flowed through Alex as Janice's beautifully sculpted face drained of color. "What do you mean mistresses? Like there is more than one? He said he doesn't have any, never had. H—He is not that type of m—man," she sputtered, drawing away.

"Marc is a very passionate person. He is rough and vulgar from what I hear. Likes to do it everywhere, but in the bed. He has many desires, but if you are accommodating, allowing him to be as...*amorous* as he needs, then I do not see why he will not give up his women for you. You can be very accommodating? You can do it often? Can you not?" Alex had to hold in the laugh as the young, uptight woman fled. *Prude.* Her information had been right. Her smile disappeared as she caught sight of her father. He glared at her in warning as the dance came to an end.

"My lady, may I have this dance?"

Her head swung toward the strained voice. She could hear the anger swirling through it, barely contained. Marc glared at her, his hand extended in invitation.

"*My lord,* of course, you may." Her sarcasm added fuel to his already smoldering anger. Marc pulled her onto the floor. His steps faltered, his ire turning to horror, as an allemande, not the next dance on the itinerary, began to play. One look at the other dancers showed he was not the only one confused.

Alex shot a quick glance at the orchestra and smiled.

"What was that about?"

"My lord?" Alex faltered. Had he seen her speaking to the band earlier? She had stopped to speak with Betty Laralline to insure the first dance she had with Marc would be the more intimate allemande. It was risky, but it was worth it.

"Stop calling me that," he growled at her before mastering his features and calming his tone. "You know just what I am talking about." The music wafted through the crowd, and they danced smoothly, perfectly. Their movements and elegance drew many looks, and just as many compliments.

"I assure you that I do not, my lord."

She pasted on an innocent look, but she had a good idea what it was he was asking. But since it could be the talk with Janice, or the smile and look at the band, or a multitude of other infractions, she thought silence was the best choice.

She had learned early in her childhood not to answer until she knew what she was being accused of. She had confessed to many a crime that was not yet known about before learning that lesson.

"I will not deign to tell you what you already know, Alex. I refuse." When her silence dragged on he bit the words out. "Why did you take Janice for something to drink?"

His arms automatically drew her close and pulled her tight before releasing her. He spun her until her smile was genuine, her voice soft and relaxed.

"I was just trying to be nice. I did not think that would be an issue. Do you not want me to be friends with her?" She tightened her grip, digging her fingers into his shoulders as they drew close. Leaning forward slightly and gave him a better view down her low cut gown. He bit back a groan. "Do you not want me to play nice, my lord? What is the problem?" She batted her lashes at him in an innocent and seductive combination.

Heat erupted in his loins. What was the problem? He wanted to kiss her right here in front of everyone. That was the problem. "If I believed that is what you were doing, which I do not. I saw the look on her face. What did you tell her?"

The music came to a stop and Marc began leading her back to Lady Hollister. "Alex, answer me."

"It is none of your business, my lord." Alex yanked away from him. "Now if you will excuse me, *Spencer* is awaiting his dance with me."

Marc grabbed for her arm as the viscount stepped in between them.

"You will have to allow me my dance, my good man." Spencer did not look at him, nor did he await a reply. He swept a low bow and held his arm out. "My lady."

She had to smile. Spencer Ferguson was a dandy if she had ever seen one, right down to his long ruffled cloak, with its many capes, which he wore to every ball and event. He had once told her it was all just so he could swish it off in a whirl of elegance and style when he handed it to the butler at the door. His tight trousers and even tighter jacket clung to his well-formed body, his arms giving away his love of fisticuffs. It was his passion, but he would never admit to fighting.

"It is a barbaric practice that might bruise my perfect face, a face I do not even allow the sun to touch, let alone man," was a well-known opinion that Spencer was fond of spouting off to anyone who would listen. He never once had a bruise, not because he never fought, but because he was not hit often and never in the face.

It was neither his impeccable appearance nor his immaculate clothing, for which she always praised his valet for his efforts when she saw him, that caused her smile. It was the fact the man—below all the dandified clothing and prissy speech—was pure steel. He was one of the toughest men she knew, but she was one of the few who saw him for who he really was. He kept his true self contained, for safety and disguise. He was a spy, an English spy, but a spy nonetheless. Keeping an eye on the higher members of society for French spies and betrayers of the crown, at only four and thirty he had moved high in the ranks.

"My dear, you must be the most beautiful woman here. How can you still be unmarried? Someone will snatch you up quickly this year. I would say if someone wants you, he had better work fast." He smiled devilishly at Marc.

Marc scowled

Alex managed to keep her composure only until they had reached the dance floor. "Stop that," she whispered. "I know why you did that, and it is pointless. You must keep this a secret, only the family knows of it." She didn't need to await his conformation. Secrets were what he did. "Marc is betrothed to Lady Janice Rutmeyer."

She laughed at the horrified look on his face.

Marc swung his head toward her laugh.

Amber pulled him onto the floor. "Brother dear, you must pay more attention to your sister. Do you think you could take your eyes off Alex for a long enough moment to dance with me?"

"I do not like the implication that you have inferred. What do you mean by that?" He caught sight of Janice making her way to him. Her eyes sparked with a dangerous anger and he cringed, knowing he would pay for this later.

He took a deep breath and turned his full attention to Amber.

"You know what I mean. You have done nothing but stare at her since the night of her eighteenth birthday ball." They took their place as the music began. Janice took a spot with Craig Connelly and Ashlee held onto the arm of Philip Moore. The partners all began in unison. The light's twinkling and swirling as the ladies were twirled around.

"I am just looking out for her. She should not be dancing with that dandy. He is only after her for one thing, and you know what it is. I will tell her she is not to dance with him, nor any man I do not approve of. I am responsible for watching out—"

"One kiss does not give you the right to take over her life," Amber said in a quiet but stern tone.

His steps faltered. "It was more than a kiss, and that's not what this is about. I—"

"What do you mean more? How much more?" Amber yanked him off the floor and into an unoccupied alcove. "I was told it was one simple kiss, just to shut her up. Is that not what it was? Did you—did you—" she stuttered and fell over the words.

"No. It was not that. It was more than one but it was just kisses." A kiss here and there and everywhere, but it was not what she thought. He pushed away the guilt of knowing the only reason it wasn't was because of Jeremy. "Now can we finish our dance?"

She held tightly onto his arm, cutting off his escape. "No, I got you over here so we would not be heard. I want to know what is going on between the two of you."

"Nothing. Nothing at all. I am just—" He took a deep breath. It came out as a sigh. "I just do not know when she got so grown up. When did it happen? I look at her and where I used to see a little child to be protected, I see this strong woman who does not need me anymore." He looked at her with a sad smile. "Both she and Ashlee needed me once. Ashlee is different, but she still needs me."

"Marc, when has Alex ever really needed anyone? She may need you now more than she ever has before. She has always been independent, always off on her own." Amber wondered if her headstrong brother even understood his own feelings. She didn't think so. Not with the look of confusion on his face as he watched Alex being led off the floor, not to her father.

"Where is she going?"

"To get a drink." Amber wrapped her fingers around his, leading him back to his betrothed.

He snorted in irritation. "Probably more brandy."

Lord Danton slid up next to her, sending Spencer off with an impatient wave.

"Now what?" Marc grumbled and took a step toward the refreshment table and the bane of his life.

"Stop. Leave her be if you plan to marry Janice anytime soon."

He followed Amber's gaze.

"Janice, yes, that is what I plan to do." *And I can be just as passionate with her as with Alex*, he thought. And he would prove it. He approached her with a determined look, nearly pulling her onto the floor, only a moment before Danton escorted Alex onto it.

"What are you doing? You did not ask me if I wanted to dance." Janice pulled away from him, his urgency scaring her. Reminding her too much of what Alex had said of his amorous nature. "I think it improper not even to ask me." Before she knew it, he was swirling her next to him on the floor. "My lord, is everything all right? You seem very…" *virile*, she thought but did not add.

Without an answer, he whisked her out the garden doors.

"What are you doing? Take me back right this instant." She jerked her arm from his grip, stepped back into the room, and looked around as subtly as she could. No one had noticed, at least not that she could tell. She slipped through the crowd and to her father.

"What happened, my dear?"

"Lord Clifton said he was feeling a bit ill and went to walk in the garden." She sighed, her body still trembling from his forceful actions. Her story was a good one, and it was one she would make sure that Marc verified.

"Ill? My, that is too bad. He has never been real excited about these kinds of parties. Always hated them and avoids them as often as he can," Lady Rosalind Johnston said. She smiled sweetly at the young girl. At forty, Rosalind was a beautiful, well-sculpted widow. One who thought a roll or two with a handsome lord was just the thing to help endure the boredom, one who was bored often.

Janice wrinkled her nose at Rosalind and, without a word, turned her back on the promiscuous widow.

Rosalind shook her head, unperturbed by the reaction. It was a reaction she received from some of the more uppity of the ton. It was not a fact that bothered her. These were not the type of socialites she associated with anyway. She grinned at the young woman's back and walked away.

A few moments later, Lady Johnston slipped into the garden. "Marcus, are you out here?" she whispered into the darkness.

Marc grasped her arm, leading her into the dark shadows. "Rosalind, what are you doing out here?"

"Looking for a diversion, can you help me?"

Marc just smiled at her. She was not one of those widows in need of another husband. Her husband had left her a wealthy woman when he had been killed. She would prove an interesting distraction for him as well. His little bride may not be willing, but he would prove his desire and passion ran farther than that damn little chit Alex.

As Marc began to kiss the tall and beautiful woman, Alex allowed herself to be pulled from the dance floor and out onto the veranda that overlooked the small, yet impressive rose garden. "Are we out here for a reason, Lord Danton?"

He pulled her into the shadows. "I believe you owe me something for the injuries you inflicted upon me the last time we danced."

"What is it you think I owe you?" she asked, striving to keep the bored tone to her voice.

"A kiss, the one I wanted last season. At least for now." Danton leaned in close, his drink laced breath overpowering her and sweeping her memories back to the first night in the garden with Danton.

All she could hope was Marc would not once again find her in this compromising position.

"I think not. I am going back inside now." She tried to pull away, but his fingers tightened around her arm. "Let me go. I can scream."

He smiled lecherously. "Go ahead. How much do you think the gossips would like to know you are out in the darkness alone with a man such as me? Do it. Then you can explain why you are out here."

He ended up being the one who let out a scream. As he dipped his head down to kiss her, her forehead impacted with a sharp thud against the bridge of his nose. He clutched at his face. "You damned bitch, I think you may have broken my nose." His voice was thick and nasally, his breathing tightening. Blood trickled between his fingers. "You will regret this."

She moved away from him and smiled. "No, I think not, and it will be up to you to explain what happened out here." She turned and slipped into the tall trees that accented the rose bushes.

"I shall tell them it was you. That it was an accident while we were kissing. And more." He waited for her to reappear, which she did, but only for a second.

Just long enough to say, in a sweet and secure voice. "I do not think you really want to marry me, now do you?" She turned to walk away but paused with a glance over her shoulder at him. "Even if you do, do you think my father will let you live to see the wedding?"

His breath hitched. No, he would not attend that wedding. He knew there was nothing he could do, but he could not leave without the last word, could not let her win so fully without at least ruffling her perfectly preened feathers. "No, your father would not, but would your lover care?" As her eyes jerked to his, he knew he had hit a nerve. "Which one of your lovers would care the most? Lord Edward or how about Viscount Ferguson? I have heard rumor that you spend time at Rose Hall and you are always hanging on that simpering sop, Spencer."

Instead of the worry he had expected, she just laughed as she disappeared into the night. She was not worried about the rumors, though she was happy her father had never heard them. Knowing she had better stay out of sight for a few moments, she wandered the flower beds. She loved the smells of the late night moisture on the petals. Night was her favorite time. It made one feel free, hiding one from the prying eyes of society.

Alex came to a stop, her breath catching as she caught sight of Marc, his kisses deepening on the Dowager Johnston as she wrapped her arms around his neck. How could he feel passion with someone else? She let out a silent sob as she raced for the back gate. Knowing it was most likely to squeal offensively if opened, she slid over it.

As Alex made her way to Hollister House to change, Marc pulled away.

"I am sorry. I cannot do this. I…well, I cannot say right now, but I cannot do this."

"Is it Alex that is keeping me from my pleasures?"

He could only shake his head. He didn't know. He didn't want to know. He watched her walk away. She would go in through the library doors, as she had come out. She had not argued with him, and, at that, Marc felt a moment of unease at upsetting the sometimes unstable widow. He pushed the unpleasant thoughts away and reluctantly headed back to the ball.

The moment Marc stepped into the ballroom, Thomas and Maxwell accosted him. "Where is Alex? Did she not find you out there?"

"No, I did not see her. Why?" A trickle of worry started.

"I saw Danton lead her out, then a moment later he returned. Blood on his face, I think she broke his nose, but he would not say anything of it. Then you came in. No one saw them go out. They have no idea where she has disappeared to."

Marc cringed. If she had gone out to the gardens, she might have seen him with Lady Johnston. Hell. How could things have gotten so out of hand? "We should look through the garden, perhaps she is still out there," Marc said it, but he did not believe it.

Without another word, all three men made a straight path to the back gate. None believed she was still in the garden.

A soft fluttering caught Marc's eye. The small scrap of material was trapped by the rough wood of the gate, the cool breeze catching it, the moonlight shimmering off the creamy silk. He plucked it off with a groan.

Maxwell shook his head. "Where will she go? Hollister House?"

Thomas just shook his head. "I hope so."

"Do you think we should tell people she went home ill?" Maxwell looked at his son, knowing him well enough to realize he was worried. "Do you know something, Marc?"

He couldn't bring himself to meet their gazes. "No."

"I do not think we should tell anyone anything about my daughter. Just tell them we do not know where she is. If last season is any indication, she will be somewhere she should be." *At least she will say so*, he thought with an inward sigh. "And, if we say anything, it will cast a shadow on her story."

"Story? Thomas, you make it sound as if she is lying?" Maxwell had a bad feeling that Alex lied more than anyone knew.

"I do not think so, but everything always falls into place so easily when she starts her explanations. Just enough coincidences that make it sound true, but not quite."

Chapter 6

M ilady, you are not going?" Robert's voice was quiet, and yet Alex heard the subtle command and stiffened. He stood in front of the surrey, his arms crossed over his chest. For a small framed man he was effectively blocking her way.

She said nothing, only raising a brow with a look of impatience that she knew would get her what she wanted. It always did. After a moment of silence, his shoulders began to slouch, and she knew victory was close.

"What if they come to find you?" His tone had softened, and a touch of concern tinged his words, leaving them sounding more plea than command.

Alex groaned. She had wasted no time in changing from the silken petticoats and gown to a light floral day dress, and now Robert's hesitation was using up what precious time she had. Knowing he was only concerned, touched her, although the results of that concern pushed at her temper.

She gathered the thick, hooded cloak closer around herself and tightened the reins on her patience. "It is always a possibility someone will come to look for me. That means we need to be going. I want to be at Edward's and back before the families get here. I promised Spencer I would speak to him, tonight."

Robert widened his stance. His frown deepened, and he didn't move. Alex lost her patience. She shoved at him, but to no avail. Finally, she grunted and lowered her voice until he had to lean forward to hear her. "I know very well how to drive this thing. I can go now, with you—or later without you. It is your choice."

He scowled but held out a hand to assist her onto the seat. Half an hour later, the surrey pulled up to the rear entrance of Rose Hall.

Alex flashed a sulky Robert a quick smile before she jumped—in an unlady-like fashion that would have made her mother swoon—to the hard-packed ground. A massive man stood guard outside the back entrance, awaiting her. She knew he was awaiting her because he was normally posted on the inside of that door, and Edward would not have thought anyone, except her, would have merited a personal guard when they arrived. She gave him a wide smile. "Good evening Brandon. How is the night progressing?"

"Evenin', Lady Rose. I'm to show ya sometin' before ya go in. Com' wit' me." Alex grinned as he turned, without awaiting her answer, and walked away. Brandon Coshtess, Edward Barlow's main bodyguard, was at least a foot and a half taller than her and outweighed her by at least a hundred and fifty pounds, none of it fat. With his dark appearance and long black hair, he looked a pirate. It made his job easier, giving him a sinister look that no one wanted to test. Not many would look close enough into those light green eyes to see the loving man beneath.

Alex turned to follow as he disappeared around the manor and into the darkness. She rounded the corner to find that he had stopped to wait.

He offered an arm, which she gladly took. The grounds on most of the estate were well kept, but beneath the trees that lined the rear of Rose Hall, the uneven ground tried one's balance and left one focused on their footing as opposed to anything that might be going on around them.

That was where Alex found herself and, lost in concentration, she let out a grunt of surprise when Brandon pulled her to a halt. "Behind the cart." He pulled his arm away from her with a gesture toward a rundown dark burgundy carriage. Alex had a moment of recognition. She was sure she had seen the carriage before, but could not place where.

Tied to the rear of the conveyance was a sad and pitiful looking creature. He was a tall and skinny stallion, his black coat riddled with whip marks. His high spirited eyes gleamed in the moonlight as they darted from side to side.

"Oh my." Alex walked toward the skittish animal.

Nervous tension thrummed through him and he quivered. Pity tightened her chest.

The closer she got, however, the better he looked. He was lanky and underfed, but that only served to show her the well-defined muscle more clearly.

He needed a soft hand, a gentle touch. A good bathing and plenty of food would do him a world of good. With the right owner, she had no doubt he would be worth a small fortune.

She had appraised enough horse flesh in her life to know a champion when she saw it, no matter the condition he was in. He would not be the first hardship case she had turned into a winner.

Even if he would never race, she could not leave him in the hands of the beast who had left him in this condition.

"Easy boy." She ran a trembling hand along his flesh. She ignored when he nipped at her, knowing that patience would get her much farther than discipline.

The wounds were both old and new, but none that would cause any permanent damage. At least to anything besides his hide, and a few scars were never a bad thing. *At least not for a stallion*, she thought with a smile. His muscles jumped beneath her administering fingers as she probed for any underlying problems. "What is his owner like?"

Brandon leaned toward her with a grin. "Lord Christopher Manning's well on 'is way to being drunken and deep into 'is house credit. 'E's been coming to the card room sometime, but it's 'is first trip to the back. Lord Barlow saw this poor creature and when Lord Ferguson said you'd be comin', 'e thought it was time to include 'im." His voice dropped conspiratorially, "Edward also holds 'is marker for other bets, least fifty thousand pounds."

Which meant he would not say anything about her being present, Alex thought with a grin. Generally, it was only trusted friends in the private room, but sometimes there were other gamblers. Ones who had enough to lose, they would not mention the goings on or the participants. She scowled, knowing, even with so much to lose, some did talk. She knew because there were rumors of her being there, rumors that could only come from loose tongues.

"Baron Manning, Perfect." With a final pat for the neglected animal, she allowed Brandon to lead her into the darkness once again. This time her mind on what was to come next instead of the unsteady pathway.

Once back at the surrey, Alex touched Brandon's arm to stay his movement, "Wait just a moment." She turned her attention to still fuming Robert. "Head back to Hollister House. I will meet you at the Pettlenosters' in the morning. Stop by and talk to Melody." She spoke quickly and ignored the look of growing irritation on his face. "I fell asleep in one of the upstairs rooms, but she did not want to tell anyone, in case it would get me into trouble."

"Milady? How will you get there?" He moved to join her on the ground, but she shook her head, waving him off.

"I shall be at the Pettlenosters' tomorrow morning. Come get me after my father has gone to White's. Tell him you spoke to Melody and that she saw me. I told him you are planning to marry her so he will not question it." With her orders given, she turned away. Robert cursed loudly, but Alex thought it safer to ignore him. She stepped through the rear entrance, and the door clicked closed behind her.

Alex stopped. Effectively hidden behind Brandon's broad back, she quickly scanned the elegantly furnished room. Plush rugs and immense pillows were thrown around the wall, and women of all shapes and states-of-undress lay upon them.

One man lay half buried below three of them, all petite brunettes, all completely naked. Alex could see his legs and one elegant hand resting on a heart-shaped bottom. No doubt, Michael Cranston, whose affinity for small and elegant brunettes was quickly becoming legend. It was the only type of woman that ever held his interest. At only twenty, he was one of the most-sought-after bachelors in London.

Every title-hunting mama sought to capture Lord Terry Cranston's son, one day to be the new Marquis of Livindale and a very wealthy man. They were never deterred by his wicked reputation or his bad choice of company. Mothers paraded their daughters before him like cattle at an auction whenever he made a public appearance. Which was often and Alex was sure it was because he loved the attention.

There was one large oak table at the center of the room, surrounded by eight matching chairs, though there was space for many more. At rare times, it had held fifteen, but most days the group was small leaving most of the chairs empty. Invitations to the back room of Rose Hall were cherished and nearly impossible to acquire.

Alex watched the men for a moment as they played their hand of cards. With a deep breath, she pasted on a wide and engaging smile and entered what many called The Lion's Den.

She pulled off her cloak before turning her attention to the tall, bare-breasted hostess. Alex smiled lovingly and handed the tall redhead her cloak. "Good evening Victoria, how is your mother? Better I hope."

"Mama is quite well. Her cough is completely gone. She's expecting a visit from you this season. I hope I can tell her you will be by, my lady."

"Absolutely. You know I would not pass on the opportunity to see her or the children. I have grown attached to them all."

Victoria beamed as she turned to stow Alex's cloak with the men's.

"My dear, how are you tonight?"

She turned toward the deep familiar grumble. Edward wore no jacket, and his shirt looked wrinkled beyond repair. His pale blue eyes, blond hair that skewed in several different directions, and secretive grin gave off a reckless and wickedly charming aura that Alex knew many women found hard to resist.

"I am fine and you, are you well?" She allowed Edward to kiss her hand and then to pull her into a quick, but tight hug.

"I am well. Did Coshtess catch you before you came in?" At her nod, he turned her toward the table.

Lord Manning, she discovered, was easy to find. At the table was Lord Porter Farthing, known to most just as The Baron. He was a tall, thin man with slick black hair and shining green eyes. Nothing in his looks or appearance gave away his fifty years, though his sweet looks were usually betrayed by his loud voice and vulgar language.

At his right was Mr. James Gideon. He was only two years older than The Baron, but he was already the most feared, and meanest, barrister in all of England. The short stocky man smiled up at her, his shaved head shimmering beneath the high chandelier and his dark blue eyes shining as he gave her a knowing look, none of the nastiness showing that his opponents saw in court.

Porter slapped the back of the man beside him, "Look, Connelly, a pretty woman, just what you were speaking of, is it not? Having a pretty woman at this table—no, wait, that was under the table on her knees—"

"Do not be such a pig, Farthing." Lord Craig Connelly punched his friend in the arm. "Lady Alex is not interested in your dirty mind."

Craig was the fifth Earl of Lasiter. His family and his money were both old and well established, but in his forty-two years, he had managed to offend ninety percent of the ton and completely alienate the rest. What Alex loved most about him? The fact that he could care less.

Edward took the chair at the head of the table and picked up the cards. One empty chair, belonging to Michael, who had apparently found more comely pursuits, sat on his right. The next chair held a man who she had seen in the main gambling room many times.

She glanced at the large oak door that led to the main club. Alex knew that on the other side of the door was a man as equally impressive as Brandon, Finch Cromby, Edward's second bodyguard and personal servant.

She took a steadying breath and turned her attention back to her target. Lord Manning was handsome, even with his chubby cheeks and rounded belly. His brown hair was wild, bedraggled even more every time his roving hands swept through it, a clear sign of aggravation. His green eyes were dull with the effects of expensive imported brandy and desperate with the lack of chips in front of him. He barely looked up at her, not noticing her at all.

"Lord Manning, I would like to introduce you to a friend of mine," Edward said, rapping his knuckles on the table to get the man's attention.

Manning finally looked up, his eyes widening in shock.

"Lady Alex, who I will take it as a personal favor, one in payment of many you have asked of me lately, that you will not mention to anyone—*anyone* that you have seen her here. Do we have an understanding?"

Manning's brow crinkled with worry and comprehension at the thinly veiled threat.

"Yes, my lord."

His words were slurred, but not nearly enough for Alex's liking. She took the empty seat to his right, leaving Michael's chair empty in case he wanted to return to the game.

"It is a pleasure to meet you, Lord Manning." She gracefully extended her gloved hand and allowed him to kiss it. She shuddered slightly when he did not immediately release it, but she allowed him to take the liberties to keep him happy and unaware of where she planned for this night to lead. "May I get you another drink, my lord?" Without awaiting his answer, she motioned to Victoria.

"Thank you, my lady, and please call me Chris."

She nodded in acknowledgment and extended the same courtesy. "Alex works best at this table." And as far as she was concerned, anywhere else. She had never been big on titles.

The game went on as before, Michael even rejoined them after some time, though he didn't stay long before becoming bored and heading back to more lively venues. Alex drank just enough for looks and to soothe her nerves. She had already had a few too many at the ball. Lord Manning, on the other hand, drank every drink she placed in front of him. By the time the sun was threatening to rise, he was so far into his cups he hardly noticed anything. Aside from the soft, caring voice and the swell of the bosom of the woman who had taken all his money.

"Lord Manning, you are going to have to fold your hand." Edward smiled at him, surprised he had not fallen from his chair with as much as Alex had persuaded him to drink. Alex had flirted and sweet-talked until the poor man's head was obviously spinning.

"I cannot fold. This is the best hand I have had all night." The words were now so slurred they were almost incoherent. "Edward, give me the money to match her."

Alex and Manning were the only two left in the hand.

"I cannot do that. You are already far above what I would do for a regular gamer. I am very sorry." His lips smiled sweetly, his voice spoke with a kind fatherly concern, but his hardened eyes allowed no argument, at least not for the sober and coherent.

"I can win, with all that is wagered I can even gain some back of my losings. Please, you must." He reached across the table to grasp Edward's hand, but Edward pulled away.

"There is nothing I can do." Edward shuddered, just looking at the man. Sometimes he worried that he should not allow Alexis Rose to come here. He knew years ago that he should tell her no. But by then she was old enough to decide things on her own and tenacious enough to get anything she wanted. She would worry something like a dog on a bone until things worked the way she thought they should.

"Either fold or match the bet, old boy." Spencer smiled his most idiotic smile, his high-pitched voice ringing through the room. He had been on his best behavior throughout the night. Saying little and what was said was inane chatter of cravats and fashion.

"Lady Alex, if you will hold my marker—" Manning had a hopeful, yet stupefied, smile on his radish red face.

"I do not hold markers. That would leave a trail to me that I am not willing to risk. Although if you were to make an offer, I may be willing to accept something else as a replacement." Leaning back, she smiled. "If you have anything of value with you."

His hopeful gaze fell and his brow furrowed in concentration. Slowly he shook his head, and Alex had a moment to think the night had been a waste of her time. Suddenly his face brightened, adding to the already drink-reddened color. She had to fight a grin as her mind compared him to an over-ripened tomato. "I have a horse. He is a magnificent stallion. I will put him up." He reached for the cards as if she had agreed.

Her hand stayed his movements. "Lord Manning—Chris, I am not a horse woman, I do not even ride. What am I to do with a horse?"

Lord Manning grinned at her hesitation. "Oh, well he is worth his weight." His voice took on a cajoling echo. "You can sell him, I am sure Lord Barlow or anyone here would help you with the sale. I am going to have to raise the stakes, though, if I am to put him up—say all you have left in front of you?"

Alex looked at the large pile of chips before her and pretended to consider. "A fine horse, you say?" At his eager nod, she looked again at her chips. If she lost, it was not much, in respect to what she had on other nights, and she truly wanted that stallion. "That is fine indeed." She focused on his ruddy face. "If this stallion is as good as you say." She paused to await his eager nod, which came quickly. "I will take your word as a gentleman that he is. I would look at him first, but I would not know one end of the horse from another." Her voice was as cajoling as his and she rubbed his arm brazenly.

Less than ten minutes later, after throwing his cards at her and tossing his chair to the side, an angry and muddle-minded Manning left the horse in the caring hands of Brandon.

"That was good playing, my dear. I am impressed." Lord Spencer's voice had lost the annoying nasal quality as he spoke to her—in fact, the moment the door had closed behind the irate lord. "I dare say you trumped him good."

She waved away his compliment and finally pushed the talk to the reason she had come. Spencer quickly explained what he wanted changed in his contract with Clifton Shipping, a lower fee for shipping in exchange for more cargo to be shipped.

"The...bobbles and trinkets are becoming quite in demand," he said in his nasally, public voice.

Alex shook her head and pretended not to know that bobbles and trinkets was code for French Silks and Brandies. She yawned and promised him it would be done.

Alex stood to stretch. "I had better depart before the morning maids beat me to a room at the Pettlenosters'. I am going to have Brandon leave the horse in the stables. I will then have him take me home." She accepted her cloak from Victoria with a smile. "I will see you gentlemen later."

As Alex reached the door, she could hear the men laughing behind her. Spencer loudly clapped James Gideon on the back declaring, "She must be talking to someone else. I do not think I see any of those in here. Perchance they are hiding under some of those cushions. You see any gentlemen over there, Michael?"

She didn't hear the answer as she shut the door behind her with a laugh. Brandon stood outside the door, holding the reins of a still nervous, but calmer horse. "I can take him, Brandon. Get the carriage ready to take me to the Pettlenosters'."

She ignored his worried gaze, the best she could, and tugged on the reins.

The stallion followed calmly. The stables, where she kept her horses, were not far from the main manor, and it was a nice night, at least since she was wrapped in her thick cloak, and the wind and drizzle could not get to her.

Suddenly from the darkness sprang a man, his body falling atop her. She fought as he pressed her into the wet ground. "You took something from me, and I want something in return." His brandy-tinted breath gagged her as he pressed his damp lips to her face.

"Let me go, Manning. You do not want to do this."

Christopher only responded by grasping at her breasts and pulling the cloak out of the way of his roving hands.

She opened her mouth to scream for Brandon, but his slimy tongue and crushing kiss cut off the words. She fought to reach her boot, to her dagger that Edward insisted that she carry. She pulled it free. Her only thought was to threaten him, to make him release her. Fear changed her plans.

She could feel her skirts being shoved up. Cold air and clammy hands pushed at her trembling thighs. She felt the bared hardness of his arousal press into the delicate skin between her legs. Without thought, she plunged the dagger into his shoulder. Blood spilled down the front of her, running under her arms and around her ribs. She kicked him solidly in the groin.

Manning let out a breathless grunt and crumpled to the side. She wasted no time getting to her feet. She leapt onto her new stallion's bare back and gave his ribs a kick. He tore through the darkness. She clung to him, not looking back until she heard a horse pursuing her. A quick glance revealed Manning, upon what appeared to be Michael's large bay mare.

Not willing to lead him to the rest of the horses, she only knew of one place that would be safe to go. She only hoped that her father had already left for White's.

✧✦✧

"Do you believe she fell asleep at Ferdinand's? It seems...I do not know? Convenient."

Thomas, Jeremy, and Maxwell all laughed. Marc scowled at them.

"If it was not for the 'convenient,' Alex would have no alibis at all," Jeremy managed to say though his laughter.

"Now, Jeremy that is not the way to speak of your sister." Lord Hollister could not hide the grin as they stepped from Hollister House. The morning had slipped away from them as they had sat and talked over breakfast.

The mist and chill still lingered in the cool morning air, and it would still be hours before the main crowds were up and about, but the men were late. The four of them were usually at White's early, long before the main crowds arrived.

"Yes, well, I hope she is going to be more in hand this season..." Marc's words trailed off as an apparition appeared on the street before them.

The massive black stallion slid on the cobblestones, feet booming like thunder across the still morning. His hide lathered and his eyes wide and panicked, he fought for purchase on the slick stones.

"What the hell?"

"He is out of control." Marc could clearly see the man on the back fighting with the reins of the heaving and lathered creature. He appeared desperate to stop him or at least turn him. The rider's dark cloak billowed behind him as he wrenched on the reins to no effect.

"Oh, please stop, turn. Something, anything. Do you not see my father there? I cannot ride up on you, you stubborn ass. How am I to explain you or the man behind me?"

The horse's hooves found purchase on the uneven cobbles and came to a sudden stop. Alex, unprepared, grasped at the mane as she flew straight over the horse's head and right into Marc's waiting arms.

"Sir, are you all right?" Thomas reached forward to steady the cloaked figure.

Marc pulled his hand from beneath the cloak. It was covered in drying blood. "Ma'am, you are bleeding." With no choice but to catch her, he had grasped anything available. Unfortunately, that "anything" had been more than enough to know a woman, a well-figured woman, was below that cloak.

"Ma'am?" Maxwell looked at the small figure in confusion. Marc and Thomas both reached to remove the cloak.

"Are you all right?" They pulled at her hood only to have her snatch it back. "You are bleeding, let us help you."

The hood almost slipped. Alex pulled away from them, knowing they would not stop until she was unmasked. Manning could be upon them at any moment. Marc pulled again at her hood and cloak. This time she slapped at his hands. "Stop. I do not need your help. I am fine."

"Alex?" All four men spoke at once.

Handing the reins of the now calmer animal to Robert, who had obviously come at the sounds of commotion, she shoved him toward the side of the building.

Around the back was a small stable that housed Jeremy's two riding horses, her carriage horse and her father's two. "Take him to the stable and send someone for that stupid doctor."

"Doctor? I thought you were fine?" Thomas pulled the cloak aside gasping at the amount of blood that covered her.

"It's not for me, Papa, I am fine." She didn't meet his eyes, keeping her face hidden beneath the rim of the hood.

"If not for you, than who?" He was feeling her stomach and shoulders as she tried to push his hands away.

Clattering hooves on the cobbles drew the men's gaze.

As Lord Christopher Manning came into view, slumped over his saddle, but still in pursuit, she said. "I cannot very well let him die."

Before anyone could respond, Manning was off the horse and charging toward them. "You stupid whore, you could have killed me."

Thomas stepped in front of the man, his sudden appearance almost causing the man to tumble to the ground. "Baron Manning, I would suggest you not speak to my daughter in that manner." His quiet warning did not penetrate the web of inebriation that clung to Manning.

The man's rank breath assaulted Thomas as he leaned closer to him. "Your daughter took ever'thi...I had a hand." His words were slurred, hard to follow. "Your daughter got me drunken, cheated, stole my horse, seduced me and then tried to kill me."

All heads swung to an indignant Alex as she protested. "I did no such thing."

Turning on her Christopher laughed. "Which are you denying?"

"All of it. I do not know what you are talking about, my lord." She tugged the cloak tight around her and managed a snotty humph as she stuck her nose in the air.

"Did you not get me drunk?" He took a staggered step toward her just to have Thomas shove him back.

"I could not have gotten you drunk. I have not seen you and even if someone did put them in front of you that does not mean you had to drink them." Alex smiled at him. "I would say, you got yourself foxed, my lord, not I, or anyone else."

"You seduced me. I was drunk and could not see my cards. That to me means you cheated me. I want my horse back."

"Once again, my lord, I do not know what you are talking about. The only horse I have, I bought, from a man who won him in a poker game." She could not stop a mischievous grin. "From a man not very good at holding his liquor or his cards."

Manning lunged at her. Thomas stopped him with a forearm to the stomach. "Stay where you are. I will not tolerate you getting close to my daughter. If she says she did not see you last night, than she did not see you."

"She saw me, she cheated me." Lunging past Thomas he yanked the cloak aside. "If you did not stab me or see me than how do you explain this?" Thomas grabbed him holding him back.

"I think you may want to take a good look at me, Manning." She opened her cloak fully, letting the hood fall back, stepping closer to him. The men gasped at the blood that splattered her face. "It would not take much imagination to picture what position you were in when I stabbed you, *if* I had stabbed you."

Alex looked at the captured man, who was quickly sobering as his adrenaline began to pump. "You did see me last night. We played cards. I would have won had you not cheated." His voice was now a whining whisper, a sullen pout of a child who knows he will not get his way but refuses to give up.

"Manning." Thomas gave him a good shake, his voice a dangerous whisper. "Where were you playing these cards with my daughter, before you ended up on top of her?" Thomas allowed Christopher to struggle from his grasp. "Where were you?"

Manning opened his mouth to blurt out the answer, only to snap it shut as Alex took a quick step toward him. "Yes, my lord, where did we play?"

He swallowed hard. "Your lover will not be able to protect you forever."

Robert stepped into view. "My lady, the doctor." He jerked his head toward the approaching carriage.

Stepping away from Manning, she smiled. "The choice is yours, my lord. I think it best that you tell the truth. You lost your horse to a man in a card game, you were drunk when you were riding and ran into...a branch in the woods. That is how you injured your shoulder, correct?"

When he didn't answer, she took another step away. "You can always tell them where you *think* I was playing cards, but I did not game last night, my lord. If I had and you accused me of cheating, that *branch* that ran through your shoulder would have aimed a lot lower. As I said, the choice is yours."

All eyes swung to the doctor as he stepped from his conveyance. When they looked back, both Alex and Robert were gone. "My lord, what happened to you?" Doctor Monroe pulled him to the stairs. "Lord Hollister, do you mind if I see to him inside?"

"No." Thomas answered, there was no way he was going to miss this.

"Now you did not answer me, Lord Manning. What happened?" The doctor ushered his patient into the house and through to the kitchen.

When Manning spoke it was without hesitation. "I was riding through the trees. I had too much to drink and did not notice a branch sticking out. I am fine. There is no need for this fuss." He hoped the doctor would not have to see the wound.

"There is a lot of blood. I had better see to it nonetheless."

It was almost an hour later by the time the doctor stepped out of the front doors of Hollister house, Christopher Manning, and all four men in tow. They waited as a carriage came to a stop before them.

ونونو

As the doctor had led them into the house, Alex and Robert made their way to Lord and Lady Pettlenoster's. Melody Chambers quietly stole her up the stairs, scrubbed her clean, and put her in the gown she had worn the night before. Alex slipped into a bed and Melody barely made it out of the room before the morning maid came in to dust.

As the young woman gave a soft scream of surprise, Alex came out of the bed. Her hair tussled from the wild night and her dress, wrinkled from the night tucked in the carriage, gave the perfect impression that she had just awoken.

She allowed the maid to assist her in adjusting her clothing and hair the best she could and then made her way down the stairs. She found Lady Pettlenoster and Lady Lisa Bickerbee sitting down to breakfast.

She quickly apologized and explained that she must have fallen asleep, "I had just wanted to get away from all the pressures of the ball and before I knew it your little house maid was waking me up."

Both ladies gushed over her, apologized for not making her more comfortable, and begged her forgiveness. Alex walked on shaky legs, that she hoped no one noticed and joined them for a relaxing breakfast.

She was amazed with the amount of gossip the two women could tell in just the half an hour she was there. Laughing and gossiping, which both ladies loved to do, Alex began to catch her breath and think that the day may actually turn out better than it had started. Which, she had to admit, was not going to take much.

Lady Bickerbee's latest tale about the newly widowed Lady Annalise Mayberry was not new gossip, but it was picking up speed in the rounds and the severity of scandals. "I heard," Lady Bickerbee continued in a soft whisper, "that Lady Mayberry killed her husband because he finally had proof that she had been unfaithful."

"Heavens," Lady Pettlenoster exclaimed, her hand flying to her heart as if to keep the delicate organ from leaping out of her chest.

"Excuse me, ladies," the butler, who had to be as old as the hills, interrupted. "Lady Hollister, your groom is here to pick you up."

Alex nodded and gave her thanks. She hoped Dr. Monroe and Manning had still been there when the message had arrived to explain her absence.

She thanked her hostess for her understanding, making sure she seemed quite contrite and said her goodbyes as quickly as dictates would allow, but, like always, it was far too long before she was securely in the carriage and heading back into the mess she had created.

Alex lay back against the rocking seat of the carriage and tried unsuccessfully to still her hammering heart. Her father, she had no doubt, was going to tan her hide for this latest bout of stupidity.

The carriage rocked to a stop jarring her from her painful musings. Robert dropped to the ground and opened the door. "Andrew March wants to see you. He sent a message to me this morning. He says it is time sensitive and that you will want to know."

Alex only shook her head. "Send him a message to meet me in an hour at Hyde Park." With a nod, he closed the door. She sighed as the horses began to move again. Alex fought with heavy lids, finally allowing them to slide closed just as the carriage came to another stop. She barely stifled a curse as the door swung open.

She contained her smile at the sight of the men staring at her carriage from the stairs of Hollister House and put on the best show of her life. Even she was impressed as she leapt from the carriage, feigned panic in her voice.

"Oh my. Dr. Monroe. What has happened? Is it my mother?" She had meant only to pretend, but swayed heavily and thought for a moment she would actually swoon. Lack of sleep and the excitement of everything that had happened in the past few hours were catching up with her.

Grasping her hands, Dr. Monroe pulled her close. "My Lady, you look exhausted." He looked closely at her and shook his head. "Do not worry. The family is just fine. Lord Manning has injured himself while riding. It is nothing to be concerned about, though." Alex saw the doubt in the doctor's eyes. She didn't think he believed the story.

Christopher bit his tongue as she turned her concerned eyes toward him. "Lord Manning, I hope you are all right. Were you hurt badly?" She could almost control the smirk.

"I am just fine, my lady. There is no need for alarm. Nothing that will keep me from mounting up. I just have to be more careful. Watch where I am going. I know as an *inexperienced* horsewoman you probably would not understand." His voice was sarcastic, his brows lifted in challenge.

Alex had a quick image of the way she had mounted the unsaddled stallion and rode off. She internally groaned at her mistake, but managed to keep a straight face. "You will have to be more careful. I would hate for anything to happen to you if you are not careful enough." His widening eyes told her he had caught her threat.

"My dear, you should go and lie down, you need to get some rest. Promise me." The doctor broke in.

"Yes, doctor. I will. Thank you for taking such good care of Lord Manning for us." Alex gave the doctor's hand a good squeeze.

"You are welcome, my dear lady. Was Lady Rachel around this morning before you left? I am supposed to go see her today."

"Yes, I had breakfast with Lady Pettlenoster and Lady Bickerbee before Dunmore came to collect me. Lady Bickerbee was only going to be there for just a few moments more so she should be alone by now. Before you go may I ask you a favor?"

"Of course, my lady." He still held her hand as he moved toward his carriage.

"It is unseemly for an unmarried young woman to fall asleep at a ball. I would appreciate it if you would keep it just between us. I would take it as a personal favor."

"Of course, my dear. I will not breathe a word of it to anyone. Get some rest."

Jeremy laughed as the doctor's carriage, followed by Lord Manning on his pilfered stallion, moved out of sight. "Alexis, that is funny."

She turned to him. "What?"

"Asking the man with the loudest mouth in all of London, perhaps the whole of England, to keep anything quiet. The story of where you were last night will be all through the ton before the morning is up." He watched her smile spread. "And that is exactly what you want."

"Better to have them think you were there than somewhere gambling, right, my dear?" With that said Thomas grabbed her painfully by the arm propelling her toward the house. "I want to talk to you. Now."

Maxwell Clifton pushed both Jeremy and his son toward the house. "She may need protection at the moment. Go." When all five people were in the study, Thomas turned on the girl he had raised.

"Tell me where you were last night."

Alex opened her mouth, an answer on her tongue, just to shut it again. She shook her head. She tried one more time, looking frustrated as nothing came out.

"You want to lie to me?"

Alex just shook her head. She could not lie to her father. It was impossible. She had once when she was six. He had found out and instead of the anger she had fretted over he had merely shook his head and walked away. His disappointment had been more than she could stand.

One day, when he caught her lying to her mother, he asked why it was she would lie to her as well as to her brother, but not to him. Her answer had surprised him. "I can tell anything to Jeremy because he assumes I will lie, Mama only wants to hear what will not upset her, whether it is the truth or not. You? You, Papa, expect more from me. You want nothing less than the truth."

He knew she had never lied to him again, but that didn't mean she told him everything either. If she didn't want him to know, she would not say anything, even though that was a strain on her as well.

"Tell me where you were last night." He repeated.

He watched as her delicate jaw tightened stubbornly and her chin rose a notch. He could see her blue eyes harden. He let out a sigh as he realized he would not get an answer. When she was determined, nothing would get her to talk. Not even the beating he would like to give her.

"Alex, I am not going through the same things that happened last season. There will be no sneaking out of balls, no disappearances, and no more *convenient* excuses like falling asleep somewhere we all know you were not. Tell me this. How did someone see you at Ferdinand's when you were not there, and how did you get in today?"

She just looked at him, her gaze cold and challenging.

"Alex, damn it, I will not tolerate this."

"Tolerate what, dear?"

Alex started at her mother's cheery voice.

Catherine had just awoken and missed all the excitement with the doctor and their stabbed guest. Alex turned back to her father, a look of delight on her face. Her glinting eyes daring him to tell her the truth. He knew as well as she that her mother would faint away if she knew.

Not willing to lie to his beloved, he turned a defeated gaze at Alex. Alex just smiled before turning to her mother. "Father was just telling me there would be changes from the way I conducted myself last season."

"Oh, and there will be changes?" Her mother looked hopeful. "I did not appreciate the rumors last season."

"I plan to be on my best behavior, Mother." Alex smiled sweetly, but something in her eyes told Thomas to be on guard.

"Fine, than I would suggest you go get cleaned up and get some rest you just look exhausted. Put a cold cloth on your eyes, it will help with the puffiness. Now, run along so you can be ready for the Rutmeyer ball tonight."

Alex arched her brow at her mother and opened her mouth only to be interrupted. "Alex, you do not plan on missing tonight's ball, do you? That would be unseemly for you to do so." Thomas gave a pained look to the men in the room, already knowing the expression on her face meant that she planned just that.

"Alexis, you are going, are you not?"

Her mother's plea hurt her. Alex knew very well she would miss this occasion. She may not be able to miss another, but she would miss their first of the season.

"Of course, I shall be there, Mama."

"Yes, you will." Her father's tight angry voiced pulled her attention away from her mother. "And you will be there with a smile. You will dance and pretend like you want to be there. You will be at every ball, every tea party. At every brunch, every dinner gathering, and every soiree that is thrown. You will attend them in their entirety." He stepped jerkily toward her, his voice rising. "You will be on your best behavior throughout this entire season, and I will hear no arguments from you on it. I will not hear of you being anywhere but where I think you will be. Most of all, I will never hear rumor of you hitting Lady Janice nor anyone else."

"You hit her?" This came from both Jeremy and Marc at once. Jeremy with a sound of delight, Marc with a sound of horror. Then Marc stepped toward her. "I had heard the rumors, but she always denied them."

Alex's little bout of temper had almost caused a scandal. Janice had denied it only because she had been terrified of Alex's retribution. Her excuse was a fall, the black eye and bloody nose causing her to miss several important gatherings. The witnesses had been few and most of those had been Janice's close friends, the rumors had been short lived.

Alex didn't even look in their direction, the ice chips in her blue eyes were smoldering in anger as she kept her gaze locked with her father's. She refused to answer.

"I mean it, Alex. You will not embarrass me or your mother again."

This caused a tremor to run through her. Sadness darkened her, so deep it jerked at her heart. "I will do my best to make you proud of me this season. Both you and Mama." Just not in the way they thought, and she prayed they would be proud, not ashamed. Her voice shook and tears threatened.

Thomas stepped toward her, a look of sadness on his own face, but Catherine got to her first. She smiled at her daughter. "I know you will, my dear."

Chapter 7

Alex trudged up the stairs, wishing for nothing more than to climb into bed and stay there, perhaps all week. Unfortunately, she knew she could not. As much as the thought taunted and seduced, Andrew March would be expecting her.

Alex knew her mother well. The proprietress of society would waste no time sending Alex's maid to attend to her and that wouldn't do. She had no time to be pampered and put to bed.

She looked at the wide expanse of soft bedding and smiled. She would just have to beat her maid to it, she thought with a tired grin. She quickly slid beneath the thick covers and pulled the folds of her dress out of sight.

She wiggled deep into the soft bedding to await the arrival of her maid, and it only took a moment to realize she had made a grave mistake. Soothing warmth began to seep into her frigid limbs, and her muscles began to relax. Fog enveloped her, and sleep threatened to pull her down. Her eyes slid closed. She jerked them open with a soft snort. She had to stay awake and began to pray that her maid would hurry.

The soft click of the door, a few moments later, startled her back awake, though she hadn't realized that she had fallen asleep again. "Milady, can I assist you?" Her maid's voice was a soft whisper.

"No, Rebecca, I do not need anything. Take the rest of the day for yourself. I am going to sleep forever." Her voice was slurred and she began to worry. Exhaustion was starting to win the battle for her worn and battered body.

Alex barely heard the click of the door as she fought the heavy pull of sleep. She waited only until she was sure the maid had gone before she pulled herself from the bed and rushed to the door. She opened it a crack and peered into the hall.

She let out a sigh of relief when she found nothing in the hall but expensive rugs and side tables. With deliberate speed, she carefully made her way to the servant's entrance, stopping at each corner to peer around it.

Alex's heart thudded painfully in her chest, sweat trickling down her temples. Her nerves thrummed with excitement, but at least the rushing adrenaline had her wide awake. She took slow steadying breaths, but at each corner, and at each door, she was sure she would be caught.

After what seemed an eternity, the servant's door was finally in sight. She opened it slowly and, with a sigh of relief, rushed for the stables and Robert, who hopefully was awaiting her.

The stables were in sight when her father's voice sent her scrambling for the nearest bushes. Tucked out of sight, she peered through the dense green foliage. Her father, Robert, and Jeremy stepped into sight. Luckily, her brother and father stood with their backs to her. Robert glanced at her and she waved at him quickly before hiding herself once more.

"Dunmore, I wish you to sell that horse. I want him gone before I get back." Her father's voice pulled Robert's attention away from her, for which she was grateful.

"Father, can we not keep him? He is a great specimen. I would love to have him. He looks to be a great race horse."

Thomas ran his hand along the smooth coat of the nervous animal. Alex could tell by his stance that he was seriously evaluating the stallion. He looked at Jeremy. "No. For two reasons. One, you are right, no matter his present condition he has the look of a champion. Which means he needs training and a constant rider. You are a pleasure rider." He gave the horse a good pat. "Two, if I leave that horse around, Alex will find her way onto it, and you saw how much trouble she had controlling him. No, it is best to sell him and get it over with." He turned back to Robert when he received nothing in response besides a petulant scowl. "Can you do that, Dunmore?"

"Yes my lord. I know someone who may be interested in him."

"Who?" He looked at Robert in question, the man stayed silent. "I have to be able to tell my daughter where the horse has gone, and that he will be well cared for. If you do not tell me, I will see to selling him myself."

"My lord, my brother works for one who is interested in horses. Raises them, trains them, and races them. The stallion will be well cared for." Robert began to fidget and Alex barely managed to repress a groan.

"Who?"

Alex could hear the edge in her father's voice. He was losing patience and so was she.

Robert faced her, but both other men still stood with their backs to her. She leaned out from behind her hiding place. Robert glanced at her and she gave a weary nod. Anything to get them out of here and to do it before she fell asleep where she stood.

"A.H., my lord."

There were murmurs of surprise.

"Do you think he will be interested in this horse?" Thomas looked over the bedraggled creature once again. He was in sad shape and Manning should be horsewhipped.

"I am sure he will be, my lord." A sly grin spread across his face.

"Take the carriage and see to it then."

With that, they were gone. Alex was surprised when her father had not questioned Robert about his knowledge of A.H, but thought she understood. Thomas was still angry. He would start his interrogation with Robert soon, of that she was sure. She was not worried, though. Robert was loyal.

Alex waited till she heard the carriage wheels rumble away from the house before rushing out of her hiding spot. "Take him to the stables. Tell Raymond to clean him up and feed him. Stop on the way and let March know I will meet him at Hyde Park in an hour. Tell him A.H. bought a horse and get the money from him to give to my father." Her words were quick and quiet and, without waiting for a response, she hurried into the stable.

She saddled Jeremy's high spirited reddish-brown stallion, Jumping Snake, and tried to ignore the irritation that was pushing at her. It galled her to pay for a horse that was already hers. Well, she had more than enough money saved up over the last six years to afford him.

Besides, she would have it back at month's end with her allowance, a staggering sum, one that she hardly spent a shilling of, investing most of it.

Riding erect, and very proper on her uncomfortable sidesaddle, she made her way through the early morning streets and directly to Clifton House. She allowed their groom to help her from the tall horse. "Thank you, Danford. Keep him saddled and prepare Lady Ashlee's mare. We shall be riding at Hyde park." She smiled sweetly and ignored Danford's skeptical look.

He quickly mastered his features and bowed low. "Do you wish me to come along, my lady?"

"That is not necessary this time. Robert will meet us on the way if he does not arrive here before we leave. I shall be right out with her."

That proved to be a difficult task.

Alex was assailed the minute she walked through the doors of Clifton House. The two attackers were Blake Jr. and Darla Fortshaw, Blake and Amber's small children. Blake Jr., who would be five in just a few months, had been aptly named. Looking just like his father, he tried to emulate him in his stance and movements. Darla, who had just turned three, looked just like her grandmother, Alma. Everyone spoiled her, but Alma most of all.

Alex scooped up both children, coddled, and kissed them. Amid squeals and giggles, she plopped unceremoniously onto a long couch and hugged the children close. "Do you want to know a secret?" she asked.

Small heads bobbed in excitement. They obediently closed their eyes and held out their hands without being prompted.

She grinned and realized it obviously was not much of a secret anymore. She slid them onto the couch, their eyes remained obediently closed and their hands, slightly tinged with dirt, remained outstretched.

She rose gently as not to disturb the two still figures waiting patiently, or not so patiently, she thought with a smile as she watched their feet twitch and bob in anticipation. In each eager hand, she placed a small, chewy caramel.

Both sets of eyes popped open, and they swept the sweetmeats into smiling mouths before thanking her profusely. Unable to scold the happy children for the bad manners of speaking with their mouths full, she only laughed and set about to leave loud trails of kisses across their cheeks and foreheads. They giggled and squealed.

Alex loved the children. Sometimes it made her wish she would someday marry and have children of her own. She pushed the thought away before it had a chance to grow. It was not in her plans to settle down and marry.

With a sigh, she turned her attention to her next daunting task, routing Ashlee from her slumber. Never an easy task, she considered the fact that she should have told March to meet her in two hours instead of one. She grinned and took the stairs two at a time.

Ashlee, who had never been one to rise early, as it was unseemly for a properly bred lady to do so, fought her friend with tooth and nail not to leave her bed.

Alex dragged the covers from Ashlee, ignored her squeal of protest, and began to answer the usual questions. No, it is not still dark. No, it is not too cold to ride. No, it will not rain until later in the day. No, the parks will not be empty of civilized people.

By the time she had her up, dressed, and finally on a horse it was almost time to meet March. Andrew March was short, fat and balding. More importantly, he was the kindest man Alex had ever met. His gentle and caring brown eyes always set her at ease as they did with everyone he came into contact with. It was one of the reasons he was one of the most sought after solicitors in London.

March had been Alex's solicitor for four years. She rode in silence. Ashlee, now awake and looking perfect, sat astride a small and docile bay mare at her side. Alex thought back to that day, long ago, when she had met the man she now considered a dear friend. It had been an accidental meeting, one she was thankful for every day.

It had been the day of her fourteenth birthday. With a mission in mind, she had slipped from the party. She had ridden Jumping Snake through the thick trees, clutching a missive from the Earl of Lasiter, *CONTRACT CHANGE FOR CRAIG CONNELLY* written upon the sheets of folded and wax sealed paper.

She had rounded the house, jumped from her horse, and instantly slid to a stop. Stuart Rodgers, the Clifton's butler was at the open door. A man she had never seen stood before him. With the missive hidden behind her back, she forced her feet to move toward them.

Rodgers wavering voice matched his tall, gaunt body as well as his ancient age. "Mr. March, I assure you Lord Clifton is not home, but if you will leave me a messa—"

"It is a matter of importance. As a solicitor, I cannot speak with anyone but my client."

"He is not here. You will have to come back." Rodgers lifted his bone thin nose in the air in dismissal. "Lady Alex, why are you not at your party? Does your father know you are here?"

"It is a surprise for Ashlee." Alex held out a small box wrapped in silver and blue. "I am just going to leave it on her bed. Then I promise, right back to the party." She smiled sweetly.

"Fine, indeed. I shall keep your secret until she finds it, miss. That is very good of you. Go on, now." Keeping the missive from Rodger's sight she had run to Marc's study.

When she had returned, March was still there. "May I speak with you child?"

"I am not a child. I am fourteen." Her lack of physical maturity had bothered her, but not as much, she soon discovered, as the sudden explosion of breasts at sixteen would bother her. They had caused havoc on her jockey career. Having been racing since she was twelve, she had hated getting use to the chest bindings and the padded chest plates that some riders wore as protection, but they had been essential to keeping her chest hidden.

"Indeed, my lady? I saw what you had behind your back." March had smiled, but panic had touched her.

To get trust, trust must be given. That was his motto. "I have clients who are using Clifton shipping. They were instructed to do so by Craig Connelly. He assured them he was happy with the agent with which he worked. Clifton's agent is a twit. Who sent you with that parchment?"

"You are a solicitor?" He nodded. "Would you work for a woman?" He nodded again. With money from gaming, the races, her investments, her horses, and her monthly allowance, she had known she needed help for some time, but had not known where to turn. "As my solicitor, you would be sworn to secrecy?"

Again he had nodded and she had told him everything, including Marc's reluctance, his absolute refusal, to get involved in his business.

March had been invaluable to her ever since.

Alex was brought back to the present as Andrew's carriage pulled to a stop not far from them. She turned her attention to Ashlee who was prattling about a hat to be delivered later that day. Alex smiled and hoped she had not missed anything important. "Stay here. I need to talk to someone."

Ashlee rolled her eyes, but Alex ignored her and made her way to her solicitor. "Mr. March, it is nice to see you. Robert said you needed to see me."

With a wide grin, March assisted her to the ground. "I have good news, but you will have to work fast, if you want to get it." At her questioning look he laughed. "Linden Manor is being sold."

"Linden? Why?" Linden Manor was the sprawling land that bordered the Clifton's country home. Its acreage spread for as far as the eye could see and was a magnificent property. The forest at the edge of the property wrapped around the back border of Paddington Manor to connect with the one that separated her family home with that of Marc's.

Although the home itself was not as important to her as the land and stables, she had always loved to visit. It was mostly because she adored George and Amanda Putney. George was as Irish a man as she had ever seen and he had been pining away for his homeland since he had moved to England. That had been when he had fallen in love with the beautiful daughter of an English lord while they were visiting Ireland.

"According to Lady Putney, whom I spoke with last night, George has inherited some land in Ireland, from an uncle. The home is in major need of repair and the only way they can restore it is by selling their home here."

"My finances? They are in good enough shape to offer for the home?" She knew they were or he would not have even mentioned it.

"More than enough, my Lady, but they have other offers. Shall I proceed?"

"Of course. You know I have been looking for a place. That is perfect, to be so close to Mother and Father." To Marc as well, though she hated knowing Janice would be there as well.

"I shall let you know in a few days if A.H. has purchased a property."

"Fine. While I have you, I need you to make up a new contract for Lord Spencer. Here are the points he wants changed, as well as a copy of the original. Write it up and I will get it back to him. His contract is up soon, so we need to rush it."

⌀⌀⌀

Thomas, Maxwell, Jeremy, and Marc had made it to White's, but the excitement from the morning had left none of them eager for socializing. They had only been there about twenty minutes when Maxwell decided on a better way to spend the day. Playing with the grandkids. The other men were quick to accept his invitation.

They had barely walked through the door when Marc's day went from bad to worse. Alma, in casual conversation, announced that Ashlee and Alexis would be upset to have missed them.

Thomas shook his head. "What do you mean, missed us? The little chit is supposed to be asleep in her bed."

Alma looked a little concerned at Thomas's irritated tone, but she smiled sweetly as she answered. "Alexis showed up here not too long ago. How she managed to drag Ashlee from her bed this early heaven only knows." She glanced at Thomas and must not have liked the look on his face. She cleared her throat and hurried on. "Yes, well, the girls left for Hyde Park not long ago. I am sure they will be back soon, though."

Thomas grunted. "If they are at Hyde Park, why is your groom still in the stables? Who went with them?"

"We assumed Robert did. Though Alex really did not say." Alma Clifton's soft brow wrinkled with worry.

Thomas shook his head. "Robert is taking care of something. He was not at the house when we left."

Marc groaned. It was dangerous for two young girls to be riding so early in the morning. He turned and headed to the door.

"Marc, where are you going?" Maxwell asked his son.

Marc turned back. Eager to be gone, he shook his head impatiently. "I am going to get my sister. She should not be out there. Neither girl knows how to ride that well, and Alex has no right to drag her out without a proper chaperon. She has been nothing but a bad influence on Ashlee for years." He turned and stomped out the door, not considering until he was outside just how her father would react to his little speech.

Marc could only hope her father would understand. He impatiently waited for his horse to be re-saddled, snapping at Danford twice in the process.

The entire way to Hyde Park he thought of the trouble that Alex caused in his life. Why could she not just be a proper young lady like his sister, at least like his sister when she wasn't around Alex?

He kicked his horse into a trot and, by the time he finally made it to Hyde Park, he was seeing red. His anger boiled just beneath his skin and, seeing Ashlee sitting alone, with no Alex and no chaperon in sight, did nothing to help his nerves. He nudged his horse forward and scanned the park for the missing Alex.

Suddenly a large, loudly baying, dog rushed around his horse's legs. Marc jerked his attention to his mount. She reared up kicking and bucking wildly. Marc nearly lost his seat. By the time he had the mare under a semblance of control, the massive canine had made its way most of the way across the park and was bearing down upon his sister. Marc gave his mount a hard kick to the side and rushed forward, but he knew that he would never reach her in time.

Her horse reared. The dog ignored them completely and continued to run. Ashlee screamed, the sound echoing across the nearly empty park

Alex spun toward the sound. "Bloody Hell." She gave a quick look around her, but did not see anyone near them. She prayed no one would see her.

As the dog rushed past her, still barking and apparently chasing nothing, Alex leapt into her saddle. Throwing her leg over the saddle in a very un-lady like manner she kicked him forcefully in the side.

Alex pushed Jumping Snake harder, urging more speed out of him as Ashlee yanked at the reins, jerking this way and that to no avail. Jumping Snake, with the constant and secret training from Alex, overtook the young mare in a short time.

The mare refused to stop, and Ashlee was too terrified to handle the reins correctly. She was as panicked as the horse.

"Do not pull so hard, not straight back. What have I told you? Gently to the side." Alex's shouts rolled across the still air, meeting Marc as he rushed toward them.

Marc almost fell from his horse when Alex came side by side with his sister. Alex leaned out of the saddle, tilted until he was sure she would fall. He held his breath. Alex grasped Ashlee's wrists and tugged the leathers toward her.

The mare had no choice, except to allow her head to follow it. It only took a few moments for Alex to get the horse stopped. Marc yanked the reins and leapt from his saddle before the horse had slid to a full stop.

He ran to them, first yanking his sister and then the infuriating Alex off the horses. "What in the bloody hell—"

His words were cut short as Alex let out a loud and dramatic squeal and began to cry loudly. "Oh, my lord, you have saved me. I cannot begin to tell you how thankful I am that you were here with us. He was so out of control. I do not know what I would have done without you." His heart stopped as she threw herself into his embrace. Her breasts pressed firmly into his constricted chest. She clutched at him in apparent terror. His arms went instinctively around her small waist, and he pulled her close before he thought better of it.

"Alex, you are going to be fi—"

"Oh, Lord Clifton," an excited voice said from behind him cutting him off. "You are a hero. What has happened?"

Marc turned to find Lady Gwendallyn Ronchester, widow of the Duke of Roche, Lord Bernard Ronchester.

Beside her sat her overprotective granddaughter Lady Tabitha Forester and Tabitha's doting husband the Marquis of Caswell, Lord Charles Forester. They were all looking at him in awe from Lady Ronchester's barouche, the hood folded back allowing in the early morning sunlight.

Lady Gwen had turned seventy this year. Her long red hair was graying severely at the temples, and her eyes were almost white and almost blind. She had not seen what had happened, but there was nothing wrong with her hearing.

"We heard the horses. They sounded out of control," Gwendallyn said. "I heard a scream and had to make sure everything was all right when I heard the crying."

Marc quickly released Alex, just realizing he still had his arm around her. He turned to the small group of onlookers.

"Lady Alexis, are you quite all right?" Lady Ronchester held out a gnarled hand.

Alex stepped away from Marc and took the offered hand as gently as she could, cautious of the old lady's arthritis. She spoke with a breathless exaggeration as she told them a story that left Marc's head spinning and made him realize that Alex had been playing a part for an audience from the moment she threw herself into his arms. She must have seen them approaching.

Alex's gripped his arm and tugged him close. She went on with her wild tale of the dog scaring her horse, leaving Ashlee out of the tale completely. She told of being out of control and Marc risking his life to save her. She went on and on about his bravery and selflessness. She clung to his arm, her breasts accidentally rubbing against it. The second time they pressed into him, he caught her impudent grin. It wasn't an accident, the brazen chit was doing it to torture him.

Marc tried to pull his arm free, but she held tight.

"Oh, my dear. That is terrible. Lord Clifton, you are indeed a wonderful man," Tabitha said, and it was apparent that she was eating up every word.

Gwen was shaking her head in sympathy.

Unfortunately for him, the older Lady Gwen got, the more she gossiped, and Lady Tabitha was no better. "My ladies, my lord, I would appreciate it if we could keep this to ourselves. There is no need for this unfortunate episode to get around." He had little hope of that, as did Charles, who only rolled his eyes at the notion.

"Of course, my dear." Gwen turned back to the distraught Alex. "My dear, you must be terrified to get back on that horse now. I do not blame you one bit. Come to tea with me. I shall give you a ride."

Alex was about to decline. She couldn't very well let people think she was afraid of horses. What would that do to her reputation as a jockey? She opened her mouth to refuse, but Marc's angry voice stopped her.

"No. She has to get home." He reached for her. "She is going to the Rutmeyers' ball tonight."

She stepped out of his reach with a grin. Without waiting for Lady Gwen's driver to dismount and assist her, she took her place beside the elderly lady. "Be a dear, *my lord,* and take Jeremy's horse back to the stables. I will see you at the ball."

"No, I told your father I would make sure you got there." Stepping forward, he was prepared to pull her out of the carriage if he had to.

"Do not be silly, dear boy. I can make sure she arrives safely. My granddaughter thinks I do not get out enough, so she is dragging me along." She smiled at the petite redheaded young woman who gazed loving at her. Alex raised her brow at Marc and smiled wickedly, an alluring combination that hit him hard.

And made him hard.

"See you there, my lord."

He took a deep breath and surrendered. Alex had started enough of a commotion with her imagination that his arguing now would only cause more. If he didn't strangle her soon, he was going to lose his mind.

He wanted to scream at her to call him Marc as she always had. He hated hearing the title come from her sweet lips. Since she had fled into the woods, she had yet to call him by his Christian name.

Alex had to fight the urge to look back, just to see if he was watching her leave. She wanted him to be. That would mean she was under his skin, at least a little.

Less than twenty minutes later, she sat in the overly plush and garishly floral tea room across from Lady Gwendallyn and her five white cats. Her granddaughter and her husband had returned to their townhouse to prepare for the ball. The spoiled cats crawled and mewed as the two women talked...well, as Lady Gwen talked and Alex tried to listen.

Lady Ronchester left her just long enough to greet the Foresters, who would escort them tonight, but in those few moments, Alex felt her eyes drift shut.

She awoke with a start to a gentle shake of her shoulders. "You are exhausted, Alex," Lady Gwen said with a warm smile. "You are more shook up then you are willing to admit. No, do not shake your head at me, you can hardly force your eyes to stay open."

Tabitha ginned. She knew Alex did not want to attend the Rutmeyer ball, and Tabitha planned to do anything she could to help her. Anything she could do for Alex, she would, since she had been the reason Alex had struck Janice last season. Janice had been tormenting Tabitha for half the season. Her dresses, her gloves, her hair. Nothing was good enough, and everything was cause for torture. When Janice had made disparaging remarks about her virtue, or lack thereof, Tabitha had broken into tears. Charles, her betrothed at the time, had wrapped his arms around her preparing to defend her honor. Alex had gotten to Janice first. Any words Charles had been going to say were lost to him as Alex dropped the pompous woman with one punch.

"We are going to drop you off at Hollister House. You are going straight to bed, and there will be no argument."

Lady Tabitha arched her brows in a challenge for Alex to protest, and her face relaxed in to a conspiratorial grin.

Alex would not have argued, even if she had been wide awake. It was the perfect reason to miss the ball, one of the few valid excuses she was going to have this season, and she was not about to pass it up. She whispered a soft thank you as she rose from the beautifully crafted Victorian chair.

Dragging herself out of the large carriage and up the stairs she waved off Rebecca's help, telling her to retire for the night. Alex was too tired to fuss and bathe. Falling onto her bed, she slipped quietly into exhaustion, her riding outfit tangling in her legs as she sought comfort.

Soon dreams were pulling at Alex's mind, pleasant ones of forest floors, Marc's arms, and amazing pleasures.

ৎ৩৫৩

Marc stepped into Meyer House, the Rutmeyers London residence, and was greeted with a dead silence. All heads turned as the Clifton and Hollister families were announced. The deadening silence grated on Marc as it dragged out. He knew what that reaction meant, a scandal. His heart caught in his tightening throat. His breath came in painful rasps. He had worked too hard for another scandal.

Suddenly the room exploded in an uproar. Everyone began to talk at once. Those closest grabbed Marc and shook his hand, thudding him on his back and laughing.

"My Heavens, Clifton, who knew you were such a hero?" Viscount Ferguson's annoying nasal voice sounded across the ruckus that had ensued. "Everyone, look, it is our own knight in shining cravats. I have never known such selflessness, such drama."

Marc struggled to remember what they were congratulating him for as Spencer congratulated him again and again, pumping his hand the whole while.

"You must have been so brave to throw yourself in the path of a wild runaway stallion, half crazed with fear from the dog pack that pursued it."

Marc groaned as understanding hit. It was worse than he thought. The story had grown.

Spencer's eyes glittered with understanding and humor. Marc realized the irritating fop was taunting him. There was no time to consider it, for as soon as Lord Ferguson released his hand, it was taken again—and again, the tales of his heroism growing as each person congratulated him.

As the tales grew out of control, so did his anger. He hated being put in this position, and she knew damned well he would not make her out to be a liar by telling the damned truth.

As soon as the uproar had died down, he was in for another shock, one that pushed his patience to its limits. Lady Gwendallyn and Lord and Lady Forester were announced. His head swung toward them. Distinctly missing from the group was Lady Alex. Marc followed Thomas as he went to greet them.

"Lady Gwen, Lord and Lady Forester, it is my great pleasure. Where is my daughter?" He kissed both ladies' hands, even as he spoke. Alex had to have known they would ensure the guests she would come and with whom she would arrive.

Tabitha's voice, soft, yet pained and regretful, carried well through the silence that had erupted once more. She shook her head in sympathy as she answered. "She was still quite shaken from her ordeal. She went home to rest." She clucked her tongue. Her smiling eyes met her husband's. "Charles, what was it Lady Alexis said to tell the Rutmeyers?"

He looked uncomfortable but just took a deep breath before relating the message. "She said to let all know, she *extremely* regrets the fact that she has to miss the ball. She was quite looking forward to it, after not being able to make it to any of last season's events."

Charles cleared his throat, and Thomas closed his eyes. He knew there would be more, one more jab. At least he hoped only one more.

Charles shook his head as he continued. "She says it is grievous to have to miss the dance to stay home and do nothing, but it was unforeseeable." Thomas held his breath hoping that was all. It was not. "Lady Alexis also asked for us to relay her wish that you have all the success tonight—that she feels you deserve."

Thomas grasped the pale man's arm as he finished Alex's little speech. His face had whitened and tightened with each word. Thomas believed it was embarrassment—or amusement—he couldn't quite decide. He gave Charles's arm a quick squeeze. "That is fine, Lord Forester."

"What is it, dear?" Catherine said from behind her husband. "Is she all right?"

He turned to her with a soft smile. "She has gone home to rest. If she is that upset, I think it best I check on her. Do not worry, I will be right back."

Thomas was angry, sure it was some kind of trick. He glanced at Marc, who looked extremely guilty every time someone congratulated him, and Thomas was getting the sneaking suspicion his little angel's story was untrue.

He made his way to Hollister House, but was convinced by the time he arrived that the trip had been a waste of effort. He was convinced that Alex was not there.

He, nonetheless, went directly to her room. Knocking lightly, he didn't expect an answer and didn't get one. He opened the door, expecting to find an empty and un-slept-in bed. He was surprised.

She was sprawled across the bed. One arm thrown over her head, her riding outfit still on.

"My Lord?"

He turned to the soft voice of her day maid. "Miss St. Talves. Will you assist me, please? Let's get this outfit off her and get her under the covers."

Alex didn't even flutter an eyelash when they undressed her. In her chemise, she lolled from one side to the other as they maneuvered her, pulling the blanket over her.

"Thank you. You may go." He didn't watch as the door closed, his eyes only on the child—no, she was a woman now. When she had become so, he couldn't recall. It seemed to have happened overnight.

His lips brushed her forehead. She groaned, leaning toward him. "I love you, my child."

He spoke softly, his words reaching into her dreams. She grasped his hand, pulling it into her embrace. Her sleepy word warmed his heart, and she was still again.

"Papa."

Chapter 8

Epsom, Surrey, England, June 1880:

Marc stood rigid, wedged between Janice on one side and her mother's wide frame pressed close against his other. The scent of matching sticky-sweet honey perfume wafted up and coated his nose and lungs, effectively cutting off any hope of a clean breath. The ladies chattered away inanely about everyone's gowns, the modistes, their bonnets, the teacakes, their hair, rouge, powders, needlework, the pianoforte…on and on they went, until he wished his ears were as clogged as his throat.

He ignored the smell and their chatter the best he could, without being rude, and looked out across the mass of bodies that packed the ball room of the Ronchester country home just miles from where the Epsom Derby would be starting in only a few hours.

Why he had let himself get pushed into arriving at this ball with the Rutmeyer family, he could not fathom. He supposed, he admitted grudgingly that it may have had something to do with wanting to avoid a certain redheaded hoyden. For the past five years of being back into society, he had come to this ball the way he had arrived at every other gathering, with the Clifton and Hollister families. He groaned inwardly. He had allowed his emotions, and he supposed his guilt, to keep him from doing what he had thought was best.

While Janice had been thrilled, Marc's father had been disappointed, and his mother had looked as if she were on the verge of tears when he had announced he would not be accompanying them.

The tall and stoic doorman announced the arrival of the next guests, his voice a deep rumble that didn't make it over the din of the crowd. Marc strained to see who had arrived. An older man, his very thin, yet pretty wife, and a tall beautiful young woman with masses of gleaming chestnut waves piled above a smiling angel's face, stood facing the assembly. Marc recognized them as the Chadwick family. The Earl of Basildon, he knew from Whites, a very nice man, but the ton thought him beneath them. An old title, but one that had not come with money behind it, and it was rumored that what little there was he had lost gambling many years before he had wed.

Marc had not yet had the opportunity to meet Lady Chadwick and their daughter. He thought to make it a point to make their acquaintance as he tried to ignore the disappointment that they were not the arrivals for which he was waiting.

To get his mind off his impatience, he turned his attention instead to the large crowd and, with a smile he let his gaze come to rest on Gwendallyn. Lady Ronchester had held the first Race Day Rout when she was only twenty, that had been some fifty years ago. It had changed to the Derby Day Rout, in 1780, when Edward Stanley, the Twelfth Earl of Derby organized a race for himself and his friends to race three-year-old fillies over a mile and a half. He had named it the Oaks after his estate. Stanley had won a coin toss to decide what the title of the race would be, and The Derby was born.

In the last few years, her granddaughter had taken over. Tabitha managed all the hard work, but had kept the ball unchanged. It was still the massive rout it had always been. People mingled, drank, and danced, enjoying themselves fully at what most considered an informal gathering, though how a guest list of several hundred people could be considered informal Marc could not guess. The rout would last all day, a gathering before the race and a ball after, with many women, not interested in racing, staying behind and playing Whist or All Fours until the rest of the guests returned.

Marc turned his attention back to the door to discover the Hollister/Clifton party had obviously just been announced. He bowed politely to both the Rutmeyer women and made his way to greet his families.

After a quick word of greeting, Thomas wrapped Catherine's hand through his arm, smiled at her, and led her to the dance floor. Maxwell and Alma were quick to join them, as were Blake and Amber. It quickly left only the two brothers and their sisters. Marc smiled at Ashlee who responded with a wide grin. He made his way toward her, ready to ask her to dance.

Ashlee had watched her brother intently, from the moment she had entered the room and had caught sight of him staring at the families, at Alex, even before he had started making his way to their sides.

Ashlee had thought of Marc a lot since Alex had left them at the park after the near disaster with her horse. In fact, she had thought of little else.

She had been suspicious of the way he had looked after Alex's retreating form. Now he held that same look. The same look Blake always held right before he kissed his wife. Even as Marc was coming to dance with her, his gaze still drifted toward Alex. It was apparent who he would rather dance with.

Marc wanted Alex. That was clear. He was just too stubborn to admit it. Smiling to herself, Ashlee thought to help him along.

Jeremy stepped toward his sister, his intention to escort her to the floor. His eyes widened as Ashlee nudged Alex aside. Smiling sweetly she took his extended arm. "Oh, Jeremy I would be delighted to dance with you."

Jeremy laughed as they walked away. "That was very sneaky, my dear. I did not know you had it in you."

"I think it about time he did what was best for himself and not what is best for his reputation. I have seen Alex. The way she is beginning to dress. The way she manipulates every situation to be the most disturbing to Marc. She knows he is jealous as well as interested. I know she loves him. I just want to help her out."

"Marc will never admit it. He has plans for the future, and Alex is not in them. I think he knows Janice is going to make him miserable. It is a price he is willing to pay."

She smiled up at him. "I know. Alex also has plans, and she does not believe that Marc is a part of that future. That is why we must help them. If they will not willingly do what is best for them, then we will have to convince them."

Jeremy laughed at her not-so-innocent look. "You mean trick them?"

"I think if Marc is tortured enough, he will admit he loves her. Down deep, he knows he does. I believe he saw a glimpse of it last season. That is why he started to ignore her. Whatever happened, it scared him." Ashlee shrugged. "When he admits it, so can she."

As Jeremy agreed with her, Marc held his hand out for Alex with a low bow. He couldn't very well leave her standing there alone. "Did you plan this?" he asked through gritted teeth.

"Why would I do that? You were not my first choice to dance with, *my lord*." She held in a smile as his face hardened. "You cannot blame me because your sister wanted to dance with my brother. You do not have to dance with me, my lord. Just lead me to Spencer, I will dance with him and not bother you again."

"Not a chance." He missed her devious grin as he literally dragged her onto the floor. "You will dance with me and not that sop of a man. If he can be called a man." He had already pulled her close and spun her around before he realized what he had said. "Hell and

Damn." He was trembling with anger and pierced her with a menacing glare.

"Such language, my lord."

"Call me that again, and I will take you over my knee." He bit his lower lip in a vain effort to call back the words.

"It is the nicest thing, as of now, that I can think to call you. Would you like to hear the others that come to mind, than you can decide which one you like the most?" Blue eyes glittered coldly at him, her head tilted to the side as she looked up at him.

Her hair was artfully swept up off her shoulders, with only small wisps escaping to tickle her cheeks and sweep down her back. Marc bit back a groan at the sight of her long, graceful neck. Her throat was exposed in an invitation to his quivering lips.

His breath hitched, and his groin sprang to attention.

Her soft pink lips smiled, the tip of her tongue peeking out to moisten them. "Well, do you want to decide on another name, my lord?"

He could not answer her. It was all he could do to breathe.

The song ended, and he dragged her from the floor almost as fast as he had taken her there. Without a word, he walked away. Alex smiled.

"How is everything going?"

Alex didn't turn to see Ashlee's face. She just laughed. "Fine, just fine." She shook her head as Marc took his place back by Janice's side and was once more pinned in between her and her mother.

"Is there anything I can do to help you?" Something devious sounded in Ashlee's voice, and Alex turned to look at her.

"Why, Ashlee, you did that on purpose, so I would have to dance with Marc. You are not being very nice to your brother." She grasped her hands, holding them tightly. A loving smile crossed her lips.

"Neither are you. Do you think he will call off his plans..." Ashlee trailed off.

Alex followed her gaze and spotted a pair of pale green eyes intent on Ashlee. Viscount Mooreland was a dandy of a man. He even put Spencer's little side show to shame, though Alex was sure his was genuine. His black hair was slicked back, and his clothing was so full of ruffles and lace, Alex always thought he should save the trouble of squeezing into his form fitting outfits and just wrap a petticoat around himself.

She dropped her head and bit the inside of her cheek to keep from laughing at the image as the man in question made his way to them. "I think we will discuss this later. Now I think you should prepare to dance."

Alex had other plans for Ashlee's husband to be, yet she hadn't pushed them, so far. Not until she decided if she just wanted Ashlee to marry Bradley Hamilton because Ashlee would not move away or because she really believed she would be happier with the younger man. Bradley was very much in love with the beautiful Ashlee, and everyone knew it, except Ashlee. He stood across the room, leaning with feigned nonchalance against the wall, watching every move Ashlee made.

Ashlee was swept away from Alex, leaving her to her thoughts. She had a lot to work out. There was the race that was only several hours away and the first race of the season always caused her a slight panic. There was finding a satisfactory excuse for not remaining at the party with the rest of the women. And getting to Epsom Downs and back without detection, when the entire male population of the ton was in attendance, was always a cause for concern.

Then there was the hope that was starting to grow that Marc truly did care for her. Her whole plan had started out as a type of revenge, but now? Now, she didn't know. The entire thing had gotten out of hand and, more, it had become a challenge. And anyone who truly knew her knew she could not pass on a challenge.

Spencer Ferguson swept a low bow before her, his frills and lace drawing her attention. "My lady, would you care to dance?" He offered his arm, but she shook her head.

"No, but I could use a drink. If you do not mind." She smiled up at him, forcing herself not to search out Marc.

Spencer saw it. "He is watching you. His dance with Janice just ended." He pulled her white gloved hand into the crook of his arm, leading her to the far side of the room and the refreshment table.

"Brandy, please," she said. Brandy would calm her nerves.

He poured her a short glass of brandy, shaking his head. "Tell me. I can help." She knew they were alone when the high-pitched, nasal sound of his grating false voice was replaced with the deep tenor of his real one.

"I am just thinking of getting to the races. That is, at least, what I am trying to stay focused on. The rest is just going to distract me. I need to keep my head." Even as she said those words, her eyes sought the one she wanted. "How can things be so hard?"

"Life is hard. Whoever told you it would be easy lied." He smiled and shook his head. "How will you get away? Fall down the stairs and break your leg? I think with as closely as you are being watched that may be the only way." He had meant it as a joke, having seen the way her entire family and Marc's were watching her. A jest maybe, but it started the wheels turning in her mind.

"They are watching me so that I do not try and escape. They do not want me to embarrass them anymore than I already have." She quickly and quietly told him of what had happened after she had left the card game. He shook his head.

"We were concerned when Brandon could not find you. The messenger we sent out to find you said you had made it home safely."

"I think I will take a walk out in the garden." Alex shot one more quick glance at Marc. He was focused on Janice and her mother, who seemed deep in conversation. Alex tipped her glass to her lips, draining it quickly.

She looked at Spencer with suspicion as his gloved hand ran gently across the soft satin of her sleeve. He just smiled and winked, and Alex realized that Marc must be watching. She rolled her eyes, realizing his intent.

He watched her walk away. A few moments later, he saw Marc disappear out another set of French doors. Those on the opposite side of the long ball room from the ones Alex had used, but they both went to the same garden. Spencer smiled.

Lost in thought, she failed to hear the footsteps that approached her. A gasp was torn from her lips as she was spun around. Regaining her composure quickly she smiled at Marc. "My lord, is there something I can help you with?" He pulled her farther into the concealing rose bushes and tall stalked hollyhocks that Gwendolyn loved so much.

He held her painfully by the arms. She trembled by their closeness. Yet their bodies did not touch. He held her at a distance. "I want to know why you insist on spending time with that man." He drew her closer without realizing he was doing it. He could now feel her breasts grazing his chest. He fought the lust that was beginning to strain the fabric of his trousers.

Standing on tiptoe, she inched her face toward his. Alex could not force the tremor from her unsteady voice as she asked. "What man, my lord?"

His lips brushed hers, their noses touched. "Stop calling me that." His hands slid down her arms finding their way around her trim waist pulling her flush against his arousal.

She whispered against his lips, brushing them in invitation, her hot breath stealing his. "*My lord...my lord...My*—"

His lips crushed hers, his hands sliding lower. Grasping her bottom he lifted her, settling her more fully against him. He deepened the kiss. The coldness of the air around them was forgotten.

He slid his tongue across her lips, and they parted. A groan escaped him as he plundered all she offered. One hand still holding her up, he fought to lower the gown she wore.

He now wished she was wearing one of her soft and loose-necked day dresses.

His lips trailed across her check, devouring her neck as he made his way to the swollen pink nipple he had managed to expose. As he grasped it in his teeth, her moan disappeared into his hair as she cradled his head to her breast, pressing kisses onto his scalp.

Setting her small feet back on the ground he pulled the nipple deeper into his mouth. The suction drawing her even closer to him as her back arched, urging him on.

Reaching beneath the hem of her gown, digging through layers of lace his chilled hands found the hot skin of her calves. The dress caught on his arms, dragging upward, as he slid his hands farther up her legs.

Alex caught her breath as the chilled winds caressed her bare skin. Marc grasped his hands beneath her bottom lifting her, settling between her thighs. She had no choice but to throw her arms around his shoulders for balance, even as her back settled against a stout tree trunk. Clutching to him desperately, she could feel the hardness of him pressing against her, his clothing and her drawers the only thing separating their most private of parts. His mouth crushed her lips once again. His kisses were getting demanding, fierce. Possessive.

Not letting up for even a breath, he assaulted her senses. She instinctively wrapped her legs around his hips. Not able to get enough, he deepened the kiss, taking all he could. Tasting her willingness and her passion drove him over the edge.

Supporting her with one arm, he slid his fingers across the soft linen of her drawers. She pressed her hips into his hand.

There was no question of stopping him, she never thought to say no. She had no thoughts about anything.

Not until she heard the sounds of someone approaching. Marc had heard as well. He let out a healthy curse against her sweaty neck before dropping her to the ground.

He turned to find the source of the voice. Within a heartbeat, he had refastened his trousers and was praying the foliage would hide his lust. A man burst through the path between the rosebushes.

Marc spun toward Alex, only to find her gone.

"My Lord Clifton, what are you doing out here all alone?" Spencer's high voice grated on Marc's ears, and he wanted nothing more than to clobber the man.

Spencer fought to keep a straight face. He had hoped he would be just in time. He wanted enough time for some kisses and a caress or two, but not enough time to complete the act.

If Marc was in love with Alex, as everyone claimed, a little frustration when it came to her would do wonders. From the blackness rolling across the young man's face, Spencer guessed his timing was perfect.

"I was enjoying the garden. If you don't mind, I shall beg your pardon. I believe I shall return to the dance." Marc tried to step around him, but Spencer reached out and grasped his arm.

"Yes indeed. I shall be happy to walk with you." Without waiting for a response, Spencer began to lead him along. He could feel Marc trembling beneath his fingers. "My poor boy, you are shaking. It is beyond a chill out here. Cold, but when you have things on your...mind, you really do not notice, do you?"

"Lord Ferguson, I would like to go on my own if you do not mind." Marc tugged at his arm, but Spencer just tightened his grip.

"I do mind, as a matter of fact, my Lord Clifton. I will walk back in with you. You see, you have come along at the perfect time. I came out looking for someone I saw come this way, and I would hate for her parents or the haute ton to think disparaging thoughts of her if I were to return alone. I never found her, but if we were both seen leaving. Well, you know, people love to talk."

Spencer almost laughed at the anger that clouded Marc's face. It darkened to a nice shade of red, if he did think so himself.

"You came out here looking for someone? Who?" Marc didn't want to know. Didn't think he would allow the arrogant dandy to walk back in the house if he had been meeting with Alex. Though it made sense. They had been talking before she had slipped out. Spencer had caressed her arm. Had she been waiting for him?

"E-gads man. I really cannot tell you that, my dear Clifton. That would be ungentlemanly of me, would it not? I am not that much of a rotter."

There was only one woman who had gone out. It would be easy for Marc to figure it out. He could feel the muscles of Marc's arm jumping under his gloved hand. Marcus Clifton was jealous. That was good.

As they walked in the door, Marc hoped to withdraw from the

annoying man. To his horror, Spencer led him straight to Alex and the two families.

Thomas looked up from his daughter's smiling face to see the storm brewing on Marc's livid one. "Is everything all right, Marc?"

"Jolly good, my lord," Spencer answered for him. "I let him talk me into a stroll with him out in the gardens. I must have been mad. Silly me. It was chilly enough to frost my cravat. I just hope the sun peeks out before the races." He looked at Alex with a smile. "I am surprised we did not run into you out there. I know how you love the gardens, my dear lady. Would you grant me this dance, before we all must leave the beauty in this room for the monotony of the races?"

"I would be delighted," Alex said with the proper curtsy and a gracious tilt of her head.

Marc almost didn't let him pull his hand free. He was throbbing inside. He was angry and, more, he was confused. He didn't understand what was happening to him. He only let his arm relax, releasing the trapped hand, at Spencer's questioning look.

Marc's stomach lurched as the couple took the floor.

"What are you doing? Why were you out there, Spencer?" She cocked a thin well-groomed brow at him with a knowing and patronizing look.

"I saw him go out. I thought to save the poor man from you. Besides, if you give in too soon, it will lessen his torment. I cannot stand aside and allow that." He gave his false—and, she thought, stupid—laugh.

"Very funny. I have a feeling I have more help in this than I want. Everyone seems to be conspiring against the *poor man*." Her wicked smile did not match the concerned tenor of her words. "I am going to need your help with something, though. I need you to help get me to the races here shortly."

"What are you planning?" Spencer asked.

"As soon as I can, Beth Raynes—" Alex motioned to a small redheaded maid who rushed between the refreshment table and the hidden doorway that led to the kitchens, "—will assist me in getting to your carriage and keeping any nosy people at bay."

Beth was a former lady of Rose Hall and was just recently added to the Ronchester household, on the recommendation of Alex. The young girl was too uncomfortable around the rowdy men and was happy with the change of employment. She was also loyal to Alex for helping her.

The music stopped. Alex looked up to see Oliver Danton striding toward them. "Shall I get rid of him?" Spencer's low voice said he would be happy to dispose of him in any way she wished.

"No, I will dance with him." She winked at Spencer. "Marc hates him."

Spencer held her hand out to a surprised Earl of Staten. "My lord, I assume you are wanting a dance. I believe it will be the last one before you leave for the races."

Danton watched Spencer walk away before turning back to Alex. "Not exactly a dance, a short stroll perhaps. There is something I need to talk to you about." He led her across the dance floor to the double doors leading to the garden.

She smiled but didn't fight him. "Do you plan to take me out there, Danton? Do you think that wise?"

"No, I think not. I just wanted some privacy."

Alex looked back at the dancers. She could see Ashlee hanging on Philip Moore's words as they spun around the room. She could see Marc looking in her direction, spine stiff, and, even from this distance, she could see him tremble slightly. In anger? Of course, she thought with a happy flush.

"What is it, Danton?"

His face darkened.

When dealing insults, you had to know your opponent. Marc hated her calling him my lord, but Oliver Danton thought it disrespectful for anyone to call him anything less. It didn't take much needling to learn what bothered someone.

"I want to offer you my protection."

"You want to what?" That brought her attention fully back to him. Ashlee and her prospective love were forgotten. As were Marc and his jealousy.

"I have it on good authority that you were seen at Rose Hall. That you stabbed a man. I know you do not want this kind of information to get out. I can help you. Look, Alexis, this person wants revenge. He is planning to tell everyone all he knows and from what I hear he knows quite a lot. I am not at liberty to tell you who it is, but let's just say he is a powerful man in London."

Alex didn't need him to tell her who it was, and she knew Manning wasn't stupid enough to tell everyone. Telling one man was bad enough, and she would make sure he understood that. But she would deal with one snake at a time. She smiled. "What do you plan to do to help me?"

"I will marry you."

"Why would you do that? You do not want to be married to me."

"No, but I want your dowry. That is a massive amount, from

what I hear. I can help you. If you do not marry me, I will tell everyone what you have been doing. The gambling, the mingling with whores, your lovers. Tell your father you will marry me." He grasped her arm tightly. "You will do as I say."

Pulling him closer, she smiled. "Danton, my dear. I will tell my father. I will tell him I will marry you." His grip relaxed and he smiled. "Not tonight, though. I will tell him—when Hell freezes over."

She jerked away from him with a laugh when shock replaced his victorious smile. "Damn it, Alexis, I will tell everyone."

"Do, if that is what you think you must. Danton, if you think I will marry a man who rapes women, then you are stupider than I thought. And that would be saying a lot."

He sputtered at her, unsure of what to say. "How dare you accuse me of—"

She waved her hand in dismissal as she interrupted him. "Lonnie White."

His face drained of color at her words. "Who told you about her?" His eyes widened. "Marcus? Jeremy?"

"No."

Danton face was as white as the tablecloths on the refreshment tables.

Alex saw the understanding in his eyes, the self-preservation. "I would think twice before you tell anyone the rumors you heard about me. Someone with such a past as you should be careful what is said."

"Is everything all right, Alex?" She turned a brilliant smile on her father before returning her gaze to the irate man beside her.

Her eyes glittered in challenge. "Is it, Danton?"

"I was just apologizing for my behavior the other night. I will leave you in your father's capable hands, my lady."

He was shaken, and that worried her. She may have started something she was loath to finish. He was not a man who gave in easily.

She just wondered why he needed money so badly as to consider marriage to her.

"Alex?" her father asked.

"Everything is fine, Papa." She smiled widely at him when he took her hands. "Are we leaving now?"

"We? You know how I feel about that. You are not old enough yet to go. Stay with your mother and play some Whist."

She smiled at him. She knew he didn't want to encourage her love of the horses and the races. It hurt her, but she was grateful as well. She couldn't very well race if she was a spectator. She always asked, though, but only because she knew he would deny her. "Have fun, Papa."

"My little girl is getting so grown up. I am glad to see you mingling more this year." His brow furrowed. "Though be careful with Lord Danton." He kissed both her hands.

"I will, Papa." She watched him walk away, one more weight lifting from her shoulders. It was easier to leave with him gone.

Not long after her father had left her, most of the other guests began leaving in a procession.

Spencer loitered behind, speaking to this woman or that, telling anyone who asked that he was waiting until the main crowd had cleared.

He was speaking to Amber Fortshaw about her children when he heard the scream.

Everyone rushed in the direction of the woman's shout. Spencer rushed forward. "What happened, my lady?" Gently he took Alex into his arms. "Are you hurt?"

He'd tried hard to feign concern when he saw Alex lying on her side at the bottom of the stairs. Luckily, he was used to acting as quickly as a situation commanded.

"No, my lord. I believe I am fine. I just took a small fall. I must have tripped." She shot a gaze up the stairs.

All eyes followed her look. On the stairs was an outraged Lady Janice Rutmeyer.

"I was just walking down the stairs when I saw her. She must have tripped over her gown. She has been known to be clumsy," Janice said.

"She just fell? Tripped on her gown?" Spencer's voice was just the right amount of outrage, suspicion, and concern.

Alex, not quite as talented an actress to compete with her dear friend, fought the urge to laugh and hug him. Her hand tightened on his arm as she pulled him toward her.

"I just fell. It was an accident." It had not been an accident. It was very much deliberate, but Janice being there was just a happy coincidence. Alex had pretended to trip convincingly. Also painfully, she realized as she felt the twinge in her ankle. Great, that was all she needed. "Please. Do not worry about it. It was all my fault."

She passed a terrified, or at least she hoped it appeared that way, look at the woman on the stairs before looking back at the group assembled around her.

No matter what was said from here on out, there would always be speculation of what had happened on the stairs. Even more so when

Janice's betrothal to a man everyone assumed would marry Alex was announced.

Alex's mother glowered at Janice, even as she dropped to her knees beside Alex. "I do not think your father has made it far, my dear. I will send for him."

"No. Do not bother Papa. I am fine." With that, she tried to stand. With a gasp, she collapsed against Spencer. Much to her relief, the twinge in her ankle was nothing serious.

"I think we had better send for him," Amber said.

"No, I do not want to worry him. Let him enjoy the race. I will be fine. I would just like to go to bed to rest."

The Hollister and Clifton families had been among the few guests to be offered rooms at Lady Ronchester's country home. The plan was to head back to London in the morning.

Alex smiled at her mother in what she had perfected as her I-get-what-I-want pout. "When he returns from the races, you can tell him I had a little spill. He will come check on me and, then if I am no better, he can call for the doctor. Please." She could read her mother clearly and knew the moment she had won.

"I will get you up to your room." Amber tried to get her to her feet, but she faltered under her weight when Alex just hung limp.

"Please, my lady. I will take her." Without awaiting their answer, Spencer swept Alex into his arms.

Catherine Hollister had a moment of indecision. It was inappropriate, at the least, bordering on scandalous at worst, but he was the only man left in the room, and the remaining women would not be able to carry Alex safely up the stairs.

Lady Forester decided it for her. "Indeed. That is most kind of you, Viscount Ferguson. It will be comforting to know Lady Alexis is in such good and caring hands."

Alex realized that her mother should not have been concerned for propriety as the entourage of remaining ladies followed him through the foyer and up the stairs. She had more chaperons than she knew what to do with.

She had never been so grateful for Spencer's assistance as he pushed her into the bed, turned with a determined air, and rushed all the ladies out of the room, "We will send a maid up to help her get ready for bed." He closed the door behind him. She could hear his mumbled words, and then, like a miracle, the hall was silent.

Within a few moments, Beth Raynes entered without knocking. "My lady, hurry this way." She led Alex through the empty halls and out into the cool afternoon breeze. By the time they had made their quick escape to Spencer's waiting carriage, Alex's ankle was aching.

Spencer's driver, who was the very image of discretion, assisted Spencer with the limping girl. As they put her into the carriage, she grimaced.

Spencer knew it was not for show. No one could see her now. "What is it?"

"I think I did too good a job. It is nothing. I twisted my ankle. It is a twinge, but I am sure it is worse just because of the fast walk to get here. I shall be good as new by the time I arrive at the track. Which I had better hurry if I am to meet Tess. Thank you again, Spencer. I shall see you at the races." She closed the door, and Spencer climbed onto the seat with his driver.

Out of sight of the manor and, once he caught sight of Alex's carriage, Spencer motioned to his driver and the carriage jolted and swayed to a stop. Alex left Spencer's carriage and entered her own. Just in case someone saw her, she didn't want to try to explain why she was entering A.H.'s. It was waiting down the road.

Robert had waited far enough from the house not to be spotted and, in the denseness of the woods about halfway to the racecourse, a sleek, black and unadorned carriage awaited her. It was a small, four-person coach that was immaculate and beautiful in its simplicity. It's thick, rich-leather interior was soft and smooth. It showed the care and pride the owner took in their possessions.

Alex closed her eyes and, what seemed like moments later, opened them again as the carriage rocked to a stop. Looking from the window, she saw her other carriage and Tess Richards.

Tess, one of the meanest looking men that Alex had ever seen, jumped from his perch. His square jaw was rigid as always, his nostrils flared as if he were perpetually smelling for danger, and his dark blue eyes glittered with a challenge to the world.

She had in a sense rescued him three years ago. He was homeless, having just been released from the Tower for murdering a man. They had imprisoned him, only to free him six years later, saying that someone else had admitted to the crimes. What had made the situation unbearable was the fact that it had been confessed to right after his arrest. The guards had just not wanted to release him.

Tess had nearly killed one of the guards on his first night there. His scar-riddled face, hands, and back were a testament to the revenge they had extolled from him for that deed. Alex had found him almost dead in the woods one night. After bringing him food and bandaging his recent wounds, she offered him a job. He had tried to get work at other places and had been outright refused. Though being a driver was not what he had any experience in, he did so willingly.

She provided him with a salary, a generous one, a place to stay, and a new found self-respect that, after his shady childhood, his disruptive adolescence, and his ill-gotten imprisonment, he never thought to have again. In return, he gave his loyalty and, if needed, would give his life.

Tess Richards opened the carriage door at the same time that Robert opened hers. She glided unseen by outside eyes from one carriage to the other. "Robert, I will meet you here as usual." He would wait where he was. If someone came by, he was to say he supposed to meet his brother, who had not, as of yet, arrived.

After a smile and word of good luck, Robert watched the carriage and the mysterious and illusive A.H. disappear into the trees.

Chapter 9

After having spent what seemed like an agonizingly long carriage ride, with the Duke of Myerdome's fat thighs and jabbing elbows forcing themselves upon him, Marc was in no mood for the man to sit by him. He had tried to move away, but Samuel had just followed, and now they sat elbow to elbow, awaiting the first of the races.

"My dear boy, with you at my side I feel luckier than I have in quite some time. I believe we will win with that horse you picked out. I had thought it might be one of A.H.'s steeds, but from what I hear he has not arrived yet." Lord Rutmeyer had hung close to Marc, betting the first race as he had and, to Marc's irritation, constantly prying him for information.

"No, he is not." Jeremy leaned closer to the fat man as if to impart some deep wisdom. "He never is. He will be here shortly after the start of the first race and will leave before the fifth has ended. He only runs the second and fourth races."

As if summoned, a plain black carriage pulled into the stable area. "Is that him?" Lord Rutmeyer seemed in awe. "Who is that dreadfully large man driving the carriage?"

"That is indeed him, your grace. The infamous jockey." Thomas snorted in amusement. "I rather think all this intrigue is done just to push the betting." He looked around at the press of people pushing at the rail to be as close to the horses as possible. "With the rumor floating around that he is to show himself at the end of the season, I have never seen the stands so full. As to the large man, he is Tess Richards. A murderer and a brigand that, somehow, two years ago was released from the Tower. It is said that man there was the one to get him out, for he has been with him ever since." Thomas gestured to the small frame that emerged when Tess opened the door for him.

Marc looked closely at the jockey who stood dwarfed behind his large driver. A.H. had been on Marc's mind a lot since Samuel had mentioned him looking at Marc before he raced. Who was he? His frame was smaller than some of the other jockeys, but not as small as others. A.H.'s hips were lean, his legs long and much too shapely to be a man's, though with the baggy pants and knee high black boots it was hard to tell. Nothing else was really discernible since he always came in full gear. The heavy chest padding—that some did not wear—was always in place, as well as the helmet and visor that, nowadays, all of them wore. The thick leather helmet would protect their skulls in a fall, and the attached visor kept the sun off of their faces. All in all, he looked the same as all the rest of the racers.

The entire assembly seemed to watch as a young man approached A.H. He spoke to the man that Marc knew to be Raymond Dunmore, Robert's brother. Whatever was said did not sit well with either A.H. or the big Tess.

Both heads swung toward a man approaching them, and Marc's gaze followed. Jonathan Reed. Marc shook his head and grunted. "When did they allow him back? I did not think his ban was up yet."

"Mr. Reed paid some heavy fines—bribes to get back on the track." Marc caught the irritation in his father's voice. Maxwell was outraged that Reed was back, and Marc understood why.

Reed was not supposed to race at all this season, perhaps not even the next. He had always cheated, but last season he had made such a bad display of poor sportsmanship, that they finally banned him from the track. The catalyst had been A.H. himself. He had beaten Reed on too many occasions, and Reed had retaliated. He had been caught cutting the girth on one of A.H.'s saddles.

"It appears they share our surprise." Jeremy gestured down to a humorous sight. The small and delicate looking rider was trying to hold off a man who was larger than the horses he rode. Tess wanted to get to the man and the small gloved hands on his chest seemed to disappear. Smaller though he may be, A.H. won out. Tess said something that did not appear to be pleasant, and A.H. pointed to the stable where Tess and Robert would stay during the race. Tess shook his head. A.H. gave him a small shove that didn't even rock the man and pointed again. Tess gestured to Reed and walked away.

As Tess walked toward the stable, Reed approached. Robert stood in between them. There was a short unpleasant confrontation between Reed and Robert.

Thomas chuckled as he looked down at the unfolding drama. "I think Reed wants to talk to him."

"That is not going to happen. He does not speak to anyone from what I hear. Not even the other riders or the officials. Does he?" Samuel Rutmeyer looked to the group for confirmation.

"No, your grace. His man, Raymond Dunmore—" Marc gestured

to the man who was standing his ground with admirable patience. "—speaks to everyone on his behalf."

"Oh, he has already given up." Jeremy chuckled as Reed threw his hands into the air and stomped off.

"That was quick. I had expected more of a show than that." Marc would have said more, but someone caught his attention with a wave. It was not meant for him, but for the object of their conversation.

A.H. made his way to the stands, weaving in between horses and jockeys with practiced ease. He accepted something from the stern-looking man who had broken off from the crowd and waved him over. Marc squinted against the light but could not tell what he had been given. It was large, square. An envelope perhaps? He stared intently at the man. He knew him. Suddenly recognition set in and his stomach tightened. It was the man Alex had spoken with in the park. Anger swept across him. "Father, who is that man? The one A.H. is talking with."

Tilting his head for a better look, Maxwell Clifton took out his opera glasses.

"That is a man you should know. He is famous around here," the Marquis of Gravenhill answered before Maxwell had a chance to scrutinize him fully.

"Yes, indeed, Blake, it is." Maxwell put away the glasses as the first group of horses took the starting gate. "I am sure you will recognize his name. Mr. Andrew March."

"The solicitor? He is the one Alex tried to get me to use instead of Taggard." Why would she have been meeting the man she had wanted him to employ? Was it just a coincidence? No, he had a feeling that nothing that little chit did was ever by accident.

"She wanted you to use him? When was this?" The horses took the track, the screams of encouragement started, and A.H. stood calmly talking to March.

Marc thought about it as A.H. finally made his way back to Raymond. "When was it? She was fourteen, not long after her birthday from what I remember." He looked at his father but, out of the corner of his eye, caught Raymond accepting the large parcel. It was indeed an envelope.

The first group crossed the finish line with a loud cheer, yet all were anxious to watch the daring and illusive jockey that hid from all. Raymond laced his hands together and allowed A.H. to mount the massive-chested stallion. A.H. sat straight in the saddle, but Marc's gaze followed Raymond as he made his way to the crowded stands. Curiosity turned to suspicion as he headed directly for Lord Spencer. Spencer nodded in agreement and accepted the large envelope.

Marc, intent on the two men that Alex knew and spent time with, had almost missed A.H. looking to find him. If not for Lord Rutmeyer, he would have. "I believe your man is looking for you. Step out so he can find you."

Marc's eyes swept back to the track. Stopped right outside the starting gate A.H. was indeed looking for someone. Marc waited and the jockey swept his gaze across the families again, across the Cliftons, across the Hollisters, and across the Rutmeyers. Not seeming to find what he was looking for he widened his search, but still made his way back to the families.

Marc stepped forward where he could be seen.

The jockey visibly relaxed. Marc gave a short bow. The jockey stiffened but inclined his head in acknowledgment before maneuvering his large roan into the starting position.

Taking last-minute bets, men in white coats and trousers moved about the stands. "Who shall we bet on this time, Clifton? We won with your last pick. Shall we go with your boy?"

Marc just shook his head. "Yes, I think I shall. Master Greg is a champion stallion. He does not always win, but it is more often than not." He nodded to the young man, they made their bets, and the shot was heard. Horses screamed, and jockeys spurred them on as the spectators flew to their feet.

The horses bolted from the gate, Master Greg taking the lead, followed closely by the big black stallion ridden by Reed. Reed spurred his mount on, his whip flying furiously. This was his first race back, and he was not about to allow this jackanapes to beat him. The first turn into the race, A.H. was still ahead. Marc found himself on his feet, rooting for the young jockey and his impressive horse.

A.H. kept the lead. Marc could see the greed in Samuel Rutmeyer's eyes as he tasted another win. Marc leaned forward as Reed began to catch up, began to move in on the outside, pressing Master Greg's flanks toward the rail.

Adrenaline rushed Marc's body, his muscles tensed, his breathing came hard and swift. He loved the races, the joy at the purity of the mounts and the challenge of it all thrilled him like nothing else. Except perhaps a certain woman's body that, even now, he was having difficulty not imagining.

He saw it in the way the jockey sat the big roan in the lead, the way he leaned almost off his mount into the turn to give the massive creature extra balance. He watched, but only saw Alex as she leaned across his sister's mare to grasp the reins, his overactive mind making it look one and the same.

The swift beat of the pounding hooves tore through the crowd, the yells of the men in the stands drowning out the screams of the jockeys and mounts. Horses pushed at each other, nipped at flanks.

Positions were changed, challenges faced. The cries of the onlookers rose in a fevered pitch, but the riders heard nothing. They felt the wind whipping at their clothing, their skin. They felt the challenge of the next turn, the demand of the other racers. To do their best, to win, to show a good sport, and to succeed. Most of all—to ride.

The last turn reared close ahead. Master Greg needed no encouragement to take it. He flew ahead, well-groomed hooves throwing dirt and dust onto the riders behind him.

Marc shouted, unable to stop it as it came out. Reed pushed his stallion into the roan's wide and muscular flank. Reed's horse stumbled but regained his footing. Reed forced the pressure onto the young jockey.

A.H. was trapped against the rail, his riding boots doing nothing to protect the delicate skin of his knee as it ground against the rough wood. His only option would be to slow. Not for him, but for his mount who had to have taken some damage.

A.H. ripped at the reins, forcing Master Greg to slow. He came in third, behind Reed and a white mare named Glory. Coming to a stop away from the others A.H. jumped from the saddle and almost fell. Small hands went to a blood red knee.

The material had been soaked through. Marc's breath stopped in his throat.

Raymond was there in only a moment, pushing at the hands to see the damage. A.H. almost fell, but other hands, big hands caught him before he could. Marc could barely contain his heart as it threatened to beat hard enough to leave his chest. "Is he all right?"

"I hope so," Thomas's concerned voice answered.

Marc thought of nothing else as he watched the play unfolding before him. He wished he could hear what was being said.

A.H. spun out of Tess's grip, only to be caught in mid-lunge going for the throat of the man who had damaged Master Greg. Marc knew there was damage even though he could not see it from this angle, from the blood on his rider's knee there had to be damage to his side.

Tess struggled with the smaller man before finally throwing him over a wide shoulder and dropping him, gently, a few feet away. Whatever was said calmed the man. His weight balanced on one leg, favoring the injured knee, he stood his ground and waited.

Raymond approached him after speaking to the official. After a heated debate, Raymond returned to the official, who nodded and walked before the now-silent crowd.

For a short, gray-haired, fat old man, Jamison Daniel's voice boomed across the enormous arena. "Due to the questionable win that Jonathan Reed just acquired A.H. has been given the chance at another race. He has declined, due to the injury sustained to himself and his mount." There was a sigh in the crowd that one did not just hear, but felt.

Daniel raised his hands for silence as he continued. "He is accepting the chance at another race, however. He has requested to pick the time of that race, and his request for the rematch has been approved. The date has been approved as well." He paused for effect. All waited with baited breath. "It will take place as a sixth race, the last race day of the season." All hell broke loose in the stands.

Marc could hear people as they contemplated what that meant. They all knew it was a ploy on A.H.'s part. It would be the match right before his big unveiling, as it were. They would be hard pressed to find seating on that day. It was promising to be quite a show.

The third race went well, Marc's pick for that race winning.

"Well, Clifton, it looks as though you are always right. I say, if it had not been for the bad business of him being cheated, your boy would have won as well."

"He is not 'my boy,' your grace. Also, I am not always right. I lose just as often as I win. I—" His head swung to the racers. He took his feet once again. "He is racing?"

There was a rumble throughout the entire assembly of the same question.

"It looks that way, though his assistant looks less than pleased." Thomas gestured to Raymond, arms crossed and face tinged with red. Tess stood not far behind, anger rolling through his features as well.

"That is probably what the argument was between them. He probably wanted to take the rematch now, not wait until the last race. I do not think they believe he should be racing." Blake looked down as A.H. was hoisted into the saddle. It took two tries. His bent knee was caught by Raymond, but as the pressure hit the knee, A.H. grasped Marylee's thick mane, doubling over her withers.

Tess stepped forward with what, Marc could guess, were not nice words. He lifted the smaller man into the air, dropped him unceremoniously into the saddle, and walked away.

Once again A.H. searched Marc out.

"I do not think he should be either," Marc said as he inclined his head.

The gesture was returned in kind.

"My lords, your graces, would you care to wager?" The young redheaded boy was so filled with freckles his face was nearly covered.

"What say you, Marc? Your boy again?" Jeremy made his bet for A.H. as he always did when on the second and fourth race. He was loyal and never wavered in his bets no matter the horse or the odds.

"Excuse me, please." Tess's low graveled growl sent the young wage-taker almost into a panic. Tess's long dark blond hair whipped in the winds momentarily covering his hardened blue eyes. Pushing it out of his face he heard the sharp intake of breath, but thought it funny that it had come from the fat man he knew to be the Duke of Myerdome. Samuel had been interested in the man from afar, but as he looked at him up close, he was no longer so curious.

There was a large scar running from his temple to his nose. It was not the only one, but it was the largest. He had been lucky to keep his eye. The jagged white line ran along the bottom ridge of it.

"Yes, can I help you?" The young wage-taker tried to be brave, but he was shaking so bad Marc thought even his freckles were trembling.

"I was sent to see what the odds are." There was no need to ask which odds he was asking about. There was no one who didn't know who the big man worked for.

"Thirty to one."

Tess walked away without a word, but with a dark look at Marc.

"He terrifies me," the young boy said.

"Yes, young man." Marc laughed softly and hoped he didn't offend the boy. "I can see that he does that to most anyone he meets."

"Thirty to one. I do not think it has ever been that bad of odds for your boy. Has it been, Marc? Are you going to still bet him like Lord Hollister?" Samuel didn't give time in between each question for any response, so Marc just waited until the end of the tirade before trying to answer them all.

"Not since his first races and that was three years ago. The reasons the odds are so bad are the same reasons that my bet will not be with him. He is injured. You see how he can barely sit his horse. On top of that—" He took a moment to survey the racing schedule in front of him. His hands, he noticed, were still shaking at the thought the arrogant ass would even push another race now. Though he was not sure why he cared. Finding the mare's name, he continued. "Marylee is a new mare. This is her first race, and she is of questionable background. Which a lot of his horses start out that way and, by itself, would not usually deter me. But with the injury and Reed being in the race, it is not a bet I would make."

"Lord Hollister did," Lord Rutmeyer said with a tinge of confusion.

Jeremy just smiled. "I did because I always do. I never fail to bet on Marc's boy, though I do fail to win sometimes." He laughed.

Maxwell could not help but taunt his son. "Look, Marc. *Your boy* is taking his spot. Are you sure you do not want to bet for *your boy?*"

"He is not *my boy* and, no, I do not. I am betting for Troy. His rider is the same as Glory's, and Troy is a better horse. He has a great chance of winning."

The shot rang out. Troy took the lead, Reed right behind him and, to everyone's surprise, Marylee was right on their heels. Marylee took herself alongside Reed at the second turn.

A.H. took the outside, urging his mare onto ever greater speed. The crowd went wild, screaming encouragement for a mare and rider most had not even bet for. They had not expected him to race, let alone take the second position.

A gasp was heard across the stands as Reed pushed his stallion into Marylee. A cheer went out as Marylee let out a kick forcing him to retreat slightly.

Reed tried to push her off pace, to distract the new mare, but Marylee was not tempted. With a quick urging from her rider, she lunged forward, taking the last turn with lightning speed. Reed was hard pressed to keep up, and the bystanders clung to the railings, leaning precariously over the edge as A.H. lightly tapped the colorful riding crop against one thick leather boot. It would make a cracking sound and, while not touching the horse, it urged her forward.

With a lunge that brought shouts from the entire masses, she pulled ahead. Taking the last turn with no one before her, they headed straight toward Marc and his group.

Marc's breath caught and held, knowing the rider had looked to him, catching his eye with a proud set to his shoulders as he swung across the finish line. It was too much. More than Marc could handle. The man knew him, and he was going to find out how. And he was going to do it now.

While the members of the audience still whooped and hollered over wins, losses, and the unexpected performance of an amazing jockey and a new mare, Marc left the stands.

In his excitement, A.H. obviously forgot he was injured. He almost crumpled to the ground at the edge of the stables as he leapt unassisted from the tall back of the bay mare. Marc rushed forward to assist him.

A.H. spotted him and nudged Tess into his path. Marc stopped when Tess turned toward him. His blue eyes glinted, and his stony features did not soften. Marc strained to see around him, but Raymond had disappeared into the darkness of the stables with the man Marc wanted to see.

Glancing back at the mountain of a man before him, Marc tried his most frightening stare, one that had put many a servant, and much of the ton in their place. No one wanted to tangle with the next Duke of Paddington.

Tess didn't so much as blink.

"Let me by. I want to see your master. He knows me. Let me by." Tess just stood in his path. "Move. I know where his carriage is. I can go around the building to get to it." His voice boomed with authority. "I will have your job for this."

"I don't think so. You don't know who you are dealin' with. I ain't worried about anythin' you can do. My master will not let me go, and if you try goin' round that stable. I'll rip off your arm." His dusty growl sent shivers down Marc's skin. He was not used to being threatened. He didn't think it had ever happened before. It was a new sensation, one he didn't like.

"You lay one hand on me, and you will end up in the Tower." It was the wrong threat. Marc knew it even as he said it, but he was unprepared for the laugh.

"I've spent a lot of time there and will go back for loyalty." Tess's big frame had stilled, his voice was low and deadly, and his smile was unfaltering. All of which made Marc more and more uneasy, yet he refused to back down when Tess took a step toward him.

"I know if you tell him I am here to talk to him, he will see me. He knows me, and he will want to see me." Marc matched his step forward until he was nose to chin with the massive man.

"Not yet." Raymond had returned after settling his master in the carriage. "Tess take A.H. where you need to. Tess—Tess you were told not to harm him. Did you not hear that said?" He now looked up at the man who was unwilling to back down. "Tess?"

"I heard." Tess's eyes never left Marc's. "You are only in one piece 'cause of that order."

Marc didn't breathe a breath until Tess had disappeared into the stable.

"A.H. is not ready to see you yet." Raymond's calm voice drew Marc's attention. "Yes, you have met, my lord. I was instructed to inform you, the two of you will talk after the last race of the season."

Master Greg gave a pained cry from where he was standing, head hanging, his reins draped over a stable gate.

"If you will excuse me, my lord. I need to see to Master Greg."

"Is he hurt badly?" Marc followed Raymond over to the horse. The roan shivered. "Easy boy." Marc's hands slid down the horse's side. The wounds, not bad, were already bathed and doctored.

"No, he will be fine. I am afraid, though, my lord, that he will be out for several races at least. I will request that, at the end of the last race, you meet me here, but not before then. I cannot guarantee your safety with Mr. Richards."

"Because he got him out the Tower?" Marc gently stroked the tall horse until he was calm and his shivering stilled.

"A.H. did not get him out of the Tower. It came after that. But, my lord, that is a story that A.H. will have to tell you." Turning his back on Marc, he led Master Greg away.

"Wait."

Raymond turned back.

"How bad is A.H. hurt?? His knee, I mean."

"I do not know, my lord. He is too stubborn to let me look, too pigheaded not to race, but Tess is to send for the doctor, with or without approval from my willful master." And, with that, he was gone, taking both Marylee and Master Greg with him.

Marc had just made it back to his seat as the fifth and final race was getting underway.

"Marc, I saw you going off toward the stables. Did you see your boy?"

With an exasperated groan, Marc smiled at Jeremy. "I saw him from afar. That big driver of his is more of a bodyguard than I had planned on. A.H. will not talk to me, but he wants to. I bet you cannot take a guess as to when he will see me face to face."

Jeremy laughed as Blake piped in his opinion. "If it is anything like the rest of his promises, it will be...let me see...after the last race."

Everyone laughed. Lord Rutmeyer just looked confused.

Spencer Ferguson watched as Marc walked back to the stands after speaking with Tess. He waited as Marc spoke with his family, waited for the messenger he knew would come for Thomas Hollister.

With Alex's bloody knee, he knew the doctor would be called, and his job would be to keep Lord Rutmeyer busy. They did not need him standing around and complaining while the doctor worked.

Spencer grinned. It was a good thing she had faked the fall down the stairs, he thought as he made his way toward the large group. He reached them as the messenger came into sight.

"My lord, Lord Hollister." Daniel Barnes was probably six foot tall and as big around as a willow sapling, but he shoved his way through the mobbing crowd without even breaking a sweat. Thomas Hollister's youngest groom's pale blond hair showed over many heads.

Thomas pushed someone, he did not stop to see who, out of the way. "Barnes, what is it?"

"It's Lady Alexis, my lord. She fell at Lady Ronchester's. It was right after you left. She has sent me to get you."

Thomas's heart lurched in his chest. "Is the doctor on his way?"

"Not yet, my lord. Lady Alexis sent me for you. That was all she said."

"What happened? Why did no one get in touch with me before now?"

Many people had stopped to look at the dark, loud voice. His worry was tinged with the fact that she had sent just for him.

When Daniel could not tell him anything more, Thomas sent him to get the doctor. He turned to his group. "Do you want to stay, I will send the carriage back—"

Jeremy, Blake, and Marc all said no at once. "We will go, Father. She may not be everyone's sister—" He glanced at Marc. "—but we all care about her."

Marc scowled.

Maxwell clapped his hand on his friend's back. "We are going with you, that is what family is for."

Thomas looked at Samuel. They had brought him. It was their responsibility to see him back to Lady Ronchester's manor, but Thomas did not feel like dealing with him at the moment.

"Your grace, I would appreciate it if you would spend some time with me this afternoon." Spencer stepped forward with a deep bow for Samuel. "Some of us are getting a card game together at one of the local inns before we head back to the rout." Spencer smiled. He pointed behind them to Lord Edward Barlow, who had just left his normal spot above them in the bleachers. "He never stays long. He is only here to see A.H. race. He may be persuaded to tell you something of the man as we play. Would you care to join me?"

"Spencer, my man. I would be delighted. I hear you are good at the tables. You could give me some advice. Plus, you are right. Perhaps he will reveal something to me." Rutmeyer walked away without waiting for Spencer to join him.

Marc caught the look of disdain that crossed Ferguson's moss-green eyes as he watched Rutmeyer's retreating backside, but when Spencer turned to look at Thomas, the look was gone. "Give my best to your daughter, my lord. I will keep him occupied and get him back to the rout after the doctor has left and all is settled."

Thomas smiled gratefully and gave a bow. "I will, my lord. Thank you."

Spencer nodded and followed behind the waddling form who was bearing down on Edward.

Once in the carriage Blake Fortshaw laughed. "I think we owe Ferguson a bit of thanks for that."

"Yes, it was nice of him to distract the man. I can actually breathe in this seat now." Maxwell looked at Marc as everyone made some comment about it. Marc just looked worried.

"I am sure she is fine. There is nothing to worry about. More than likely a sprained ankle."

Marc looked at his father's sympathetic gaze. Was his worry that obvious that his father—no, from the matching looks that circled him, that everyone—knew he was overly concerned?

It was not just about the fall, though. It was about Spencer Ferguson and his damn jab of giving Alex his best. It was perfectly acceptable to say something like that, yet he could have done it without the snide glance in Marc's direction.

Alex danced too much with the dandy for Marc to be comfortable about it. Plus, Spencer had gone out to the garden to meet someone, and Alex had been the only woman out there.

The question remained, did Spencer go on his own, or had Alex been waiting for him.

The doctor was coming out of Alex's chambers as the men reached the door. "My lord, are you her father?" At Thomas's nod, he continued. "I am Dr. Canton, can I speak with you privately."

"No, it will only mean I have to repeat what you say later to them, anyway." Thomas's worried gaze went to her door. "You got here quickly."

"I was next door with the Satterfield's little girl. She is sick but fine. I was just coming out when Lady Forester came to get me. She had seen my carriage. I know Daniel is out looking for me. I must have gotten here right after he left."

"How is she? Can we see her now?" He didn't care about any little girl but his own at the moment. He just wanted to see her, to hold her, and know she was safe.

"You can see her, but she needs her rest. She twisted her knee pretty good. She didn't want me to tell you, but I think you should know. She scraped it up fairly bad. It must have hit the edge of the stairs. She needs several days of bed rest. I would let her rest tonight and go easy on the way back home. Have your doctor there check her when you get back and then keep her down for at least three or four days. If anything changes tonight, let me know."

"Thank you, Doctor." Thomas held his breath as he opened the door.

Beth Raynes smiled up at them. "She is sleeping, my lord. Dr. Canton gave her some laudanum."

Marc walked slowly to the end of the bed, concern etching his normally jovial features.

She looked so pale. Gently, he touched the long, smooth material of the canopy. Its pale cream silk billowed around the four corners of the bed, leaving the sides open.

Alex was covered to her chin in thick blankets. Her head snuggled down in the thickness of her feather pillow. Her eyes opened sleepily. His breath caught. He forgot everyone in the room as her blue eyes focused on him.

They drifted partway shut only to struggle open again. "Did you see her do it?"

Marc moved closer to the bed, tracing the outline of her foot beneath the coverings, before taking it gently in his grasp. "Did I see who do what?"

Her groggy mind was distracted. She didn't answer. Thomas walked past Marc, laying his hand momentarily on his back as he passed.

"Papa." She gave a weak smile. "I do not think I much like whatever that doctor man gave me."

"Just something for the pain. May I look?"

Without waiting for her answer, which she never gave, he pushed back the covers and, with no concern for the men in the room, pulled her nightrail up over her knee. Pulling back the bandages he gasped. "That looks like more than a little fall." Her skin was rubbed nearly raw. Bruises could be seen around the damaged knee.

"I did not fall, Papa. I was pushed."

The men looked at each other as she struggled to rise. Covering her leg Thomas assisted her. She fell into his arms. Wrapping her own around him, she returned to sleep. He nuzzled against her soft hair as she buried herself farther into his embrace. Kissing the top of her head, he sighed. "I love you, Alex."

Once she was settled back into her bed, the men went in search of the women and some brandy.

Ensconced in the warm, comfortable drawing room, a brandy in his hand, Thomas asked the ladies what had happened. Catherine looked at Marc with hesitation. "She said she fell."

The men all looked at each other, each remembering her words. *'I did not fall, I was pushed.'*

"Catherine." Thomas's voice told her more than she wanted to hear. He always knew when she was trying to hide something, and he would not tolerate it.

"He will find out soon enough. That rumor is too juicy for them to ignore. It will be better if we tell him." Alma smiled at her son. "Marc, I will tell you first that Alex did indeed say she had fallen." She took a deep breath. "There was a scream, and everyone ran into the room. Alexis lay at the bottom of the stairs."

Catherine took over the story. "She defended herself too quickly. She said she had been coming down the stairs when Alex fell, but she had nothing to do with it."

Marc had a bad feeling rip through him. "Who said?"

"Alex swears it was not as it looked. She defended her. She said she fell," Alma said.

"*Who*, Mother." This time it was not a question, his voice betraying his impatience.

She swallowed hard, but her youngest daughter saved her the pain of breaking it to him. "When we found Alex lying at the foot of the stairs. Lady Janice was the only one around. She was standing halfway up the staircase," Ashlee said in quick, but soft tones.

Anger burned at Marc. "What?"

Alma Clifton rushed to stand by him, laying her hand on his shoulder. "Alex said it was nothing, that she fell." She looked closely from man to man, and something she saw in the looks that passed between them made her ask. "What is it?"

Thomas sighed. "When we got here, Marc walked to the end of her bed. Alex awoke to ask him if he had seen her do it. She was feeling groggy with the effects of the laudanum. Before she slipped into sleep, she said she didn't fall. She was pushed."

Ashlee gasped loudly. She knew the fall had indeed been staged, and she also knew the only way Alex would have been hurt badly enough for a doctor would have been an accident at the race. "I think we should wait until the effects of the medication wear off before we make any decisions."

She could only hope they would not try to talk to her while she was influenced by laudanum. That was all Alex needed—to slip up and tell a secret while drugged.

"You are right," Thomas said. "What happened after she...fell? Why did someone not send for me immediately?"

Catherine shook her head. "She made us promise not to send for you, she did not want to bother you, and she made it seem like it was a minor fall. Lord Spencer said she was fine, and..."

"What?" Thomas was on edge and nearly shouted. "Why would that man not tell me that she was hurt when I saw him?"

Amber stepped forward. "I am sure she made him promise not to tell you, as she had made the rest of us promise. She was very worried about upsetting you and making you miss the races for what she said was just a little fall. Lord Spencer had remained behind for a few moments when Alex fell. Since he was still here, he carried her up the stairs to her room."

"Alone?" Marc's heated voice boomed through the room. "How could that be allowed? That is indecent." His anger at Janice was overshadowed by suspicion of Alex's relationship with Viscount Ferguson.

"Marcus Reyes, it is no such thing." Catherine Hollister slapped his arm. "It was in the middle of the day, and there were many women who chaperoned."

"That is enough for tonight." Thomas placed a hand on Marc's shoulder. "We should all get some sleep for a long day tomorrow to get us home.

Chapter 10

Rock, old man, how are you today?" Marc said in a loud and cheery voice to Percival Rockford, Thomas's valet. Rock, as unmoving as his nickname, one he didn't deign to acknowledge, gave a small bow. With a straight and serious face, he walked past Marc to close the door Marc had left standing open. "Not even a good morning to me, old man?"

Rock turned with the same quiet dignity that always surrounded him. "Good morning, my lord."

Marc grinned and opened his mouth to ask about Jeremy. "Is Alex up?" he said instead, cringing as the words tumbled from him. He had told himself the entire way that he was coming only to breakfast with Jeremy. He had almost convinced himself, at least until the first thing out of his stupid mouth was about Alex. "Since she was injured," he added quickly, "I thought to check on her."

Rock inclined his head, and Marc would have sworn he saw the edge of his lips twitch, if it would not have been beneath his dignity to do so. "No, my lord. None of the ladies have yet to come down to breakfast. The gentlemen are in the parlor if you would like to join them there."

"Yes, indeed, my dear man." Marc gave a small bow and gestured for the tall, thin man to lead the way to the always cozy breakfast parlor.

Positioned in the northeast corner of Hollister House two walls were covered with massive windows allowing the warm morning sun to caress the entire room and all its occupants.

The furniture was simple, comfortable, inviting an informal and relaxed atmosphere that Marc hoped to have in his own house one day.

"Lord Marcus Clifton, my lords."

"Rock, old man. Thank you. Are you answering the door now as well as pressing father's clothing?" Jeremy gave Marc a wicked smile. "Come sit with us. Break your fast, old man."

Blue eyes widened slightly, and his nose raised another notch giving the only indication his dignity was ruffled. "My lord, that would be most inappropriate, as you well know. And I did not answer the door. I was in the hall when he let himself in. If that will be all, my lord?"

"Jeremy, be nice to Rock. You know how you annoy him. He is very dedicated to his position. He is a proud man. He has been with your father for many, many....many years." Marc could not help a grin as he stood regally and spoke in fair imitation of the elderly valet. "He never bends, you know that."

Thomas shook his head and laughed.

"Ignore them, Rockford. You may be excused." As Rock walked out of the room, Thomas turned to the boys. "You two should learn not to tease him. He could still decide to take you over his knee. It would not—"

"Alex!"

The concerned shout, that sounded so different from Rock's normally gentle voice, got the men into the hall in an instant. Stopping just inside the archway they could see Rock and Alex, but neither looked their way.

Thomas pulled the boys back with a shake of his head and a finger to his lips. He wanted to see just how hurt she really was. He didn't think she would tell him. He knew it was because she didn't want him to worry. He worried anyway.

Alex sat on the bottom stair, obviously where she had fallen, and Rockford stood, his back to them, with his hand outstretched to assist her to her feet.

"My lady, are you all right?" Rock asked.

Alex smiled, tried to stand, only to plop back down. "Oh, just fine. I hurt my pride more than my rear, so I think I shall live. If father had not insisted on that vile concoction the doctor left I would be steadier on my feet." In a fog or not, she had plans this morning, and she could no more sleep it away in a drug-induced slumber than she could spend it wallowing in her pain. Life moved on and, unfortunately, sometimes you just had to cinch your stays and move on with it.

"Shall I get your father, my lady?" He turned, but her soft voice stop him.

"Percy, please."

Percival Rockford turned to her with a glow in his eyes. Alex was the only one to call him that and always had been. No one else would dare. She started calling him Percy when she was only three. Tenacious even then, as soon as she had realized it had bothered him, she tore into it and held on tight. Rock had learned then she would not let up as long as he let it show that it annoyed him. Percy was beneath his status. Percy was a fun and carefree kind of name that did not fit with his solid, secure image.

He had finally asked her why she did that. Why she wanted to annoy him so badly. She had looked up at him with childish adoration and told him simply. "I love you, and you need to smile. If I call you Percy you...you do something."

It had been her young way to get any reaction out of him. He had squatted before her, telling her she was more than welcome to call him whatever she would like. The name had stuck.

"You need to get your rest." His granite face seemed transformed by the loving smile that he bestowed on the young lady. To the men behind him, he seemed the same impassive figure as always.

"No. Percy, I want to eat breakfast with Father before I get ready for Lady Hamilton's tea." She struggled to rise again and failed with a grunt of exasperation. She had planned to use her injury to get her out of Hamilton's gathering, had indeed planned it when she pretended to fall. She just hoped she could accomplish what she needed to, but she was beginning to have her doubts.

Her knee hurt her more than she imagined it ever could, and the laudanum slurred her vision and her words. She had not taken the full dose as her father had asked, just enough to take the edge off the pain, yet it still affected her. She had not taken the full amount, partly because of her need to leave the house, but mostly because Rebecca had told her she had blurted things out when drugged the night before. Luckily nothing to get her into too much trouble, but she was not going to take any chances.

"Your father is not going to allow you to go to tea today, my lady. You need to return to your room, honey pot." Rockford smiled at the woman, who he would always see as the four-year-old he had found up to her elbows in the large honey pot in the pantry.

"I cannot." She began to cry.

Rock dropped into a crouch. "Do not cry, my lady. It will all be fine." He withdrew his sparkling white handkerchief to dab away her tears. Caressing her face, he shook his head and smiled. "It will turn out for you in the end, I have no doubt."

She sniffed loudly. "Do you know what a handsome man you are when you smile?"

"So my wife tells me every day." He brushed an errant curl away from her red and watering eyes. "This is not about missing the tea or even your knee, now is it?"

Alex wrapped her arms around his neck. "Are you happy in your marriage?"

"Very much so. Why?"

"Do you love her and she you?"

He turned to sit on the bottom step, pulled her into his lap and held her close to his chest as her tears threatened once again.

"I love her as much, or more, today as I did when I married her thirty-five years ago. Come now, honey pot, why do you ask?"

She sniffed loudly, accepted his handkerchief and laid her head against his shoulder. She took a deep breath to control the hateful tears. "I have cried more in these past few weeks than I have in my entire life."

Looking toward the doorway, Rock didn't see anyone coming from the breakfast room, so he relaxed a little more. "Tell me."

"I just—I have never considered marriage before. I want it. I did not think I did, but I do. I have seen my parents and the Clifton's marriage, as well as that of Amber and Blake. I know they are happy and in love, but I also know they are an exception to the rule of society marriages. I do not want to be unhappy in my marriage. I do not want him to be either and I know he will." The tears came again, silent this time, wetting the shoulder of his immaculate coat.

"Honey pot, why do you think he will be unhappy married to you?"

"I do not." She pulled her head up to look at him. "I mean. I can make him happy, but he…"

Then he understood. He pulled her close and kissed her wet and puffy cheek. "Do you have someone in mind you would like to marry?"

Alex smiled, but all she could do was look at him and nod.

"I take it you think he is marrying someone else?" He had begun to rock her gently back and forth, her eyes sliding slowly shut, her head slumping against him once again.

It was a moment before she answered, and he thought she had fallen asleep. Rising to take her back to her bed before anyone caught him in such an undignified manner he started at her small voice.

It was soft and almost silent, but it carried well. "I do not *think* he will marry her. I *know* he will. It does not matter if he loves her or not, does not matter if someone else loves him or not, because he does not care about anything, except his wretched reputation."

✐✑✐✑

A few hours later, after Alex had been deposited back into her bed, Marc sat in silent thought as the carriage pulled away from Hollister House to meet with the Cliftons, the Blakes, and the Rutmeyers, who had insisted on going to the tea party with them. Luckily, the Rutmeyers would meet them at Clifton House, and they did not have to trudge all over creation to collect everyone.

He could hear Jeremy and Thomas chattering in the background, but his mind was consumed by Alex.

Did she truly want to marry him? Would it matter if she did? Marrying her would not help him or his reputation, would indeed undo all of his hard work. Her outrageous behavior was getting worse and, though scandal had yet to touch her, it was only a matter of time before it caught up with her. Then where would her husband be?

It was not that he cared only for his reputation. There were just some things that took precedence over everything else. That included his own happiness. He knew Janice was going to make him miserable, but would Alex make him any less so. No, she would make him more so. He would learn to care for Janice. He would get his heir, his business, and the life he wanted, and nothing was going to stop him.

Jeremy elbowed him painfully in the side. "Marcus, are you going to get out so the rest of us can or are you going to sit there staring into space thinking about pretty little girls?"

Marc glared at him until he caught the amused grin of Alex's father. "I was not thinking of…of any pretty little girls." Marc snorted. "Shut up and let's go in."

He slipped from the open carriage door and came to a stop. Everyone was awaiting them at the front of the London Townhouse.

Blake stepped forward hand outstretched and grasped Marc's arm. "Smile, my boy, I have a way to get rid of that scowl. I have it on good authority that someone wants to sell you a ship, but you have to go look at it now as he has several people who are interested."

That indeed got Marc's eyes shining, a smile brightening his face. "I will send a message to Taggard, he can see to it—"

"No. You have to go yourself, I'm afraid. The messenger was very specific. Now, how did he put it? Ah, yes I remember. That drunken blackguard is not allowed to go near them, or there will be no deal." Blake laughed as Marc's scowl returned.

"I am tired of that rumor. I have had no issues with the man in my dealings with him." Marc felt indignation rising, but refused to allow it to get the best of him.

"We can figure that out later, for now we have plenty of time before the tea. Let us go and check out this ship." Maxwell smiled at his son. He knew him well enough to recognize the interest in his green eyes.

Marc hesitated. He did not see to the buying of ships himself and did not plan to start now, though he was interested in seeing the ship. "Father, we will be late for the Hamiltons."

Maxwell shook his head. "We are still quite ahead of schedule. We will be the first to arrive at the Hamiltons if we do not dawdle."

"Yes, my boy, I would love to see one of your ships."

Marc caught the groan before it could escape as Samuel stepped forward with his encouragement.

Marc looked at the ring of interested faces and admitted defeat. "Of course, your grace. We can send the women on to—"

"No." Janice smiled shyly as Marc turned to her. "I mean, I would love to see a ship as well, Lord Clifton. I have never really been to the docks." Janice needed to reinforce her claim on him in the eyes of society, especially since the meddling little child was injured and out of the picture. Janice almost wished she had pushed her. She may as well have since everyone seemed to think she had.

Marc cursed almost silently. Not quite low enough, he realized, as Blake cleared his throat to disguise a laugh.

"Of course, my lady."

℘⅏℘⅏

Alex opened her eyes, sunlight stung at her vision. "Bloody Hell," she whispered into the quiet room. Glancing at the mantle clock she realized she had not slept long.

Her knee was stiff, but moving it proved less painful than she had expected. She swung her feet out of bed and prepared herself for the dizziness, but the effect of the laudanum appeared to have worn off while she had slept.

She looked at the ceiling and said a quick thank you and a prayer to make it through her day without getting caught. She took a deep breath, dressed quickly, and rushed to the stables.

After assuring Robert her knee was fine, an argument that took much longer than she would have liked, he finally helped her into her carriage. She was sure her eyes had drifted shut before they had reached the first turn in the crowded London streets.

Opening the carriage sometime later, Robert smiled at the dozing woman inside. "My lady."

She smiled without opening her eyes. "Sorry, that medication is still making me groggy, but it is helping with the pain. Help me out."

"No, stay. I will get Miss St. Johns and the boxes and bring them to you." Robert shut the door, not allowing her to argue.

"Mr. Dunmore. Where is Lady Alex?" Malacinda St. Johns, only four years older than Alex, still felt as if she should take the young girl under her wing.

Robert looked up at the tall woman with a smile. "Lady Hollister is fine. She had a small fall, but is waiting in the carriage." Robert picked up one of the large boxes that sat just inside the doorway.

Malacinda relaxed, picking up a smaller box, and following Robert to the carriage. He took her box and helped her in beside her small friend.

"Malacinda, good to see you."

"Alexis, I hear you took a fall."

Alex smiled. Malacinda only called her Alexis when she was upset with her.

"Are you sure you are up to this today?" Malacinda continued.

"Of course." Alex looked at her with pain in her eyes.

Malacinda knew it had nothing to do with her fall. She was looking at her with jealousy, a look she had not noticed in quite some time.

"Alex?"

Alex just shook her head and smiled. "I am fine."

She had met Malacinda at Chariton House a little over a year ago and was instantly taken with her. She had known her for three months before she found out what her profession was and worse that Marc was her protector. Alex had made the mistake of talking to her about Marc. Nothing real personal, but enough she was afraid that Malacinda had guessed to her true feelings.

She had avoided his mistress for two weeks, but found she missed her more than she could bear. She liked her and wanted nothing more than to be her friend. They had made a silent pact to not mention Marc and had not spoken his name in ten months, but Alex was still jealous. Malacinda knew Alex didn't know that she and Marc were no longer intimate. She had considered telling her on several occasions, but just didn't know how to bring it up.

"Alex, we do not—"

The carriage jolted to a stop and rocked under Robert's weight as he stepped down.

Alex waved her words away. It was better not to know anything. Both heads turned to Robert as he helped a third girl into the carriage, her big box packed onto the rear of the conveyance with the other two.

"Victoria, how are you?"

Victoria Chariton smiled at the pair. Alex had met Victoria two years ago when Victoria had been hired to be hostess in the backroom of Rose Hall.

"I am fine. I told Mama you were coming by. The children are excited beyond words to see you." Victoria's mother, Vanessa Chariton, was the owner and headmistress of Chariton House, one of the many orphanages that dotted the outskirts of London.

Arriving at the large two-story white house, Alex leaned heavily on her two friends. A dozen children came running out the open door only to be caught by both women and Robert before they could plow into Alex. To erase their hurt and confused expressions, Alex smiled sweetly.

"I have missed you all." She reached over and took a small five-year-old-boy by the hand. "I have taken a fall, hurt my knee. So I am happy to see you and want you to hug me and tell me you have missed me as well, but I need you to be careful with me, all right?"

At their worried nods, they were released. This time, they were slow with their approach as she gathered them to her in a massive group, trying to hug them all at once.

She visited with the children, handing out toys and clothing from the large boxes while Robert unloaded a large parcel of food items. Her visits with the children were always the highlight of her trips to London. She loved them all dearly, but today was straining to her.

Vanessa seemed to realize this without being told. She ushered the children into the house after Alex promised to see them before the end of the week.

"How is Rebecca doing?" Vanessa asked the limping woman before she was helped into the carriage.

Rebecca St. Talves had been in the orphanage since she was three and, by fifteen, she was out of place. She was ashamed of who she was. Her mother had abandoned her after her father had refused to continue to support his mistress and her young child.

Alex had fallen in love with the young girl on sight and had immediately hired her as a ladies maid. Taking her out of Chariton House helped them financially as well. Less mouths to feed and bodies to clothe. The same day, she had taken another child as well, though he was no longer a child, having just turned eighteen. He had no prospects and no idea where he was going with his life. He had been with the orphanage since birth.

Reeves Dalton was now, and had been for a year, the man responsible for taking messages to Marc. He was to tell Marc they were from Taggard if he was questioned, but Marc had only done so once, with his first message. Alex did not trust anyone else to take the missives, and it was too much of a risk to do so herself.

"Rebecca is fine. I shall bring her with me when I come at the end of the week." She hugged the elderly woman tightly, then allowed Robert to assist her into her seat.

Having sat for almost an hour with the kids, and the long ride toward the docks where the home was located, Alex could not bring herself to reenter the carriage after they delivered Victoria to her door.

"Robert, take the carriage to Malacinda's. I want to walk. My knee is starting to throb it is so stiff."

Without a word, Robert did as she asked. He had lost the argument for her to stay home. His worries she was much too injured to make the trip fell on deaf ears, so he didn't even bother. He would not win a fight with her unless he absolutely refused, and he would not do that.

ৎ৲৩৴৩

Marc had seen the ship, had bought it, and had tried his best to ignore the simpering woman who clung desperately to his arm.

Now, he sat as close to the door as he could and watched the town houses go by. This was Malacinda's neighborhood. What he would not give to be sitting in her sitting room, playing chess and listening to the sound of her laughter.

Laughter that floated to his ears as if to tease him. He could almost hear it. With a frown marring his high brow, he leaned out the window. He was not imagining it. She was indeed in front of them. He recognized her sweet swaying. Her long black hair was silky smooth and swung seductively across her slender back. She was laughing with a much shorter woman. They clung to each other in laughter. Both sweet voices floated to him as he leaned farther out the window.

He watched the second woman, a familiar knot began to grow in the pit of his stomach, though he could not place why, or who the woman was, though she was indeed familiar.

The short woman said something that caused gales of laughter to come forth once again and, as they started walking toward Marc's rented house, his breath stopped in his throat.

The woman had taken no more than four shaky, limping steps when Marc cursed loudly.

Thomas, who had been intently watching Marc's varying expressions, leaned out the window the best he could to follow Marc's line of sight. With a curse that set even Marc's to shame, he pounded on the top of the carriage. Then, without realizing the women were leaving their carriage to follow, Marc and Thomas stormed toward the two friends.

Marc got to them first. "So you are why I am not getting what I pay for?" He ignored the shocked gasps from behind him. "How could you do this to me—"

Malacinda cut him off. "She doesn't know."

That irritated him even more so. How could she think he was taking this woman and still be friends with her? Friends? Is that what they were?

"Right. You followed me here, didn't you?" His voice raised, he stepped toward her. "You planned this."

Alex stepped forward until her chin was at his chest, her blue eyes glittering up at him. Her voice louder than his as her temper began to smolder. "No, I did not, my lord. You think awfully high of yourself to think I would do such a thing just for you. Yes, everything I do, my lord, is just for you. I met her when I was visiting a friend. I did not know what she was or that you were involved until I had known her for several months, my lord."

People were starting to stop and ogle the large group. Thomas grabbed Marc by the arm, forcing him to back away. Maxwell pulled Alex back by the arm, quickly grasping her waist to steady her when her leg came down heavily. She wrapped her hand around his forearm and bit her lip.

Alex's face paled and she began to sweat slightly, but still she patted his arm to let him know she was once again steady.

Thomas was too angry with her to notice. "What friend were you down here to see?"

"Vanessa Chariton." The name sounded familiar to Thomas. He knew the name, just not why.

"And are you stupid enough to wander these streets alone and unprotected?" Thomas was starting to feel the anger subside, knowing she was safe.

"I am not alone, I am with Malacinda, and I am not unprotected." She gestured to Robert. Thomas followed her movements. He caught sight of Robert and yelled for him. Robert made it to them within a moment.

"You better explain very carefully why you would leave my daughter in danger while you sit so far away." Thomas had been having his doubts about the man, and this might give him good reason to let him go.

"Papa, he could see me the entire time. I was never in danger." Alex stepped away from Maxwell to reach for Thomas. He just pulled away. She swayed, but held her balance.

"What good does it do, when you are that far away, if you can see her? What if someone grabbed her or threatened her, how would you get to her in time?" When Robert didn't answer, just looked at Alex, Thomas's voice boomed across the cobblestones. "I pay your salary or do you not realize that with the amount of time you spend with my daughter. I want an answer from you now or you will find yourself a new position."

Robert Dunmore was not concerned about his position in the slightest. At the end of the season, he would be a jockey for Alex instead of her driver, though he fought a smile, thinking of her father's reaction to her new driver. Lord Hollister may burst a vein when he saw the big Tess.

Alex couldn't afford to lose him just yet, though. It would make things too complicated. Grasping his sleeve, she nodded her head in permission. Thomas's eyes grew wide, and Janice gave a small gasp of fright as a massive pistol was pulled forth from beneath Robert's coat.

"That weapon is bigger than you, are you good?" Thomas glanced around at the few people who stood by and watched the play unfolding.

"Yes, my lord, I am. No matter where your daughter goes, she is always well protected." He slid the weapon back as he spoke.

Jeremy was as much a weapons man as he was a horse lover. He had a large collection. In fact, he had a gun much like that one, the one Marc and himself had used to teach Alex how to shoot—in secret, of course. If their parents knew they had done it, they would have had the switch taken to them. The fact they had been in their twenties would not have saved them. How Alex had ever talked them into it he still could not remember. "Who would you shoot with that?"

"Anyone who threatens to hurt my lady." His words were gentle, but the challenging glare he pinned on Marc betrayed his soft voice.

"I am glad to hear that, Dunmore. That answer saves your spot with my household. I will take her from here. Take my carriage back to Hollister House."

Alex stiffened. "That is my carriage, Papa."

"I bought it and allow you to use it, but that carriage, that servant, and everything else you seem to take for granted are not yours. They are mine, as are you until you marry. We will have a long talk when we get home."

She stepped out of his reach when he moved to take her arm. "I am sorry, Papa. My knee is bothering me, and I need—"

She was only going to say she needed her medication, but Marc's commanding voice cut her off. "Your knee is good enough to wander the streets like some common woman for any man to see. If you can go traipsing all over this wretched place, you can sit through a bloody tea."

Thomas almost laughed as he watched her jaw tighten and her beautiful eyes narrow stubbornly. "I will do no such thing. I will not go to that tea with you. I have plans and they do not include you, my lord."

Thomas thought to finish this before it escalated too far out of control. "No? I have to disagree, you will go to that tea." He didn't leave her a chance to argue. "Boys, if you please."

Marc grinned and stepped toward her. Blake left Amber's side to take her on the right. Jeremy sidled around until he was on her left, then they all three boys moved in. They had caught her in the same way time after time when she was a child. They fell into the same routine they had used then to capture the unruly chit.

"Stop, I mean it. Leave me alone. I am not going anywhere with you. Jeremy!" Alex screamed as her brother lunged toward her.

She spun away from him only to be confronted with Blake as he grabbed her arm. Ripping away from him she let out a whimper as her knee twisted. The ground spun before her, and she found herself upside down over a hard shoulder.

It had been habit, the way they worked together. Marc thought nothing of it until he saw the enraged look on his betrothed. She was nearly sputtering. Great.

"Take her to the carriage. Dunmore, she will be fine, take her carriage to the house." Maxwell turned with a low bow and a friendly smile to Malacinda. "My dear, it was a pleasure to meet you."

Malacinda watched Alex kick and fight Marc the entire way to the carriage.

"Bloody hell." Marc hurried on as Alex cursed, clutching at him, her fingers digging into the back of his coat, her head buried into his back. Her legs trembled as she whispered even more curses, the pain shot through her as her knee connected to his hard chest.

"Let go, baby. I need to put you down." She pried her fingers free. Marc's smile disappeared at the pale shaky face before him. "Bloody Hell."

"Marcus! What are you doing?" Janice cried as Marc pulled the long skirt of Alex's dress over her knee.

Alex lifted a brow at the use of his name. "Yes, my lord, what are you doing?" Grasping her skirt she tried to keep it down, to keep her modesty. "Hey." She jerked her hands back as Marc slapped them. "Ow."

"Marcus, this is inappropriate. Stop it." Janice hit his shoulder with her reticule. He just rolled his eyes at her.

"First names already, I guess with you getting married it should be quite proper, right, my lord?"

Grinding his teeth, he was saved a response. Thomas stepped in between Janice and Marc.

"Is she all right?"

The concern in his eyes dissipated Alex's anger.

"I think so. She caught me in the stomach, with the wrong knee." Marc turned it gently in his soft hands, looking for any sign of blood.

"Is she bleeding?" Maxwell asked, peering over Marc's shoulder. Alex grunted.

"If she is, it has not soaked through the bandages yet." Marc gently pressed on the white wrappings, cringing when her leg tightened under his hand. He looked at the small indent his finger had left in the bandage, it was still white and clean. "I do not think so." He ran his thumb along the back of her calf, hoping no one noticed.

"Is she in much pain?" her mother asked.

"Is she going to able to walk today?" Blake asked.

"Do you think she is hurt too bad to go to tea?" Thomas asked.

Alex jerked her skirt down. "It is too bad she is not here, or we could just ask her."

Marc turned his most charming smile on her, one that stopped her heart. It lodged somewhere in her throat, cutting off her breath. "Is your knee too bad to go to tea?"

"I do not want to go." Her weak voice was a bare whisper.

"That is not what I asked. Is your knee bad enough you cannot sit through tea with the Hamiltons?" Marc smoothed out the material of her skirts, caressing the thigh beneath.

"It will be a long day for me."

Marc smiled. "Still not what I asked."

Blue eyes darkened, her breath deepened. Alex opened her mouth. Words died in her throat. She looked into his eyes, his trusting smile. He was another like her father. He would accept nothing less than the truth from her. He always had expected it, and she had never felt the need to lie to him before. He had never asked her anything personal that she didn't want him to know and it was unsettling to discover she could not outright lie to him.

Thomas took in her angry scowl, her exasperated look as she ground her teeth. A look he knew well. So he was not the only one she could not lie to. He would keep that in mind.

Marc arched an eyebrow. "Do I take that as a concession you are fine enough to go or do you want to tell me you cannot manage to sit?"

"I do not seem to have a choice in the matter so we may as well go, my lord. Father likes to be the first to arrive at this particular tea party, you know that." With an evil gleam shining in her eyes, Alex shot a glance at Janice before looking back at Marc. "But then, you have been with us so long you know everything there is to know about—all of us. So there is no need to remind you of anything, is there?"

Marc didn't trust himself to a response, wanting nothing more than to shut the two of them in the carriage. An image of a speeding conveyance rolling through the long winding roads that ran through the woods rushed through his mind. He was in it, Alex sitting astride him, riding him as the carriage careened through the trees.

Hoping no one would see his expanding breeches, he helped Alex the rest of the way into the carriage. Janice was standing next to him, so he had no choice but to assist her next, though he was nervous about sitting them so close together.

Janice clutched her reticule tightly as she slid across the seat, ramming it into Alex's injured knee. Amber, grasping Marc's hand as a support nearly lunged into her seat as Alex cursed.

Janice smiled sweetly, "I am so sorry. Did I hurt you?"

Amber grasped Alex as she lunged toward the infuriating woman.

"Alex." Her father's voice did nothing to stop her, only Amber slamming her back against the soft leather did. "Alex, I think when we get home we will have that talk again as well. That talk seemed to have done no good either, none at all."

Alex paid no heed to his voice, only glared at the woman across from her.

Chapter 11

They were indeed the first to arrive at the Hamiltons'. Opening the door for the ladies, the men waited to take the one they were designated to take. With the addition of Janice, it was, for the first time, an uneven number.

With Alex missing the Rutmeyer ball, it had still been even, but now Jeremy had opted to take Ashlee as well as his sister. He would enjoy escorting two women on his arms.

Jeremy stepped forward to take Ashlee, handing her down and stepping off to the side to await his next turn. The look on her face stopped him in his tracks. Marc, unnoticed, listened behind them.

"That dreadful woman did her best to injure Alex. She hit her with that weapon of hers at least a dozen times. All with a sweet apology only to do it again. She is hurt, I think bad now. I know her arm is going to be bruised by the force Amber had to use to keep her from hitting that woman."

Catherine and Alma had both relayed the same thing to their husbands as they moved to the rear of the group. Lady Beatrice was helped down by her husband as Thomas started forward.

Marc cut him off, stalking angrily toward the two women who were driving him insane, both in such different ways.

Jeremy looked up as Amber, pale faced and angry, accepted Blake's outstretched hand. His concerned question stopped on his lips as Marc brushed past him.

Janice smiled down at him, reaching for his hand.

He gave it to her. Without even a look at her, he put her on the ground. Turning back without pause, he reached for Alex. She was near tears. He could see the pain and fury in her delicate features. "Baby, come let me help you."

The words caused her eyebrows to shoot up and a flush of embarrassment to touch her cheeks. Those words brought on the memory of what had happened the last time he had said them to her.

Nonetheless, she gave him her hands. Pulling her close he made sure her weight was supported by him as her small feet touched the earth. Pulling his hand away to tuck her hand into his arm, he gasped. There was blood on his glove.

Grasping her hand once more he turned the palm up cursing at the small crescents cut into her delicate skin, perfect imprints of her short and immaculate nails. "What is this?"

"That, my lord—" She pulled her hand away, teetering as she did so. Thomas caught her arm before she could fall. "—is the only thing that kept me from throwing a woman out of a moving carriage."

Thomas whispered with a smile. "Janice or Amber for holding you back."

With her nose in the air, she snorted in disgust. "At one point or other during that much-too-long ride, both went through my mind."

Thomas looked at Janice, who stood off to the side with a deadly look on her face. She was again in the background while everyone's attention was on Alex. Didn't she realize that this was a close family and even marrying Marc was not going to make her a part of it? She had to earn it, and he didn't see that happening. "You do not have to stay. You can take the carriage home, my dear."

"Not a chance." Her voice was low and poisonous. There was no way she was going to allow that woman to win. She would not back down to her.

"But—"

Catherine grasped his arm, stopping him with a shake of her head. "I will tell you later, just do not argue."

Thomas was surprised by the anger in his sweet wife. She had lost the demure and proper look to her green eyes sometime during that ride. The hurtful words that had spewed forth from Janice had shaken her resolve to be the perfect woman. Janice had, the entire trip, spoken of Alex as a weak woman, a disgrace to society and her family.

It had taken all Catherine could do to sit there. She wanted so much to tell Amber to let her daughter go. Instead, she told Janice that was not true. Janice hadn't even looked in her direction. She had been relentless, telling Alex it would be best if she just slithered home and hid her shame and embarrassment away from the world. That she was the only thing that had brought her family down, and she should hide away and admit she was useless and shameful.

He looked again at the Rutmeyers who stood, waiting impatiently off to the side, both women had the same indignant, yet self-satisfied look. "Fine, but I want to look at that knee before anyone else gets here."

Giving Alex his arm, Thomas left Marc to reluctantly escort his soon-to-be betrothed, though that thought was becoming less and less appealing by the moment.

Walking through the double doors of the massive and elegant town house, they were greeted by a loud and squealing woman. Lady Nancy Hamilton wrapped a confused Alex in her arms.

Turning to the wide-eyed group she, gushed with praise. "Oh, you must all be so proud of such a wonderful girl. Such caring and devotion to see to things when you are injured. Are you not so proud, Lord Hollister?"

He sputtered, not sure what to answer, or exactly what the question was. Luckily, she didn't need an answer. She didn't even wait for one, just continued on in a rush. "Oh, my dear, you must sit down. Can I do anything to help? I know they must need a lot. You must let me help."

Alex grabbed the sixty-five-year-old dowager by the arm, giving her the gentlest of shakes to stop the flow of words. "My lady, I really do not know what you are talking about."

"Yes, you do. It is all right. There is no need for secrecy with me. I know."

Alex bit her lip.

Nancy clasped her hands over her heart. "Bradley saw you on his way back from the docks. He saw you coming out of Chariton House, but when he had circled the block, you had already gone. Though your choice of friends, I must say, did surprise me."

Thomas was the one to interrupt her monologue this time. "Chariton House—as in Vanessa Chariton?" He looked at Alex for confirmation.

"Yes, Vanessa is the owner of Chariton House. She and her husband started it before he passed away," Lady Hamilton answered for her, which suited Alex just fine. "I know you must be so proud of her work at the orphanage." She turned back to the small woman she was congratulating, not noticing the paleness of her face, the effort it was taking just to stay standing.

"I am sorry, my lady. It just slipped out," said a young voice.

Alex smiled at the young man who approached shyly. She had met Bradley in their first season. He had been taken with Ashlee from sight, but she had her sights set on Philip Moore. Bradley was a dear friend to Alex, but she knew his grandmother wanted more from her than to be his friend.

Nancy beamed at them with matchmaking on her mind. "There is nothing to be concerned about, my boy. My grandson thinks a lot of you, my dear."

Alex glanced at him and rolled her eyes, no one noticed it but him. He bit back a grin.

Alex shook her head. "I know, my lady. I do have one favor to ask of you, though. I would appreciate it if you would not mention anything to anyone about my trips to Chariton House. It is unseemly for a young unmarried woman to be going to that part of the city alone."

Nancy patted her hand gently. "Unseemly or not, you will only come out looking charitable for it. It will not tarnish your reputation."

"But what of my future husband? He will not like it said that his bride was alone at the docks. I am sure my husband will be more than willing to help me and then, when I am safely married, you may tell anyone you want."

Wanting nothing more than to see her grandchild settled down with this enchanting woman, Nancy would agree to anything. "Yes, of course, and I am sure your husband—" She looked meaningfully at the uncomfortable young man who had taken his place by her side. "—will be more than happy to help you."

"I am sure, whoever he is, he will." Bradley Hamilton, Count of Reagin, could not bring himself to outright argue with her plans for him. She would know soon enough.

Nancy frowned at him momentarily then turned a smile on Alex once more. "I just have a question or two. How is it that you came to go to the orphanage and how on earth did you meet—" She glanced at Marc. "—a woman of that profession."

With a look at her father and at Marc, Alex smiled. Shaking her head slowly, she sighed in defeat. "Actually, those are both the same answer. I met a young lady, a serving girl, Victoria Chariton. Vanessa's daughter. She approached me almost a year and a half ago when Chariton was falling into disrepair. They were having a hard time. No food, no clothing, and the roof was leaking." Nancy gasped in horror as Alex continued. "She only wanted a donation of money, but I had to see for myself how bad things were. They were worse than she had described. I have been there on a regular basis ever since."

The families didn't want to say anything that might cast doubts on Alex's whereabouts nor her convenient excuses, but they all wondered if that would explain at least some of the disappearances. They thought that it would. Unfortunately, for Thomas, he was sure it didn't explain all of them.

"And that *woman*?" Lord Rutmeyer couldn't help his interruption.

He had been looking forward to casting disparaging doubts on the seemingly untouchable reputation of the woman who was looking to be more of a threat to his future than he had wanted to admit. He still wanted something for ammunition against her.

Alex looked back at him, but her eyes strayed until they were locked with Marc's. She smiled cautiously. "I had been going to Chariton for about four months or so. Malacinda was a friend of Victoria's. She also helps out with the children. Our paths finally crossed. I had known Malacinda for several months and had grown quite attached to her. She grew on me with her joyful view of life and her infectious laughter. When I found out what she did and who she—" She titled her head with a sad ghost of a smile on luscious red lips that trembled as she fought against tears. "—worked for, by then it was too late. I could not turn my back on her, no matter her choice of profession."

Marc had been angry to think she was so heartless as to not care that he was taking another woman, but at her sad words and the sight of the too-shiny blue eyes, he knew better. She did care, and, what was more, she didn't know he no longer took his rights with his mistress, nor anyone else for that matter. He stepped toward her.

Nancy Hamilton, the dowager Duchess of Reagin, pulled Alex away from him without even realizing she had. "That is fine, my dear. No one here will say anything about it, though I still believe it will only serve to enhance your standing. Now come with me, stand at my side, and help an old woman greet her guests."

Janice finally found the voice that had been frozen in her throat when she saw the man, who was supposed to only be thinking of her and their marriage, reach for the woman she hated. "My lady, Alexis is much too injured to stand for that long before your guests. I think it would be better to have her sit somewhere out of the way and rest, or to go home."

"Oh, my dear, Alex. I had not thought of that. She is right. You need—"

Smiling widely, Alex shook her head. She knew what Janice's fear was. Standing alongside Nancy who, by her own right, was a wealthy and powerful woman, Alex's standing would increase. According to Janice, it was too high as it was. "All I need is someone to lean on while I stand there and then a good stiff brandy when I am through."

Janice gasped as Nancy laughed.

"You are right. I will make sure my tea, as well as yours, is liberally laced. It shall be our little secret. Do not meet many women who like the stuff. Shall we?"

Alex hobbled along, grabbing a stunned Ashlee as she did so. "You shall be my leaning post, my dear."

Marc caught the pleased look on Bradley's face as he fell into step behind them. Marc ground his teeth and forced himself to stay rooted to the floor. It would not do to pummel the poor boy for being besotted with Alex, though Marc would not admit even to himself that he was as well.

Thomas watched Alex as she leaned into the dowager countess. Within a few moments, Alex put Ashlee's hand, one that she had been leaning on, into Bradley's. Thomas could not help the smile when he saw the young man's glowing response. His eyes shone with love as he gazed at her. Ashlee seemed confused by his look. Bradley just pulled her hand through his arm, laying his over the top of it. Holding her closely, he turned them to greet the first of the guests.

They bowed and greeted several guests, and when a lull came, Thomas made his way to the group. "My lady, may I steal away my daughter. I would like to check her knee."

Nancy patted Alex's hand and smiled "Of course, my lord. Use the library and then make her comfortable. I will join her in a bit."

Out of earshot, Thomas chuckled. "That was very good, my dear. Does Ashlee know Bradley is infatuated?"

It was unseemly for Ashlee to be standing by him, but since everyone would be told she was there at the countess's request, it would not be commented upon. No one argued with the powerful woman.

"Not yet, Papa. But she will soon. I plan to help it along—" Alex grasped his hand as a pain shot through her leg.

"Come, let's have a look at that knee, and I want to know what happened on the way from the docks." He gestured for Catherine to follow, and Amber stepped away from Blake to trail along.

Marc watched as they disappeared into the library. He stared at the door even when Janice stepped in front of him.

"Marcus, will you come sit by me?" Running a hand seductively along his arm, she clenched her jaw as he just shook his head.

"In a moment, my lady."

The door opened, Amber called to a servant.

"A moment? I think you should remember who you are to be engaged to. If you want this marriage to continue as planned, I would suggest you come and sit."

Marc looked at the library door with pain and confusion, but he knew what his future was, and he accepted it. He took a chair next to Janice, who now wore a smug grin.

He may have sat, but he did not miss the return of the servant, who now carried fresh strips of linen, brandy, and a bucket of water. Alex was bleeding again. He tightened his fists to keep from lashing out at the woman beside him. He was jeopardizing his future.

What was he going to do? He wanted so much to barge into that room and make sure she was all right. He wanted so much to be the man he had always dreamed of. To have a successful business, to be a respectable duke and the envy of the ton. He was being torn in two.

Those were the things he could have with Janice, the things she wanted him to have and to be. With Alex, he didn't think he would be those things. She would not want him to be. She didn't care about respect nor success and she didn't care about the ton. She was carefree and careless. He needed a wife who was serious. One who knew what she wanted in life.

He looked at Janice. What did she want in life? Status, a rich and successful husband, the respect and awe of her peers. That was all he needed in a wife.

Alex hobbled from the room, a smile on her face, but not in her eyes. She was in pain. Why did she not just go home? She didn't want to be here.

Taking a seat as far from Marc as she could, Alex nearly collapsed into the chair. Janice tightened her grip on his arm when he went to move. "I am not stupid, Marcus. If you leave my side to go to her, I will walk. There will be no marriage, and if you think your business will not suffer from what my father says, you are very much wrong."

Marc struggled with himself once more. It was one thing to give up his happiness in order to thrive, but she was beginning to press into his pride.

Well, he would get her married, get his heir. Afterward, he would be so far away from her, she could not torment him.

Marc had been so involved in his own thoughts, he didn't even realize the tea room had filled until he saw Lord Ferguson walk past him.

"My dear girl, you look absolutely miserable. Can I talk you into a walk in the garden if your knee is not too awful? We shall stay in plain view, and you are always welcome to lean on me." Spencer bowed low and kissed her hand. "If you do not mind, my lord," he said to Thomas, who stood protectively at her side.

"If she is up to it, but do not take her far." Thomas cast a quick glance at Marc. He was glowering. How long was Marc going to let this go on? Thomas didn't think even Alex was this stubborn.

"I would like that, Lord Ferguson. You cannot imagine how stiff my leg gets just sitting on my—"

"Yes, well." Spencer pulled her to her feet. Even he was hard pressed not to laugh.

Catherine patted Alex's hand and leaned close to the pair. "Keep an eye on her. She has already started on the brandy, my lord. Keep her safe."

"You will have to excuse my wife. She has had a trying day." Thomas patted her arm, concerned at her irate tone. For almost nineteen years, she had hidden her true self from witnesses. Only the family saw her for who she was. Fun, loving, and playful. He hated when they came to London, and she disappeared behind her shell.

"No fear, my lord. I would think nothing of it. If she is anything like her daughter, she has a fiery spirit." Without waiting a response, Spencer helped Alex out the patio doors.

Alex moved farther into the garden, where she could still be seen but not heard. "Fiery is not a word for it. She is raging in anger right now."

A deep tenor voice showed his concern. "Not at you, I would hope."

"No, Spencer, not me this time." She told him what had happened in the carriage with Janice. She placed a hand on his chest to calm his ire. "It is nothing. I am fine, I just was not about to crawl off somewhere like I had lost."

"I have the contract signed. When would you like it? Would you like me to get it to March on my own?"

They walked in slow circles, her limping becoming less pronounced as they went around.

Spencer watched Marc staring out the doors at them. He was trying to be discreet about it, but Spencer had been a spy much too long to miss it.

"No, take me for a ride in the morning to the park. I need to be on a horse. I have another race coming up, and I need to be ready. I need to see exactly what damage was done. I will have March meet us there."

"Certainly." He stopped her pacing with a gentle hand on her arm. "You know I will do anything you need me to. Can I help you with anything else? To talk?"

She shook her head. "I love him."

"I know." If they had been in private, he would have taken her in his arms. The best he could do was wrap his arm around her waist, to assist her on the way back. He pulled her close. "I will truss him up and stash him in your bed if you like."

Her laughter was the first thing to reach Marc's ears.

Marc ground his teeth and stood.

"Marc." The single word was spoken with warning, not question.

"I am going to speak with my father. I shall be right back, my lady." He kissed her hand, cringing at her smile.

"Marc, are you all right?"

Thomas looked up at Maxwell's words. Marc didn't look to be anything close to all right. He was miserable.

"I want to know why she stayed. Did they tell you?" Marc looked at Thomas with reluctance. He didn't really want to know, and Thomas saw it.

"Let's just say, for now, it was a gauntlet thrown," Thomas said. "Alex accepted the challenge. I will tell you the rest later, if you really want to know."

Marc shook his head.

As Alex was assisted into her seat, her back to Marc, Lord Pettlenoster clapped him on the back. "Tell me, my boy, did you win good money on your boy last night?" His cheerful mood was dampened some by Marc's dark scowl.

"No, I did not. Jeremy, however, did. He wagered for the new mare to win." Marc almost missed the next question when he noticed Alex's sudden smile and interest in his conversation.

"So what is your boy like?" Noticing Marc looking, Alex turned back to the group of ladies she sat with, a grin fighting to come forth. She pretended to listen to the latest fashion tips, but Marc could tell her attention was still on him.

"I have not met him. I understand people think I have. They are mistaken, and he is not my boy."

His voice was rough with anger, even though he tried to keep it at a reasonable level. Alex wondered how many times it had taken A.H. being referred to as "his boy" before it warranted that response. *Another thing to annoy him with. How pleasing.*

"Yesterday, everyone saw you go talk with him, and since he has been shipping with you for so long, we figured you had met."

Marc's eyes snapped away from Alex's smooth profile to Bradley Hamilton's smiling face. "What?" He looked at Maxwell. His father just shook his head and shrugged his wide shoulders.

Bradley looked at the men in confusion. "Has he not been shipping with you for the last six years?" He had spent his life on ships, going to and from the docks since he was a small child with his father. Had continued to ever since his parents death in a ship wreck three years ago. He had missed the trip in order to stay with his grandmother, who had been ill. His parents had loved ships, taking many trips on them.

Bradley continued to see to his shipments of textiles and silks in person, though he knew the ton frowned upon it. With who his grandmother was, he figured he could practically do whatever he wanted and get away with it.

He used Clifton shipping but did not trust Taggard as much as he trusted a snake. He had heard good things about the agent for Clifton. Bradley had been disappointed when he had met him. So he saw to every detail himself. His life on ships gave him an advantage that most people did not have.

Marc just shook his head at the younger man. "Why would you think that?"

Alex no longer had to pretend to ignore them for the men's discussion had drawn the attention of nearly everyone in the small tea room.

"I have seen A.H. at the docks when your ships come in. At least I assumed it was him. He is secretive that man. He does not get out of the carriage. That big fellow that works for him—" Bradley looked at Marc to make sure he knew who he spoke of.

Marc nodded. "Tess Richards."

"Yes, well, he gets the information and takes it back to the carriage. I also see his solicitor, Andrew March, there as well. Sometimes I have seen him speaking with that solicitor of yours. Taggard."

"Taggard, good man, that fellow."

All eyes swung to Baron Robert Dinmont.

"I deal with him myself, comes to my manor whenever I need him." His rum-laced breath was potent, even this early in the day. He had been drunk when he had arrived, and now he was nearly tottering. Dinmont was one of a few men, all drunkards who cared nothing for their money nor their merchandise, that still worked with the slovenly man. He was their type of man. He spent his time at their manors drinking and taking advantage of any young maids who wandered too close to him.

Bradley snorted, and Alex groaned before she could stop it. Luckily, no one noticed.

"Yes, I am glad you approve." Marc had not heard many praises for the man. He was beginning to wonder if he should have let him go three years ago when Alex had nearly begged him to. His eyes snapped to Alex. If she cared nothing for success, why had she been so adamant about his solicitor? How indeed had she even known?

Spencer smiled at Alex who had begun to look uncomfortable with the direction of talk. She raised her eyes pleadingly at him. He tried to change the subject. "Lord Clifton, I hear you are interested in purchasing Linden Manor."

Before he could answer, Bradley laughed. "I hear he is not the only one. A.H. is looking to buy as well."

Jeremy looked at Marc with surprise. From the look of surprise on Marc's face, he hadn't known.

"Just think, your boy living next to you. How exciting, my lord," Jeremy said with a wide grin.

Alex almost laughed as Marc's jaw clenched and his eyes clouded with irritation.

"How do you know he is considering Linden?" Maxwell asked the young man.

"I was told by Lord Putney. He was in London yesterday, seeing to some last minute investments before they leave."

The story of their moving had spread quickly.

Jeremy looked at Marc. "Do you think he has the money to buy such a property?"

Marc just shrugged. No one seemed to know.

Thomas made their excuses early to take Alex home. Her eyes were nearly drifting shut by the time they had her in the carriage. Thankfully, Lord and Lady Rutmeyer decided to accept Spencer's offer of an escort home. Janice didn't. They dropped her off, with Marc doing his duty by escorting her to the door. Kissing her hand, he could think of nothing but the black smudges beneath Alex's eyes.

Later that night, Maxwell found his son behind his large desk in the warm study. Marc sat in just his trousers, his bare chest glistening with sweat. The large fireplace was dark, but several lamps cast light over the somberly decorated room. It was all man—leather and mahogany overpowering ones senses.

"I assume you are here for the same reason I am. Did you find anything?"

Marc looked up, a brandy snifter sliding through his fingers, shattering on the hard wood flooring beneath the massive mahogany desk. His words were slurred, his eyes bleary. "Indeed I have. He was right. A.H. has been shipping with me for six years. He was one of my first clients. How could I not have known that? I have been sitting here, looking over the books, and I realized something. I have no idea what I am doing. Taggard is the man in charge of it all, but his paperwork is so damned confusing, I do not know what to think. I hardly ever look at it. Here, you look."

Maxwell looked over Marc's shoulder, ignoring the smells arising from his foxed son.

Before him were two piles of paper. Writing on one was signed by Taggard. The words were ragged and raw. Some made little sense.

The second pile was vastly different. Its wording showed intelligence and did not contain a signature. If one did not know better one would think it was written by two different people.

Maxwell laid a comforting hand on Marc's large shoulder. "Perhaps he is not drunk as often as one would believe."

"You think so. That would be good." Marc bit his lip. "You liked working with the people, right? I have tried it, but they are unwilling."

"You tried?" Maxwell knew his son had been approached, but he was under the impression Marc had stuck to his convictions and refused.

"Yes, a few months ago. I went to see some of the ones who had come to me before. They said they were happy with my agent. Do you think they meant Taggard?" Marc almost fell from his large chair, reaching for the decanter of imported brandy.

"Who else would they mean?"

Marc just shook his head, swiping the papers from his desk, with a bare forearm, watching them flutter to the floor.

"Come let me help you to bed. I think you are in need of some rest."

"I am fine, Father, just let me be." Marc stormed out of the room without a look behind him.

Maxwell shook his head. He had never seen Marc in such a state of agitation.

Chapter 12

M y lord, I did not expect you this morning." Catherine Hollister swept into the sitting room after receiving Viscount Ferguson's calling card.

He had noticed the raised brow on the butler's round face when he had given him the small white card. Assuming it was nothing more than the usual speculation of how often he was beginning to see Alex, Spencer had thought nothing else of it. He knew rumors were starting to swirl that he was courting her. Neither of them had done anything to dissuade it.

"Lady Alexis did not tell you I was coming, my lady?" Spencer smiled at the older version of his friend, taking her hand to delicately place a chaste kiss on her bare knuckles. Catherine was beautiful but hidden. He always thought there was more to her than she let on. Perhaps it was just the resemblance that made him believe she was more like her daughter than she let on. "She agreed to ride with me this morning. I hope she is well."

"I shall see if she is up to a ride."

Catherine turned to find her daughter limping into the room. She was surprised at her attire. Her normal colorful day dress was replaced by Catherine's tan and black riding habit that was elegant and respectable. It brought out her features to their fullest, hinting to curves and softness that lay hidden beneath the soft material. Its low cut bodice showed a bit too much cleavage to make it acceptable for an unmarried woman, but it was beautiful, and Alex was stunning in it.

"I am up to it, Mama. I am stiff, but I think exercise is better for it than sitting around. I am sorry I did not let you know last night that I was planning to go out with Lord Ferguson." A weak smile played across her soft lips. "I was out before I ever got home, my lord. I had to be carried to bed."

Her mother laughed nervously, sending a pleading look at Spencer. "Alexis, that is personal."

He just shook his head. Catherine had no need to worry about his discretion. He knew her daughter well, but even he was surprised by her choice of outfits. Her long fiery hair was swept under a large bonnet, tan with long black ribbons trailing down her slender back. He noticed, as he bent over to kiss her hand, that even her gloves and boots matched the ensemble. This was a new version of his longtime friend. Marc was a good influence on her, it seemed. The changes were all for the better.

"Have you taken your medication today? Are you sure you are up to this, my lady?" Spencer took her arm. "I can always take you riding another day."

"Yes, I am fine."

"Good, shall we?"

Catherine wrung her hands in worry as Viscount Ferguson handed Alex into her saddle.

They were quiet on the way to the park. Alex concentrated on her knee and, looking around, she was glad Hyde Park was still empty. Nodding to Spencer, she threw her leg over the saddle. Riding beside him, she laughed, and they picked up speed until her long braid was flying behind her.

"All right, stop." Spencer was laughing as he caught up with her. "I gave you a slow horse, so I would be able to beat you. How do you coerce such speed from such a docile animal?"

"We understand each other. We both wanted to beat an arrogant male." As if in protest, the massive stallion swung his head and snorted in indignation.

He pointed. "There is March's carriage."

She followed his gaze, spurring her mount to a run once again. This time, she was beaten. Her mare was, indeed, nothing but a pleasure ride. The first run had taken everything out of her.

"My dear, I am glad to see your knee is mending well." March looked at Spencer, his green eyes smiling. He had his doubts about the man. He just didn't know what caused them, but he didn't trust him. "Lord Spencer, a pleasure to see you." His voice said it was anything but.

"March, my dear man, how are things in your world?"

March glowered at him, Alex just rolled her eyes.

"My Lady, I need to speak with you privately." March paid no heed to Spencer's question or his grin. The man's voice grated on his every nerve. The fop.

She looked at Spencer, who moved to take his leave. He understood that March didn't know he was privy to a lot of Alex's secrets. There had been no need to hide them from him, knowing what it was he did. This was not the first time they had met with March. They met with him on many of their early morning rides, but the meeting had usually pertained to shipping.

Alex placed a restraining hand on Spencer's immaculate coat sleeve. She looked back at her solicitor. "He is fine, Andrew. What is it?"

She handed him the large envelope containing Spencer's revised contract. March threw it into his carriage as he stepped out. He would get it to Alex's messenger, Reeves Dalton, and he, in turn, would get it to Marc. A run around that would be so much less complicated if Marc were not so stubborn.

His hands beneath Alex's arms, March lifted her from her mount. Spencer took his place at her side. "It is of a sensitive nature, my lady."

She just nodded, encouraging him to continue.

March took a deep breath, finding the right wording. "A.H. has just purchased Linden Manor."

"Oh, Alex. Congratulations," Spencer said. "That ought to drive your man crazy." March looked at them with suspicion as Spencer wrapped his arm around her shoulders, pulling her close. "That is just superb."

She laughed. "When can I start taking the horses over?"

Assuming now that Spencer was privy to the jockey's true identity, March relaxed. "As soon as you would like. The Putneys are staying with some friends, and their belongings are already on the way to Ireland. They plan to attend the Clifton Ball tomorrow night before leaving. If I am informed correctly, they are making a farewell ball out of it." March froze as the young lady squealed, throwing herself into his arms. Grinning, he held her close for only a moment before setting her aside. "That is not appropriate in the least for a respectable young lady of society." March looked at Spencer to see his reaction to her exuberance.

Spencer was not surprised. He just smiled. "I must agree with you, March, but she has never been a true member of the haute ton. She may not be a society bee, flitting from flower to flower, but she is so much better. She is strong, loyal, determined, and she has a plan for her future and the willpower to see it through." He coughed softly moving away from her. "She is also pigheaded, willful, arrogant, conceited, and full of herself."

Both men laughed as she took a swing at Spencer's head. "And you are an ass. For that, I may not include your invitation to the Hollister Ball tonight." She stuck her tongue out at them when they just laughed.

"My lady, who says I shall deign to attend your quaint little fiasco, as it is. How I should lower myself to be acquainted with someone of your low standards."

March listened to the nasal twang, watched as his nose rise notch after notch and smiled. "He has a point, my dear." He did a good job of imitating Spencer, whose eyes widened in surprise. "Your standards are lacking, after all, look at the riffraff you sink to taking your morning ride with."

ભ્ય૭

Laughter echoed from the trees of Hyde Park as Marc was let into Hollister House.

Maxwell smiled at his son over his tea cup. "What are you doing here this fine morning, my boy?"

Thomas shook his head. Maxwell had come over, knowing Jeremy had taken the Earl of Lingfield's daughter, Lady Melinda Denizli, on a carriage ride though London. He was taking her to the shops to find a new hat, a task they all knew he loathed. Jeremy would have agreed too much of anything in order to take the beautiful blonde on a private morning outing.

The Earl of Grunby and the Duke of Paddington were planning to spend the morning relaxing, without the children, like the old days, before the wives and families. Lady Hollister had gone with Alma to Lady Pettlenoster's for tea and lemon cakes, leaving the two old friends alone for the first time this season.

"Jeremy should have told you he was taking Lady Denizli for a ride today, he is not here." Thomas knew full well his son would have told him.

"Yes, my lord, he did. I was looking for Ashlee. I told her I would take her to get a new dress before your ball tonight. She said she would meet me here."

Why on earth she wanted to do that, he had no idea. He could only imagine.

Ashlee walked into the room as if summoned by the sound of her name. "Lord Hollister, where is Alex? I had hoped to take her with me today. She is so good at picking out dresses. I could really use her help."

All three men just stared at her. Ashlee knew she had gone too far. She just shrugged at them, challenging them to call her a liar.

"She is not here, my darling. Lady Hollister informed us before they left that Alex has gone on a ride in the park with Lord Ferguson." Thomas watched as Marc's eyes glazed over, the cords in his neck beginning to pulse erratically.

Ashlee's full pink bottom lip quivered as she pushed it into a pout. "How can that be? I need her to go with me."

"Perhaps we can go to Hyde and get her. I am sure she wants to go with you as much as you want her to."

The fathers tried to hide smiles as Marc made the offer they both knew was not for his sister but for himself.

Ashlee squealed in joy, running from the room.

"My lord. Father. I had best get to her before she rushes off without me. Heaven forbid, I shall not have the pleasure of chasing after two little girls, while one of them tries every fabric and hat there is, and the other pretends not to be bored out of her mind."

With Marc gone, Thomas smiled. "With as long as Alex has been gone, poor Ashlee is going to be upset, but I think her little plan is going to go astray."

"Yes, that would be terrible." His eyes sparkled as Maxwell thought of how to help. "If Alex shows up here, we could always send her after them, Ashlee was very adamant about her help. You do know where they will go first?"

Clapping each other on the back, they sat back to wait.

Marc missed them by only moments. "We cannot have missed them. Should we go to Hollister and see if they have gone back there?" It was out of his mouth before he could stop it.

His groan was no deterrent for Ashlee's joy. "Oh, Marc, may we? Thank you so much. I did not want to tell her father, but I would like your advice on Alex's wardrobe. You always have such good taste in women. You always pick out the best of outfits for me. I would like your help in getting a few new gowns for her. Will you help me?"

He had never been able to tell his little sister no, even if he had wanted to. This time, he did not, the idea of picking out clothing for Alex made his lips numb and his pulse race. He could say nothing at all. All he could do was nod.

Marc looked up fifteen minutes later, as they approached Hollister House, to see Lord Ferguson and Alex riding toward them. Bringing the calm mare alongside Marc's small carriage, Alex smiled. "I was told you would be at the shops, my lord. I was on my way to meet you when Spencer spotted you coming this way."

"We were coming back to wait for you," Ashlee said. "I want your advice on some gowns. I thought to get a new one for our ball tomorrow. You should get some new ones as well." She changed seats. If Alex was going to accompany them, she now had to sit next to Marc.

Marc did not miss the smile that passed between Lord Ferguson and the irritating hoyden on the horse.

Neither Ashlee, nor their respective fathers, realized Alex was going to the shops, anyway, this morning. Spencer was escorting her to her mother's carriage, which would be closer to his townhouse, anyway.

Catherine had asked them to meet her at Mademoiselle Rhamninose's boutique for fittings when her ride was over, by then tea with Lady Pettlenoster would be completed. They had stopped by Hollister House long enough to make sure Catherine and Alma had not returned when Thomas had informed her to meet them.

Though Alex had said she would only pick out a few, with the purchase of Linden, she was now prepared to fully stock her new wardrobe. Catherine had plans for her daughter's attire. It was time to turn her little girl into a woman. Alex had taken a liking to the ball gowns she had worn just for Marc. She still preferred the day dresses, but even today she had opted for something more conventional. Seeing Alex wearing her own riding habit had been what had convinced Catherine she was ready.

Alex really didn't have any clothing that was just hers. With the exception of a few gifts from Thomas and Jeremy, all the gowns she had worn, including the riding habit, were her mother's. The perks of being a mirror of each other.

Alex reached for Spencer's hand. "Spencer if you do not mind, I shall see you at the ball tonight. If you would help me down—"

Marc was already out of the carriage before Spencer could so much as lift his leg to swing off his saddle. "Do not trouble yourself getting down. I can help her."

As he assisted her to her feet, his eyes roved along her body. Taking in the exquisite lines of what was obviously a Rhamninose original, he forgot his annoyance at the simpering man. The contours accentuated the curves and mounds below, causing a lurch in the lust he had thought controlled.

The mademoiselle should not have made the bodice so revealing. She usually would not have been so dramatic with an unmarried woman. It was good he was going. He would make sure she was properly clad.

"Thank you for the ride. I shall see you at the ball, Spencer."

Leaning over his saddle, he kissed her hand gently, holding the fingers longer than necessary. Marc could not stop himself from pulling her hand free.

Viscount Ferguson only smiled. "As I said, someone will marry her quickly this season. It would be a shame for someone to miss out on the opportunity. I do not intend to miss mine." Turning his charm back to Alex, he smiled at her frowning face. "You should not mar your brow so, my girl. You know I love you and would give you the world if I could, and I plan to give you what I believe you need. Now you go along with your friend and her overprotective brother and save me a dance or three at the ball if you be of a mind to, my love."

Alex grabbed Marc before he could go after the man who rode calmly away. "Would you be so kind as to help me into the carriage, my lord?"

"Do not call me that." Without a thought to her knee, he nearly threw her into the seat beside Ashlee. His sister frowned at him when Alex could not stop a groan of pain that escaped. "Sorry." He slammed the door on their surprised faces. Taking a place next to the driver, who looked at him in shock, Marc growled at him, "Just go."

"You are not planning on marrying that man are you, Alex?" Ashlee's voice was shrill as she turned on her redheaded friend. "And what are you wearing?"

Alex hugged her close as she laughed. "No, I am not. I plan to marry no one at the moment. I do not see that changing and, even if it was, Spencer is not the one who would even offer for me. He loves me as a dear friend, as you love me. He is also trying to torment your brother. He has it in his head, like many others in this family seem to, that the man is interested in me. If Marc was interested in me in any way, he would not be marrying someone else. He will marry her because he believes it is the only thing he can do. Nothing is going to change his mind, and I think it would be best if we all leave him alone about it."

Even after everything that had happened between them, Alex was still certain Marc would not change his mind. It was more than she could take. She knew the same things the rest of London knew. Marc was attracted to her, he even cared for her. She also knew something the rest didn't see. It wasn't enough.

The carriage came to a stop, and Alex shook her head at her mother's words echoing from beside the carriage. "Marc, what are you doing up there?"

Marc jumped to the ground. "My lady. Mother. What are you two doing here? I thought you were spending the morning with Lady Pettlenoster."

Marc waved off the driver, opening the door himself and helping the girls to depart the conveyance.

"Oh, you brought Alexis, good. My dear, I am glad you decided to meet me here." Catherine pulled her, slowly to accommodate her slight limp, into Mademoiselle Rhamninose's large and roomy shop.

Stepping inside the massive room, Marc shook his head, anger starting to worm its way through him. "You had planned to come to the shop today?"

She had made it sound as if she were coming just to help his sister.

Alex didn't answer directly. Running her hand along several materials, she began to decide on the ones that would do for a dress tomorrow night. "Of course, I came, Mama. You did ask me this morning if I would."

The arrival of a robust black-haired French woman stopped all conversation. "Oh, Lady Hollister, I am so glad to see you. You do wonderful justice to my creation. I am pleased to see the way the lines fall along your frame. Lady Hollister informed me you would be along so we have taken the liberty of picking several bolts of cloth that would be exquisite with your coloring." Her roving brown eyes found Marc standing protectively behind the young lady, nearly on top of her. "Ah, I see you have brought Lord Clifton with you."

Alex looked over her shoulder, her eyes widening at the closeness of him, his chest brushing against her shoulder. Her breath thickened, coming in tight gasps as she looked up at him. She smiled into his green eyes, biting her lower lip. His hands itching to caress the satiny skin, Marc stepped farther behind her.

"It is good he is here. We shall depend upon his excellent taste when it comes to his loved one. He always knows just the perfect designs to show off a woman to her best."

Alex looked back at the elderly lady with a wide smile. "I know. I have seen some of your best displayed to perfection. I have one in mind, in fact, that I would love you to do for me."

"Which would that be?" Mademoiselle Sylvia Rhamninose looked at her doubtfully. She could not see the dresses and gowns Marc picked for the young Lady Clifton doing any justice to the vivacious red head.

"I cannot quite recall right at this precise moment, but I am sure by the time we get in to do the measurements I shall drag it from my memory."

The seamstress just looked at her with a knowing smile. "Then I would suggest we do some measurements. If you will excuse us my lady, my lord, duchess. We shall be back before you even know we have been missing."

Marc watched them disappear behind the long curtains in the rear of the building, followed closely by Catherine.

Mademoiselle Rhamninose spoke quietly to the young girl as she assisted her to undress. "So, now what surprise gown is it that you have in mind?"

Alex looked at her mother in concern. Taking a deep breath, she knew she would not walk away without the dress she wanted, her mother's approval or not. "A red dress, long and elegant. A wide collar—"

"Low cut and tight through the waist? That, my dear, is not the dress for a young lady." She began to take her measurements as they spoke. Pausing only for a moment when Catherine spoke.

"If it is a gown she wants, it is one that we will take. Nothing too graphic, though. It must be tasteful. I will trust your judgment and Alexis's." Catherine sat back in a tall backed chair to await her turn.

"Just so I know if I have the right outfit in mind. Where did you see this particular gown?" Mademoiselle Rhamninose thought she knew which gown it was, but there was no way this young lady would have seen it.

"It is one of my favorites of Miss Malacinda St. Johns." Alex ignored the sudden pallor of the face that now stared up at her. "I do have some changes in mind. I am shorter, so it needs to be slightly less revealing. I also do not want it in red. I want it in beige and black."

Gathering her composure, the seamstress asked her to hold out her arms. "You are right, tan and black are wonderful colors on you. We shall make a delightful creation. When shall we need it for, my lady?"

"Tomorrow."

"I don't know if I can—"

"I know you can. I also want several more gowns, at least fifteen. I also want riding habits, walking dresses, and day dresses. I need new chemises, I like the batiste. It is my favorite. I will leave them to your and Marc's discretion, although whatever neckline he decides on, I want it lowered. I want less than what I am showing now, but I am not interested in being prudish. I want an entire new wardrobe as I only have my day dresses. I want it in all within a month, just deliver them as they are completed."

Catherine nodded her agreement as her daughter talked. She was surprised to hear the amount of outfits Alex was requesting. Usually, she would not ask to have anything bought for her. Catherine was pleased.

She was next to be measured. With that done, the seamstress showed them out and called Ashlee and her mother in. Marc watched in shock as Alex walked through the shop picking out expensive bolts. Silks, satins, linens, woolens, and brocades. Each went into an ever expanding pile to be held up before her by two of the mademoiselle's assistants. Marc either nodded yes or shook his head no. He was just amazed she was not sitting bored as she had on the last trip he had accompanied the girls on.

One cloth, a light gray silk slid smoothly over her skin as Marc nodded. "That is perfect. The gray is almost a silver, put it off to the side."

Within moments, Sylvia nearly flew from the back room. Shooing away the two young assistants, she took Alex by the arm, leading her toward dozens of already finished pieces. Alex stood impatiently while Marc decided on gown after gown. Sylvia didn't even look toward the women as she took notes. Alex was not dissuaded though, leaning over to whisper her own opinions in Sylvia's ever-listening ear. Sylvia would just smile and nod at Marc, while making the additions Alex wanted.

Alex watched Marc. He was in charge and confident. She wished he would do the same things with his shipping. If he would take charge, she knew he would be so much more successful than he was now.

The ton, at least those who wished to ship with a trustworthy company, would learn to accept him as a tradesman.

Marc offered his hand as she stepped away from Sylvia. Ashlee took her place. When all the women were done, none with the extravagance Alex had shown, they bid farewell to Mademoiselle Sylvia. Alex was the last to leave the shop, stopping to speak with her when they were alone. "Mademoiselle, I wish to pay for my clothing myself. Send me the bill through a messenger, and I will the get the money to you through Robert Dunmore, my groom. Do not accept any payments from anyone but me. I also like that pale yellow gown that Marc wants done in the gray silk. Can you alter it for me to wear tonight? I will need it by six?"

Sylvia smiled, saying it would be in her hands by five.

At the next shop, Jeremy peered around a massive stack of packages and parcels with a weak grin.

Catherine grinned. "Jeremy, I see you are making yourself useful."

"Mother, what are you doing here?" Jeremy looked across the small room at the exquisite blonde who was gathering more items, even as Alex joined her with a small hug. He knew his sister, who had never approved of his choice of women before, truly liked Melinda.

Catherine lowered her voice to a soft whisper. "You will not believe it, but we are here because your sister wants to purchase some items." She quickly relayed what had happened at the boutique.

"Really?" His eyes followed Alex throughout the shop. Her small hands ran along each item. With the advice of Melinda and Ashlee, Alex purchased gloves, hats, boots, and fans. Everything she bought was wrapped and placed in Marc's carriage.

Alex stopped her mother as she began to pay for the purchases. "I have it." When Catherine raised a brow at her, Alex just smiled. "I do not ever spend my allowance. Let me now."

Marc took her by the elbow, ignoring the gasps from around him, his fingers digging into her flesh. "Are you sure it is not from your beau? Does he give you money for your time?"

Pulling her arm away from his she smiled menacingly. "How dare you? Are you suggesting I am his mistress? Is that what you are implying, my lord?"

"No." Marc stormed out into the early afternoon light, Jeremy right behind him.

The shopkeeper disappeared into the darkness behind the curtain. He would enjoy spreading the news of Alex and her lover.

Jeremy grabbed his friend by the arm, yanking him around to face him. "I do not want to have to call you out, my brother, and that is what you are to me. But if you ever say anything disparaging about my sister again, I will. What the hell was that about?"

Marc didn't even bother to pull away. "I do not know." He took a deep breath, forcing himself to hold Jeremy's gaze. "I overheard the men at White's speaking of her *affiliation* with Spencer Ferguson, as well as Edward Barlow. I know it cannot be true. She does not even know Edward, but Ferguson. She knows him. She was riding with him again today. I am under the impression she does quite often..." His voice trailed off as Melinda walked up to them, taking Jeremy's clenched hand.

"I think I would like to go home now. Mother is expecting us for tea." Nervously, she glanced at the man who had always fascinated her. He tried so hard to be polite, it was almost painful to watch. She wanted to tell him just to relax, take a deep breath, and enjoy life. Instead, she allowed Jeremy to help her into his carriage.

Alex fought to calm down. She forced her clenched hands to ease open. "Well, I think it is getting late. We should be getting home. I need a nap."

Alma took her daughter's hand leading her out. Catherine and an angry Alex followed next.

Having gained control of his emotions once again, Marc offered his hand to Alex.

"My lord, I shall be riding to Hollister House with my mother. If you will, please drop off my packages when you retrieve your mother, I would be very grateful, my lord."

"Damn it, Alex. Do not do this. I am sorry, all right? I did not mean to say those things, they just slipped out." He reached for her only to have her move farther out of his reach.

"They slipped out because you were thinking them, my lord." When she moved to leave, Catherine stepped in front of her. "Mama?" Her brow arched, her hands rested on her hips in a casual pose that spoke nothing of the anger that rolled through her.

"I am sorry, my dear, but Alma and I are not going to the house immediately. We have a stop to make—and—well, you need to go with Marc and Ashlee. You know he did not mean what—"

Alex interrupted with a whisper. "I understand more than you think I do, Mama. I do not need this kind of assistance. I do not want it or him either." She stomped past Marc, flopping into the seat next to Ashlee, all the good feelings of the morning gone.

She was angry, mostly with herself, as the carriage jolted over the uneven cobblestones. The buildings went unnoticed as she stared out the window, her thoughts on Malacinda. She had gotten offended when Marc had accused her of being a mistress, yet what was wrong with it? She was not ashamed of Malacinda, though Alex didn't like what she did, and she realized it was more than it being with Marc. Malacinda was worth more than that.

With a smile, she looked at Marc. He was staring out the window, an angry scowl firmly in place.

Returning her gaze to the city, Alex knew why she had been so mad. Even Marc looked at a mistress as something lower than himself. If it was so bad for Alex to be one, than it stood to reason that it was bad for Malacinda to be one as well. Her smile spread as an idea took root in her mind. She was going to have to start furnishing her new home. She was going to need servants and someone to watch over them. Malacinda had been running her own household for quite some time and already had two servants under her command. Her day maid and her cook. It would not take much more to run a larger staff. Alex settled back, content now with her decision to hire Mala-cinda as the housekeeper of Linden. She would not be required to do anything, except keep everyone in line. She would still be allowed to keep her day maid and her cook—who was wonderful, in Alex's opinion—could cook for them all with a kitchen staff of her own.

Marc would just have to find himself a new mistress. That thought caused her smile to spread.

That smile caused a tightening in Marc's throat as he glanced at her smooth profile.

Chapter 13

Precisely at five, Alex stood, damp from her recent bath, admiring the new gown lying across the foot of her bed. It shimmered lightly in the flickering glow from the small fire that crackled across the large room.

"My lady, may I assist you. I have put your purchases away— ohh, that is beautiful."

"Thank you, Rebecca. I need to be dressed and ready in two hours. There will be arrivals of gowns and outfits every day or so for the next month. Just press them and put them away. A message will come for me from Mademoiselle Rhamninose. If I am not here and Robert is, give it to him. Tell him to take care of it for me." Alex had already informed him of the billings. He would take them to March, and her solicitor would give him the money needed so he could pay for the gowns.

It took almost an hour to ready herself. The only thing that was refused was the corset. "I want to look glamorous tonight, but more, I want to breathe." Rebecca just laughed. "Get me something to drink. Brandy."

"Yes, my lady."

Alex sat before the large dresser, looking into the mirror as her young day maid shut the door.

The reflection in the mirror looked like her mother, more now than ever. Her brilliant hair was wound high in a coiffure, elegantly piled with loose tendrils streaking across her lightly powdered cheeks. She had never been as proud of her looks as she was now. Of course, she had never taken the time with it as she had the last few days. Alex had made the decision with the purchase of her own home and the upcoming unveiling of A.H., that she could be a beautiful woman as well as a business woman and, looking in the mirror, made her realize that.

When the door opened, she didn't even look up. "Just put it on the table, Rebecca, and head to the kitchen for something to eat, I will not need you till tonight." She gasped and jumped to her feet when Marc's reflection came into sight before her. "My Lord."

Marc had come to apologize for the way he had behaved at Sylvia's shop, but those two taunting little words pushed him over the edge. Without a word he grasped her arms dragging her into his embrace, kissing her painfully before she could object.

He silently cursed her power over him. He could not understand this loss of control over the slightest touch of her, the sweet sound of her voice. It had to do with the length of time he had been celibate, of that he was sure, and now he blamed her. She had been the one to ruin his setup, push his mistress away, ruin his life.

She struggled for only a moment before her hands slid around his neck and her lips parted. Her unabashed response to him baffled him.

He would not admit that she truly cared for him, for that would mean he was taking advantage of her love, and that he didn't think he could bear.

Pushing back the guilt, he lost all thought as her tongue darted forward, caressing his, urging him on. Marc slid one arm around her waist lifting until she was sitting on the dresser. His other hand searched out the rounded tops of her breasts, caressing them roughly as he deepened the kiss.

Alex gasped, arching toward him, as his hand slid into her bodice grasping a nipple between his finger and thumb.

Her tongue captured his as it plunged into her warm mouth. His groan rumbled through her every nerve. Marc forced his knee in between her thighs, pushing her farther onto the dresser as he wedged her legs apart.

Digging through the layers of ruffles beneath the beautiful yellow gown, he found her warm calves. She pulled him closer, his lips trailing kisses across her cheeks, running his tongue into her ear, biting gently down her neck. Alex braced her ankles behind his thighs, allowing him to push her skirt farther up her trembling legs.

Dragging the soft silk bodice down, he grasped a hardened nipple in his teeth. Lathering them with kisses and gentle nips.

A knock sounded at the door. "You have to be kidding me." His frustrated words rumbled against her lips. Alex pushed him off as the door began to open.

"Rebecca, what are you doing? Is that brandy?" Her mother's voice was heard from the hall, the door stopped. "She does not need that. Take it away, and I will get her down to await the guests."

Alex shoved Marc behind her dressing screen as she tried to readjust her clothing. "Stay back there," she hissed urgently as she pushed him to his knees.

She took a deep breath as her Catherine came into the room.

"Are you all right, my dear? You look peaked. Is it your knee?"

"My knee is fine. I'm just excited about tonight." Walking away from the screen, Alex tried not to limp.

Catherine looked at her daughter with suspicion. "Are you sure you're all right? Your neck is all red. Do you have a fever?"

Marc cringed when he remembered how rough he had been with his kisses and his teeth.

Alex's hand went self-consciously to her neck. "No, Mama, I am sure I do not. I was a little too rough when I was washing my face, but I am fine."

"You have to be more careful. Come to my chambers. I have an ointment that will help."

Not risking a look at the screen, Alex allowed her mother to drag her from the room.

Marc listened to the footsteps fade and took long raged breaths. It was several minutes before he could no longer hear his heart thudding in his ears. He took one long more long breath and crept from the room. He did not allow himself to relax until he entered the main hall without being seen.

Tension seemed to flow from his shoulders, but did not make it far, as he turned a corner to come face to face with Jeremy and Thomas.

"Marc, I did not know you were here yet." Thomas raised his brows at him as he took in his ragged breath and reddened face. "Is everything all right?"

"Indeed. I just thought to spend some time with Jeremy before tonight. I promised Lady Rutmeyer I would pick her up for tonight so I wanted to stop by first." He glanced at the front door and at the high polished tables, but could not seem to bring himself to look at her father and brother.

"You are going to bring her here?" Jeremy just shook his head. With as volatile as Alex's temper had been lately, he could just picture how well that was going to go over. He should warn her.

Hearing voices behind him on the stairs, Marc began to walk to the door. "Yes, I should get going. I just wanted to tell you I would not be arriving with the rest of the family. I will be here shortly, though."

The two men looked at each other as Marc rushed from Hollister House. "Is it me, or was he in a hurry to leave?" Jeremy asked. They both looked up as Alex and her mother walked down the stairs. "You think he was here to see her?"

"Perhaps he lost his nerve when he heard her voice." Thomas looked up at the identical pair that swayed down the stairs. "My loves, you look amazing." He took Alex in his arms. "I hear you have made a massive purchase. I am glad you are starting to come around. This does not mean we will not be having that talk later."

"I know, Papa." It would not be the last talk they had. All heads turned as Edmond Windrow, Hollister House's short and thin butler, announced the arrival of the first carriages.

As the family went forth to meet the first of the guests, the Clifton and Fortshaw families, Jeremy pulled Alex to the side. "Marc is not going to be with them. He is getting Janice."

Alex didn't say a word, just walked into her place in line with a tight jaw. Thomas shook his head as he saw the tears she was fighting. "Alex?" No response. She didn't even look his way. "Alex, please."

No response.

She fought for control and found it. By the time the guests had reached them, she had a smile on her face and, ignoring all the worried looks, she held her emotions in check. Her resolve did not waver as guest upon guest was announced.

It held firm until the Rutmeyers arrived.

With her hand possessively wrapped around Marc's arm, Janice Rutmeyer pulled him closer with a smug smile on her pale pink lips.

Marc fought to keep his anger at her in check. The carriage ride had been straining, to say the least. She reminded him several times he was to treat her in the manner she deserved, telling him the marriage was not an official decree as of yet, and he had better walk a tight line.

"Good evening, Lady Hollister, I hope *we* are not late. We did so want to be here early." Janice smiled at Alex with malice, all the while pulling Marc closer to her, holding on tighter to his arm while her eyes never left Alex's cold blue stare. "Is that not right, Marc?"

The only emotion Marc could detect was the tightening around Alex's eyes as she forced a smile. "My dear lady, it is as pleasurable to see you as always. My lord, so nice to see you again. I hope you had no difficulties sneaking away."

She hid her smirk well, as his eyes widened in shock at her blatant taunt.

"Marcus?" Janice looked at him for an answer. Her small foot tapped lightly on the floor. "What is she talking about?"

He stuttered as he looked from one lady to the other. Alex could not hold back the grin as the others of the family looked at her.

"She only meant that it is difficult to get away from the family when we are preparing for a ball."

"Indeed, my lord, it is the first time that the family was torn apart in as long as I can remember," Alex said, her voice calm.

His brilliant green eyes pinned hers as he fought anger. He wanted nothing more than to tell her he did not tear apart anything, but more guests were arriving behind him. Ice blue eyes held his in challenge. His were the first to drop away. He would settle this with her later.

Hours later, Alex walked with her arm wrapped through Spencer's toward the dance floor, her balance faltering slightly. She had just left the floor, only to be led right back to it. For the last several hours, she had danced almost every dance, and she was exhausted. Her knee throbbed with a vengeance, as did her head.

It seemed the only one she had yet to dance with was the one she wanted to the most. The one who had been avoiding her since his arrival. Who had, in fact, doted on his soon-to-be betrothed at every turn. It was that sight that had drove her to the brandy decanter between every dance.

"Are you all right?" Spencer did not stop to consider what the other guests would think as he pulled her past the dancers and into the library. He had taken one look into her pale, shaky face and acted. He had come to care for the young girl more than he had ever cared for anyone before. The dark circles beneath her eyes spoke of the pain that trembled through her body. He could rightly guess it was an emotional pain that haunted her so.

Without awaiting an answer, he pushed her into the black leather chair that sat snugly before the warm fire. Leaving the door wide open, he thought they followed decorum closely enough. "Is it your knee?" He knew it was not.

Her breath was coming in short gasps, her vision beginning to darken. She could only shake her head. "I have just overexerted. I am fine. I shall sit here and rest, go back to the others." Several deep breaths and she was feeling better. "Perhaps some brandy will fortify me."

Spencer had a feeling that she had overindulged already, but he refrained from saying so. He left her without a word. He would quietly retrieve her father to see to her. Thomas would know how to best deal with her.

Marc slipped into the library, shutting the door behind him. Alex stood before a small table that held a large brandy decanter, a glass in her hand as she stared at the fire.

"Alex, I want to talk to you." He was not sure what he was going to say, but he would start with her rendezvous with men in the library.

Spencer approached Thomas, pulling him away from the others. "My lord," he whispered quietly. "I am worried about Alex."

Thomas raised a questioning brow at him.

"She is drinking more than normal lately. Her temper has always been capricious, but lately it has become erratic. She tries to act like there is nothing astray, but I can feel there is, my lord. I know I am out of line, but I do care for your daughter."

"I know you do, Ferguson—Spencer. She cares for you a great deal as well. You have been there for her a lot over the last couple of years."

More years than he knew, but Spencer refrained from comment.

Thomas nodded. "I will see to her."

"I left her in the library, my lord. She implied it was her knee, but…" Spencer let his words die, the rest was obvious.

Jeremy caught up with Thomas before he had made it more than three steps. "Is she all right? I saw Ferguson take her into the library then come to you. Marc is in there with her now. Is everything all right?"

"He is in there? Not with the mood she is in, Hell." Grabbing Blake on his way past, Thomas told both boys to come with him. He would be prepared for either kissing or fighting, but he wanted help, no matter which he encountered. They would help pull Alex off the young man if she was that angry, and if Marc was taking advantage, which Thomas did not believe he would, well then they would help drag him off Marc.

Inside the library, Marc stood face to face with an enraged Alex. "How dare you tell me who I can and cannot come into the library with, my lord? You have shown me absolutely no consideration tonight in the least. You have not even danced with me, my lord."

Marc took another step closer to her, his body responded to her heaving breasts even as he fought to control his anger and confusion. "I did not know that was required of me, you should have told me."

She cringed at the sarcasm in his steely voice. She did not think she had seen him so angry, at least never at her.

"And what was that little comment about me sneaking away supposed to accomplish?"

She stood her ground as he took another step toward her. "Perhaps if you were not such a horse's ass, you would not have to ask that question. By now, you should you know the answer."

They were now body to body and face to face.

Alex swung her fist into his rock hard chest, cursing, as it only served to hurt her hand. She swung harder, this time at his face.

He grabbed her arms, pulling her closer as she fought to injure him. One hand pulled free and the three men entering the library were greeted with a resounding echo as her fist connected with Marc's clenched jaw. They pulled the door closed.

Marc shook her roughly. "You damn hellion, you will not do this to me. If you insist on hitting me, I will take you over my knee and blister that round little bottom of yours until you cannot sit."

With tears fighting to come forth, she began to struggle more violently, her feet connecting with his shins as she spat curses at him. Words he thought would shame some of the sailors he had known. Where had his little minx learned of such words? She mocked him even in her anger as two words were riddled through the curses over and over. Two words she knew he hated hearing her call him.

"Damn it, Alex, stop doing that. Stop it."

Again, she called him my lord, accompanied by several none-too-savory choice animal parts.

Before he could shake her again, he felt hands on him.

An enraged voice shook them as hands began to rip them apart. "Stop it, the both of you. What the hell is the matter with you two?" Jeremy and Blake held a struggling Marc while Thomas fought to control his daughter.

Marc pulled away violently. "Nothing." He started toward the doors and Jeremy and Blake both reached for him. All three spun back as they heard a curse from behind them. Not Alex this time, but her father.

Alex had kicked Thomas hard in the shin, taking the opportunity to slide from his grasp. Before he could stop her she grasped a, now empty, decanter and flung it at Marc. Missing his hip by a breath, it crashed into the wall beside him. He gaped at her, wide mouthed in shock.

Thomas once more had a firm hold on her. "You three go back to the party, tell them I knocked over the table. I am sure all the guests heard that crash." He shook Alex, his fingers cutting into her arm as she continued to struggle. "I will be out shortly."

His growl sent shivers down Alex's spine, yet her struggles never ceased. Marc was reluctant to leave. He knew Thomas was angry with both him and Alex, but he had to get to Janice and make up some excuse for even being in the library with the woman he was supposed to be avoiding.

Thomas waited until the library door clicked shut before releasing his beloved little girl. What was he going to do with her? For as tiny as she was, she held a hurricane of emotions inside her. "What has gotten into you?" He tried to sound angry, but his voice was low and shaky. Never had he seen her so angry, so hurt.

"Sorry for the glass, and the kick, Papa." Alex struggled against the hateful tears. She had always prided herself on her strength, but, lately, she wanted nothing more than to slide beneath her bed and hide. "Did you come in because you—heard us?" Her breath hitched as she swallowed a sob that tried to escape past the tight knot of tears lodged in her throat. So far, she had been discreet about her activities when in London, but she had lost control tonight.

"No, love." He could see the tears trembling in her blue eyes— like the first thaw of winter, the water shimmering along the surface of a frozen lake. "Viscount Ferguson said he thought you could use me."

Her eyes lifted to his, a tear trailing down her face. Alex's trembling lips parted to speak, but a sob tore free. Falling into his arms, she let go. The tears fell painfully onto his immaculate evening coat.

Neatly lifting her into his arms, he pressed her head onto his shoulder, rocking her back and forth as she cried. He knew not what he said to her, just nonsense words of love and comfort. Words he had used on her as a small child when she had awoken with a nightmare.

He remembered how she always wanted to be so strong, so independent—that was until she was scared or hurt. Not physically—no, physical pain she had always been well in control of, like her knee now. Emotional hurts were different. Then she would run to him, fling into his arms, and let him hold her. He was the only one she would run to.

Slowly the sobs subsided and her face lifted. Kissing him gently on his weathered cheek, she gave a shaky smile. "I love you, Papa."

"And I you, my little hellion."

She giggled as he set her back on the floor. Wiping her face gently with his handkerchief, he smiled. "Perhaps we should let you get some rest. I can make your excuses." He knew he needn't ask any more questions of her. Indeed, had he not been so surprised by the confrontation he had walked into, he would not have asked her any. He knew what was wrong with both of them. He just didn't know how to fix it.

"Not yet."

Thomas led her to the door and was now watching Marc sit stiffly beside his betrothed. He wondered briefly how he had explained his actions, or if he had.

"I want one more dance first."

"I do not think you will pry his arm loose from that woman, my dear." He looked down and started at the look of love in her eyes, surprised at the power of the emotion in them.

"I meant you, Papa."

"You have danced with me many times tonight. Are you sure you want one more?"

Smiling, she hugged his arm tightly. "Papa, I know one thing. No matter where I go in life or what happens from here on out, I will always want one more dance with you."

Marc watched with a knotted stomach as Thomas wrapped his arm around Alex's shoulders and led her to the dance floor. He had not been able to tear his eyes away from her since they had appeared. Her eyes were red and swollen as though she had been crying. Again. And again it was because of him. Last season, he had upset her by avoiding her, now he could not seem to stop himself from searching her out to do the same thing.

He felt fingers clutching his arm, but could not make himself look at her as he spoke. "Would you care to dance, my lady?"

"Not now, Marcus, and can you not call me Janice?"

He looked at her now. Her batting lashes and wide smile made him cringe. "Shall we announce the betrothal tonight?" He smiled inwardly while keeping his features serious as her smile fell away. A small shake of her now pale face was her only answer. "Then I should perhaps keep it at my lady until that time."

"You do not call *Miss* Hollister by a title." *No*, Janice thought angrily, *he calls her baby*.

"No, I do not call *Lady* Alex by a title, but she calls me my lord." He could hear the anger in his own voice but could do nothing to stop it.

"What were you doing in the library alone with her, *Marcus*?" She deliberately put accent on his name as she said it.

He had put her off the first time she had asked, but had spent the time coming up with a story. Close to the truth if he would admit it to himself. He wouldn't.

"I had seen Ferguson take her in the library and was concerned." *And angry. And jealous.* The thought stopped him for a moment. Jealous? No, not him. He had several mistresses over the years and had never once felt anything close to jealousy, even when he learned they had strayed. He pushed the thought from his mind and ignored

Janice's next questions as Philip Moore approached his sister.

He didn't like the man. Didn't want him bothering his sister, but found a moment of hatred for the man as Thomas and Alex stepped into his path.

Alex had talked Thomas into letting her stay. She had seen the way Moore was watching Ashlee dance with the Count of Reagin, his eyes full of lust and evil. Alex didn't believe he had any notions of marriage. He would use Ashlee and set her aside, and she would not be the first.

Telling Thomas her plan, he reluctantly agreed to let Alex play the distraction for a while and give Bradley Hamilton a chance to dance again with the woman he had fallen for. He only agreed because Thomas didn't like Moore either. So after leaving Alex in Moore's hands, knowing she could handle him, Thomas slipped a quiet word to Bradley to dance again with Ashlee.

The dance went well, and Alex was dragged to the refreshment table when Philip saw someone he knew. Two dances went by, Alex asking twice to return to her father. Both times Philip smiled and agreed. Both times he would take a step with her in that direction only to be stopped by someone else.

Alex struggled with the urge to walk off and leave him there. She had already had one brush with scandal tonight and was not quite to the point to do so again. Instead, she looked at her family. Thomas, Blake, and Jeremy, as well as Maxwell, were on the dance floor. Spencer was talking with Michael Cranston, Porter Farthing, and Craig Connelly by the garden doors. Four of the six men she had invited. The only ones not to show were Gideon and Edward, but she had not expected them. No one was available to come save her.

Glancing at Janice who was involved in an animated conversation at Marc's side, completely ignoring him, she allowed herself look at him. Their gazes caught and held.

Marc caught his breath when Alex smiled. He grinned and fought a laugh as she dramatically rolled her eyes in exasperation at the man beside her. He wanted nothing more than to go to her rescue. He had seen her pleading eyes, searching for help. He had to fight the urge to go to her. He had never felt so comfortable with any woman as he always had with Alex. But that had changed last season when he had so wanted to kiss her. His desire had been so sudden and so severe, he had run.

His smile disappeared, and his indecision must have shown on his face for her smile quickly fell away. Shaking her head, she looked away, but not before he read the pain in her eyes.

He bit back an oath as her eyes swung behind him, his stomach churning as her face lit with pleasure. He felt that feeling that was certainly not jealousy ripple through him. Even knowing who he would see coming to her aid, he could not stop himself from turning as her eyes pleaded for help once again, the small incline of her head begging for salvation.

Marc was dumbfounded by the sight he saw. It was not Spencer as he had thought, but who it was confused him. He was sure he was mistaken. She could not have gestured to this man. Then his heart dropped as the short, yet muscle-riddled man, with the shiny bald head discreetly motioned for her to wait.

James Gideon disappeared into the gaming salon. Marc looked back at Alex, who now held a true smile while she watched Moore talk with someone new.

Marc had never met Gideon, but he knew who he was. He didn't think there was a soul in London, or anywhere in the surrounding areas for that matter, who didn't know of Mr. James Gideon by mere reputation alone. He was a barrister without equal. A man of unquestioning power and loyalty. It was said he won some of his cases just because the jury had been afraid to go against him. But it was also said he only took cases that he truly believed in.

Everyone knew, without question, that once he decided you were worthy of his friendship, he would do anything for you. No one in Marc's family had met him, but it was he who had kept the rumors of his father being a spy from going to court.

He was the reason that, twelve years ago when Rutmeyer renewed his efforts to destroy the Clifton reputation, no charges were officially brought forth.

Twelve years ago, Samuel Rutmeyer had approached Maxwell to agree to marry Janice to Marc when she came of age. Maxwell had refused. Marc had been angry, knowing full well the ramifications of that denial. Even then, the Rutmeyer family had been sinking in debt.

Sure enough, rumors of charges being filed were heard, even though the Clifton's were no longer in the shipping business. All because Maxwell Clifton had not sold his ships.

Marc remembered vividly the tears Alex had spilled when she had eavesdropped at the study door. Several days later, the rumors had slowed, and the courts refused to hear the indicts.

It became common knowledge that Gideon was responsible. Marc thought it strange at the time that no one knew him and yet he had stepped up for them.

No one knew him—except Alex. But that was just ridiculous.

How would a six-year-old know a man like that?

Within moments, the powerful and dangerous man was out of the gaming salon. Marc watched him closely. Staring at Alex, Gideon shook his head in indecision. Taking a deep breath, he seemed to decide. With a smile, he approached her.

"My lady. May I have the pleasure of this dance?"

Philip turned to him in outrage. "Now see here, I am—" His face paled, and he stepped away, leaving Alex to fend for herself. Marc wanted to pummel him for his cowardice.

"You are what?" Gideon's soft voice carried a threat that bore no chance of an argument. When Moore didn't respond, Gideon pulled Alex onto the dance floor to await the next song.

"We will dance." Marc's growl left no room for argument as he pulled Janice onto the floor behind Alex.

"You should not have gestured to me, what if someone saw you? I almost did not dance with you." Gideon looked over her shoulder at Marc. He grinned to see who he was with. His gaze only touched Marc's for a moment, but long enough to let Marc know he was aware of him.

"Then why did you?" She spoke softly, though she did not realize Marc was behind her. Anymore, she didn't really care who heard her nor saw who she danced with.

"You looked ready to injure the boy."

Her eyes swung to him. "Why, you make that sound as if I have a violent nature. That is scandalous. Who have I ever been violent against?"

Gideon smiled as his gaze skimmed Janice, whose face flushed scarlet. He looked around the room, his gaze stopping on Michael Cranston, who she had kicked out of his chair, and then hit him with it when he had pawed at Victoria Chariton. Then he raised a brow in the direction of Lord Manning, who she had stabbed. "I can think of three, right here in this room."

Above her guilty look, he saw Marc look at her hands with an angry scowl. "Or is it four now? You hit a man tonight." He spotted the small red scrape on Marc's tightened jaw. "In the jaw, if I am correct."

Alex looked up at him with narrowed eyes. "How do you do that?"

He just smiled. "What were you doing with that simpering sop? I did not think you went in for the lacy kind of fellows. Other than your beloved dandy, that is."

"I can tell you that Spencer, at his best, could still learn a thing or

two from that irritating man. He puts Spencer to shame." Her laugh
washed over the man behind her as she told Gideon what she had
been doing.

Marc lost the trail of the conversation as the music began. He
was not able to get close enough to hear anymore, and didn't see
right away when Gideon pulled her toward the door.

Thomas did. He followed, only stopping when he realized Gideon was only taking her to the door and no farther. They spoke as he
slipped into his coat.

"I wish you would stay. That is why I sent you an invitation. You
are more than welcome in my home."

"But this is not your home. It is your father's home. I am out of
place among the ton." He clasped her hand tightly, watching with
satisfaction as Marc stared toward them. Gideon felt the mischievous
urge to pull her out the door. He fought it.

"That is what Edward says as well. Both of you are welcome.
When I get back to the country, I will throw a tryst like none other,
and I will expect you to be the first to arrive, with Edward at your
side."

"I shall be delighted, my dear. I shall see you tomorrow." He
kissed her hand for longer than necessary, just to see the vein pulse
in Marc's neck. Gideon wondered if Alex knew the way Marc felt
about her. She had spoken of him many times over the years. A blind
man would see she was in love with him. And he was certainly not
blind.

"No, tomorrow is the Clifton ball. I cannot miss it. I will have to
miss the game, though I would love to come." Her smile was whim-
sical.

"I meant at the track. My money is on you." With that he strode
out of the door, leaving her wide mouthed in shock. *How does he do
that?* she wondered for the hundredth time since she had first met
him so many years ago. She had not told him she was A.H. and she
was sure Edward had not either.

Shaking her head, she came face to face with Thomas and Maxwell. Where were the women of the family, why was it they never
came to her aid? It seemed they avoided the confrontations whenever
possible. Alex was sure if she looked, they would be in a small clus-
ter silently praying she would use her head and remain silent. That
would never happen.

Thomas was angry and scared for her. She could see it in his features. "What were you thinking accepting his offer to dance?"

Marc, Jeremy, and Blake approached. She wondered where

Janice was. She smiled when she noticed her being detained, quite effectively, by the charming Michael Cranston. The future Marquis of Livindale was smiling his most asinine smile, one that told Alex he was not the least interested in the woman, not even as a conquest.

Alex wondered momentarily why he was doing it, then Craig winked at her, inclining his head toward the angry Marc as he did so. She knew then they were also trying to help her. If she got any more help in the matter, she was likely to scream.

"Papa, he is a barrister, and a very respectable one" She leaned heavily on her uninjured knee and tried to keep her eyes open. She had to get some sleep unless she planned to fall from her horse at the track.

"Respectable or not, it is still improper to dance with a man you did not know. You must wait for a proper introduction."

"I am sorry, Papa. You are right. I should have waited, I was just so anxious to get away from Moore that I did not think." She hadn't. She refrained from walking away from Moore to keep from creating gossip and then did something worse. She had just been so excited to see him.

"I know, love. Now, you look about to fall off your feet. Go to bed. I shall see you when I return from the races."

Alex kissed him gently on the cheek once more, not caring who saw, and walked past him. She had seen not censure in his eyes, but love. That gave her hope for her future with him. Perhaps he could look past the dictates of society and see her for the girl he still loved.

Alex stopped docilely in front of Marc, her face serious and the look in her eyes remorseful. "I am sorry, my lord, that I tried to throw that decanter at your head."

"I shall just be grateful that you your aim is bad and you could not get it that high," Marc said, his spine stiff.

"Oh, not that one, my lord. I was aiming for the one that carries your brains."

Blake burst into laughter. Jeremy slapped him on the back as he agreed with his sister, and both fathers looked on in horror while Alex calmly walked away. Her parting words were at least low enough only the family could hear them, but she had said them with such a serious expression, it was all Marc could do not to laugh.

Chapter 14

Sitting at a small table at White's, Marcus could not get his mind off of Alex. Indeed had not been able to since that first kiss. Now he didn't know what to do about her.

He had heard rumor after rumor of her lovers and, with the way she responded to him, he was beginning to think she was not the innocent he thought she was. What's more, he didn't know why he cared so much. The thought of her with another man tore at him.

Snatches of conversation came to him from the table against the wall behind him, pulling him painfully back to reality. Looking up into the boiling eyes of Thomas, Marc knew he was not the only one to have heard the insolent words.

"I know how it sounds, but I believe it is true. Edward Barlow is the newest lover of Alexis Hollister. The way she flaunts herself around—" The words were cut off as Marc spun from his chair so fast it crashed to the floor. Grasping Viscount Gregson by the throat, he threw him against the wall, setting the wall sconces to rattling.

He slammed Randy Gregson once more into the wall before anyone could get to him. "If you ever say anything like that about Lady Alexis again, I will call you out, do I make myself perfectly clear."

Thomas Hollister and Maxwell Clifton each grabbed an arm, rock hard and trembling beneath their grasp. Randy stood six foot and was thick as an ox, but in his anger, Marc had lifted him off the ground.

Jeremy slapped him hard on the back, drawing his attention away from the sputtering man. "Marc, let him go."

With a growl, Marc dropped the dark-haired man to the floor.

"Let's get down to Epsom to see to the races, my boy." Maxwell kept a firm hold on his son's arm, leading him out of the room. "What was that? You never lose your head like that."

"It was nothing, and you can let go of me now," Marc said in a deadly calm voice, through tightly clenched teeth. How could he tell them what had happened when he didn't understand it himself? He had just snapped. Perhaps he was losing his mind.

Several hours in a rocking carriage had actually gone a long way to relaxing Marc, and he was beginning to start thinking ahead to the races.

"Look." Jeremy pointed at the sleek black carriage driven by the massive Tess Richards. "He is here before the first race? He is never here before they start."

"Indeed, he is not. This is a first, I believe." Thomas took a long look at Marc. "Perhaps your boy somehow knew you would be here quite early today and is here for you."

"He is not my boy." Marc's voice was low and full of malice, his relaxation threatening to abandon him.

They all just grinned. He watched the young jockey with speculation. Was he indeed here just because Marc was here early? That made no sense.

The young man in question was now standing between his large driver and Raymond Dunmore. Both the jockey and his assistant looked like small children beside the large man. Raymond and A.H. conversed on what were probably the other riders, horses, and the races to come.

Before the men could take to their seats, A.H. looked to where they normally sat, obviously looking for Marc, as usual. As A.H. began to scan the crowd, he was knocked into Raymond as Tess shoved his massive elbow into the small man's shoulder. Grasping his shoulder and catching his balance, A.H. looked up at his driver then followed his gaze.

Marc watched as the jockey's small hands flew up to cover his mouth in a very feminine gesture.

"My God," Jeremy said.

Marc completely concurred with Jeremy's comment as he followed the jockey's gaze.

Walking alongside the Viscount of Mooreland was Viscount Ferguson. Spencer was as dandified as he had ever been; his frills and lace were now in competition with Philip Moore. Walking beside Philip, Spencer looked like an exact copy.

A.H. had stepped behind Tess, his forehead now laying on the boulder-sized back as Tess craned his neck over his shoulder to smile at the trembling form. Marc realized the jockey was laughing. Struggling for control, A.H. stepped around Richards, making sure Spencer saw him, holding both hands, palms up, in a gesture that could only mean, what the hell? Thoughts that mirrored Marc's own.

Spencer stepped forward, giving the most elaborate bow, ruffled cuffs shimmering in the late morning sun. Spencer could hardly move his head without hitting the high starched collar that rubbed against his neck and chin.

A.H. shook his hands at him in a questioning move. Spencer only waved a glove. Several pairs of eyes followed his direction to see James Gideon, sitting beside Edward Barlow not far from where Marc would soon take his seat. Gideon gave a low bow as A.H. put his hands on his hips and shook his head in what appeared to be exasperation.

Marc remembered the dance the barrister had with Alex. She had told Gideon that Spencer could use some lessons from the superfluous man his sister had somehow taken a liking to. Lord, what Ashlee saw in the man, Marc could not fathom. Gideon must have told Spencer what Alex had said.

"Where are you going, Marc?" Maxwell looked at the grin that spread across his son's face, the problems with Alex forgotten, at least for a moment.

"I have a matter to see to, Father." Without a look behind him, Marc strode determinedly toward the jockey and his odd entourage, as Raymond disappeared into the stables.

With a start, A.H. stepped behind his bodyguard.

"Can I help you, my lord?" His extensive scars lent him an ominous air, one that had sent many a man slithering away in fear.

Marc stopped several steps away from him. "I want to have a word or two with your master. It has to do with his shipping contract. I would like to discuss it." He stepped a little closer, trying without luck to peer around the bulk of the frightening man.

Scars could not be determined individually, with the exception of the one that had almost taken his eye. His face seemed riddled with crisscrosses and gouges. Whatever had happened to him had been gruesome and over a long period of time. Marc looked past his face and scars, into brilliant blue eyes that sparkled with amusement. Tess was struggling to regain the intimidating composure he had used the last time Marc had faced him.

"If you have business with A.H., then I would suggest you wait until the end of the races. My master is very serious about his races and likes to keep his mind on his work."

Tess's face wrinkled in the effort not to laugh. He had to get back to himself. The jockey always had a strange effect on him, causing him to laugh or get angry. Once, he had been well in control of all his emotions, but his small master had destroyed all his walls.

"Serious, yes indeed. I saw just a moment ago how serious he is." Marc looked around the hard shoulder trying to get a look at the man who snorted. Marc knew he was trying not to laugh again. "I cannot say that I blame him though. Did you see Spencer? Lord, he has more frills than a petticoat."

That did it. In trying to hold in the laughter, A.H. began to choke and cough. Tess was unprepared for the shove that came from his small friend and ended up bumping into Marc as both men tried to hold in the laughter.

"You are going to have to go now." Tess's voice was strained.

Marc just shook his head and walked away. He turned back after he had made it only a few feet. A.H. watched him walking away. Marc made a poor attempt at the extravagant bow Spencer had performed. This sent A.H. back into hysterics, hands over his mouth, until Tess had to support the small trembling frame.

Seeing the angry look on Raymond's face as he emerged from the stables, Marc decided enough was enough and, with a nod of his head, he went back to the family. Once there, he watched the first race begin, surprised to see Raymond would be the jockey for one of A.H.'s horses in the first race.

Looking at the racing schedule, Marc saw that he would be in the third race as well.

"Marc, what is your boy up to?" Jeremy looked at him in shock when the taunt didn't work as it usually did.

Marc just grinned. "From the look of this—" He shook the itinerary gently. "—A.H. now has another jockey and is in four races, instead of two. He is not here early just to see me." He chuckled, remembering the scene he had just had. It was out of his character to play, especially in such a public arena.

As if to remind him of the situation he had put himself in, Rutmeyer, who had just joined them, spoke up from beside him. "I thought you did not know the boy. You seemed awfully familiar with him down there. I do not recall seeing you so at ease."

Jeremy gave him a knowing look. "I have."

Marc scowled as Alex once again slipped into his thoughts. Jeremy was right. Before Marc had begun to lose his mind, as he was sure he was doing, he had been most at ease when it just the three of them. Marc, Jeremy, and Alex. They had been inseparable.

Marc knew Jeremy was speaking of the many times when, in order to give Jeremy privacy with whatever girl he was wooing at the time, that it had been just Alex and Marc. They had spent those times, lying in the grass awaiting the return of her brother, talking and laughing.

Jeremy had always teased him to be careful. *'My sister is easy to*

*lose your heart to. I should know. I have, and look at my father and
yours. Watch your heart.'*

Marc's smile disappeared, replaced by a dark scowl. "I do not
know him. I did not even get to talk to him, just that big guard of his
again. I can pass a joke with someone and not know them."

"How can you stand that close to the man? He is a cold-blooded
murderer. What if he was to kill you? It would be easy to anger such
a man as that." Samuel Rutmeyer shuddered.

"I do not think that was a problem. I can handle a man like that."
Marc held in the smile. He had worried about the man the first time
they had met, but not this time. He had seen something in his eyes,
something that spoke of compassion and a joy of life that Marc had
not seen in many other faces. He was a man who had seen the worst
in life and now wanted to enjoy the best. That did not mean he would
not turn into that other man if he was provoked, or, Marc was
certain, if someone was to threaten his little master.

"Who shall we bet for this race, my lord?" Rutmeyer would bet
as he had the last races. Whatever Marc did, he would do. He was
sure to win that way. "Shall we go with your boy's stallion?"

"I do not think so. I do not bet on new jockeys. I go with more
sure winners." For some strange reason, Marc did not bristle at A.H.
being referred to as his, for indeed he did look to him every chance
he got.

Jeremy turned to him with a patronizing smile. "Captain Jack is a
good stallion. He has won many a race. His bloodline is much sought
after."

Marc grinned. "Yes, but is that enough to make up for an inexpe
rienced rider on his first race out?"

"I think so, especially if that rider was probably trained by A.H.
himself." Jeremy raised a challenging brow to him. Seeing Marc's
stubbornness, he smiled. "Do you want to wager on it?" At Marc's
sudden grin, he smiled. "Shall we say, Alex?"

"What is that supposed to mean?" Marc growled, taking a quick
glance at Samuel.

Rutmeyer was ignoring them. He had, indeed, wandered to a fellow bystander to gossip until the men taking the bets came around.

Jeremy laughed. "Relax, I saw him walk away. I would not do
that with him standing there. The wager will be to see that she gets to
the Rutmeyer ball tomorrow night. If your horse beats the Captain, I
will shadow her and make sure she gets there. If Captain Jack and
Dunmore beat your horse, then I will not have to put up with her
temper, you will. Deal?"

Samuel was laughing when he walked back. "You will never be-lieve what I just heard." It was said with such apparent glee that Marc's stomach clenched. "I am sure it is just one more rumor, or you would be sure to know about it, Lord Hollister."

Thomas started when he realized he was the one being addressed.

"What would I know of, your grace?" His tone was carefully neutral.

"I just heard that your daughter knows A.H. She was seen getting out of his carriage not long ago. I assured the man that was not true, but one would hate for that kind of information to get out. I do hope your daughter will see fit to join with our little group at the ball to-morrow night."

As Thomas reassured him that she would, Marc bristled at the blatant threat. Turning to Jeremy, he spoke just one word through his clenched teeth, not deigning to explain what it meant to the question-ing Rutmeyer. "Deal."

Captain Jack, to everyone's amazement, came in first place, while Marc's wager had come in third. The second race went equally well with all parties winning as A.H. crossed the finish line first on a known winner, Mistress Penny. Raymond came in second on a big bay stallion, Torrent Rays, in the third race, and A.H. won the fourth on Marylee.

Marylee had overtaken the other riders in the fourth race by a large margin. She had won by at least four lengths. When A.H. came off of her, he was literally tossed into the air and caught in the arms of the big Tess. Marc could almost imagine the laugh that was issu-ing forth, but it was the wrong laugh.

He could almost hear a laugh he knew well. One he had to shake his head to dispel the image of. It was a laugh he not only wanted to hear again, but he wanted to be the one who caused it, but he didn't think he would ever be able to get Alex to laugh for him again.

Jeremy looked at his friend. "Are you all right, Marc?"

Marc nodded as the fifth race began and A.H's black carriage disappeared from sight.

The Hollister carriage was the one that had been taken to the rac-es, and their first stop would be at Clifton House to drop off Marc and Maxwell before the remaining men headed home.

The carriage rocked to a stop in front of Clifton house. Marc pushed the door open and jumped lightly to the ground. He turned to get out of the way of his father and then froze.

"What is it?" Maxwell stepped out behind him. "A.H.?"

"That's his carriage. Let's see if it is actually him that is in there." Marc shook his head knowing full well it would not be.

"Do you mind if we come in as well?" Thomas asked as the remaining passengers nearly tumbled from the carriage.

The five men were greeted not by A.H. but by a terrified butler. "Your grace, I am so sorry, I tried to stop him from going in, but he growled at me and said if I didn't move he would eat me."

Stuart Rodgers was shaking so badly, Maxwell feared he would have a fit right in the middle of the foyer.

"Easy, everything is fine. Just tell me where I can find the big man."

Everyone made their way to the small parlor, even knowing they were not going to meet with the infamous jockey. Though the big driver was just as much of a curiosity to them.

"Richards, how may I help you?" Marc looked at the man who stood beside the doors that led to the garden. "You are not the one I expected to see. I want to talk to your master."

"That is not gonna happen right now. He was very specific about that." The smiling man Marc had encountered earlier in the day was now hidden once more. His face was impassive once again. He was indeed living up to his reputation.

"I will only discuss it with A.H. It is private."

"Fine, then there is nothing else—"

His words were cut off as a slight wind swirled through the door led by a red-faced Alma, who had needed a few moments of fresh air in the gardens. Her scream brought Ashlee running down the stairs, even as Tess caught the now unconscious woman who had swooned in his arms.

Maxwell rushed forward to help his wife, only to be drawn up short by the impish grin bestowed upon him by the startled man.

"Well, don't stop there. Come get her. Waking up to this beautiful face is not going to make her feel any better."

Maxwell laughed as he retrieved his wife. By the time he had her laid comfortably on the settee, Tess had retired to the shadows by the door and Ashlee had come in beside him.

Unaware her brother watched her, she quietly asked Tess if everything was all right.

He shook his head. "I was in the wrong spot." He inclined his head in Marc's direction.

Her face paled when she noticed he was watching her. Luckily, he was the only one. "Alex is going to kill me for this," she whispered as Marc began storming toward her.

Alma saved her as a moan cut across the still air. "What—" Her eyes widened as she remembered what had happened. "Where is he? Are we being robbed?"

"No, my dear. That is a servant of one of your son's shipping clients. It is all right." Maxwell motioned for Tess to step forward as Ashlee dropped to her knees beside her mother.

"Oh, dear. You are a big man, are you not?" Alma asked with a shaky laugh.

"Yes, your grace. That I am. I beg your pardon for scaring you."

She just smiled, still unsure whether he was a threat or not. He definitely seemed one.

"Ashlee, take your mother upstairs while we finish with this business," Maxwell said.

Tess watched them until the door closed, and then Marc's angry voice drew his attention back. He had been thinking of what Alex was going to say when she learned of her friend's mistake. She should never have talked to him.

"That is my sister, Ashlee Clifton. She is a good friend of Alexis Hollister."

Tess's head swung back to Marc as he wondered why that was mentioned. Surely he didn't suspect her of being A.H.

"Do you know my daughter?" Thomas stepped forward with a raised brow.

"Why would you think I know her, how could I?" Tess tried to control the worry. He had told her he didn't think it was a good idea to come here, but she had been worried about her shipments.

Thomas, wanting a true reaction, thought a little shock might work. "It is rumored that my daughter is the lover of A.H."

Tess's face contorted in rage as he advanced upon the men. "Who said such lies about her? Tell me."

Thomas opened his mouth only to have Marc cut him off. "I do not think so. I think that is something we will keep to ourselves."

"Why?" Tess's eyes blazed, and his trembling fists were clenched at his sides.

"Because you have the same look on your face you did when you threatened to rip off my arm." He ignored the shocked looks from around him. "Only more so."

Taking a deep breath to calm himself, Tess gave a gruesome smile and said in a sweet low voice that sent chills down five sets of spines. "I was only curious. I did not plan on doing anything about it."

Blakley broke the tension as he burst out into laughter. His voice trembled as he stuttered out the words. "Good G—God man, is that supposed to be your innocent l—look."

Tess chuckled. "Not good, eh? Fine, just tell me why someone would say such a thing?"

Thinking that safe enough, Thomas explained someone had seen her leaving the carriage.

"If all it takes anymore to be qualified as a loose woman is to step out of a man's carriage, every woman in the whole of England and beyond would be in that same spot."

"Why was my daughter in that carriage?" Thomas's temper was fraying, and his voice was showing the effects. He waited for Alma to burst in to calm him down as she sometimes did. She didn't come, more than likely because of the big man's presence.

"I don't recall sayin' she was."

"I know very well she was, or you would not know her well enough to be so protective, now how do you know my daughter? You will tell me, or I will—"

Tess drew himself up to his full, frightening height and stared down at him. He smiled sweetly. "Or you will...what, your grace? Take a good look at me. Just what do you have to offer as a threat that could intimidate me?"

They all looked at him closely, realizing the scars that covered his face disappeared into the collar of his shirt. How much of that big body those scars covered was a question that ran through every mind. Maxwell put his hand on his friend's chest to push him back. He knew Thomas well enough to know he would not back down, even from this giant of a man.

Tess smiled. "If there is nothing else, I shall take my leave."

Before he turned away, Marc stepped in between him and the door. "I would suggest you answer him as to how you know Alex. We already know she has at least one lover."

"Move." Tess's fists tightened at his sides as he fought his temper. Marc could see it on his face.

"Still under orders not to hurt me, are you?" Marc fought through pain and anger. He was tired of the rumors and was now convinced Alex was indeed a fallen woman, and it ripped at his very soul. There was no other explanation for her knowing the big Tess.

"That, and you are beginning to grow on me. Like mold, I suppose," his low voice growled as he clenched his fists tighter, his whole arm shook as his knuckles turned white. "The fact that I like you, nor the order given will keep me from killing someone who hurts my little master."

It took all Marc had not to back down before the look of rage, but he held his ground. "I have no intention of hurting your master."

Tess leaned closer, his blue eyes twinkling dangerously. "You already are." He shoved past Marc and out the door.

Jeremy gave a weak laugh. "If that is him liking someone, I would hate to think what would happen to the one he loathes."

෧෨෧

A carriage was heard in the drive of Clifton house later that night. Knowing the first arrivals would be the Hollisters, the entire family went into the foyer to meet them.

The large oak front door was thrown open before Stuart Rodgers ever got to it. In flew an excited Alex, her gown causing Marc to nearly swallow his tongue. Its bodice and skirt were dark beige with black ruffles and seams. It was beautiful and brought her tanned skin to a glowing bronze.

Tight through the waist and pressed high in the bodice, her upthrust breasts jiggled tauntingly above it, perfectly framed by the high collar that swooped up from the low cut square neckline. He knew that dress style. He had indeed picked it out for Malacinda. There had been slight changes, but he knew she had worn it purposefully to torment him again. She was even dressing the part of a whore now. The anger he had been fighting all day was beginning to swell.

She raced past them all, unaware of her family calmly following in her wake. She pulled Ashlee Clifton off to the side and began excitingly recounting what had happened at the track. How good Marylee had done and especially what Spencer was wearing.

Thomas walked over to stand beside Marc, ignoring the black look on his face. "What has gotten into her?"

Not me, Marc thought angrily. He started guiltily and hoped he had not spoken aloud. When her father only looked at him, he relaxed slightly. "I do not know, but she is sure excited about something."

By the time the guests had arrived and had been greeted, he had himself well in control and was now standing beside Janice, who clung insipidly to his arm, as he watched the dancers.

Marc had asked Janice to accompany him to the floor twice. Both times she had declined. He had the feeling she didn't like to dance with him. It had changed ever since her talk with Alex. Janice seemed scared of him now, and that included dancing with him.

Janice pressed herself closer to Marc, her arm linked through his.

When she smiled up at him, she realized with annoyance that he was not even looking at her. He was looking at his sister.

Marc was blessedly unaware of the woman on his left arm. His attention was at his right, his youngest sibling. Ashlee was beautiful in her pale green taffeta gown. Looking down at her, his brow furrowed as he followed her gaze. She was discreetly watching Bradley Hamilton, the Count of Reagin. Seeing him shyly return the look, Marc decided he had mistaken the man's interest in the beautiful Alex. Well, Bradley would make a fine husband for his little sister, if only Marc could get her mind off that powder puff Moore.

If only he could—his thoughts came to a crashing halt as a firm, yet supple form pressed against him, the smells of lilacs and roses telling him, in the unsettling tightening in his groin, whose hip and shoulder brushed intimately against him.

Her excited whispers forced him to acknowledge her. Looking down at them, he was in time to see his sister's eyes widen as she looked around him. "Oh my. You were right." She fought a laugh. "He looks ridiculous in that costume."

"He looks ridiculous? Look behind him."

Ashlee's eyes widened even farther as she took a good look at Moore. Not wanting Spencer to outdo him, he had added even more silks, lace, and ruffles. "You were right. A petticoat would have been easier." She smothered a laugh, ignoring her father's censorious glare, the subtle shake of his head that told the girls they were once again being impertinent.

Marc's scowl darkened with a murderous look as Spencer made a straight line for them. Automatically, Marc stepped forward, leaning until his shoulder was in front of Alex in a protective stance. With a flourish of flipping sleeves and billowing lace, Spencer performed a flamboyant bow over Alex's hand, while Philip did the same to Ashlee. "My lady,"

Lord, Alex thought with a grin, *the voice is getting worse.*

"May I have the pleasure of a dance?"

"Spencer." Her voice cracked with laughter. "Why are you dressed like that?"

"A beautiful woman was heard to say I could take some lessons."

He raised a mocking brow at Marc, who only sidled closer to Alex, dragging Janice along when she refused to relax her grip on his arm. He feared he would permanently have her finger marks grooved in his now crushed evening jacket.

"Now, you did not answer me, my dear. Dance?"

"He should not have said anything and, no, I cannot dance with you dressed like that." She couldn't, she would laugh so hard she would fall.

"You danced with Philip."

"That was different." She tried now not to let the smile burst forth.

"Yes, indeed my good man. I am much better looking than you," Philip Moore said as he led Ashlee off to the dance floor.

Spencer gave her a wicked grin as he turned to the red-faced man who now practically stood on top of her in a decidedly possessive gesture. "I saw you, my lord, doing a fine rendering of my bow, but I would be glad to show you where you went wrong. First, you must flick your wrists to flip your cuffs—"

Marc's vein pulsed in his neck as he clenched his jaws. His fists came up as he tried to step forward only to be stopped by Alex's small hand and the alarmed look in her ice blue eyes. He held her gaze, her soft smile was nearly his undoing, until he remembered she was just saving her lover. He jerked his arm from her beneath her fingers.

Her small smile disappeared as she pushed past him taking Spencer's arm, but to her horror, Spencer was not done. He continued instructing the enraged man as if nothing had happened. Jerking on his immobile arm, she hissed at him, finally making his words stop.

"Are you stupid? Would you poke at an angry bear?"

"If I thought it would bring me some enjoyment." He winked at Marc, completely ignoring Jeremy as he stepped in front of his infuriated friend to keep him from pummeling the fop. Ferguson led a gasping Alex to the floor and, while everyone was watching to see what Marc would do next, he slipped out into the garden with her.

"I wanted to tell you how proud I was today. Your little filly surpassed anything I ever thought she would. It was amazing—"

Before she knew what was happening, he was gone.

Leaning her head back against the rock wall that surrounded the garden, she sighed. What was she going to do? Things were getting out of hand. She would tell everyone to back off. It was not fair to Marc, nor to her. Every time she saw Marc, she loved him more, and she missed him so much.

The easy relationship they had once shared was now lost to her forever.

The life she had secretly hoped would be hers someday, that he would be hers, would never come about. Those were hopes she had refused to admit to herself when she was younger, and now they were hopes that she had to abandon, for it would never happen.

She started when she heard footsteps approaching. Looking up to Marc's enraged face instead of Spencer's lightly powdered one surprised her. "My Lord, what are you—"

Marc didn't give her a chance to finish. He had had enough of being interrupted and since he was sure she was no longer chaste, he planned to take her quickly. He brought her painfully into his embrace, his lips crushing hers as he jerked at her skirts. His fingers dug deeply into her arm as he pulled her closer.

Alex could feel the power and the passion in his kiss. She could also feel the anger. She was worried but was not scared. She knew he would not force himself upon her if she wasn't willing, but she could not see herself adamantly refusing him if he insisted.

Marc was surprised by her response to him. What's more, it built on his anger. It convinced him that he was right to doubt her feelings for him. He was not the type of man to take advantage of a woman's love, but she did not love him. She was using him the same way she used her other lovers.

His kisses and hands became more aggressive, but not painful, at least not yet. It was so unlike the other occasions Alex was able to keep her head and pull away. "We cannot—do this."

"Why? You have not told me no before." His hands fumbled with his breeches trying to hold her skirts up and free himself at the same time.

She struggled against him. "I know you, you are honorable. If you take me, you will feel obliged to marry me. I do not want you to be forced to do anything."

"You are right," he said. She felt the first tendrils of doubt as his words hissed across her lips. "If I took your maidenhead, I would, but since we both know you have lost that long ago, I will not feel so obliged. My honor will not be offended."

"I think we—" Alex jerked her head away from him and began to struggle. "What did you say? How dare you?" He tried to kiss her again, but she fought him. "Stop, you are hurting me."

Before Marc could step away, he was torn from her. Spinning to see the seething features of Alex's lover, all Marc's anger burst forth. Swinging at him, he caught Spencer under the chin with a full blow, following it with an uppercut to the abdomen. His fists met with a strength and power he had not expected from a sop. He had thought the man all softness and fluff, but his best hits had barely staggered the man.

Before Spencer could get to him, Alex was between them. "Stop it, now."

Spencer was the first to back down. Not trusting himself to speak, he just shoved her toward the library door before disappearing into the ballroom.

The first sight Marc saw was Spencer in a small group, the same one he had been in the night before. Spencer was surrounded by Porter, Connelly, and Michael Cranston. Ferguson caught and held Marc's murderous look with one of his own.

"Marc, have you seen Alex?" Thomas had seen Marc go out and was hoping he had seen her in the gardens, which would be preferable to her sneaking off again.

He struggled to contain his ragged breathing. "She was upset. She went to the library."

"Upset? Should I go see to her?" Thomas's brow furrowed as he looked at the library door.

"No, that will not be necessary. Here she comes now."

"Upset? My dear boy, that I think is an understatement of some proportions. She is livid, I am not sure I have ever seen her looking so enraged."

Marc had not either, and he could not get over what a glorious woman she was even when angry.

Chapter 15

Marc rode, straight and stiff, upon the back of his black mare Isabel, looking very much like the duke he would someday become. At his side, on a peaceful gray palfrey, looking the part of a proper soon-to-be duchess, was Lady Janice Rutmeyer. He could see the picture that they presented to the ton. A gentleman with the perfect catch, a woman of grace, breeding, and high society standing.

He knew what they saw, and it was exactly what he wanted. Mostly.

They had left the Rutmeyer residence less than twenty minutes ago, and he was already at the end of his patience with her, and her puling ways.

It had been everything—nothing was good enough. Starting with the fact he had not brought a carriage. She had not been prepared to ride and, for this lapse in his judgment, he had waited well over an hour for her to change. He learned quickly, not from her words, but from her tone and her stance that she did not care to ride.

This was a disappointment, but it was one he kept to himself with a smile and a nod.

He enjoyed his morning rides, and he loved his horses. He knew very few women who enjoyed a good ride. Oh, they would all do the smooth walks in the park, but few liked to actually ride.

His mind automatically replayed the ease in which Alex had pushed her brother's horse into a gallop to catch his sister. The instructions she had screamed to the terrified Ashlee echoed through his mind and drew forth another image. One that he looked back on with a different set of eyes.

The morning she had outrun Lord Manning appeared in a different light, now that the numbing fear at the thought of her bleeding was no longer blinding him.

She may have not had full control of the massive stallion by the end of the run, but by the lather that had covered both her mount as well as Manning's, the ride had not been a short one.

She must have more ability in her seat than he gave her credit for. In order to stay atop an unsaddled mount for any amount of time, especially at that speed, meant she had to be more than just a little competent.

"Are you listening?"

Janice's voice grated against him, bringing him back to the present and the very unpleasant ride.

"I am sorry, my lady, please forgive me, the beauty of the morning swept me away momentarily, but I am back now." He smiled sweetly, or at least as sweetly as he could muster.

She rolled her eyes. "How far do we have to ride before we can return?"

"Any time you want to return, I will take you home." *I told you that already* were words he barely caught hold of before they could escape. This had been the third time she had posed that question. He waited for the other complaints to continue, the ones she had rambled on and on about ever since they had reached Hyde Park.

The air was too cold, the morning too foggy, the wind too strong, the mount too rough, the ride too long and too fast, even though he could get off and walk faster. Something in his tone or his expression must have spoken of his growing anger because none of those complaints came.

He looked over at her and cringed as she sidled up to him with a smile, running her hand down his arm, leaning into him until she almost fell from her saddle. He had to reach out and steady her. "I am sorry. I usually like my rides more. I guess I am just out of sorts today. I am beginning to get anxious about the upcoming announcement. It is getting close, and I was thinking we could…"

He waited in the silence and, when she didn't continue, he reluctantly asked. "We could what, my lady?"

"Tonight is my family ball. I believe it would be a good time to announce our intentions." She had seen the way he acted around the little chit she was truly beginning to hate, and though she didn't want him, she found she didn't want Alex to have him either. She really did not want to marry this man, but if she could get him under some semblance of control, she could manage. He was too scary, too big, too strong, but the sooner she could get him tamed the better.

She had never been one with a strong stomach. She was weak and a coward. She knew this and had no inclination to change it. Her only defense against this very virile and amorous man were threats to his reputation, but she was afraid they would not work for long once they were married.

They would be enough to get him married, but may not be enough to control him.

"Announce our intentions? Is that what you really want?"

It was not what she wanted. Her father was well aware of the undercurrents of emotions when it came to the redheaded hoyden. He wanted to get Marc committed to her, and once Marc revealed his intent to his peers he would not back out. No, Marcus Reyes Clifton was a man of honor.

Janice found herself more than a little reluctant, but as her father had pointed out many times in the last weeks, if Marc didn't go through with the wedding, the Rutmeyer family would be ruined. Her father would go to debtor's prison, and that was not something she could stand by and allow to happen. So she looked at Marc and mustered a smile. "It is what I want."

Taking a deep breath, Marc nodded. "Let us return to the house to inform your family of the plans, and I can announce it to mine when I arrive back home."

They rode in silence, and neither spoke until they were in the Rutmeyer library.

"My father will be home soon, the family went to the shops. I thought this a good time for us to get to know each other and what is expected from this arrangement." Taking a deep breath, Janice kept her gaze on a deeply frayed carpet. She released her breath and the words tumbled quickly from numb lips. "There will be three children, two boys and a girl. At that point the...physical—" She swallowed hard. "—relationship will end. There will be no...lurid and vulgar scenes. The lights will always be off, and you must touch me as little as possible. I cannot help your insatiable amorous needs, but I am not some street trollop."

Marc wondered, quite annoyed at this point, what she was talking about. He did indeed enjoy his mistress, and he was never long in between visits, at least not until the last ten months, but he was not the sexual deviant she seemed to think he was. My God, he had been celibate for almost a year now. He opened his mouth, but she did not allow time for comment.

"There will also be no more mistresses. I will not be made a fool of." He thought she tried to sound in charge, but she just sounded like a spoiled child. His anger was starting to build.

"So I am not to have a mistress, but I am not to have you either. Is that how it will work?"

At her nod, he reached for her and dragged her roughly against him. Her body was soft and supple. The slight curving of her hip flared from a thin waist, but she lacked the lean, lithe essence that spoke of health and activity, a body such as—he forced his mind to stay on the woman in his arms, and not the one who captured his thoughts.

She struggled against him. "What are you doing? You cannot do this."

"I think we should go over what I want out of this marriage. I do not know that I want to give up this body after our three children."

He grasped the back of her neck, kissing her roughly. There was no response whatsoever in her cold lips as she continued to struggle against him.

No thawing on her part and, to his annoyance, no response on his part either. He broke away and put several steps in between them.

"How dare you? You cannot treat me like some…some prostitute. If you expect me to respond to this kind of torture after we are married, you are sadly mistaken. This betrothal is based on you doing what I—"

"There may not be a betrothal." His angry voice boomed across the silent library before he could stop it. He turned to leave—hopefully, before he said something to permanently damage his future.

A trembling hand stopped him. "Please, I am sorry. I did not mean it. You can take me, Marcus." She suddenly wrapped her arms around his neck and yanked his lips to hers.

In her clumsy, and unconvincing, attempt at seduction, she managed to knock their heads and teeth together. Marc tried to reach for support, for anything to keep them upright, but he failed. They fell to the settee. Breath whooshed from her as he landed atop her, but to her credit she didn't fight. Her hands slipped away from him.

He deepened the kiss, determined now to keep it gentle. "Open your mouth."

She did. There was still no response as she lay lifeless beneath him, her hands clasped to the soft material of the small couch. She was not a participant, but willing enough to lay there and take what he gave.

His hands roamed her body, caressed her breasts, her waist, her face. She trembled as his hand slid beneath the bodice of her gown, her fingers tightened on the couch. She lay stiff beneath him, but, unfortunately, she was the only thing that was.

Marc still felt nothing, but if he was going to marry her, he would have to become accustomed to it, or children—three or otherwise—would never be a possibility.

He told himself that the lack of response on his part was just in response to her own coldness. He forced away the image of the night in the garden with Rosalind where her unabashed responses had brought nothing to him either.

Trailing kisses down her neck, his lips met with the small nipple he had uncovered. He would bring some response to her if nothing else.

"Can you not just do it and get it over with?"

Her words chilled his blood, showing him beyond any doubt what he could expect in the marriage bed for the rest of his life.

c/ɔc/ɔ

"I came to offer you a position." Alex smiled at the surprise that lit Malacinda's face. "You cannot tell anyone about this, though. You can tell them you are going to work for A.H. but not who the jockey is."

Malacinda looked confused, but agreed, as she took a seat, motioning for her unexpected guest to do the same.

Alex grinned and sat prim and proper on the offered chair. She waited a moment, smoothed her skirts.

"Are you going to leave me waiting all day?"

Alex smiled at the impatience in her friend's voice. "A.H. stands for…Alexis Hollister."

"You are the jockey I hear so much about?" Malacinda clapped her hands and laughed. "That is perfect. I know how you love horses."

Alex shook her head and laughed. "Only you would not even bat an eyelash at that announcement."

"Oh, my love, after all the years we have known each other, and all the shocks you have put me through, it will take more than that to surprise me."

Alex relaxed against the back of the chair and grinned.

Malacinda rose and walked to the wine decanter on the side table. She offered a glass, but Alex shook her head. "Now, what is the position you are speaking of?" Malacinda asked.

"I want you to come and work for me. I have just purchased Linden Manor in Barnet. I would like for you to be the housekeeper. You can keep your day maid and your cook, who if she is willing will cook for the entire house, with a staff. I will hire anyone she needs. You will not have to clean and cook and things like that, that is not what I am offering at all. What I want—what I need, is someone I trust to run things. Make sure the household runs smoothly and I will hire anyone you feel needs to be hired."

"You are willing to do that for me, even though you know what I am? What I do?"

Alex went to her, drawing her into her arms, as tears started. "I love you, and I would do anything for you. As for what you do, I want that to be in your past. I know what you did for me. I also know you tried to talk to me about it several times. I am sorry I did not listen. You should not have risked your place with—him—not for me." Alex ignored the tear that slipped down her cheek.

Half an hour later, Malacinda and Alex stood at the door. It was all settled. Malacinda and her servants would begin packing today and, within two days, Tess would be around to collect them. They would be set up in Linden Manor. It would be just them for the time being, until the end of the season and all was revealed.

"Are you sure about this, my lady?" Malacinda asked. "What if I cannot do it?"

"You have run this house for quite some time. Just decide on what is needed at Linden and let me know. Now, remember what I said about Tess. He is not as he looks. He is a sweet man. I already have a butler and a footman, though they are not in residence yet. Whatever other staff is needed, just let me know. I will send Tess out to check on you every day, if you need anything in the meantime, just come get me."

Robert helped Alex into the carriage, she turned to bestow a beautiful smile on Malacinda.

"I will be fine there. Just go before you get into any more trouble. Your secret is safe with me."

Miss St. Johns had been in her home packing for no more than fifteen minutes when the door was pounded upon once again. Melissa Mayes led an irate lord into the drawing room.

"Get out now." His words were harsh, but his tone was quiet and the smile he gave to the plump day maid was kind. She bowed gracefully and didn't argue.

"Lord Clifton. Are you all right?" Wrapping an arm around him, she led him to the big four-poster bed. His face was ashen and dark circles rested beneath his troubled eyes. "What has happened?"

He allowed her to push him to the bed. "I saw the future."

She left his side only long enough to bring him some sweet wine. "Drink this."

He took the glass and drank, not knowing what it was and not caring. "I came here to take you, to make you lay with me." His hand snaked beneath her silk dressing gown gripping a full breast. He closed his eyes and, much to his dismay, Malacinda didn't pull away. He could feel her watching him as his hand gently kneaded the warm flesh.

Closing his eyes had been a mistake, as images of Alex swam behind his close lids, tormenting him. Jerking his hand away, he lunged to his feet. "I cannot do this. You have to go. I have to find a new mistress since you are unwilling to lay with me. If you need time, I will give you what you need as long as it is reasonable."

"That is not necessary. I will be gone in two days' time." She turned back to her packing.

"Two days—you are already packing. Where do you think to go?"

Dropping heavily to the bed he stared at her. This day was getting worse and worse. He had not come to ask her to leave, nor had he really come to bed her. He had come to talk. He needed to tell someone about his problems, but now that he was here he just couldn't bring himself to do so.

"I am going to Linden Manor, I will work for—"

"A.H. You met him?" His booming voice echoed across the room as he once more lunged to his feet, making her jump, swinging around to face him. The negative shake of her head didn't register to his swirling mind. "You are going to be his whore."

"No. I am going to be his housekeeper. He is not interested in me in that way." She tried to keep the worry from her voice as Marc paced the entire length of her bed chamber. "I am no longer to be a mistress. It is a good position."

"That bastard. He cannot do this to me." He seemed to be talking more to himself than to her, she wondered if he even remembered she was in the room. "He cannot satisfy himself with tormenting me with looks and gestures, with stealing Linden out from under me, now he takes my mistress as well as the woman I—" His feet stopped, his breath hitched at the word he had almost said, and for a moment, the room went black. He staggered, the anger within him swelling. "No!"

"Marc?"

He turned and ran from the room.

Throwing himself into his carriage, he pounded on the top. When his driver asked where to, he just cursed at him. The driver clicked the reins over the beautifully matched steeds and just let them take the roads as they would. When his master got control of himself, he would give the instructions, until then he would let the rocking of the carriage soothe him. It wouldn't be the first time.

Lying back across the seat, Marc pulled his legs up, bracing them against the wall of the conveyance, and stared up at the ceiling. What had been about to say. *The woman he loved*—that would have been disastrous. That was not possible. He could admit that he cared for Alex, but love. No, he would know if he was in love. Everyone he knew seemed to be well aware when they were in love. And what if he was?

Could he love a woman who was working with three lovers—two? He was sure, no matter what he had blurted out in Malacinda's chambers, that the jockey was not Alex's lover. Tess had been convincing in his arguments on that case, and Marc believed him. He also believed A.H. thought himself a friend and would see that as a betrayal.

How his clouded mind came to that conclusion, Marc could not fathom, but he could not dislodge the surety of the notion.

Then how to explain taking his mistress? If Alex had told the jockey Marc was no longer intimate with her, perhaps he was trying to help her. Give her an honorable position, after all? That would be a better thought.

Of course, where she was going would be an issue. How would Janice react to having his prior mistress in the property next to theirs? It would be bad enough for him to be living next to Alex and her family.

Without getting up, he kicked his booted foot into the carriage ceiling, yelling his directions at the startled driver.

He had lost his bet with Jeremy at the track and now had to escort Alex to his future wife's home. What had he been thinking? He would not do that. First Janice was going to hit the ceiling if Alex walked through the door with him, second...well, second, was the rage he had seen in Alex's beautiful face.

Alex was not one to get over things easily. She was just like her father. And like him, she could hold on to anger for years, perhaps forever.

Lost in self-absorbed misery, he didn't notice the wheels had stopped, nor did he take into account when the door opened.

"Marc?"

Leaning his head back, he looked at the upside down image of Jeremy. "Shut the hell up."

"I did not say a word. I would like to, but with that look in your eyes, I shall control my wayward tongue." Jeremy could not stop the laughter as Marc regained his composure and landed in the dirt at his feet.

"If you could control that wayward laughter, it would be appreciated as well." Marc's dark scowl and rough growl only brought peals of laughter, ones that doubled Jeremy over. Marc gave him one hard shove and, to his dismay, the laughter continued even from the ground.

By the time Jeremy had control of himself, Marc's spirits were lifting. "I am here to fulfill my deal. Where is that *wayward* sister of yours?" He offered his hand to Jeremy, but faltered when the laughter started again. "Hell and damnation, that better not mean she is not here."

"No, she is not. She went for a ride with Spencer this morning, but after he brought her home, she disappeared with Robert in the carriage before anyone could stop her. But I wish you well in your search and can honestly say I am glad it is you and not I."

Without a word, Marc returned to his carriage. He tried to ignore the laughter that followed the carriage as the wheels rattled against the cobblestones.

"Where the hell could she be?"

She would not still be with Spencer. That would be too easy. She was not at Malacinda's. He was just there. Where else would she be? Where had he seen her lately?

In Hyde Park? No, he was just there.

With March? No, he had seen March disappearing into his office.

His mind went back to Malacinda. He remembered for the first time her admission she had not met the jockey. If she had not met him, than how did she accept—Alex? She didn't need to tell A.H. the details, just to tell him she knew someone. She would take care of the rest.

If she had gone to Malacinda's and was no longer there, where would she go?

His mind began to spin, and his breathing became ragged. Where? Chariton House, it was close, and Alex would no longer be worried about being seen there, not since the ton apparently were behind her charity work.

It took no time before he was ushered into Chariton House by a young girl, no more than ten. "I am looking for Lady Alex Hollister, is she here perhaps? She is my…"

What exactly was he going to say? His friend? That didn't sound right to him and, though he wanted her friendship, it was not all he wanted. He could no longer deny that he wanted her.

"Yours? Yes, Lady Alex is here. She brought Becca to come and visit with us again."

"You know Rebecca?" He allowed the clean and smiling child to take his hand, leading him to the rear of the house. Looking around, he could see the effects of money. He had only been in one orphanage, and it was nothing like this. It had been more of a work house, which he was sure was the way of most of them. This one had the look of a home. Someone had spent a great amount of money on it, and he smiled, knowing who it was. Alex may not spend much of her allowance, but he could see the results of what she did spend.

"Yes, I know Becca." The sweet angelic voice tugged at him. "She used to live with us."

That brought him up short. "Truly?"

Her blonde curls bobbed as she nodded.

"What is your name, sweet?"

"Heather. What's yours?" Her big blue eyes sparkled at him, and he could not resist picking her up.

"Marc." He was going to say more but he could not. Before him was Alex. She sat in the center of eleven children, Rebecca at her side. She was just beginning a story. Her soft voice caressed him, and he smiled. What else would he have learned about her last season had he not been so pigheaded and avoided her? He could have helped her with this.

One small boy, three or four perhaps, crawled across the floor and into Alex's lap. She paused in her story long enough to pull him closer and kiss the top of his carrot orange hair. "My little Irish man," she whispered before continuing with the fairy tale of the lost princess whose true love came to her rescue.

Her words ground to a halt, and her eyes widened when she saw Marc standing at the door. His smile widened. He took a seat on the benches that ringed the small room, sitting beside a startled Robert and smiling a greeting to whom he could only assume was Vanessa Chariton herself.

Everyone was staring at him. Heather saved him as she relaxed in his arms. "This is Marc. Lady Alex is his."

His startled look took in Heather then Alex's raised brows. He just blushed, shaking his head. "That is not exactly what I said." But he realized it was close since he had not finished his sentence. "I do not want to interrupt the story. I had not wanted to distract you."

Alex gave an indelicate snort, telling him he had not succeeded. He knew he distracted her. It tugged at his conscious, building on his guilt. Whether she had two lovers or two dozen, she cared for him.

He could see it in her eyes. Had she had the lovers before she knew he was lost to her, or had it been just lately? Had he driven her to another's arms? It didn't matter. She would never be his, and he could never trust a woman who had a lover.

Taking a deep breath, she began the story where she had left off. Her voice was strained now, but soon it smoothed out as her composure returned.

Her eyes kept going to Marc, sitting so silent, just listening to her. There was something different about him. A sense of loss and defeat that she had never sensed in him before. He looked at her with regret and pain. She could not help but wonder what had happened.

She wanted to ask him, wanted to let him know she would always be there for him, like she always had been, but she knew better. Things had changed too much to return to the same natural ease that they had once enjoyed.

Marc fought the urge to go to her as the small boy wiped a tear from her pale face, saying in a soft Irish accent. "Tis just a tale, milady."

Nestling in his bright curls, she finished the story. Setting him aside she rose, striding toward Marc. "My lord?" She had no need to ask what he was doing here, or how he had found her. She knew there would be no way to miss the Rutmeyers' debauchery now. He had come to drag her home.

His lips pursed but he did not comment on her use of his title. He wanted to. He wanted to grab her and shake her until she called his name over and over.

"I have come to escort you home."

She didn't look surprised, just shook her head.

"Vanessa, this is Lord Clifton. My lord, this is Vanessa Chariton, a good friend of mine."

'My pleasure, Mrs. Chariton, and please call me Marc." Since *she* won't, he wanted to add.

The names of the children swirled around him as Alex introduced them all. They all received a warm smile and a greeting that brought tears to her throat. He was the man of her dreams. He was the man she had pictured coming to her rescue the entire time she had been telling the story. She was that lost princess, awaiting her knight to come to her aid.

She realized, as he took his place next to her in his carriage, that he had not come to rescue her from this sadness. He had instead come to feed the damsel to the dragon. Even as that thought made her chuckle, she could feel the tears stream down her face.

"Baby, please—" He reached for her hand only to have her jerk it out of his reach.

The concern in his voice had been more than she could stand. Anger gave her strength to control the tears.

Her blue eyes were cold as she turned her wet gaze at him. He withdrew his hand. "Do not pretend, my lord, that you care."

She turned back to stare out the window and stayed that way until the driver opened the door in front of her home. Stepping up first, she jumped to the ground without assistance, anything to keep him from having to touch her. His touch would turn her into a sobbing pile at his feet, begging him to love her. She fled into the house.

"Alex!" His words chased her. She slammed the door against his plea.

Alex threw herself on the garden bench and let out the tears that she had feared would come.

"Alex?" Marc's soft voice was full of regret. She didn't look up. "Please. You need to get ready for tonight. It takes time to get prepared, and you want to look your best—"

"I am not going, *my lord.*"

Her voice was tight. He could not tell if it was from anger or tears, or perhaps both.

"Yes, you are. I am going to make sure of it."

That got her on her feet to face him. "Oh, yes, my lord, we would not want to upset your little bride, now would we? We would not want to upset her with some scandal that I would not show up at her fiasco. Believe me, no one will be surprised. I will try to keep my opinions to myself, so I do not cause you any embarrassment, my lord." Her voice had steadily risen as she had advanced on him.

"It has nothing to do with me or her. It has to do with a bet. I lost a bet with Jeremy, so I have to take you."

Her face paled. The tears once more came to the surface, but she held them. "You came to get me, sat with the children, brought me back, and pretended to be concerned because of a goddammed bet. You lost, and your punishment was me—Me!"

She shoved him hard as he reached for her. He missed her as she ran from him. She collided with Jeremy as her family emerged from the house. One look into her ice blue eyes, and Jeremy backed up. He had never seen such pain.

"Me?"

Thomas grasped her arms as she entered the library. "I am sorry. It is not as you think. No one thinks you are a punishment."

His kind words were cut off as her tear-filled voice filled the room. It's quietness so startling in its unusualness that they were all silent as she talked. "No? Not a punishment? Just an embarrassment? Just an undisciplined hoyden without a wit of common sense?" She refused to cry one more tear. She fought for control as she began to struggle for freedom from her father's vice-like grip.

The three men knew to what she was referring as the scene from the library before she had left for Aunt Levita's replayed in their minds. Marc cringed, knowing those were his words she was spitting back at Thomas. They may have been his, but he could tell she was just as angry that her father had not defended her.

"My dear, you are not those things. Why would you think such a thing?" Her mother's panicked voice stilled her like nothing else could. Alex instantly stopped struggling in his tight grip.

"I do not know, Mama. I must have imagined them. Surely no one would have said them about me, at least no one from my own family." She smiled sweetly at Thomas, a smile that did not melt the ice in her gaze. "For we know they are not true, I do have some common sense." She was not about to argue with the rest. God would surely punish her for such blatant lies if she were to do so. "Now if you will release me, I would like to retire to my room."

Thomas tightened his grip. "I do not think so. You will go get ready for tonight. I already sent your maid to your room to set out your clothes and a bath. You will be going tonight."

She knew not to argue when he looked so angry and, as she opened her mouth to do so, she decided she should not have claimed any common sense, obviously she had none. "I am not going tonight, Papa. You cannot force me to do this." She tried to hold her ground as he dragged her though the house, but she was no match for his size and strength.

"You are going tonight, or you will regret it. I will not have you do this to your family."

Her eyes narrowed. "What? Embarrass you once again?" She began to truly struggle, pulling from him she bolted for the garden only to be caught once again by Marc. He wanted to let her go, but he had made a deal. He would make sure she got there.

Holding her shoulders tightly, he spun her to face her family. His grip painful, his bearing unyielding.

"Papa, you do not want to do this to me. I want to stay. It goes against my every principle to go tonight." His face remained impassive. "This is your final choice, Papa." Her brow raised in question, her head tilted to the side. "This is how you want it?"

"Yes." Even as he said the word, a knot of worry started in his uneasy stomach.

"Fine." She relaxed completely and smiled. "You can get your hands off me, my lord." Marc's grip momentarily tightened, but he released her. "I shall be in my room preparing." She gave Marc a cold grin. "Since I am your loss, I expect you will be the one to escort me up the stairs. Just do not walk too close." She walked away, her entire body shaking with rage. "I would hate for *you* to *fall*."

Catherine waved him off. "I am not sure what is going on about a bet, but I will take it from here. I do not approve of either of you using my daughter as a pawn in your gambling. I am disappointed."

Two young heads hung in shame, unable to meet her gaze.

"And you." She turned to her husband. "I do not want her making any more of a scene than she already has, but she *is* a little version of you. Do you think it would be wise for someone to force you into doing something you felt so strongly against?"

Chapter 16

Marc glanced up, and his heart stopped. Alex stepped through the drawing room door in a low cut pale blue gown covered with the same sparkling beads that adorned her upswept hair. She was exposed more now than she ever had been, and his desire and his anger suffered a painful spike.

She would be a spectacle in her dress, if nothing else. He awaited with baited breath for one of her glorious breasts to spill out of the tight laced top of her gown. He could tell from where he stood that she had donned the corset, he figured, for the first time in her life.

It made her already sculpted figure exquisite. Her head was held in pride, her smile pasted on and as false as any he had seen on the other belles of the ton. She had outdone herself.

He recognized the dress. He had ordered it for her, but he had not ordered it in its present condition. He could picture Alex now, leaning her head down to whisper to Mademoiselle Rhamninose, obviously conspiring against him as he had given his orders.

Thomas stepped forward quickly. "You are not wearing that. That is indecent. You cannot—"

His words stopped as his small and normally well-mannered wife stepped from behind his rebellious daughter. "Why not? She is well within fashion. She is no more indecent than any other woman there will be. I helped her dress." She stood proudly beside her daughter, both women standing firm in the face of the enemy.

Alex had already apologized in advance to her mother. Catherine had looked worried for only a moment then smiled. She was still concerned about the truth getting out, but her need for revenge on Janice Rutmeyer and that pompous mother of hers overruled Catherine's normal fear.

Thomas shook his head at the change that one carriage ride had brought in his wife. She herself was dressed much like her daughter, with the exception of her gown being a pale green, instead of the sky blue that so brought out her daughter's eyes.

The families knew well that when the two women—who normally fought against each other at every turn—banded together, there was nothing to stop them. Thomas didn't even try. "You are right, my love. It is just a father's love and protectiveness that caused me to speak out."

His wife melted before him, as he knew she would, but he was concerned when the ice didn't thaw in Alex's well-powdered face.

Alex was docile and meek the entire way to the carriage. Thomas Hollister was beginning to feel an uneasiness spread through him. Looking at the other men, he knew he was not the only one.

Once alone with the other men in the carriage he spoke his concerns.

"I know what you mean," Maxwell replied. "I am beginning to feel the same way. Like the tingle in the middle of your shoulders when you are expecting a knife to be embedded in your back. She gave in too easily. It is very unlike her."

Heads nodded all around.

When the families descended the carriages and began to pair up to enter the ball, Alex stepped out of line and took her father's hand. She took it because he was the one who had upset her the most. He refused to defend her, refused to listen to what she wanted. He refused to allow her to have some say over her own life, and he had called her an embarrassment one too many times.

Up until this point, she had tried to remain in the eye of society, in the good graces of the elite. Everything she had done had been to the same end. Her future. She had never done anything that should have embarrassed anyone. They should be proud of her. They would see how well she *had* behaved. He thought she was an embarrassment. "So I will be," she whispered.

Thomas glanced at her, but then they were announced, every eye on them to see if they had managed to convince their rogue daughter to attend.

Thomas knew he had made a mistake when he saw the disappointment riddled on nearly every face in the crowd. They had secretly cheered her. No one having the courage to stand up to the Rutmeyers and their underhanded ways, they had lived vicariously through her. His regret died when the faces changed, grins fighting to break out. He realized his docile escort had dropped back and was now digging in her heals and struggling, making it clear to everyone that she had been forcibly dragged there.

When he saw the knowing looks on the ton, he groaned. "Dammit, Alex. That is enough," he whispered to her.

She jerked from his arm. "That is just the very beginning."

Striding out of his reach, she marched like a soldier going into battle, right past the receiving line and not giving so much as a glance at the enraged Rutmeyers.

"Hollister, if that is the way she is going to behave, it would have been better to have left her at home." Samuel was almost purple with embarrassment. "She has flaunted herself around this town too often. It will not be long till the rumors catch up with her."

The threat was too obvious to miss.

Bowing low to his host, Thomas tried to be nonchalant on his way to Alex, who now sat at the edge of the room, alone. Bowing in front of her, he motioned to the floor. "May I have this dance, my dear?"

She could hear the anger in his trembling voice. "Only if you want to drag me out there." She could not meet his eyes. She wanted nothing more than to dance with him. To make everything all right, but she had a feeling nothing would ever be all right again.

"I thought you would always want another dance with me?" His words were not regretful, they were filled with annoyance.

She met his eyes, tears sparkling in her own. "I would not want you to have to dance with an embarrassment."

He could see the hurt in her eyes. He had not realized his words had cut her as deeply as they had. "Do not do this. You have not been an embarrassment. I—"

"You are right. I have not been. What I am, you do not know, because you care more for your reputation than you do for me. I do not care what any of these people think of me. I only cared what you and the family thought of me. I thought you cared for me. I thought Marc—I was wrong. The only ones who care about me are the ones who care about me when I am myself. You only want me to be what you want me to be, not what I am. So, no, I have not been an embarrassment, so far. I have tried to keep myself in check, but since you and everyone else I love thinks so poorly of me…well, why should I try anymore? I will not dance, I will not eat, and I will not socialize. You can force me to be here, but you cannot force me to act the dim-witted socialite."

Her voice had started to rise, and she was drawing more attention than he wanted.

"You will not do this to me. If this is the way you want to act, I would suggest you prepare for the consequences."

He stormed off, leaving her to consider his words. A cold smile spread across her face. She knew the consequences of this rebellion only too well. She was risking everything she had worked for.

She had lied, though. There was one man she would dance with, but he would never ask her. Not at the party of his beloved. She stood from her seat to make sure everyone saw her. She smiled benignly and awaited her first offer to dance. It came quickly, and it was not the last. The men came, one after another, all trying to be the one to get her on the floor.

Janice, from what Alex could tell, was getting angrier and angrier. After Alex had turned away the first, there was no end to them. She knew the effects of a challenge and, despite her promise not to socialize, she was soon surrounded by men. Janice was being ignored for the first time in her life.

Marc was enraged as her laugh floated across the sea of men.

"Do something to stop this." Janice pulled on his arm and Marc was afraid she would soon be in hysterics.

"What would you have me do, my lady?" Marc had some thoughts of his own, but they all ended with bloody and battered men strewn across the floor and him disappearing with Alex lying across his shoulder.

"Go dance with her. I know her. She will not turn you down." He looked at her in shock. "I only want you to dance with her once. Then she will have no reason to turn down the others, then they will leave her alone."

"And flock around you as normal." His voice was tired and defeated, not angry.

A big man with a wide smile sidled up next to Alex, pulling her away from her admirers. "My dear. Can I speak to you quickly?" His dark brown hair was pulled back in a brown ribbon, and his brown eyes sparkled with merriment.

"Of course, Captain." Baron Jamas Levees spent the first thirty years of his adult life as the captain of the *Miss Hannah* and those who knew him well still referred to him as such.

"I see your man coming toward you. I think Miss Rutmeyer wants to put an end to your mutiny." His smile never wavered.

"What can you tell me of mutiny, Captain?" She leaned closer to him as she whispered for his ears only.

The other men had backed away for the captain to have a private talk with her.

"If you want to pull this off, I would suggest one dance. It has to be with the one who will cause the most commotion. The Rutmeyers deserve every scandal they get. Every time they turn around, they are carelessly slandering someone. Everyone is afraid of what they can do. Here he comes. Everyone will expect you to dance with him, but look at the door." Captain Jamas slipped away.

Her eyes widened as Marc approached. He pushed his way through the crowd. "May I have this dance, my lady?"

"My Lord, I do not think so. Thank you for the kind offer, my lord." Her smile never faulted even though he could see the pain in her eyes. "I would not want to put you out or offend your sense of honor."

His eyes widened.

"I do not think with two lovers—" His voice caressed her face as he almost silently whispered the words. "—that you should expect me not to be offended. How is someone to marry you now?"

He had not realized anyone had approached, nor was he aware anyone could hear his soft, angry words. A responding whisper right in his ear told him otherwise.

"And since you are a chaste virgin, you would have the right to condemn?"

Marc spun on the man, drawing his hands up to push the man back until he realized who it was. Then only the pain and anger swirling through his every nerve stopped him from pummeling the man.

"Excuse me, but if you are through insulting the lady, I would like to ask her to dance. Shall we, my lady?"

The pain was so deep in his chest when the infuriating man offered Alex his arm that Marc could not breathe, let alone move. He hid it behind a mask of anger.

The look on Marc's face was one of pure outrage. It was good revenge. She was getting tired of his high-handed ways. He was so concerned he might shock or discomfit his beloved Janice or his precious reputation. Why could he not just be upset because she was dancing with someone else? She had given up on the fact that he was beginning to care for her. Any hopes she had had of that happening had been destroyed when he had accosted her in the garden.

Looking back on it, she should have let him take her, then he would know how wrong he was, but that would put her in the position she didn't want, a forced marriage. Slipping her hand through Edward Barlow's extended arm, she let her troubles slip away. This was the best man to dance with for the mutiny to be complete, and she didn't know how it could get better.

But she soon would.

The music started, and Edward spun her around.

"What are you doing here, Edward?"

"I heard someone was complaining that I never accept invitations, so when it came to my attention that you needed rescuing, I thought I would at least steal one dance with you beforehand." His eyes slid to her mother, but Catherine refused to look up. Her face was white. She needn't worry, with everyone thinking he was her daughter's lover, her secret was safe.

"What do you mean rescue?" Alex shook her head. "I am confused."

"Spencer informed me that when you two went for your ride this morning, you were concerned you would not be able to attend the card game at Rose Hall tonight. I was told that if you didn't show up, that you might need to be rescued."

He tore his eyes away from the woman he still cared for, but he had long since known her heart belonged to no one but Thomas. He looked down at the woman he was proud to call his daughter.

Alex grinned. This was perfect. Oh, this was the perfect mutiny. "What do I do?"

"Do you see Michael and Craig over there by the front of the hall?" She nodded. "When they distract everyone—" He inclined his head to the two men as he danced her close to the veranda doors. "—you will go straight to the back gate, where Spencer is waiting for you with two horses." As the men in question started to argue, their fighting starting to get physical, Edward frowned. "Can you ride in that outfit?"

All heads were turned to the now overpowering ruckus the two men were creating. Alex slid from Edward's grasp. "I can ride in anything." With that, she was gone.

Edward pushed his way noisily through the men to make sure he was seen. She would already be on her horse and on her way by now. "Stop it, stop it. I let you convince me to come to this ball, and this is the way you reward me, by embarrassing me. Let's go." He shoved both men toward the door before bowing low in front of Lady Beatrice Rutmeyer.

He gave his most charmingly rakish grin, eyebrows cocked as he swept up her hand. His eyes grazed her impertinently, even as he rolled the wrist of her glove down with his thumb, exposing the thrumming vein beneath it. He placed a warm, improper kiss on that pulsing spot. He smiled against her cool skin as she let out a soft moan. Looking up, he didn't let her break eye contact. He reveled in her response to him.

She may be over her prime and out of shape but there was a woman of passion buried in there.

Her face flushed and she smiled shyly. He wondered if she had ever been loved properly. "I am sorry, my love, that I am unable to stay, I was looking forward to dancing with you." He gave a mocking bow to her husband, daring him to make a challenge.

Rutmeyer wisely kept his tongue. When Edward turned to follow the two now contrite men he was stopped by five large bodies. Maxwell, Marc, Jeremy, Blake, and Thomas, all staring with menace at him.

"Where is my daughter?" Thomas asked.

"I left her—" Edward stopped as his hand swept a now empty spot. "I left her by the garden doors with an apology when the fight started. Now if you will excuse me, I need to take those two boys home. I never should have let them talk me into coming."

He didn't even look at Catherine as he walked past, but he was aware she was looking at him. With a smile? Was she aware of what her daughter had done?

"Oh, Thomas. You must go look in the garden." She stepped in between Thomas and the retreating Edward. "You must do so now before she can get far."

The five men disappeared into the garden. Catherine flicked Edward a look of mischief, which left no doubt she was aware of her daughter's dissension, before disappearing after her husband.

Edward realized he had no regrets when it came to her. No, he would not have been a good husband. He cared for her, but it was not love. He didn't think he had ever experienced a true love. Not like the one he knew Thomas and she shared.

☙❧☙

Slipping into the rear entrance of Rose Hall Alex allowed herself to breathe a sigh of relief. They had made it undetected.

"Alex, look at you," Victoria said. Spencer helped Alex out of his cloak as Victoria came to retrieve it. "You look amazing. Just beautiful."

"Thank you, Victoria." Alex took her seat to await the other three men who would be along with enough time in between not to draw suspicion to themselves. Ha, like that was going to happen. "Gideon. How are you tonight?"

"I would be better if a certain girl I cared about would use her head. The only reason they came to rescue you was they were sure you were going to do something rash." He took a seat next to her.

Victoria set a brandy in front Alex and stepped away from the table. Several brandies later, Alex was well relaxed and smiling when her knights of rescue came in.

"Thank you, gentlemen. I truly appreciate it. They will think twice before making me go into that house once again. I may have had a setback, but I do believe I shall still win the war."

The third hand of cards had just begun when a loud commotion was heard outside the interior door. Finch's handsome face appeared for just a moment with a gesture to Edward. "Five men."

In spite of herself, she grinned, this was an unexpected bonus. Not only had she deserted, but so had her men. Including Marc. She wondered if the surprise announcement the Rutmeyers had hinted to was regarding the betrothal. She had thought it might be. She laughed softly.

"Take her home, Spencer. Get her out of here." Edward waited until they had disappeared out the back, before leading the rest of the men into the front gaming area.

Edward was all business as he approached the man. "Can I help you, Hollister?"

"What have you done with my daughter?"

Edward smiled when the words came so easily to him. He was not upset, because no matter what, even though he loved her dearly, she was indeed Hollister's daughter. He saw it every time her temper flared and her dignity was challenged.

"Your daughter is not here?"

Thomas could detect no sarcasm in his words. He also knew he was a man of his word.

"Where is she?" He fought the urge to tear the home named after his daughter to pieces. The only thing that stopped him was the number of men who sat watching him.

His gaze landed on Lord Manning who sat not far away, trying hard not to look at anyone, especially one of Alex's family. His face was bruised and swollen. No wonder he had not been seen lately. Thomas glanced questioningly at Manning and raised a brow to Barlow. He wanted to outright ask if his condition had anything to do with Alex, but could not find a way to do so.

Edward only smiled.

It had been a reminder not to mention what went on at Rose Hall. Manning would not make the mistake again. Not after Alex had requested Finch and Brandon *talk* to him, let him know that she was well aware who had spoken to Danton.

"Your daughter is not here, as you can see." Edward gestured around the room to remind him of all the eyes and ears in it. "My best guess, if she is not where you think she will be, then she has gone home. She has not set foot in this room tonight."

Thomas looked toward the massive guards that stood between them and the infamous back room. Barlow gave a soft shake of his head. There was no need to cause any more of a scene than they already had. If he said she was on her way home, she was. Edward turned a menacing smile toward Marc. Marc stepped closer and arched his brow. Marc was seething. Edward could see the effort it was taking to keep his temper in check.

"Not now." Thomas literally dragged him to the carriage. When they were all inside and the conveyance was rocking toward Hollister House, Thomas spoke again. "She was there. She may not have gone into the main area, but she must have been in the back room. There must be a back door. Do you want me to drop you back off at the Rutmeyers?"

"No." They all looked at Marc as he quickly answered. He gave a shake of his head. "It has been a long day, perhaps we should just head home, Father." He would not admit it, but he could not face the betrothal announcement after everything that had happened. He was surprised she still wanted to go through with it after he had walked out of her library without a word, though she had looked relieved he hadn't taken her.

Jeremy took his father's arm as they walked through the quiet foyer of Hollister House after dropping off Blake, Maxwell, and Marc at Clifton House. "Look." Under the door was the wavering glow of a candle. It could only be one person.

"Go to bed. I will talk to her."

Jeremy hesitated before deciding to let his father handle it. Perhaps he could make her see some sense. He looked up as his mother passed him in the hall.

She smiled warmly at him. "Thomas?" The women had left the ball not long after the men had gone in search of the missing Alex.

He didn't even look at her, afraid of what he might see in her eyes. "Go to bed. I will handle this. Stay out of it." He waited until she disappeared up the stairs before turning back to the door. It was opened just a crack as if she had expected him.

He opened the door quietly. She stood in the center of the room, watching the door. She had not changed from her beautiful gown, her hair disheveled and her face still red from the fast ride to beat her father home. She was so delicate looking, but he knew it was a misconception.

He approached her with fast angry strides. "I know you were

there, and you will make this go easier on you if you admit it now."

Her jaw tightened, her eyes flashed. "You know I was where, Papa?"

He was right before her now, his anger was almost a physical sense that caressed her. "You know damned well where. You are lucky I did not kill that man for the scandal he has caused us."

"How can it be a scandal to dance with someone?"

"When you had not danced with anyone else, then you dance with the one man that all of London is sure to believe is your lover you have to ask why it would be a scandal?" His fists were clenched as he struggled to make her see her folly.

"I will admit there will be scandal, but it was from me, not him. He is a good man and—"

"He is no such thing. He is not a man to be trusted. You will not see him anymore." His anger he knew came from pain and fear. Fear that she would learn that Edward was her father and she would love him more. Thomas was terrified of losing her.

He knew Edward would protect her from harm, but he was not doing her any good by allowing her to go to Rose Hall. Thomas's anger was not with Alex, but with Edward. He was not even angry with Catherine, not anymore. She had been young and with a seductive rake like Barlow, Thomas didn't think Catherine had had much of a chance of fighting him off. Not with the brandy that she had drank. No, Thomas was no longer angry, now he was just scared.

"He can be trusted, Papa. I know the kind of man he is. Just because he does not conform to society standards does not make him a bad man."

"You do not know what he did, what he is capable of. You cannot be around him. I will put a stop to it. Dammit, he will hurt you if he gets a chance. You—"

"He can be trusted. He is a wonderful man. Nurse took me there when I was a baby, and I have been going there ever since. I go there all the time. I care for him, and he—" Her words were cut of as a resounding slap sounded across the room, his hand driving into her cheek to stop her painful words, knocking her to the soft carpet.

"Oh God, Alex." He knelt beside her, gently touching her trembling shoulder. She pulled away from him, completely silent. "Alex, love, I am so sorry."

No response.

As the tears threatened to overcome Thomas, he had to leave. He hated himself and knew she could do no less now.

Alex didn't move for a long time after the library door had closed behind the man she loved more than her life itself. She lay in self-pity, the tears finally coming. Her heart wrenching sobs filled the entire house with sadness.

Deep into the night, long after she had cried herself to sleep, Thomas opened the library door. He had checked her room, but her bed was still made. Turning back the covers he went in search of his beloved girl.

He smiled when he saw her young maid curled at her side. Shaking her gently, he put his finger to her lips. Motioning for her to follow, he gently scooped a sleeping Alex into his arms. She was so peaceful when she slept. How could such a delicate looking flower turn into such a vulgar hellion when angry? She was stronger than he had ever given her credit for. He would never try to force her hand again. He had to grin at the reference to card games.

He knew then, for a fact, why Manning had looked as he did. That was where his daughter gamed. It was not wise to speak out against Barlow. He had not told the family where she was, but it was obvious he had told someone. He didn't think it would have come to that because he had tried to take advantage of her. No, she had taken care of that herself. But he had told someone. Thomas's only question now was who, and what would they do with that information?

After laying her on the bed, he kissed her check before turning to the sleepy Rebecca. "She should awaken to help you get her prepared for bed. If not, come get me, and I will help you."

Slipping into his own bed, he felt the warm body of Catherine automatically curve against him. Sliding his hand across her soft skin, he gave a low groan. She arched her naked body closer to him. She usually kept on at least her chemise when sleeping, in case one of the children may come in.

Tonight she had not. He had paced the study for hours before going to Alex, sending Jeremy to bed so he could be alone. His wife had obviously felt the need to be with him tonight. It had been several days since he had taken her. His groan caressed her, calling to her. She turned her body to him. Wrapping her arms around his neck. She still slept. He knew why she had done this. Because they had seen Edward. She wanted to assure him of her love. He smiled, taking a hardened nipple into his mouth. Her hands snaked into his hair. He looked up at her. Still, she slept.

"Thomas…" Her soft word touched his heart. She was dreaming of him.

The tears he had been fighting all night fell onto her cheek as he crushed her against him, kissing her roughly in his passion. Awakening suddenly, she fought against him. He held her tighter, kissing her deeper. She felt the tears on his cheeks even as she realized who it was.

"Thomas?" She tried to pull away only to be dragged underneath him. He groaned when her legs opened with no encouragement from him.

"I cannot wait, I have to have you, now."

His ragged voice tore at her. She had not heard that pain in so long, not seen him so desperate, so unsure of himself, in over eighteen years. She arched against him as he buried himself deep inside her. Pounding furiously, he tried to free himself of his pain and doubt. He kissed her and roughly caressed her breasts, her back, her thighs, her face. He could not touch her enough. He wanted her all at once. To know she was his.

Catherine was not aware of her own discomfort. She opened herself farther accepting him fully, drove against him to encourage him. She was only aware of the hot tears that stained her face, his tears.

He broke his kiss, bringing himself up on his arms. "Wrap your legs around me." He thrust into her again and again. "Tighter, hold me tighter."

Thrust after thrust, in and out, his speed and depth increasing until she could feel the passion in him swim through her. Thomas fell against her, wrapping his arms tightly around her hips bringing them higher as her muscles tightened around the shaft buried so deep inside her. "Yes, please. Come for me. Love me."

This time it was she who delivered the painful kisses. He could feel her breathing increase, her cries healing the hurt he had been feeling. When she cried his name, when her warm juices spilled onto him, he cried out. "I love you. You are my life."

His seed was hot against her womb, and, when he collapsed onto her, she held him tight.

When he tried to pull away, concerned he had hurt her, she held him tighter, cradling his head with her sweat-drenched arms, drawing him deeper with the thighs that still held him prisoner in her sweet cell. He held her as tightly as his trembling arms would allow. Tears still clogged his throat. He didn't know how long he had held her before the fear started to ebb. It did not go away, but it was controllable.

He tried again to draw away. "Do not leave me."

"Never."

Her words rumbled against his chest. He turned onto his back taking her with him.

Chapter 17

Wanting to avoid the rumors he knew would be swirling of Alex and Edward, especially after that scandalous escape last night, Marc had taken his time getting to the track. He had debated on skipping it altogether, but could not quite admit defeat, at least not that completely.

Instead, he settled for arriving after the first race had begun and after, he hoped, most of the bystanders would be intent on the racers and not the other watchers.

Marc looked at the small crowd of awaiting horses and riders, but the secretive little jockey was not among them, not that he had expected him to be. He was at the race, that Marc knew. He had already caught sight of the sleek black carriage. The crowd erupted around him, drawing his attention back to the track in time to see Raymond Dunmore bring his mount into second place, neck and neck with the first place horse. Marc smiled.

"Where have you been, Hollister?"

Marc's smile fell away as Samuel Rutmeyer's blaring voice raked at his nerves. It bothered him almost as much as the taunting face of Edward in the stands not far from them. "Your boy has been pacing back and forth down there unable to find you."

Marc followed Samuel's gaze to find the jockey in the shadows of the stables cheering Raymond's near win. Marc stepped to the front of the crowd and waited.

It did not take long, and, though Marc was disappointed that A.H. didn't acknowledge his presence, the jockey did visibly relax. Marc shook his head. There was no denying that the jockey looked for him, though Marc still could not fathom why.

Tess stepped from the shadowed interior of the stables, and Marc's breath caught. There was no mistaking the massive animal that tugged at the end of his lead. It was the black stallion Alex had ridden the night Manning had accosted her. His hide was well healed, and he had put on some weight, but it was definitely the same horse.

Marc searched the racing schedule. "'Raven Blood,' appropriate at least."

He looked at Thomas who just grinned and shook his head.

Jeremy smiled and, without a word, they all placed their bets on Raven Blood. The race was trouble free, but A.H. came in a surprising second, surprising because it was not at the fault of the horse. His rider was stiff in the saddle, his body lacking its usual graceful and fluid movements that made him one with the horse.

Rutmeyer grumbled. "I thought with all of you betting on him it was a sure thing." He crumpled his ticket and threw it to the ground.

"Nothing is a sure thing." Maxwell said. "We have seen this horse before with its previous owner. This is his first *professional* race." He grinned, and Marc rolled his eyes. "Though the jockey does not look to be his normal self. Perhaps something is wrong with him. Do you think him still bothered by that knee?"

Marc watched him closely as he patted the horse and accepted the congratulations from both Tess and Raymond. He appeared in good enough spirits down there. "I think he is fine, Father, at least he seems to be now."

After A.H. came in third in his last race, Marc wondered if there was something wrong with him, after all. The jockey appeared listless when he leapt from his mount. It wasn't his knee. That was apparent when he hit the ground without even a wobble, but something was bothering him.

A.H. looked to the group of men who surrounded Marc, but when Rutmeyer wrapped an arm around Marc's shoulders, A.H. slumped and disappeared into the stables. Before Marc could get disengaged from the meaty embrace, he watched the carriage slowly pulling away.

Marc had wanted to talk to him, to find out why he was taking Malacinda to Linden, to find out if he did indeed know Alex and how, and to see what was bothering him. He knew it was ridiculous since they had never really met, but he was beginning to feel a friendship with the man.

"Do you boys want to come to the house tonight, or are you taking in a soiree somewhere?" Thomas asked.

Blake smiled and clapped him on the shoulder. "It will be nice to go somewhere I can take the children."

"We shall be there tonight as well," Maxwell added with a smile, "We have some shopping to attend to first. I need to buy something for my lovely wife, and I have coerced Marc into helping me."

Marc had volunteered to help his father, happy to have something to get his mind off his problems, but the shopping, he decided an hour later, was doing nothing to help him.

He had been in a fog through the last two shops, and would be hard pressed if asked what shops they had been at and what, if anything, had been purchased.

"Look, there is Alex," his father said.

At the sound of her name, the fogs seemed to lift. Marc cursed himself. From the shadows of the awning, Marc looked out in time to catch sight of the back of her, her long red braid hung low against the back of her billowing cloak.

She was just leaving a shop, a large bag in her hand. It brushed against her leg as she walked slowly to the waiting carriage. Whatever she had bought appeared to be heavy.

Maxwell raised a hand and opened his mouth to call out to her. His words died as a carriage came careening down the cobblestones, its passenger pounding violently on the carriage roof and calling out to his driver to stop.

The carriage slid to a stop not more than a few feet from Alex's carriage. Robert stood, his hand sliding into his coat before jumping from his seat. He landed beside her as a small framed Frenchman bolted from his conveyance. "Mademoiselle, mademoiselle."

Alex's hand stilled Robert's arm.

"Vous avez à venir pour le navire! Vous avez à venir pour le navire!" the Frenchman yelled swiftly over and over as he raced to her.

Marc scowled. "Something is wrong at the dock. I know him. He ships with me. He is not going to get any help from her. She does not even know French."

"Then perhaps we should rescue her and see what the problem is. It must be serious for him to begin yelling at the first person he sees…" Maxwell's words faltered when Alex grasped the man's coat sleeves, giving him a hard shake, her words clear and crisp.

And perfectly French.

"Monsieur Pierre, you need to stop. I cannot understand a word you are saying. What is wrong with the ship?" Her words were quiet as she looked around, making sure she was not seen. Not many people were out right after the races. The men would be back at White's and the women, more than likely, were still abed.

Pierre was almost in tears as he clung to her cloak. "That beast is threatening to throw my silks into the sea."

"If that drunken bastard does not learn his place, I will throw *him* into the sea. Piece by bloody Goddammed piece. Where is Jon Luke?"

"He is making sure Taggard leaves my merchandise on the *Lady Catherine*. Please, you know what water will do to my silks, my sweet. You must come." Pierre returned to his carriage, opening the door to await her. "Come. Come."

"Robert, follow me to the docks. There is a problem with Taggard. I'll ride with Monsieur St. Croigh." Her transition to English was smooth as she handed Robert her large purchase.

"I heard the *Catherine*'s name. If there is a problem with Taggard, would he—"

She cut him off with a wave of her small hand. Looking around one more time, she smiled. "He is not that stupid."

A.H. had a shipment of French lace on board the *Lady Catherine*. She already had a buyer for it., It just needed to be delivered.

She knew Robert's concern, but it was unnecessary. Keith Taggard had tried to squeeze money out of A.H. only once. His short visit with Tess had insured it didn't happen again.

Alex, talking away to the French merchant, allowed him to help her into the carriage. She paused on the step, turning back to Robert. "Please be careful with that. It is very special."

The carriage door shut behind her and the moment the Frenchman's carriage pulled away Maxwell stepped from the shadows and grabbed Robert by the arm, almost dislodging the package he was placing beside the seat. "Robert, you are taking on a couple of passengers." Robert hesitated and looked after the disappearing carriage. "If you let her know we are here, I will go straight to her father with what I know."

Robert watched the carriage with reluctance as it turned a corner and was lost from sight. He sighed and turned back with a smile and a slight bow. "It would be an honor, your grace."

Settled in the carriage, Marc could see inside the bag Alex had been so worried about. Inside was a large box, wrapped in expensive silver paper and covered in golden ribbons and bows. He irritably wondered which lover would receive that special gift. He had an urge to kick it. He resisted. Barely.

At the docks, Alex jumped to the ground, nodding to Robert as he brought the carriage to a stop close behind her. She turned her attention to Marc's solicitor, who wobbled his way toward her.

"Taggard. What are you doing here?" Several dock workers turned to stare, but Marc had the impression they were not as surprised to see her as they should be. This was obviously not her first visit to the docks.

"I see this little frog ran right to you." His words were slurred.

"What have you done now? Why are you trying to get more money…again?"

Marc could see the effort it was taking to control her temper. He knew it would not be long before she lost it altogether. She veritably shook with anger.

"I am just getting what is owed. It has been approved already. You know that sometimes—costs go up. Problems with—shipping and—the sea."

He over-corrected his sway, and Marc waited for him to fall. He didn't. Marc was disappointed.

He was disappointed by more than the fact that Taggard kept his feet. He was appalled by the whole situation. How could he have been so blind? He had met with the man on many occasions, but Taggard had never been in this state. *He always had plenty of notice that there would be a meeting though*, Marc thought with disgust, both at this man and himself.

Alex took a deep breath and spoke calmly. "You are right. There are problems that arise, but you forget who you are talking to. I know the *Lady* is here two days early, and I also know there were no problems with the weather nor the shipments. Nothing that would warrant you trying to swindle money from this man."

"I assure you, there…were issues—"

Alex interrupted his blubbering protests. "If it's approved, perhaps you can show me the paperwork."

"I don't—I don't have it, but Lord Clifton will not object."

His whine grated on Marc's nerves, and his assertions on what Marc would or would not do was more than he was willing to stand for.

Marc had heard enough. With a grunt, he slipped from the carriage and made his way through the crowd with his father right at his heels. Alex, distracted, didn't look behind her and, to Marc's relief, Taggard didn't notice them either. He wanted to hear all he could about the man before he interrupted.

Alex threw her arms in the air. "Of course, he will not object, because it will be like every other damned time you have done it. You just will not tell him. Very seldom does anyone come to me, they just pay your extra fee so you can go drink off the money somewhere, and you will not bother the people who really try to work. I must assume that you have finally gone for the big money, and that is why they are coming to me now. How much are you asking?" Alex's voice was strained as its volume rose.

A short stocky sailor with blond hair and bright blue eyes began to push his way through the crowding people toward her. The captain of the *Catherine* stood behind Taggard with a horrified expression on his weathered face.

Taggard sputtered before finally yelling at her. "The only reason these damn frogs work with you is because no one else will work with them."

"The reason I work with these *gentlemen* is the same reason I work with ninety-eight percent of Clifton clients. It is because you are a drunken mongrel bastard, and no one wants to deal with you. I will not allow you to ruin this man's business nor tarnish the reputation of Clifton Shipping—" She swung her hand behind her to to gesture at the shipping offices. Her hand connected hard with something soft. She heard a low growl and felt pain shoot through her arm as someone gripped tightly onto her wrist.

Alex looked over her shoulder with horror at the image of Marc's doubled over body. He seemed unaware that he still gripped her wrist as he tried to draw breath, unaware of anything.

Marc could still see white flashes in his vision, like bright fireworks that had originated from an area where no man should ever be hit.

"Are you all right?"

Marc cringed at the barely suppressed laughter he heard in his father's voice. It was painful if it were you, funny if it were someone else—sad but unfortunately true.

Another deep breath, the pain lessened, at least enough to allow him to straighten. He released her hand and tried to ignore the way she massaged it. Dull red finger marks began to surface. He cringed. He glanced up to see her looking over her shoulder at him. He spoke through clenched teeth. "I guess I should just be glad it was not a knee."

Taggard suddenly began speaking so fast and garbled that Marc could not understand much of what he said, and what he could understand he didn't know anything about.

"Taggard, shut up." Maxwell waited for the man to quiet before turning to Alex. "Alex, since you have been handling this problem so far, you may finish it."

"Your grace?" Shocked, she glanced around her then back at the men behind her. She was sure she had heard him wrong.

"For today, you are in command of Clifton Shipping."

She took a deep breath, her heart thrumming in her ears. She turned to face the captain and Taggard again, but now she was unsure of how to continue. "How much are you asking?" Her voice shook. She had lost the command and confidence she had held just moments ago. That changed when he reluctantly disclosed the amount. "*What*? That is twice what was agreed upon for the shipment."

"It's not. It's—" The solicitor stopped, but not soon enough.

"It is not? How the bloody Hell would you know? I am the one who set up the contract." Alex hesitated, concerned Marc would step in if she did what she wanted, what she had wanted to do for years. She took a deep breath and decided to put it all on the line, Marc be damned. "Taggard, consider yourself no longer employed by Clifton Shipping."

"You can't let me go! Lord Clifton, you can't mean—" He tried to step around her only to find her in his path.

"I am the one you need to deal with. Did you not hear him say I was in control? I have the authority to do things my way. Do you want to do it my way?" She glanced at a large and burly sailor who took a large step toward Taggard.

Taggard glanced at the big man and took a step back. It would not be the first time he had been dumped into the sea at her request. "Fine, you can let me go today, but by tomorrow I will be back in my position. I will talk to Lord Clifton in the morning."

"Good. When you do, make sure to tell him how much money you have stolen from clients in his name and exactly who has smoothed over the problems for you. If you are, by some miracle, reinstated to your position after your performance here today, I will no longer do my part. You will be completely on your own. How long do you think you can hold your place then?"

Alex was unprepared for the panic that swept him. He lashed out at her like an injured animal, lunging at her, his fists raised, murder and hatred in his eyes. "You bitch."

Marc grasped her arm, pulling her roughly behind him. "Touch her, and I will rip you apart."

With a malicious smile at Alex, Taggard turned and walked away.

Marc took a deep breath, but control over his rolling emotions was slow in coming. He turned on his obstinate little negotiator. His eyes widened, his jaw clenched. He grasped her under the chin and turned her head into the light. "What happened? Who did this to you?"

Maxwell walked around her and frowned. "My dear, are you all right?"

He had a bad feeling he knew who had left the prominent bruise on her cheek. The make-up she had applied did little to disguise it.

"I am fine. It is nothing important." She pushed Marc's hand away and stepped toward the captain, who now stood, head hanging, off to the side.

"I am sorry, my lady. I know I should not have gone along with him, but Taggard did have the authority."

"I know, Captain. He is gone now, and I think you value your position, correct?" He nodded. "Good. Get the shipments off of that boat, now. And, Captain, as long as I have no more issues with you, we will consider this in the past and put to rest."

The captain bowed low and thanked her. She watched him yell at the men to carry out her orders. With a deep breath, she turned to face the Clifton men and hoped her courage would hold out just a little longer.

Robert stood behind them with a sheepish smile. "I am sorry, my lady. They came with me from the shops."

Another notch of courage slipped from her. If they had been at the shops, they had heard her speaking to Pierre. There was nothing for it now. She was too far into this hole to dig herself out. She could only hope that it would not ruin the rest of her plans.

"That is fine, Robert. You did the right thing." Turning to Pierre, she smiled and, with a tremble of nervousness, spoke in French. "Pierre, your merchandise will be on the pier shortly. I am sorry for all your trouble, but you will not have to deal with that man anymore. I will let you know what is going to happen and who you will deal with from now on." Smiling at the tall black-haired man standing at Pierre's side she continued. "Thank you for watching the boat, Jon Luke. I appreciate it. If you will, please go with Pierre, I will get in touch with you later."

The burly sailor who had stepped up to do her bidding with Taggard made his way to her side. "My lady, are you all right?"

"Yes, Adam I am fine." She patted his arm. "I just hope that all the excitement is now at an end."

"That is a nice wish, but in shipping the excitement is always just around the corner." He glanced at the men waiting behind her and cleared his throat. "Um, Melody is hoping you will come by some night for dinner to thank you for helping us with little Meg."

"I would be honored. I have plans tonight and the next, but the night after that I am free."

Adam looked again at the men behind her. He wrung his weathered hands and shifted from one foot to the other and back again.

Alex smiled up at him. "Is there something else?"

He looked from one man to the next. "Perhaps if I could speak to you alone."

"Does it have to do with the ships?" He nodded, a bare movement she almost didn't catch. "Well, I would say it is a little late for secrets or discretion now. What is it?"

"The mast on the *Lavender Rose*."

Marc cringed at the name. He had christened that ship with Alex in mind only last year, right after he had desperately wanted to kiss her. It was a scent he seemed damned to always remember.

Alex twirled her fingers for him to continue. "What about it?"

Adam cringed. "The mast is bad."

To Marc, it looked as if he was expecting a blow up. It came.

"What do you mean it is bad? I just approved that damned mast. It has not been long enough for it to be damaged. You tell that man that he will have it replaced within the week, and he will do it for free. If he does not, you may tell him I will get my masts from somewhere else, even if I have to ship my timber in from America."

"Yes, my lady." Without a glance at the men, he was gone.

Alex turned back with a smile, one she didn't feel. Marc's eyes went back to the bruise. He reached for her. She stepped away.

"Now what?" She looked from one man to the other and waited with a facade of calmness, even though her insides felt on the verge of coming out.

"Now we go to the office and have a talk," Maxwell said.

No one spoke until they had climbed the stairs and were in the overly warm office. A large room, compared to the others in the building, it was on the top floor and had a beautiful view of the harbor, though no one noticed.

Alex slung her cloak over the iron coat rack and asked without turning to face them. "What would you like to know first?"

"First, I want to know what clientele you deal with," Maxwell said.

Alex took a deep breath, turned, and pushed her way past the wide shoulders of the man she was trying hard to ignore. He was hard to ignore. Since he had caught sight of the bruise, he had not taken his gaze off her.

Adjusting the skirt of her floral day dress, she sat behind the massive desk pulling the ledger from the second drawer on the left hand side. Marc raised his brows. He would be hard pressed to find anything in this office, but then he was rarely in it.

Opening the ledger, she named off six men, one of which was Robert Dinmont, the man who had come to Taggard's defense. "These are the men I do not work with, they are loyal to Taggard. The rest, in one form or another, I work with."

"In one form or another?" Maxwell took a seat across from her and told Marc to do the same.

"I work with some personally. Pierre St. Croigh, of course. The rest of the Frenchmen I work with through Jon Luke Le' Rone, the man you just saw down there. I also work personally with Porter Farthing, James Gideon, Craig Connelly, Spencer Ferguson, and Michael Cranston."

"With the exception of Cranston, those were my first clients. I do not understand how this happened." Marc lurched to his feet. "How can you do this to me? Why can you not sit quietly by, knit, and be a proper lady?" If she was a proper lady, she would not have any damned lovers that she was giving special gifts to. If she was a proper lady, who did what was expected, perhaps he would not have to marry the miserable Janice. "You would never see someone like Janice doing something like this."

That brought her to her feet. Leaning across the desk as he was, they came face to face. "That is because your beloved does not have the brains to do so, my lord."

Maxwell gave her a shove back into her chair and pulled Marc into his. "That is enough, from both of you. You will stay on your side, Alex, and, Marc, you will stay on yours. And you both will be nice to each other. Understood?" He waited for an agreement from both hostile people. They glared at each other over the desk. "Good, now explain to me how this all came about?"

"I am sure Father will tell you soon enough, so I may as well." She took a deep breath and looked at the ledger in front of her. "I have been going to Rose Hall since I was a baby. I met all of the original clients there. One day I was sitting in on a game when they were complaining of Goldfie. I convinced them to try Clifton instead."

"I remember they came to me with a bargain." Marc stared at her, but her eyes remained on the ledger. "How did you convince them to pay so much more for the shipments?"

She fidgeted with the paperwork on the desk. "That was easy. I told them to try you before they signed a contract. Offer you thirty percent more than you were asking for the right to a trial. The thirty percent more was still less than what they were paying that crook Goldfie."

"How did you know what they were paying?" Maxwell was growing more in awe of her. It seemed he had always taken the young girl for granted. She was a handful and a tornado at times, but this—this calm-speaking businesswoman—was something he had never imagined.

"I asked."

"And how did you know what I was charging?" Marc asked.

She looked at him for the first time, but did so without raising her head. "I have my sources."

"You will tell me, or else I will—"

Maxwell cleared his throat. "I do not think threats will get us far." He turned his attention back to Alex. "How else do you work with the clients?"

"Mostly, I work through Andrew March, my solicitor. He deals with their solicitors. They do not even know about me. Most of them will have no problem switching if you want to hire a new solicitor, or maybe take over for yourself."

Marc scowled at her. She grinned.

"The ones you will have some difficulty with are the men I deal with directly. You will just have to earn their trust since they have already come to you once with problems."

Marc didn't answer, but something else had come to mind. Gideon. "You have known James Gideon for how long?"

She looked confused by the question, but shrugged. "I do not know. He has been at Rose Hall for as long as I can remember. Why?"

"You are the one who convinced him to help with the rumors right?"

Alex gave another shrug of her thin shoulders, but that was all the response she offered.

Marc sighed. "You hired March because I refused to hire him? That is how you knew Taggard was causing problems."

She smiled. "There are only two clients who will not work with you. Randy Gregson and—"

"How do you know about that? Do you think because I threw him against the wall, he will not work with me?" The words were out before Marc could stop them.

"No, my lord, but why did you throw him against a wall?" When the only answer was in the form of Maxwell's laugh, she continued.

"The reason is because I deal with his mistress, and I do not think he will take kindly to your visiting her."

Marc was appalled. "You deal with his mistress?"

"Why not? I dealt with yours." Before he could respond, she quickly moved on. "Besides, I put her in place. When his old mistress came to work at Rose Hall, I spoke to her. She told me he was a strange man. While engaged in sex, he liked to talk and listen to shipping contracts, merchandise to ship, the best ships, the best commodities—that sort of thing. So I sent Keira Montaya to be his new mistress."

Marc stared at her in shock as she went on about such delicate subjects without so much as a stutter or a blush.

Alex looked up at the slack-jawed men and, when they didn't comment, she went on. "The other one that will only deal with me is Ferdinand Pettlenoster."

The surprise in the answer pulled Marc back to his senses, or at the very least gave him control of his tongue. "Why will he not deal with me? I do not think a man of seventy holds a mistress."

"No." She gave a short snort of laughter. "At least not that I am aware of. Quite an image, though."

"That is enough of that," Maxwell said, but he grinned as well.

"Yes, well, he does have a wife. Rachel Pettlenoster. I work with her. It is her money and her merchandise. We only put it in his name because the law forbids her to do her business in her own name. If you will remember her first husband was Evander Connelly, Craig Connelly's father. When Evander died, he left her nearly penniless. He was just as much a wastrel as her new husband, but at least she knows this now. Craig convinced her to talk to me. I have helped her with the shipping and making some investments. The contract may be in her husband's name, like all of her contracts, but the money is hers."

"I guess that explains how you could be seen at the Pettlenosters' when you were not there," Marc said. "Lady Rachel has mentioned that she saw you that night."

Alex just smiled.

"As to the people you have hired, who are they and what do they do?" Maxwell asked.

"Jon Luke. He acts as my translator so I do not have to go often to the pier. March is my solicitor. Adam Speltzer takes care of the everyday inspections and repairs to the ships. Reeves Dalton, he is the messenger who brings you the paperwork that needs your attention." She looked sheepishly at the ledger, refusing to meet their eyes.

"Is that it?" Marc asked.

"The only ones I plan to tell you about. So there you have it. Now what do you plan to do, my lord?" She looked at his father but he knew the question as well as the title was directed at him.

"Long term, I could not tell you right now. Short term, however, I would think that if the two of you can work together for a while, Marc can gain the trust of the clients." Maxwell shifted his attention to Marc. "That is what you want, is it not, to work with the everyday things in shipping?"

Marc nodded. "But it will not go over with—"

Maxwell waved off his protests. "We will deal with one thing at a time. Alex can continue to deal with the mistress and the wife and help you get acquainted with the others. After that, it should help with some of the disappearances at least."

Alex nodded. "It will free up quite a bit of my time, my lord."

Marc shook his head. "I am still not sure this is a good idea, but I will do it. I will take on all the workers that you hired and take over March as my solicitor, and you will no longer need to deal with them either."

"No. Adam is the only one who was hired just for the purposes of the shipping company, and he will want to stay. He is very good at what he does, and I would suggest you keep him. If you want to hire March, you will have to talk to him yourself to see if he is available. As to whether or not he is still my solicitor is none of your concern. However, Jon Luke and Reeves have prior engagements that make it impossible to work for you. I was going to have to find someone to replace them soon anyway." They were her butler and footman, and she was sending them onto Linden within a few days.

"What prior engagements?"

She didn't answer, just that little shrug.

"All right, if you two want to discuss who is shipping what, where, I will tell Robert to send our carriage home and, when he returns, we should be ready to leave." Maxwell took a deep breath and watched them from the doorway.

Drawing forth several more ledgers, Alex began a detailed instruction on the contracts. Marc was leaning forward, trying to read upside down as his father took his leave.

He took just a few moments to speak to Robert before heading slowly back up the stairs. By the time, Maxwell looked into the room, Marc, unable to read upside down, had taken his chair around the desk to see the ledgers before him better, but he was no longer looking at the ledgers. He was staring at the bruise on Alex's small cheek with a scowl as she continued to talk.

Her words cut short when his hand grasped her chin forcing her to look at him. Carefully, he ran the back of his knuckles along her injury, concern deep in his eyes. His darkened eyes went from her discolored cheek to her full red lips. He opened his mouth to speak, then instead drew her lips to his.

It was so different from the other kisses he had given her, she was unable to move. It was soft and slow, passionate but kind. His tongue slid easily between her teeth as she opened for him with a soft groan. He tasted the warm sweetness, the inside of her trembling lips, and deepened the kiss with a responding groan of his own.

Maxwell held his breath as he watched this kiss, so full of love and compassion he felt his throat clog and had to blink several times to keep his eyes from tearing. He smiled as his son drew the woman he loved closer to him, her hand laying upon his arm, the kiss never changing from the euphoric tenderness as he held her gently.

When Marc slid his hand from her face to cup a soft breast, Maxwell decided he had better intervene. Withdrawing down several steps, he stomped up the last three loudly. "I think these stairs are getting steeper and steeper. Not to mention I think they added some," he called out louder than necessary as he ascended the steps. He had been lost to a kiss many a time and only a loud voice would break the spell.

They sat apart, still on the same side of the desk, but at least pretending to go over the ledgers.

"I thought I said on your own side of the desk." Maxwell scowled at his son as if he were trying to attack her again.

"I know, Father, but I could not see properly from there. It was giving me a headache to try to see all those upside down figures. I have been...nice...to her, I swear." Marc had been about to say he had been on his best behavior, but since that wasn't true, he wasn't sure what to say. Then he remembered his father telling them to be nice to each other.

"I bet you have been."

Marc heard the sarcasm and wondered if his father didn't believe him. "I have not yelled once." He wanted to defend himself further, but was afraid of what would come out.

Look at what he had already done. He had opened his mouth to demand who had hurt her and ended up kissing her instead. And the kiss. He had never kissed a woman like that. He was painfully hard beneath the desk, a deep lust that should not have happened at that gentle kiss. If his father had been but a few more minutes, he would have found his son burying himself deep inside her as he pushed her over the desk.

Chapter 18

Marc rushed from the office as Alex slid the first of many ledgers into the desk drawer. He hesitated at the door, but forced himself not to look back.

He didn't understand what had just happened, didn't understand what was happening to his well-organized life. He still planned to marry Janice, still planned to make his way up the social ladder and become the great family they once were, but now his plans seemed far away, like an island of sharp rocks through a pounding storm.

The wind was blowing him dangerously close to capsizing, but the dark menacing form of rocks was looking less and less like salvation. His rolling nerves were more or less settled by the time he entered the carriage, but, by his father's look of concern, it was not as well hidden as he had thought.

"Marc, are you all right?"

Marc didn't answer, wasn't sure what exactly to tell him.

A few moments later, Alex allowed Robert to assist her into the carriage. The carriage rocked as Robert took his seat, the sounds of reins snapped and carriage lurched forward.

Marc and Maxwell sat on one side facing Alex, her brow furrowed and her breathing erratic. Maxwell was about to repeat the questions that Marc had left unanswered to Alex when she spoke. "My Lords, will you please do me a favor?"

"You know we will do anything we can for you. What is it you need?" Maxwell responded.

"Will you wait to tell my father until tonight is over?" She gave a weak smile and dropped her gaze to the pointed toe of her kid slipper that peeked from beneath the soft folds of her cloak. "I would like him to enjoy the family before he is upset any further."

She jumped when the Duke of Paddington laughed. She gazed at him, not worried or scared, but clearly annoyed.

"You are such a precious girl, my love. Most women would be begging me not to tell anything. You are only worried that he will not enjoy his night."

"I would do no such thing, your grace. I know you will tell Father, and I would not dream of asking you to lie to him. Besides, it is not for such unselfish reasons that I ask. I too would like not to be subjected to any further humiliation in front of the family. I would, at least, like to discuss it with him in private."

"I can wait to tell him, if you yourself would like to be the one to do so," Maxwell said, glancing at the bruise and wondering if humiliation was all she was concerned about.

She shook her head. "I would like you to tell him. I am not sure I know how to broach the subject."

Marc snorted. "You never seem to have an issue broaching any subject, or else you wouldn't be dealing with so many men's mistresses." He flushed and dropped his gaze.

Maxwell watched his son with a mixture of amusement and pity and thought that Marc had just remembered his was one of those mistresses. Maxwell turned his attention back to the problem at hand. "We plan to go riding in the morning. I will talk to your father then, while we are alone and far from the house."

He and Thomas had spoken of the tensions between the two young people on several occasions. They had also discussed their hopes for them and their future, a future together.

Maxwell was sure that Marc now knew what he wanted. How could he not be after that kiss? Maxwell would be happy to tell Thomas that all would be well between them. It would at least ease the blow from the other news he planned to deliver.

His hopes for a smooth future and happy children began to crumble as the carriage drew them through the crowded streets. Marc gazed out the window at the passing shops and bustling people. Alex inspected that toe of her slipper. And neither of them looked at the other or spoke a word.

When the carriage rocked to a halt, and Marc left it without a second glance or a word of farewell, Alex looked just as confused as Maxwell felt. His son was still fighting it, and Maxwell could not understand why. Society was not as important as Marc was making it out to be. So what if they were not the belles of the balls? Happiness was more important. All he could hope was that Marc was doing all this for himself because it was really what he wanted for his own life, and not out of some misplaced honor for the family.

Barely through the door of Hollister House, Alex braced herself for attack as Blake Jr. and Darla came barreling through the hall. Marc, removing his coat behind her, turned in time to catch her before she fell under the weight of both small children.

Alex could feel his strong hands. The heat from his body engulfed her. She wanted to tell the kids, one held tightly in each arm, to go play. She would wait patiently until they disappeared and then she would turn to Marc with a smile and throw him to the ground and beg him to take her. Alex looked over her shoulder at him, his face stern. She sighed and let go of her fantasy.

Marc pulled her closer, unable to bring himself to put distance between them. The lavender and rose scent that always surrounded her was inlaid with a scent that was all her. Soft, warm, and intoxicating, it rushed through his blood and sent heat to settle deep in his loins.

He released her suddenly as he felt the stirrings of arousal. He had to control himself, especially with two small bodies present.

He stormed away, leaving his father to assist the irresistible little hoyden. He wanted her so badly it was all he could think of. What terrified him more than anything was he found he wanted more than to take her once. He dreamed of her at night. Laying across his chest as she slept, waking to her beautiful smile every morning. God, what was he doing?

Thomas looked at the small group who had arrived and smiled. He had followed the children when they had bolted from the drawing room like the room was on fire. He had not heard the front door and wondered how the children had known that Alex had arrived.

"I am glad you are all here." Catherine rushed forward to take one of Amber's darling children from her daughter. She stopped with a soft gasp and reached for the bruise.

Alex pulled back. "It's nothing, Mama, do not ask." Catherine's eyes narrowed. She opened her mouth, but Alex just whispered, "Not now, please."

Catherine glared at Thomas as she took her seat in the drawing room.

He could not meet her eye. He had never struck Alex before, and guilt had eaten at him since it had happened. He had allowed fear, the horrible knowledge that she had spent her life with her true father, to sweep his common sense from him. He had no excuse. He just hoped he had not done irreparable damage to their relationship.

If she did go to her father now, he would have no one to blame but himself.

Unable to bring himself to look at Alex, he glanced around the room. His gaze fell on Marc who sat glaring at him. He shook his head and, unable to come up with something to say, allowed his gaze to drop.

Marc no longer wondered if he was right in his suspicions. The guilt on Lord Hollister's pale face told it all. He thought to confront him about it, but, from the pain on his face, he thought her father was feeling enough remorse, and Marc didn't need to add to it.

The ten members of the families sat comfortably as they awaited dinner to be announced. Marc watched Alex, sprawled on the floor with the kids, as she played with several of their toys. He watched the smile spread across her face, going from a forced facade to a comfortable grin, as she pretended right along with them. Her blues eyes darted to his face from time to time.

He acted as though he didn't notice.

Trying to imagine Janice on the floor with their children, he found he could not. He could picture his children, though. A strong and strapping son whose smile lit up the room. A boy who looked like his father, but had a relaxed air to him that Marc could never quite manage. He could also see his little girl, sweet and small, her bright red curls bobbing as she laughed.

He silently cursed himself and his roving imagination. He had given his daughter, not the features of Janice, but those of Alex. Right down to the bright blue eyes and dancing freckles that swept across the bridge of her nose.

Windrow appeared in the doorway. "That was fast, my man, is it time to eat already?" Thomas asked.

The look on the butler's face said it was not, and his reason for interrupting was not good. "Indeed not, my lord. Lord and Lady Rutmeyer and Miss Janice Rutmeyer to see you." He waited with a look that said he would be all the happier to throw them out.

Thomas looked at Alex for the first time. Her lips were glued in a grim line, her eyes too shiny. Taking a deep breath, he was saved an answer as Lord Rutmeyer pushed his way into the room.

"Your grace, I hope you do not mind us finding you here. You were not at home, so we thought this was the best place to look—" Samuel stared slack jawed at the young woman lying on the floor. "My god, child, what are you doing down there? Have you fallen?" He reached forward and pulled her to her feet. "You are on the verge of crying, are your hurt? The least they could have done is help you up, my lady."

"I am fine. I did not fall I was playing with the children." She smiled at him, surprised by the concern that he showed. The surprise slipped away when his hands became too familiar brushing imaginary dirt from her backside.

Marc was on his feet the instant the disgusting man's hands ran across her bottom.

The shocked looks told Marc he had made a mistake. To cover it, he moved quickly to Janice's side, realizing as he did that he had not even risen when she had entered the room. It was a good thing Rutmeyer had taken liberties, or Marc might still be sitting there.

"Lady Rutmeyer, how pleasing it is to see you. We are just preparing for dinner. Would you and your family do us the honor of staying?" Marc asked.

Janice smiled widely sending a triumphant glance at the stunned Alex.

Maxwell was angry at his son for the first time in years. He knew Marc wasn't using Alex. If he had doubted it, their kiss would have cleared any doubts, but he also knew he could not allow him to lead her on. Maxwell knew she was expecting more. Hell, he was expecting more. How could she not be?

He opened his mouth to ask to talk to Marc privately when Alex swept up the children and fled the room.

"Please, have a seat, my lady." Marc ushered Janice to a chair and took the one beside her. It was all he could do not to go after the fleeing Alex.

Alex didn't return until it was time to eat. She had not changed her clothing, but had applied more makeup to her already plastered face. Marc could still see the bruise and the puffy skin beneath her eyes from tears he had once more caused.

Dinner was a silent affair. Nothing like it would have been without the unexpected guests. Samuel shoveled food into his face faster than one would think possible, and he filled his plate several times. Alex was the opposite, pushing her food around on hers until it was acceptable to allow a servant to take it.

Marc and Janice talked of mundane things. Her clothes, her hair, her seamstress, her maids, her…her…her. That was all it consisted of. When he tried to speak of anything else, business, horses, ships, nothing was enough to draw her attention away from her favorite topic. Her.

Marc had never completely understood the tradition of separating the men and the women after dinner, but he was relieved when the sitting room doors swung shut, cutting off Janice's voice.

Marc retreated to the library with the men, brandy was drunk, and cigars were smoked, but it was not the escape that Marc was looking for. The atmosphere in the room was gloomy.

Rutmeyer talked of nothing but gaming, and, though his subject was vast, including everything from the track to the tables, Marc could tell he was not the only man who was bored. When Rutmeyer tried to get them into a friendly game of chance, all politely refused, and Thomas stood.

"Perhaps we should rejoin the women," Thomas offered and headed to the door without awaiting a response. He pulled open the library doors, and the group of men were greeted by angry shouts coming from the sitting room.

"I will not have you speak of that place in such a tone." Alex had had enough of the stupid woman and her insipid comments.

Janice had insulted Alex, she had run down Marc's mistress, and now she had moved on to Chariton house, calling it a home for miscreants.

"I will speak of it however I want. It is not right, you know? You do not care about it, nor anything else, and all you do is use your time there to get attention. All you want is to have Marc to yourself, and that is why you dragged me away to get a drink at the ball, so I could not dance with him. That is why you told me all those things about his mistress and his—amorous ways."

"You told her what?"

Alex nearly swallowed her tongue at Marc's shocked voice. She glanced behind her to see not only Marc, but the entire male entourage.

Marc supposed he should have known. He didn't know why he was surprised, nor was he surprised when Alex ignored him and turned back to Janice.

"His lordship has nothing to do with this. I care for those children."

"Please, that place should be burnt to the ground, with all those bastards in it." Janice's eyes widened as Alex advanced on her, fists clenched. Wisely she moved back. "You would not hit me here, there are too many witnesses."

"Witnesses? There were more people around the last time I hit you. Do you think anyone here has control over what I do?"

Janice's panic stricken gaze found Marc.

Alex gave a soft laugh. "Hardly." She swung her fist.

It was caught in Marc's iron grip before she could connect. "Alex, dammit. Stop this foolishness. I cannot allow it."

The look she gave him as she tore her hand free was of such anguish and betrayal he felt it in his bones. He was only trying to protect what was left of her reputation. He was not taking sides. He wanted to hit Janice himself for her spiteful comments about the poor children.

Alex shook her head sadly. Her face was withdrawn and remorseful, but in it was a pitiful acceptance. He wanted to cry, to hold her, and tell her all would be well.

Instead, he just watched her walk away.

∾∾

The Earl of Grunby and The Duke of Paddington rode though the early morning fog in Hyde Park. No one else was about. Both men were silent for a long time. Thomas was lost in thought, and Maxwell was happy to let him remain in it until his friend was ready to talk.

Suddenly Thomas reined in his mount and dismounted. He looked across the empty park and blurted out, "I hit her."

Maxwell dismounted and came to him. He didn't speak until he had tied both sets of reins loosely to a branch and leaned against the tree. He looked at Thomas and sighed. "I know. When I saw the bruise, I suspected as much. It was about Edward." It was not a question for he already knew the answer.

"Yes. She has been going there since she was a child." His words were not angry, but tinged with regret and sadness.

"I know." Thomas's head jerked back up. Maxwell smiled. "Does Catherine know?"

Thomas shook his head. "I spoke to her about it, and I do believe she hadn't known. The nurse took her. How do you know and why have you not told me?"

Now Maxwell could hear the anger building.

He quickly told Thomas the whole story of what had happened at the pier and in the office, including her telling them that she had been going to see Edward, but leaving out the kiss. That could come later, after Thomas had calmed down.

Thomas was quiet for quite some time, and then he laughed.

"Laughter is not the response I was expecting."

"Well, the orphanage explains some of the disappearances, and now the ships explain some more. Do you think that is it?"

"I would like to say yes, but I do not think so. When I asked about the people she had hired she seemed to cut the list short. When asked if that was all, her response was 'All I plan to tell you about.' As much as it pains me to say, there is something else she is hiding."

∾∾

"Alex, you have taken care of my shipping contracts since the very beginning. I am not sure if I want to deal with Lord Clifton. He was not interested in seeing to his own business then, why do you think he is now?"

Janice could hear the whispered voices of Alex and Craig Connelly in the library at Lady Bickerbee's ball. She carefully pushed the door open a little farther.

"Craig, he is serious about this, and I will not just turn you over to him. I will be involved for some time yet. He is still learning the ins and out of who does what and how it all runs on a daily basis. All he wants is to meet with you and talk it over. I will be there to smooth things out. It will be fine."

The library had been silent for several long moments when Janice spotted Alex walking in through the garden doors. She jerked away from the door before Alex could see her and relaxed when the little chit didn't look her way.

Janice made her way, with as much grace as she could muster, to Marc, who was standing beside his father speaking to the two families.

She grasped his arm with a smile and pulled him away from the others.

He looked down at her in surprise, but allowed her to lead him where she would.

After the blow up the night before, he had offered her a ride home. In the carriage, he had broken the engagement. Telling her that, no matter his reputation, he could not bring himself to marry a woman who was so heartless as to wish the harm of innocent children.

The whole time he had listened to her wails and threats of her father's wrath, he had pictured the scene in Chariton House. Alex surrounded by such sweet faces as she read her story. He had hoped for a clean break but knew it was a dream that would never come to be, and he was right. He had acted in anger, and now he was concerned what the repercussions would be.

He had thought she would be happy not to have to marry him. He knew she was afraid of him, no small thanks to Alex for this.

Janice had at first been relieved when he had broken the engagement. It had not been announced, and she could make a public display to let all know it was her idea. The relief was short lived, though. She knew she could not be free that easy. She could not allow her father go to debtor's prison.

She pulled him out the garden doors, still in sight but out of hearing range. "I do not think you want to call off the betrothal." Her soft words were full of malice.

"I cannot marry you." He was still not sure what he was going to do about her father and his rumors, but he would think of something. It could be no worse than now. When they had arrived at the ball, he saw several people give Alex the cut direct. She had gone about her business as if it didn't bother her. Whether it bothered her or not, it was killing Marc.

If Alex didn't do anything else, perhaps he could smooth over this latest rumor and get her out of the trouble she had landed herself in. He felt partially responsible for the extent of the rumors since he was positive they would not have been so bad if he, and the others, had not stormed into Rose Hall demanding to know where she was after her daring escape from the Rutmeyer soiree.

He heard whispered rumors of her love affair with Edward, words that ground to a halt when he was near. They had heard also of his behavior at White's and, though it was unlikely he would act in such a way here, no one seemed to want to risk his wrath.

He saw several people look at him in sympathy, as if he was the jilted suitor. He was not going to marry her for God's sake, why would they think he would care if she had a hundred lovers?

"You will marry me because I think you care for that girl more than you would like to say. I can see the anger in your eyes as you watch her." His eyes narrowed as he realized he had been staring at Alex and Spencer Ferguson as he twirled her across the floor. "Do not try to deny it. I see it. I also know of her little escapades with Clifton shipping."

He swung his gaze to her. "How do you know?"

She smiled. "You will marry me, or I will not bother with just destroying Clifton shipping, I will ruin your little angel over there. With the way she behaves, it will not take much."

"And if I marry you, you will leave her alone?" She nodded. "Fine. Shall we announce it now?"

"No, but I want to make it at the end of the midnight dinner, before they serve desert." With that she turned and walked away.

He looked back to the dance floor to see that the song had changed, and Alex's dance partner with it. He could see no way out of this announcement or this marriage now. It was all the fault of Alex. He tried to be angry with her, but could not. He sighed. He could not make this announcement without at least warning her that it was coming.

He was waiting for them as she and her father left the dance

floor. He took her hand before her next partner had a chance to intervene. "Shall I have this dance, my lady?"

No smile, just a slight nod.

On the floor, he held her close. This was the hardest thing he had
ever done. He could not make the words come out. She looked so
defeated that he could not bear to destroy what love she might still
have for him. The understanding that, if she were not forewarned of
his announcement, it would be much worse than just telling her now,
unfroze his tongue.

"I am announcing the betrothal tonight." She stiffened, but didn't
respond, nor did she look at him. "After dinner." Still nothing.
"Please, Alex, do not do this to me." The only indication that she had
even heard him was a thin tear that ran silently down her face.

He could not bear it. He was angry, angry with Janice, her father,
the damn rules of the ton, and mostly with Alex who had no right to
make him feel such pain. His quiet words came through clenched
teeth. "You brought this on yourself with your careless and selfish
acts. If you knew how to behave like a woman instead of some
whore, we would not be in this mess. How can you be angry with me
when you have spread your legs for everyone but me? At least Janice
knows how to act—"

Her hand connected loudly with his jaw, not a punch this time,
but a stinging slap. Gasps were heard around them as everyone
stopped to stare. She turned and fled out the garden doors.

Without a thought to consequences, he chased after her, unmind-
ful of the knowing stares that followed. He almost lost her in the
turns and twists of the garden, but the moon was full, giving light
through the soft cloud cover.

He caught her by one of the big marble benches. "How dare you
embarrass me like that?" He sat on the bench dragging her across his
lap. Marc heard the arm of her gown tear.

"Stop, what do you think you are doing?" Her high squeal could
probably be heard all the way to the ballroom, but he didn't care.

"I am doing something your father should have done long ago."

He held down the struggling form with one arm and jerked up her
skirts and petticoats baring her to her drawers. The soft silky material
was warm under his hand as he yanked them down as well. His hand
hit her bared flesh again and again. He could hear her sobs as she
begged him to stop, to release her. She struggled and fought against
him. Still, he delivered the swats she so richly deserved.

"Marc."

The sound of his name torn from her lips stopped his hand—and his heart. He looked at the deep red hand prints on her pale white bottom and cringed.

"Oh, Alex." Turning her gently in his arms he cradled her to his pounding chest while she cried. Her skirt still around her waist, her drawers around her knees, she clung to him. "Forgive me, baby."

Her sobs were silenced as he kissed her deeply, tender and with regret. His hand smoothing along the damage he had done to her tender skin.

"What the hell did you do?" Before he knew it, Alex was ripped from his hand and he felt a fist connect with his jaw. Maxwell grasped Thomas as he lunged again at the man who, for all it looked like, had just raped his daughter.

One look at her tear streaked frightened face as she pulled up her drawers and adjusted her torn clothing was all the proof needed. "Let me go. I will kill him now. You dare to violate my daughter in such a barbaric fashion. You could not contain your lusts with a mistress and a wife-to-be, you had to rape my daughter as well."

Thomas tore free, but before he could get to Marc, Alex was standing in his way, her small hand upon his chest.

"Stop. He did not rape me. It is not how it looks." One quick look down at herself, and she realized it was bad. She would never convince them of that unless she did something drastic. Standing before them was her father, his father, and Jeremy, all looked ready to do Marc some bodily harm. She cringed and turned to face Marc. She shook her head. Her eyes were emotionless specks of ice as she raised her skirts showing the damage done. Marc winced.

Jeremy started to laugh.

"Shut up, boy. Let me go, Maxwell." As soon as Thomas was released he tugged her skirts down and turned her to face him. "Are you all right?" She nodded. He took a deep breath drawing her into his arms and was surprised when she clung to him. "Forgive me, love." She nodded against him. When she whispered "I love him," he turned to Marc. "Sorry, my boy, I know you would not do such a thing, and it was only shock that made me speak in such a way."

Marc understood. He looked at her now, and that was how it appeared to him. The only thing that had saved him was Alex. Not only had she responded to his kiss, even after he had spanked her, she had thrown herself in front of him to protect him. "You protected me?"

He almost smiled until her cold words stopped him. "I protected my father, my lord. There is no reason he should hang for killing you. I would hate to lose him, my lord," she said from the safety of her father's embrace.

Maxwell's reasonable voice broke the tension. "Nevertheless, whether you had given her the spanking she deserved or not, that was not what was happening when we came upon you, and there is no telling what was heard in the ballroom. You will do what is right and marry her. We cannot get out of this scandal without it. Do you think she can just go walking back into the ball with her dress torn and her lips kiss swollen?"

Before Marc had a chance to answer, Alex broke free and turned on them. "I will not marry him. You cannot do that to him." How could she marry him, force him into a marriage with a woman he hated? He had to hate her. The angry words he had said to her, the beating he had just delivered. No, she could not allow Marc to be saddled with her. She loved him far too much for that. "You cannot force him to marry me. I will not allow it."

"You have no choice, my love, either of you. There is no way—" Thomas halted and listened. Voices were heard, guests were starting to come look for them. Hell, this was getting worse. Thomas turned to the man who would now be his son in law. "Get her out of here. We can only hope they have not heard anything, and it will be better to let them think you took advantage of her willingly, than what they will think if they see her in her condition now."

"I will not go anywhere with you, my lord." She pulled her arm away from him when he grabbed for her.

He gritted his teeth and, without a word, he slung her over his shoulder and disappeared into the garden.

Throwing her into his carriage, he climbed in after her. "Take us to Hollister and then return."

It was all he said until he had her safely in her father's library.

"My lord, this is—"

"Do not call me that. Dammit, Alex, we have no choice. Do you think this is what I want either." She looked as if he had physically struck her. "That is not what I meant. It is just—"

"I know what it is, *my lord,* and no I do not think you want to marry me. That is obvious." She looked at the chair, went to sit, then changed her mind. Marc winced. Staring out the window into the darkness, she began to cry.

"Alex, we do not have a choice." What was he to say to comfort her? She knew he didn't want to marry her. Did she truly want to marry him? She had told Rock that she did and her arguments with her father had consisted of getting Marc out of the marriage, not her. "It will be all right. We will marry and as soon as I know you are not increasing we will—"

He ducked as a vase full of roses flew at his head.

"Get out! Get out!" When she began to search for more objects to throw, he wisely escaped the room. Windrow came flying into the hall, sliding to a stop before the library door as something crashed against it.

Marc leaned against the wall not far from the door. "I would not go in there if I were you."

"My lord, what is going on in there?" Edmond Windrow reached for the handle, shook his head, and pulled his hand away as something else crashed against the door.

"I have just asked Alex to marry me. She is in the process of agreeing."

The butler looked at him with unease. "Yes indeed, my lord. Congratulations." He shook his head as something thumped against the door, probably a large book, or as angry as she was perhaps the bookcase itself. He added in a whisper. "I think."

When the families came to Hollister House, the driver telling them where he had taken them, they found silence. Marc still stood beside the library door, but there was no sign of Alex.

"What is going on, where is Alex?"

Windrow gave a snort as he took the coats. "She is in the process of agreeing to Lord Clifton's proposal."

They all looked at Marc in alarm. "What is he talking about?"

"Oh, my lord, I am sorry. I thought you knew he was going to ask her. I did not mean—" The butler shook and sputtered until Marc shook his head.

"It is fine, Windrow. They know." Marc glanced at the ladies and looked at his father in question. Maxwell nodded. Marc relaxed and looked back to the butler. "Now, we just have to wait for the young lady to come to terms with it."

"Good luck on that, my lord," Windrow said with a sympathetic smile.

Marc scowled.

"Not good?" Thomas asked.

Marc reached over and knocked on the door. Nothing. Carefully he tried the door. The moment it creaked something crashed against it, he pulled it closed. "She is just fine. She is coming around."

Thomas shook his head. "I am sorry. It was as we feared it would be, though. It was all the guests could speak of after we returned to the ballroom. Some of the guests had overheard the end of our conversation, about the kiss and the dishevelment of her clothing." He sighed. "There will be no getting out of it."

"Alex," Amber knocked lightly on the door. She pushed it open a crack. "Ashlee and I are going to come in and talk to you, all right?" Amber pushed it open farther. "Please do not throw anything at my head."

The response was a pitiful stream of tearful words. "Be careful, there is glass by the door."

When they opened the door, they found the remains of a brandy decanter, four vases, flowers and water strewn everywhere.

Amber turned to the family. "I will take care of her. We will get her to bed." Ashlee picked her way through the rubble, but Amber hesitated. Turning to her brother, she smiled. "I think it may be best if you were not outside the door when we bring her out."

In the study, the rest of the family sat in silence waiting for the library door to open. It did in moments. Marc walked to the door to watch. His sisters walked a limp Alex between them.

"It is not fair. How can my father do this to me? He wants me to marry a man who hates me. It is not fair."

Her voice was spiteful and angry. She had loved him at one time. He knew it in his heart, but he thought now he had ruined it all.

Behind her closed bed chamber door, Alex fell into her bed.

"You have no choice, Alex. Will you do the right thing? It is not just your reputation but his as well. If he does not marry you, he will be ruined. You do not want that, do you?"

Amber brushed her hair back out of Alex's blue eyes.

"No, I will marry him. How can I love him still?"

No one had an answer. Rebecca crawled into bed beside her and held her close. Ashlee took the other side, keeping her warm and letting her cry herself to sleep.

ೲೲ

"Marc, what happened?" Maxwell pulled his son away from the door and pushed him toward a chair.

Marc gave an account of her tantrum when they arrived here. He left out the part that he was not going to consummate the wedding and why. He just couldn't bring himself to tell them.

He felt bad that he had hurt her feelings, but he would not raise a bastard child as his heir. If she was pregnant, he would raise the child, but he would not give him everything. His heir would be from his blood. He would do nothing else. If she was pregnant, he prayed for a girl and prayed she would look like Alex and not Spencer or Edward.

"She will come around." Marc knew he sounded unsure. Amber appeared in the doorway. "Is she all right?"

"No, Marc she is not. She will marry you, but she thinks you hate her."

Marc just stared at his feet.

"Perhaps we should leave the men to talk, ladies," Catherine said, standing and leading them out.

Amber turning to Maxwell after the ladies had passed her. "Papa, Ashlee is staying the night here. She is already in bed with Alex and her little maid."

The door closed and Marc looked up. "Father, have you spoken to him about the docks?"

Maxwell nodded. That just left Jeremy and Blake so he gave a quick account for their benefit, and, like his father, he left out the kiss.

"Somehow Janice has found out about it." Marc took a deep breath. "After Janice's horrifying comment about Chariton house, I told her the betrothal was off. When she got to the ball, she threatened me with her knowledge of Alex's involvement with the shipping company. Saying she would not let me break the agreement. If I did, she would use the information against her. This marriage will help with some of the rumors and scandal, but not all. If I cannot control Alex and her temper, she will ruin us both."

Chapter 19

W here is she? She cannot have bolted. Could she?" Marc didn't like to think so, but he knew it was a possibility.

"Marcus, your bride is not even late. You are not getting nervous, are you?" Jeremy smiled at his jittery friend. Marc stood at the front of the small church in Barnet.

No one had wanted to endure the scrutiny or snide whispers of the ton during such an auspicious occasion, and they had all been quick to agree to Alex's request for a country wedding.

They had left London the morning after the Bickerbee Ball, special license in hand. That had been three days ago, and Alex had not spoken one word to Marc in all that time, not even to call him the dreaded title that she spat at him every chance she got.

In fact, he had hardly seen her since the night in they had arrived in the country. She was always off in the woods doing God knows what.

Alex had, in fact, been at Linden most of the time, getting it situated and everyone in their posts. She wasn't sure what she was going to do about Linden now, but she needed to set everything to rights before she told Marc. First she had to tell Marc who the infamous jockey was, and she had not gathered enough courage for that.

The wedding was not a small occasion, with family and close friends, and the servants of both houses, people filled the small church, nearly from pews to rafters. It was not small, but it was filled with all the people that Alex cared about.

The doors opened, and Marc smiled. Vanessa Chariton, a young woman who must be her daughter Victoria, and a passel full of children made their way into the small church.

His smile faltered as he noticed Malacinda followed close at their heels.

One beautiful little girl with bright blue eyes and bouncing blonde curls broke from the group and barreled straight for him. "Marc!"

"Heather, my dear, I am so glad you could make it. I know Alex will be pleased." Swinging her into his arms, he looked at his father. "Did you say it is not quite time?" At his father's nod, Marc strode toward the awaiting group.

He had invited Vanessa Chariton and the children. He could even see her bringing her daughter, but he could not fathom that Alex was going to be pleased that his mistress, ex-mistress, was a wedding guest.

"My lord, I am so pleased." Malacinda wrapped her arms around him in a tight hug. "I know she will make you so happy," she whispered in his ear.

He returned her embrace without thinking and heard a gasp from behind him. Turning, he saw the most beautiful sight.

Alex wore a sparkling white gown, with gold highlights and hem work. The sleeves were lace showing off her smooth skin, and the bodice was cut low showing off just enough skin to make his throat grow tight. Her hair was piled high on her head, and white roses were entwined through the bright red curls. Loose stands were left to frame her beautiful face. His heart stopped at the sight of her tears.

"Alex, I am sorry." Even as he spoke, he stepped away from his mistress.

Alex ignored him. She rushed to their guests sweeping both Malacinda and Victoria in a tight embrace. Then, turning, she knelt on the floor, oblivious to the damage she was doing to the delicate stitch work as the skirts swept across the floor. She gathered as many children as she could into her arms.

"I heard Heather's rambunctious voice. You made it, after all?" She looked up at Vanessa with love swirling in her eyes.

Vanessa had regrettably informed her that there was no way for her to make the journey with all the kids, but she would be there if it were possible.

"You bridegroom invited us. He said he did not think it right for your wedding to go on without us. He even sent several carriages and servants to help me with all the children."

Marc caught her in mid lunge. Alex threw her arms around his neck and kissed him deeply. "Oh, Marc. Thank you."

Holding her tightly, he chuckled. "I am not supposed to kiss you until the Vicar says I can." His laughter stopped as the door opened again. "What the Hel—" Marc glanced at the Vicar. "What are they doing here?"

The men from the back room at Rose Hall, all seven of them, including Brandon Coshtess and Finch Cromby, came into the church, escorting an elegant older lady.

Alex looked back at them as the two big men took a stand on each side of the door, standing at attention, but each with a big smile for her. Michael spotted a lovely young woman with no one at her side and joined her. Alex just sighed and shook her head.

Porter Farthing, with a smile, and Spencer Ferguson, with a lavish bow, took a seat at the back of the room. Craig Connelly helped his mother, Rachel Connelly Pettlenoster to her seat before joining her on the pew.

James Gideon accompanied Edward as he walked toward the couple. "Am I too late?"

Alex forced herself not to throw herself into his arms. She just smiled sweetly. "No, we are just getting started."

"What are you doing here?" Thomas growled darkly at the man he would so much like to hate.

"Papa, I invited them here." She dropped her voice to a whisper. "I am sorry, but this is the only day I will ever get married. I wanted them to be here. They have been part of my life for so long." She took his arm and wrapped her arms around it. She hugged it to her chest and looked up at him pleadingly. "Please, Papa. He needs to be here."

Thomas looked down into her soft blue eyes and grunted. Edward had known her all her life. He had helped her out when she had needed it and had beaten Manning when he had tried to hurt her. Throughout all the years, he had never tried to contact Catherine and had never said anything about being Alex's father, but whether Thomas liked it or not, he was. He was her true father, and he did deserve to be there.

Thomas looked at Edward. "Indeed." He said it without a hint of the anger he was feeling. He could not allow his fear to stand in between what was right for his daughter.

"Thank you, Papa." She turned her eyes to Marc. He had withdrawn from her, once again angry and suspicious.

Edward stepped toward Marc. "If you tell me to go, I will, I will even take Spencer with me, because I know you are suspicious of him, as well. I would ask that the rest of the men get to stay."

Edward waited patiently for Marc to decide. He would abide by the man's wishes though it would kill him not to see his daughter married.

"Stay, both of you. I have my mistress here. She may as well have her lovers." Ignoring the gasps around him, he started to walk away, but he was in for one more shock.

The doorway was suddenly filled with a body, and Marc wondered for a moment if Tess Richards would make it through the narrow doorway. He did, and behind him came Raymond Dunmore. They both found a seat next to Robert. Those close by gasped and moved away from the large man.

Alex smiled at Tess. Marc growled before taking his place at the front of the church.

Alex watched her soon-to-be husband take his place before turning to her friends. "Gideon, Edward please find a seat up front." Alex pulled on Thomas's arm leading him to the back of the church.

They had disappeared into the small waiting room before Thomas had calmed his anger. Catherine looked pale and shaky, she must have seen Edward. Well, perhaps she would comfort him the way she did last time. Thomas tried to push that selfish thought out of his mind, but it didn't seem to want to go. "Papa, I know you are angry, but I—"

He waved away her words. "You have every right to invite whoever you want, whether it be that man or your soon-to-be-husband's mistress—what were you thinking?"

Wrapping her arms around his waist, she pressed her head into his chest. His heart was beating too fast. It thudded against his chest. "I was thinking that I care for her. She is one of a very few I would consider a close friend. I wanted her here. It would almost be like asking Ashlee not to come. Are you ready to give me away?"

"No." Thomas tightened his embrace and fought back the tears. He wasn't at all, but he gave his wife a nod and she rushed from the room to let everyone know they were ready. "It does make it easier knowing you are so close. With as much time as the two families spend in each other's home, I figure not much will change."

She looked up at him with a beaming smile. "I love you, you know."

He dropped a kiss on the tip of her nose. "Yes, I know, but I love you more."

The wedding was brief but beautiful, and everyone met at Clifton Manor home for the reception. The courtyard was full of carriages, surreys, and people upon people. One by one, they congratulated the couple as they made their way into the dining hall. Marc was surprised to see the Rose Hall men in line. He had heard their debate with Alex that it was not proper for them to come. He agreed, but it appeared that Alex had won.

Edward congratulated them both with a wide smile. He took Alex into his arms with a tight, but brief hug. "I am so happy for you, my darling." He kissed her cheek, turned, and held his hand out to Marc.

Marc scowled at it, looked at the crowd, and took it. Edward held it longer than necessary, placing his other hand over the top of their clasped hands. "Take good care of her."

Marc tugged his hand away without a response.

Spencer took his turn next. He wrapped Alex into a large hug and kissed her soundly on the cheek. "I am glad for you, my love."

Marc opened his mouth to object just as Spencer turned on him, catching him off guard, and throwing his arms around him as well.

"Get off me, Ferguson."

Spencer just laughed kissing him loudly on the cheek before releasing him.

They were making good progress through the guests when a path opened up before them. Through the middle came the big Tess. "Alex, my tiny lady." His voice was clogged with emotion.

Tess took her into his hands and threw her into the air, catching her in a tight bear hug. "Tess—Tess you have to let me go." Alex was laughing even as she struggled. "I cannot breathe."

He dropped her suddenly. She reached for Marc's arm to regain her balance. "You know how I adore you, Tess, but you need to remember I am a small and weak woman."

He just laughed, hitting Marc on the back so hard he staggered. "Weak, that's a good one, huh, my lord?" Marc could smell brandy as the man leaned closer to him. "You think she's weak m' lord?"

"Not at all, but I do think I like you better when you have had a few. At least you're not threatening to rip off my arm."

Tess staggered, Marc did his best to support him, but he felt his knees begin to buckle under the weight.

"Quite so, I will still do it, though, if you don't treat my guardian angel right."

With that, he was out, and Marc had a moment of panic when he pictured himself underneath the large man. Edward appeared before him, along with his two big guards.

Alex sighed in relief. "Oh, thank goodness. Brandon, Finch, take Tess if you will, please. I told him not to drink before he came."

"He was nervous, my lady." Robert smiled at her. "Congratulations on your wedding."

"Thank you, Robert. Take Tess to the green room and lay him there. No, Raymond, you stay and enjoy the party. He will be out for some time."

The bride and groom walked into the banquet hall, surrounded by the orphans from Chariton. "Shall we extract ourselves from the pack of mongrels, my lord, and dance the first dance."

"Do not call me that."

Everyone watched as the young couple danced. They were perfect together, as always, and both of them forgot their problems, at least, for the space of the dance.

"Do you think everyone is having a good time, my lord?" Alex asked, looking at the guests going by as she twirled.

"I think with the amount of food and drink my father and yours are providing, everyone will have a good time. I think we had better keep young Cranston away from the drink, though."

Alex tried to catch sight of Michael, but couldn't. "Why is that, my lord?"

"He has already tried his luck with every unattached woman in this place. If he drinks too much, he may try the ones with husbands at their sides." His eyes whipped back to her as her laughter caressed him. Damn, but he wanted her.

"It does not take drink to accomplish that, my lord. All it takes is for him to open his eyes in the mornings. If a husband is not standing at her side, he will wait till he is. I daresay it is more sporting that way."

"My God woman, you cannot speak that way." He laughed, despite himself. "Are you sure you do not want to go on our honeymoon now?"

"No, I want to finish the season. If we leave now, the ton may think we are sneaking away to hide, and that will do neither of us any good, my lord."

The night wore on, the guests began to dwindle, and Alex began to get anxious. Marc watched her closely. "Are you tired, baby?" She smiled at him. He had called her that since she was indeed one. He had just never stopped. She was glad he no longer thought of her as one, though.

"No, just ready to go upstairs."

"All right. Let's sneak out before they notice we are gone."

Most of the guests had already left, leaving just the servants and the families, and most of the servants had already found their beds.

"She does not know how to keep that mouth of hers shut, Marc. If she gets too loud, put a pillow over her face." Jeremy ducked as a plate came flying at him from two directions. Amber smiled with satisfaction that her plate as well as Alex's hit their target. "Witches."

The newlyweds left the hall, laughing at the commotion behind them as everyone retired for the night. The laughter stopped when they were in the room, alone and the door shut. Marc walked to the bed and looked at it. Taking a deep breath, he knew there was no way he could share her bed. No way at all.

He had planned to sleep with her, not to let anyone know there was something wrong, but he knew if he was in that bed he would take her. He was aching with the need already.

"I will sleep in the chair, you may have the bed." Marc planted himself into the chair and slipped off one black Hessian.

"What? You are not serious, are you? You do not plan to share my bed tonight?" Alex stormed at him.

"I told you. I will not have a bastard child as my heir. I will not take you until I know you are not breeding."

She stared at him with her jaw hanging loose. She had thought everything would work itself out now that they were married. He would have to consummate the marriage and then he would know he had been wrong.

"Marc, I do not have a lover. You are the closest thing I have to that and even you have yet to take me." She tried to keep her voice low, but the anger was starting to worm its way through her.

"Do not shout or I will put that pillow over your face. I will not take you and that is it."

"Put a pillow over my—you go right ahead and try. If you would only take me like you have tried to so many times, you would see I am telling the truth. I have heard there are ways a man knows. From what I understand, you cannot fake that."

"I will not take you." He could not. Even if he found she was not a virgin, he would not be able to stop once he had started. Then he would never know if the baby was his or not. It was not a risk he was willing to take.

"Why? You were going to force yourself on me before. Am I no longer good enough now that I am your wife? Do not take it out on me because we had to get married. You are the one who took me over your knee, not the other way around."

She was sure everyone in the house could hear them now, but she was beyond caring. She would be grateful later when her anger had dissipated that the guests had all left, leaving only family and the big Tess who was still out to the world.

"Yes, I took you over my knee. I should do it again for inviting your damned lovers to my wedding. And what the hell were you thinking inviting Malacinda?" He had spoken to Vanessa Chariton at the reception to find out why she would bring his ex-mistress. She had been surprised at first but then had just laughed telling him that his bride was the one who had invited her. She had invited Vanessa and her daughter as well but until Marc had sent the carriages and the men to help she had no way of transporting that many children at once.

"Too bad she is not installed in your home anymore or you could go to her tonight, then at least one of us can be happy."

"You are right, you little hoyden, that is what I need. There is no need for both of us to go without. I have gone without for too long now. I will see you in the morning." Marc slipped his boot back on and lunged to his feet.

"Where are you going?" Alex grasped his arm only to have him jerk it away. She fell to her knees as he yanked open the door.

"I may not have a mistress, thanks to you, but there are plenty of whores out there who will be more than happy to satisfy a man like me. When I know you are not breeding, I will take you. Until then, I will take my pleasures elsewhere."

With that, he slammed the door closing off the sight of her kneeling frame.

He expected something to smash into the door, expected screaming and shouting. He heard neither. What he did hear tore at his heart, she didn't yell nor curse, but the broken sobs coming from inside his chambers was more than he could take.

As Marc turned his carriage toward London, he felt the guilt hit him. He had heard her tears, had wanted to go to her, but, still, he had fled. Fled from the feelings she was invoking in him. Feelings he neither wanted nor understood.

He wanted nothing more than to hold her, but he was afraid if he did, he would not stop. He wanted her. He could feel her body beneath him, as if it was still there, he could see it when he closed his eyes, could see the love in her eyes. Love he had destroyed with his betrothal to Janice.

He had only made it a few miles before pounding on the roof and telling the driver to take him back home. He had no taste for a whore. He only wanted one woman, the same woman he had been too stupid to take last season. She would have let him. She would have been his wife then. He should have just asked her, instead of letting everything else get in the way. Now he was afraid it was too late, the woman he loved, and yes he knew now he loved her. The woman he loved, now hated him, and what was just as bad, she thought he hated her.

Marc opened his bed chamber door slowly, truly expecting a vase to be thrown at his head. A voice behind him caused him to jump. "She is not there."

"Dammit Tess. You scared me witless. What are doing roaming the halls this time of night? I thought you would still be sleeping." Marc waited for his heart to calm, which it didn't. "What do you mean she is not here?"

"I came to check on her because I heard the fighting. I saw her leave and decided to wait for you in case you cannot guess where she went." Tess swayed until he rested against the wall.

"Come on." Marc pulled him into the chamber and pushed the big fellow onto his bed. "Now, where is she?"

As if he couldn't guess.

"She said that if you were going to go see a whore, she would at least spend her wedding night with someone who doesn't hate her, doing something she truly enjoys." His eyes slid closed.

"I do not hate her, I love her."

Tess didn't hear. He was already snoring.

Saddling his big stallion, Marc rode hard straight to Rose Hall. The beast was heaving for breath by the time they arrived. Rose Hall was close to London, but a hefty ride from Barnet.

Remembering the last time they had arrived there, he wondered if indeed it did have a back door. He rode around the building and found Robert, who had just finished cooling his horse and Alex's mare. Handing him the reins, Marc waited for him to speak, but Robert just motioned to the door. When he pushed it open and stepped, inside his jaw dropped open.

Along the wall were piles of pillows and upon those pillows were all kinds of women, some a little clothed, some completely naked. Michael Cranston was in his favorite spot kissing one woman and grasping the breast of another. There at the table were all the men who were at the wedding, with the exception of the two guards who stood at the other door and looked about to throw him bodily out.

The most shocking of all was his bride. Alex sat, still in her wedding dress at the end of the table with cards in hand and a pile of chips in front of her. Victoria was handing her a brandy, her bare breasts next to Alex's face.

Marc's eyes glanced over the young woman as they had the other's in the room, including the men, but when they lit on Alex, his gaze dropped down to her cleavage, which was more than amply displayed, and stayed.

Spencer laughed at the look on his face. "Shut the door and your mouth and come on in, my lord groom. I think you are looking for your bride, yes?

Snapping his jaw shut, Marc shut the door. "Alex, let's go. I am here to take you home?"

"Are you here to take me, or just take me home?" She refused to back down to his scowl.

"I told you already—"

"Fine," She waved away his words. "Then I will stay here. If I am not going to get what I want, I will play cards instead. Tell me, would you rather go home, fight and sleep in a chair or stay here and play cards? Stay. Sit and play with me." She gave a small laugh. "Do not worry, I will go easy on you."

"Just do not enjoy the scenery overly much, my lord, least your little bride here gets it into her head to hurt you." Connelly laughed at his own wit when no one else would.

Marc sat straight across from her, between Gideon and Spencer. "Why not? I should be able to take in the atmosphere as much as I like." He reached for Victoria, but Gideon stayed his hand and shook his head.

"Not her."

"Why not?" Marc looked from her to the rest of the women and wondered what the difference was.

"She is off limits," was Gideon's only reply.

"Who says?" Marc waited for Edward to speak up, but it was his wife instead.

"I do. She is off limits. She will get you your drinks, a cigar if you want one, but you do not touch her. If you want to touch some- one, there is a room full of girls if you can fight one away from the amorous Michael."

Michael laughed from the cushions. "If she tells you not to touch, listen. I did not listen, and it got me crashed on top the head with the very chair I had been sitting in the moment before she kicked it out from under me. All I wanted to do was grab a breast that ran in front of my face." With that thought, he grasped the breast next to him.

Alex just shook her head.

"If I cannot enjoy *her* charms, which woman can I have?" Marce looked at the woman lounging about and found one that pleased his eye. "How about you? Come here, my sweet."

Becka Rannally approached to a safe distance away then looked at Alex. Alex crossed her arms across her chest, leaned back, and smiled wickedly. The young woman backed up a step.

Marc knew the woman was afraid of his wife. He was startled to realize he liked that. Alex nodded and the naked woman sat upon his lap. His eyes widened as he looked at Alex's passive face.

Marc wanted to see her upset, jealous as he was, but she had played games of chance long enough that no one could out do her bluffs. It was easy to bluff when you knew the others' hands. Marc was easy to read. Tonight she would bleed him dry, and not only in cards.

Victoria set a drink before him, and Edward gave him the chips he requested.

Marc tried to play a decent hand while trying to look around the woman who perched naked on his lap, but he could not. It was not excitement that he felt, he felt uncomfortable and a scoundrel. After the third hand he had lost to Alex, he smiled at the lovely Becka. "My dear, I will have to ask you to take yourself where I am not so distracted. I fear, with your beauty and charms upon me, I cannot concentrate to win."

She rose to leave but leaned down to whisper in his ear, loud enough for all to hear. "You will need all the wits you can muster if you think to win over your wife." He knew the young woman was speaking of deeper things than a game a chance, but then love was the biggest game of chance of all.

Marc looked at Alex, his eyes roaming to her breasts. She smiled. Slipping off her slipper she raised her foot, pressing it into Marc's groin. He jumped trying to get away, but she pressed harder.

"Alex, what are doing—" Spencer's voice cracked. He didn't think he had it in him to still be shocked, but he was. His true voice was straining to come forward.

Marc spared him a suspicious glance as he tried to disengage her foot from his quickly raising manhood.

"Alex, stop? What are you doing?" Marc's voice sounded as high as the one Spencer put on normally.

"I was just checking." She dropped her foot with a knowing grin.

Edward laughed at Marc's sneer "She is unbeatable in the bluff, but always curious."

"What is that supposed to mean?" Marc looked at his bride with malice. "Tell me now."

"Fine, my lord. I knew you were bluffing because I can read your face. I have known you long enough to know the reason you do not play cards is because your handsome face gives you away, but, even though I know my opponent is bluffing, I still like to see what cards he holds to see how right I actually was."

Marc didn't like to think he was that readable, even though he knew she was right. "How did you know I was not going to take that woman off with me later?"

She took a deep breath while deciding on if she should tell him. "If I tell you, will you stay and play cards tonight? And be civil to everyone?"

He nodded, reluctantly.

"Good. When you walked into the room, your eyes went straight to me and my breasts. Even when you were looking at the other girls, your eyes stayed on their faces, *for the most part*. Though I cannot begrudge you that, for I am sure if I were to see a naked man, I would be hard pressed not to at least glance."

"I see you glance and that man will lose whatever it is you glanced at." Marc glared at Edward and Spencer in warning.

"Even when you looked at the girls, it was not for long, and your eyes came back to me. To judge my reaction, to see if your ploy was working and if I was getting angry. But for your ego, I will tell you that I was relieved to find you soft beneath that naked woman...well, at least you were until my foot began to—"

"Enough!" Marc was beginning to get hard again just thinking about it.

"So you see, I knew there was no chance of you taking that woman anywhere with you, besides if you had wanted another woman you would be with the whore now and not with me."

She gave him a wide smile. Marc sucked in his breath, She was absolutely magnificent.

"There is also no chance because our Becka is not stupid enough to cross Miss Alex." Spencer laughed his hideous laugh and Marc grabbed him by the arm.

When Alex opened her mouth, Marc just waved her off. "I will make a deal with you, Ferguson. I heard you speak just a moment ago and it was more than shock that changed your voice. I will ask no questions, of any kind, if I do not have to listen to that insipid voice of yours, at least for the rest of this night."

Spencer looked at Alex, but she just waited. She could tell him Marc was a man of his word and could be trusted, but the decision was Spencer's, and she did not want to interfere.

"I would guess that it must be easier on you not to do that." Marc probed at him. He released his arm. "I am a man of my word, I will not say anything to anyone, and I will not bother you with tiresome questions. I would, however, enjoy the night more if you would not screech in my ear all night." Marc picked up the next hand of cards and waited.

Spencer burst out laughing. "I can see why my little lady here loves you so much."

Marc didn't even notice the deep voice that said the spy had decided to trust him. His eyes darkened as they jerked to Alex's horrified face. So much for the perfect bluffer. She looked up at him and shrugged.

He wanted to jump up and dance. She didn't hate him. That look said she did indeed still love him. Now as long as she was not pregnant, he could move on, past her being unchaste. Hell, he was a long way from a virgin. He supposed he could ask no more of her.

Alex had known the minute he had walked into the room that he didn't hate her. He had not gone to a whore, and in a room full of naked breasts his eyes went to her. He cared for her, he did. She knew it now.

Before he had arrived, she questioned Spencer on why Marc threw Gregson against the wall. He had laughed when he told her. She had felt her heart cry out for him. Then he had defended her at the docks and was angry that someone had struck her. And tonight he had threatened any man she even looked at. Plus, if he didn't care he would not have tried so hard to make her jealous.

Gideon laughed at Marc as Edward dealt another hand. "You have not heard a word I said. Boy, if you want to keep any of that money of yours out of your wife's pocket, you had best pay attention."

Marc tried his best to focus, but every time he did, his little bride leaned forward and smiled at him, and his mind went back to Spencer's words. She loved him. Yes, he had no doubt he could look past her mistakes. She would make him a good wife. Now that he could help her at the orphanage, and he would soon be in control of his shipping company there was no reason for her to go sneaking around.

The night passed quickly, with lots of laughter and joking. Marc found that he was having fun. Sitting in the midst of these men, he was beginning to find it hard to believe that any of them were her lovers.

Edward looked at her like a father would, and Spencer spent more time with his arm around Marc than looking at her. Marc was no longer sure about any of his assumptions. Perhaps he would risk the consummation of the marriage.

They stayed late into the night, and the more Marc drank, the more sure he became that he had been wrong, and the more she ran her bare foot up his leg, the more he found he didn't care.

Chapter 20

Thomas Hollister tried to control his worry as his horse and Maxwell's were saddled, and the family watched the last of their baggage being piled into the two awaiting carriages.

Rebecca had informed Amber and Ashlee that neither newlywed was there when they had inquired with concern as to how things were going between the couple. The fight the night before had been fierce. Thomas knew Alex well, and more than likely she had run, and now her new husband was out searching for her.

"Return to London, and do not worry. We will find them—" Maxwell's words ground to a halt as three horses came into view around the curve of the long tree lined drive. The exhausted looking couple and Robert, trailing behind them at a safe distance, rode sedately to the manor, as if they had not been missing all morning and half the night.

Alex rode behind Marc's big stallion on her favorite racer, Lady-bird, now trained to perfection. She would be in the races next season without a doubt.

Alex looked back at Robert, who she had dragged from his pallet in her mad dash to be away from the manor. Not wanting to take the carriage she had saddled her mare instead and had ignored Robert's protests of the use of the horse as well as her attire.

She probably should have listened, riding in a wedding dress was more difficult than she had imagined. Alex, for the thousandth time, sighed deeply. The horses plodded along at an excruciatingly slow speed. She had not ridden this slow since she was two.

"You do not have the proper saddle," Marc repeated, as he had for at least half the trip from Rose Hall.

"I did not ask."

Marc looked back at her and shook his head. "You did not have to ask, again, your continued sighing is asking for you."

Alex went to throw her leg over the saddle, in the same fashion she had ridden in to get to Rose Hall, and Marc pulled his horse to a stop. "I do not think so."

"We are almost home." She grinned. "I will race you. First one to the family wins." She smiled. If he was willing, she would just tell him about A.H.

"Absolutely not, someone might see you," he grumbled and tugged on his horse's reins to get him moving again.

Alex felt her heart drop. Well, so much for that. Marc seemed even more concerned with his reputation now that she was his wife. Which, she supposed, was understandable, but now she was even more concerned about telling him about A.H. He was not going to understand, and he was never going to approve of her racing.

"Where have you been?" Thomas pulled Alex down. He looked at her filthy, smoke-scented gown and shook his head.

"We were out." She smiled at his groan, hugging him tightly. Her gaze went to her husband as he dismounted.

Marc was glad to see her eyes no longer held the disappointment they had when he had refused to race, but what had she expected him to do? Be seen racing though the countryside with a woman in a wedding gown?

She wanted to race. He would give her a race. When she was dressed properly for it. He was thrilled to know she was willing. Not many women were. He would not even take it easy on her, not since she had pried away every shilling he had at the card table, even going so far as accepting his marker for a future claim. When he demanded to know what she wanted, she just grinned.

"Are we going back to London today, my lord," she asked as he approached the family. The horses snorted behind them.

"Do not call me that, hoyden. We will return if you want to." He was really thinking he would like to stay, but it was too much of a temptation to be alone with her.

Now that he was sober, he was once again in control of his lust and waiting seemed like a good idea. Even if he did forgive her and try to forget, he could not risk putting a child in that position. Would he be able to love a child fully, give it the attention it deserved if he was always in the back of his mind wondering.

"I suppose that would be best." She didn't want to go, but she didn't have a choice and was glad she did not have to make up some excuse.

The last race of this season was in three days, and she was too far away from her stables at Rose Hall to make it plausible to train them in the mornings.

Marc nodded. "If you will give us just a moment to change we will be right along. We will ride with you in the carriages. Robert, take the horses to the stables and turn them over to the grooms. We shall not be long, be ready when we are."

෧ා෧ා

The tall chestnut stood patiently as his rider twiddled with his mane. Janice sat like a stone in a well manufactured calm, only one finger twirling through the long hair to give away her nervousness. Outwardly she smiled. It would not do to allow people to know she was a wreck inside.

She had debated on the decision to talk to Lord Danton for days and had finally given in to her need for revenge. She had asked Lord Danton to meet with her to discuss the little chit who had stolen the life she had strove to get for so many years, and now the Earl of Staten was late.

He had kept her waiting for more than ten minutes. If she was not so desperate to get back at both families, she would have left at least five minutes ago. It was rude to keep her waiting, and there had to be some consequences for such ill-bred behavior. She now watched him come toward her at a leisurely pace, as if he had not been so rude and misguided.

Danton smiled into her statue-like face, knowing full well she was angry. He knew her well, had gotten to know her over the last couple of years as she paraded through the season like she was a queen.

His smile did not reach his light gray eyes, but he was enjoying himself immensely. It had been a goal of his to see how mad he could get her. The angrier she got, the more of a facade she wore. He also knew she would not say one word to him about his tardiness. No, she wanted something from him.

He was not surprised by much, but her message to meet him had confused him. She had to want something desperately to come to him.

"Good afternoon, my lovely little thing. How can I be of assistance to you?" He pulled her gloved hand into his and pressed his lips to it, lingering longer than necessary. It was bad etiquette, but it would be worse for her to pull away.

She didn't disappoint him, she allowed him to hold it until he felt the time had come to release her. He dropped her limp arm and smiled at her.

"My lord, I have some news that may interest you." She was seething, but there was no one else she could turn to. She would never get the life she had planned without help, and she would be damned if she was going to allow that little snippet of a woman to take what was hers.

"And what would that be, my dear?" His smile widened as she stiffened further. He had yet to call her my lady, because, in his opinion, it took more than breeding to make a lady and there were few that he called a lady.

"I do not know if I should tell you or not. Although I am sure that you will know what to do with the information. That is why I asked you meet me, but it is not information that I will just give out for free."

To her surprise, he just laughed. "You cannot negotiate for something that you are wanting. If I do not give you anything, you will not tell me? But if you do not tell me, then how can I do anything for you? So I will tell you what I will give you for this information. I will give you me." He smiled as he watched a smile play on her thin lips.

"No, do not look at me like that, I am not wanting a wife." His smile spread as her face fell. It was a real emotion that he had finally gotten out of her. "I will have you until I am tired of you. If you are lucky enough to find a man stupid enough to marry you, I will still take you when I want and where I want. Is that clear?

Her stony exterior had returned in full icy force. "No. I will not accept that. What I have to tell you is something you will want to know. I want a husband out of it. I will tell you nothing unless you can promise to get me Marc as a husband."

"My dear, I cannot do that. He has a wife, as I am sure you are well aware. What exactly can I do to fix that? You are not suggesting that I kill her, now, are you?"

He was surprised by the look on her face. Her normally calm and collected features took on a wicked and demented gleam.

"I will do what I can to help you, but I will do nothing unless I get my part of the bargain as well."

She smiled menacingly.

∽∾∽

When they arrived back at Clifton house in London, Marc excused them and led Alex to his bedchamber. "Do not forget we have the Cranston ball tonight if you two are up to it," his father called after them.

"We will be. After a short nap."

They were both exhausted. Neither had slept in two days, and he was not looking forward to sleeping in the chair.

Alex, in a soft day dress, didn't bother to change, only slipped under the covers. She stared at him from the bed. "Are you really planning to sleep in the chair?" He nodded. "We only have a few hours to sleep, and I am too tired to molest you if that is what you are worried about."

He smiled, his eyes drooped, and he walked to the bed. He lay on top of the covers and heard Alex's irritated groan. He heard nothing else.

When he awoke, he was under the covers, Alex was gone, and a pale tinge of red-orange light was peeking through the curtains, and he could hear the wind blowing outside. He felt like he had slept for about five minutes. He closed his eyes.

A knock came to the door. "Come."

Jeremy opened the door and grinned. "Are you ever getting up? The Cranston ball is in an hour."

"What do you mean an hour?" Marc had blurry images of a sleeping Alex wrapped in his arms, her head laying against his chest and her hair tickling his cheek. He could smell her on his skin, and he smiled.

"Your pretty little bride has been at our place for hours and everyone is ready, except for you, sleepyhead."

Marc groaned and threw a pillow at him. Jeremy slipped from the room with a laugh, and Marc rolled over in the bed. He pulled the covers over his head and was overwhelmed with the soft lingering scent of lavender and rose.

He threw the covers off and got up.

The Cranston evening ball was not a massive affair as some went, but it was big enough to let all the mothers with marriageable daughters fight over their son. This was something Michael Cranston loved and took full advantage of. He even took several mothers into the library for some quick fun while their husbands danced with their daughters.

Carriages already lined the drive when the families had arrived, to everyone's pleasure without the company of the Rutmeyers, though Marc had an uneasy feeling about the retribution he would be receiving for the broken betrothal, even though it had not been officially announced.

Marc assisted his wife to the rain-drenched ground.

Alex groaned inwardly, hoping any major storms would hold off until the race was over. It was not impossible to race in the rain, but it was more dangerous for the horses. Even a small slip could tear tendons and ligaments and, in the rain, a small slip could easily turn into a large fall.

Alex slid her hand into the crook of Marc's extended arm as small raindrops began to patter against her.

Smiling down at her, Marc could see her fear, could feel the tight trembling grip that she had on his arm. Laying his hand over hers, he gave it an encouraging squeeze before bringing it to his lips.

His lips were warm against her cold skin, she had not donned gloves as she should have, but he would rake her over the coals for it later. Now it took all his concentration just to walk as she laid her head against his shoulder, both arms wrapping his arm in a tight hug.

"Are you all right, my dear?"

Without raising her head, she smiled at her father. "Just nervous."

Thomas patted her hand and smiled. He turned back to the door and knocked.

"I was just thinking." She looked up at her husband and whispered. "I have always been surprised that with as muscular and big as you are, you are not as hard as you look. It has always been so soft and warm in your arms when you hold me."

"And I have always thought that with as prickly and sour as your temper is that it is amazing that beneath it you are so soft and supple and so sweet to the taste." His husky voice was brimming with lust as he thought of her soft and supple curves.

Passion flared in her eyes, and the couple was lost to the world. All Marc could see was her head leaning against his shoulder, tilted up so she could gaze at him. The look of love in her blue eyes drew him closer.

His lips had barely brushed her parted ones when Jeremy's offending voice interrupted. "We have been announced, you two." The laughter in the hall set the mood for the evening. If only it would stay that way.

"Was that not clever of me to draw attention to you?" Jeremy asked. "That way, no one will wonder why it is you were married so fast."

He looked so smug and proud of himself Alex almost didn't have the heart to hurt him. Almost.

"You will get plenty of attention when everyone wonders what you did to deserve a broken nose." She stepped toward him, fist raised, and was hauled back against Marc's chest.

Stepping back, Jeremy laughed.

After greeting everyone they knew well, and those they passed on the way to the dance floor, Alex was laughing in joy. The night was going far better than she had hoped. Her marriage to Marc seemed to have put to rest the rumors of her lovers, and so far the Rutmeyers had done nothing to slander the shipping company.

Alex had already left messages for many of her friends and associates about the possibility. They were already spreading as many good stories of the man who was now taking responsibility for his company as they could.

Glancing up at Marc's smooth jaw, no tension in it so far, she gave his arm a tug. "My lord, would you humor me with a dance?"

Growling, he pulled her closer. "I would be delighted."

He led her into a dance but did nothing to follow the steps. He spun her in his arms and danced at the outskirts of the other dancers. She smiled up at him, her eyes sparkling, as if he was the only man in the room.

"You little minx. You planned all this, and I fell right into your hands. Now that you have me, what do you intend to do with me?"

Her laughter died, a serious expression falling over her. "No, I did not plan it. I did not want you forced."

He pulled her closer, spun her faster. "I know. You have made that abundantly clear already. Now, do not do this. I have missed your laugh so much in these last two seasons, have missed you. Laugh for me, baby."

He spun her faster and faster until she could not deny him anything, including the laughter that rang through the rafters.

The music drifted to a close and Marc pulled her close. They turned, his grip tightened when he saw the Rutmeyers being announced.

Janice had her arm slung loosely through that of the Earl of Staten. Danton's gaze had locked onto Alex, but Marc knew she had yet to see him since her attention was directed beside them. He followed her gaze and found Spencer Ferguson coming their way.

Spencer stepped into their path with a wide smile and a low bow. He kissed her hand and spoke in a soft voice. "Danton just arrived on Janice's arm, love. That cannot be good."

"Ferguson. Good to see you," Marc said in a cheery voice and grasped his hand. He pulled him closer and whispered, "How bad?"

"Bad." Spencer smiled suddenly, his jovial voice rose to its normal, and irritating tone. "Are you going to deny others your wife's company, or are you the type of husband who knows how to share?"

"I have never been good at sharing what is mine." He had meant to keep his tone light and friendly as Spencer's had been, but it came out gruff.

"Easy, big man, I was only wanting a dance."

Marc looked down into the hopeful eyes of his bride. He was surprised that he did not feel the jealousy he had before last night's gaming with the man. Plus it made it easier to know it was now his right to watch out for her and who she danced with. "I suppose you may have a dance with my bride. There are other beautiful women I want to dance with." He smiled and walked away.

He bowed low in front of his mother, grasped her by the waist, and swung her onto the floor. He may not feel the sting of jealousy, but his eyes darted to Alex throughout the entire dance.

Janice felt her anger rise as she watched Marc's attention stay glued to his new bride. She had planned only to come with Danton because she thought to get a jealous rise out of Marc. When that was apparently not working, she decided on another plan of action. Smiling, she waited for the dances to end.

"Have you heard the newest rumor?" Jeremy asked as the couples ended their dance. "You will never believe it. They are saying A.H. is a woman."

"That is ridiculous, how can that be?" Blake said. "What do you think, Marc?"

Marc just shook his head. "I think that is stupid. I mean, he has been racing for what six years. Surely, by now, someone would have noticed if it was a woman."

Spencer laughed. "Oh, that is terrible, what if it is true? Could you imagine if she had a husband?"

Alex sucked in a breath and tried to hide behind Marc. This conversation was getting worse and worse.

"The poor devil," Marc said. "Could you imagine? The embarrassment that poor man must go through. Well, we can only hope he is not a man of status, society would decimate him if they learned what his wife did."

Marc's head jerked up as Alex walked away without a word. Ashlee hit the back of Marc's head painfully with her fan.

"What?" Marc looked at Bradley Hamilton, who stood possessively close to Ashlee.

Bradley shook with laughter "Well, my lord, I do not know a bloody thing about women, but even I know you should not insult one when there are others around."

"I was not insulting women." As he watched his wife's slumped shoulders, he knew it didn't matter. He had said something to upset her and he planned to fix it. Before he could reach Alex, he watched as Janice sidled up beside her.

"You know, I was just speaking to Lord Danton. I had to tell him I overheard the strangest thing. Lord Connelly and you were discussing the way you *work* for Marc's shipping company. How disgraceful. I was not sure what to do with that knowledge, but I thought Lord Danton might. There is no need for my family to say anything about a scandal. You will take care of that yourself."

"He is Lord Clifton to you now, but then you should never have been calling him by his Christian name." Alex turned and faced Janice. "I will tell you nicely only once. Get the hell away from me."

"You will make Marc miserable with one embarrassment after another. You do not know how to be a good wife, you are too selfish."

Marc walked up in time to catch Alex's hand as it left her side. There were too many people in the hall to get out of a scandal, this time, if Alex hit her.

"Stop it, Alex. Can you act the lady just once, please? I do not need this embarrassment."

Janice smiled smugly at his wife's deep intake of breath. Alex's eyes showed she was deeply hurt, but her slacked jaw firmed into a smile. It was a smile that froze his heart.

"Sorry, *my lord.*"

He groaned loudly before he could stop it. She had only called him by his name a time or two, and only when she was excited or upset, but she had ceased to make the title sound like an insult. That affront was now strongly apparent in her voice.

His remonstration caught in his throat, knowing something was different. Timidly she wrapped her fingers in the soft material of his sleeve. "You are right, my lord. I apologize. If you will excuse me, I see Ashlee by the refreshments. I would like to speak to her."

Bradley Hamilton, with his palm resting possessively against Ashlee's waist watched as Spencer stepped away from the sideboard to meet Alex. "From the look on her face, I think she wants to speak to you privately," Bradley said. "Promise me you will save me a dance."

She nodded. She would tell Alex later that Bradley had asked her to marry him, and that she had said yes. Right now her friend looked defeated. "What is going on?"

Standing in between her two dear friends Alex stunned them with her quite words. "I love him more than life itself. I cannot do anything to hurt him, and, as such, I cannot race again."

She could not risk Marc's reputation and the life that he was building. He was more important to her than anything else. Including her dreams.

She walked away without another word, going directly to her father as she fought tears of defeat. "I need you."

"Of course, love." Thomas gently cupped her face in his wide palm, looking out over the crowd to find his new son-in-law coming toward them. "What can I do?"

"Dance with me. I just need to feel your arms around me. I have need of your strength." She needed all the strength she could get to turn her back on her dreams, but Marc was worth it. If she acted like the woman he wanted her to be, he would be happy with her. If she was the kind of wife he dreamed of, maybe he would not regret having to be forced into wedlock with her.

The silent tears that refused to be held back ripped at Thomas's heart. "Do you want to tell me about it?" The dance was slow, allowing plenty of time to talk if she so decided, but she was unsure what to say.

"Yes, I do. I do not know if you would understand, though. I have done some things that perhaps I should not have done."

Thomas smiled softly. He could not argue with that. "I know of a few, I am sure there have been more."

"Yes, but I do not know where to begin to tell you. Will you be there when I am ready?" She didn't even need to ask, but, even knowing the answer, she wanted to hear the words.

"You know I will always be here when you need me. I want to help you in any way I can and when you are ready, when you have the words, I will be here." He knew he had let her down in the past. He could not tell her it had been out of fear. The fear that people would learn the truth. That she would.

છ৯৫৯

The night passed slowly for Alex. She danced with her husband most of all, but the laughter was gone. She held herself properly aloof and in control, even when Marc spun her. To Marc's horror, she acted the lady, as he had requested.

She believed he was right. It was one thing to risk her own reputation, but to risk his was quite another matter. Marc and his family had been through enough, without her making things worse on them. A lot of what she did in the past had been to help his family and their business, and she could not bring herself to ruin everything she had worked for.

The hardest part was not knowing what she going to do now? She still had Linden and a household full of servants to contend with. A stable full of horses that still needed to be trained and raced. She would just have to sell them. Her breath caught in a silent sob at the thought.

"I am sorry I snapped at you." Marc had taken about all he was going to take of her vacant look. She did not even appear to be in the same room with him while they danced, as if her mind were a million miles away.

"It was my fault, my lord." His teeth clenched. "I am the one who needs to apologize. I was not thinking." Her voice was cold and distant. "I will do my best to be the wife you deserve."

Marc wanted to make her smile and thought he knew how to do it. "Tomorrow we are going to buy you a new mare. Your father and I are going to Tattersall's. Would you like to join us?"

"If that is what you want, I will accompany you, my lord. Perhaps you can help me pick out a respectable mare." She tried to smile at him, but it just wasn't the same.

"I will take you, if you will promise me that you will try to be happy for the rest of the night." Marc wanted to cry. It was so painful to watch the vibrant woman he had always known turn into a proper woman.

"I will do my best for you, my lord."

Chapter 21

Alex had sweet dreams of the races that she had performed in and, from each dream, she would awake to a cold and empty bed, knowing that those dreams were now just a memory. Looking across the darkness of the room, she could see the silhouette of the man she loved. The man she was sacrificing everything for, who wouldn't even sleep in the bed with her.

He was cramped and twisted in the chair, but she knew that his stubborn pride would drive him to it every night until she bled. She had finished not long ago, so he was going to have many an uncomfortable night. Several times she had considered seducing him while he slept, but her own pride kept her under the covers instead.

Getting up long before Marc, she moved restlessly about the manor. Normally, she would be deep into training at this time of morning, but she was just going to have to accustom herself to a new way of life.

"What am I supposed to do with my time now?" she whispered quietly to herself.

"Are you lost, my child?"

Alex gasped in surprise. She looked up to Stuart Rodgers who had been the Clifton butler since long before Marc was born. His pale blue eyes were now almost white, but his thick hair was still a pale blond with only a speckling of gray. She was always surprised that he still had his hair or his teeth at this advanced stage in his life.

"You could say that."

He patted her hand. "Are you having a hard time adjusting to not being in your own home, my lady?"

"It is not that. I have spent so much time here that this is my home and you are all my family. I am just—" She sighed not knowing how to continue. What was she supposed to tell him?

"Does it have to do with the fact that you are still here at this time of the morning, my child?" He just smiled at her when she looked at him in suspicion.

"What are you trying to say?" She wondered just how much he

knew. It wasn't a secret that she left every morning, but it was the way he said it that made her question him. When he just smiled and arched one white brow she laughed nervously. "What do you think you know?"

"I know a lot more than you think. I know, for instance, that your new husband has left his chair and is on his way down the stairs as we speak." Alex turned to look at the stairs. They were empty. Turning back she found that the hall was empty as well.

"How does he get around so fast?"

"Who?"

Alex spun around grabbing her chest as Marc's voice sounded right behind her.

"What are you doing, my lord?" Her breathing refused to calm, but then her heart always pounded when he was around.

"I am coming to find you. I thought we could eat breakfast together before we go to Tattersall's."

She took his outstretched arm, laid her head against it, and allowed him to lead her to the breakfast room. Nothing was said through the morning meal, but Marc's eyes never left his new and usually rambunctious bride. He had dealt with the hoyden all her life, and he missed her loud and obnoxious ways.

It made the house seem so quiet without her. Indeed, although she sat across from him, his baby was gone and, in her place, was the bride he had thought he wanted.

After everyone had eaten, Marc helped Alex into the awaiting carriage and, after the newlyweds were situated, Thomas settled himself across from his quiet daughter, and Maxwell stretched his long legs beside Marc's.

Thomas touched Alex's knee. "What is the problem today, sweetie? You do not seem to be yourself."

Alex just smiled at him and shook her head. "I am fine, Papa. Just fine."

The three men looked at each other and shook their own heads.

The carriage ride was long and awkward. The three men tried to make small talk, but the look of despair on Alex's face put an end to all conversation.

Relief swept through them when the conveyance rumbled to a stop and Robert pulled open the door.

Alex thought she was doing good. Her smile was firmly in place, and her emotions were well in check. That lasted until they passed the first horse stall and she fought tears.

Tattersall's had always been her favorite place. The smell of fresh horseflesh wafted through the building and across all the buyers. It was an aroma that used to make Alex relaxed and happy. Now it just reminded her of all she had lost.

Looking at Marc, she smiled. What she had gained was well worth it.

The three men looked at horse after horse on their way back to the gentle riding mares. Alex plodded along behind them, trying, unsuccessfully, to ignore what was going on around her. She was doing fine until a loud crash and a scream pulled her from her dreary musings.

A massive chestnut stallion crashed into the stall door several times. Throwing his weight into the thick wood, he was determined to free himself from his small cage.

"I do n—not understand it. He has n—ever acted this way b—before. He is of the highest breeding," the small man who was obviously the steed's owner sputtered to the man who had been considering buying him.

"Well, I thought you said he was a good horse. I am looking for a racehorse, not a monster. How can I get a jockey on that creature? Just because he has a good bloodline does not make up for bad temperament." The irate man stormed off in a huff.

"You stupid monster. Why could you not just behave yourself for five minutes? This is why you are not allowed out of the stalls anymore." When his owner swung a whip at him and walked off, Alex made her way to him.

"Easy, boy." The muscular creature was a fine specimen. He shook and trembled with pent up energy. The definition in his legs and flanks were loose from lack of exercise, but the power was there. He needed a gentle hand and a disciplined routine. "You are just beautiful." He laid his muzzle against her outstretched hand and stood while she mumbled to him and stroked the white streak down his nose.

He would make a good addition to her stables. Not only would he make a powerful racer with his long and sinewy legs, but if he did indeed have a good line, he would produce good stock. He would be a money maker for her—

She stopped in mid thought. There was no A.H. anymore.

"Do you want me to purchase him, my lady?" Robert whispered as Marc began walking back to them.

"No. I will not be purchasing any more horses. I am no longer going to be racing. We will work out what is going to be done with everyone." As Marc came upon them she quietly added, "I will not let anyone down."

Marc's eyebrows rose as Robert irritably said, "You already are." He scowled at Marc and walked away. "I will be with the carriage, my lord."

"What was that all about, baby?"

"Nothing at all."

With one last longing look at the rambunctious steed, she slid her arm through Marc's and headed over to the mares.

Marc glanced down at her, back at the beautiful horse, and back to his wife several times as they walked away.

After picking out a dainty mare that looked as though she had never run in her life, a long life at that, they all piled back into the carriage, with an angry Robert nearly slamming the door behind them.

The ride home was slightly more animated with the men talking of the horses and the races coming up. The talk turned to A.H. Alex closed her eyes and dropped her head against the door of the carriage.

After feeling the vibrations and jolts from carriage the entire way home, her head was splitting. She tried a smile at her father but was sure it fell short. "I am tired, Papa. Would it be okay if I just went to my room and take a nap here?"

"Of course, love. Do you need a maid to come up to assist you?"

She shook her head, pushed past Marc without even a glance, and plodded up the stairs.

"Do not forget, baby, that we are going to the theater later tonight," he called to her, but she didn't even look back.

"Yes, my lord."

In her room, she didn't even bother to undress before she fell onto her bed.

⌯⌯⌯

Several hours later, Marc sat with his hand resting comfortably on the leg of his now docile and respectable wife. The wife he had always wanted. The wife who was now driving him crazy.

The play was a wonderful rendition of Romeo and Juliet, played by a local troop of actors.

He assumed they did a marvelous job, as they always did, but Marc could see nothing but the statue of a woman next to him.

Alex held her opera glasses daintily to her face as she laughed and moaned in all the right places. When the curtains closed for the intermission, she laid the glasses delicately in her lap.

"Shall we go visit some of the other boxes?" Catherine asked as Thomas pulled the curtains open behind them, allowing the light to spill in. "I see the Pettlenosters are here tonight and a few others are opening their curtains that I would like to sit and visit with a spell." Catherine gestured across to the other boxes as they lit up. She smiled at her daughter and her new son in law, but they both declined.

Marc patiently waited until the family had left, the curtains closed behind them, and they were once more in darkness before he turned to his new bride. "I see you have come to your senses and are ready to act the way a proper wife should act."

"Yes, my lord." She now had what she wanted. She had Marc, and he was happy with her. That was all that mattered anymore. At least she thought if she told herself that long enough, it would become true.

"Is there something wrong?" Marc reached across and ran a fingertip down the smooth skin on her arm.

"No, there is nothing wrong, my lord."

"There is something going on, and I would like to talk to you about it." He just was not sure how to start. What was he going to do, complain that she was acting the way he had told her to act? Tell her to stop being the way he had told her to be? He wanted to fix this horrid situation, but he didn't know how. "Talk to me, baby."

"There is nothing to talk about, my lord. Everything is fine, my lord."

"Stop calling me that, brat. You are my wife and, as such, you should do as you are told. I want you to call me by my name." He pulled her into his arms and didn't give her a chance to respond as he kissed her passionately.

When he slid his hand across her perfectly coiled hair, Alex pulled away. "People will notice if my hair is in disarray, my lord."

"I do not give a bloody goddamn hell what they think." With that, he wrapped his fingers through her hair and yanked her into his steely embrace. He pressed his lips into hers and forced her lips apart with his tongue.

Alex struggled only nominally as he slid his hand down the front of her beautiful gown to a pair of breasts that were, in his opinion, overly exposed. Snaking his hand beneath the silky material of the soft gray gown he caressed the warm skin and grasped a hardened nipple.

All pretense of a fight was given up as she wrapped her arms tightly around his shoulders and deepened the kiss. Marc slid his hand down the tight bodice of her gown and pressed the skirt between her legs.

Alex spread her legs wider and gasped as the cold silks brushed against her warm moist folds. Marc began to pick up the tempo as he kissed her roughly. Pressing the silk into her, he could feel the moisture begin to soak through the gown.

Throwing her head back, she wrapped her long fingers through his hair, pressing his head into her throat. He ran his tongue around her neck and ears before kissing and biting her bared shoulders.

Marc kissed his way back to her lips and slid his tongue into her mouth. He pulled her closer and freed himself from his trousers. He led her hand to him and guided her fingers around his engorged shaft. He groaned deeply as her warm fingers tightened around him and he began to pull her skirt out of the way.

Her knees were bared and Marc had just begun to pull her onto his lap when the curtains behind them moved and the voices of their families were heard. "Bloody hell, you have to be kidding me."

Thomas and Maxwell laughed at his whispered words. "What was that, my son?"

"Nothing Father, did you enjoy your visits?" Marc leaned forward to hide himself and was now desperately trying to decide how to put away his still hard member without the entire group knowing what they had been up to.

The answer came when the stage curtains were drawn and all attention was turned back to the play. The curtains were pulled behind them and the box was thrown into complete darkness once again.

Marc made a move to hide himself, but before he could take care of what needed to be done Alex leaned against his shoulder.

Being the newlyweds, they had earned the seats at the front and with their backs to everyone Alex was feeling brave in the darkness.

Marc bit his tongue to keep a groan from coming forward as Alex's small warm hand encircled him again.

He didn't know exactly what to do, but he did know that if he tried to move her, everyone would know what they were doing. He could only sit stiffly as she calmly lay with her head on his trembling shoulder and caressed the entire length of his manhood. Up and down her hand slid, up and down the shaft, she gently massaged and fondled him. He had never done anything like this, and it took everything he had not to finish right there on the theater box floor.

When Alex let loose sometime later, Marc realized that the play was complete and people were beginning to cheer. He quickly put himself away and tried somewhat successfully to will away the hardness that was fast becoming painful.

He needed her, he wanted her, and he was through with waiting. She loved him, and he knew it, and he was willing to take the chance that she was telling him the truth.

And he was doing it tonight.

"Shall we go, my lord?" She smiled wickedly taking his arm as he rose stiffly from his seat. This was more like the girl that he had tormented him all his life. Maybe he was beginning to get through to her.

"Minx." He pulled her close to him and looked into her beautiful eyes. This would be the last time he was close and not able to finish.

Alex could see her future in his eyes as she peered up at him. This was the man she wanted and the life she had always feared to dream of. A life she never thought would be hers.

"Rake." Laughter danced in his eyes as he pulled her close. They walked out of the theater with her hand clinging to his arm and her head on his shoulder.

Outside the theater, Ashlee pulled Alex away from the crowd who milled around awaiting their carriages. "I want to talk to you," Ashlee whispered almost silently and led her to the hedges that lined the building.

With a quick look around, Ashlee gave Alex a short but violent shake. "What are you doing? Do you not know how many people are counting on you? You have an entire staff and more employees than a woman needs, and they are all depending on you to take care of them. What is going to happen to everyone when you are no longer A.H.?"

"Shh." Alex glanced around to make sure they were still alone. "Do you want everyone to hear? I will take care of everything that I need to, and no one is going to suffer because of me. I will take care of things." Alex turned and walked away to take her place at her husband's side. The happiness she had just been filled with seemed to leak for her like a punctured hot air balloon. Was her happiness worth all of this? There were a lot of people counting on her.

Walking calmly up to the men, Ashlee balled up her fist and punched Marc as hard as she could in the arm. "If you were not such a horse's ass, you would know what was going on around you. Do you not see what you are causing?" She was almost in tears when she walked away from the slack-jawed people who stared after her.

"What was that about?" Maxwell looked after his daughter with wonder. Ashlee had never made such a spectacle of herself before. What had gotten into her?

"Alex?" Marc looked at her in confusion, but all she did was shrug her shoulders.

As the carriages were pulling away from the theater, Alex looked at Ashlee. Ashlee did not meet her eyes.

☙❧

In the men's carriage, not far ahead of them, Marc thought about what had happened at the play and what he was going to do about it. As soon as they got home, he was going to calmly take his bride upstairs and consummate the marriage.

He would not be waiting until tonight after the ball to take her. He would make her smile again.

Maxwell looked across the carriage at the sudden grin that spread across Marc's face. "Well, Lord Hollister, what do you think that smile could mean?"

Thomas just laughed at his longtime friend. "Well, Lord Clifton, I believe that is the look that says we will soon have grandchildren."

All the men were laughing hard until they stepped from their carriage. Marc's laughter was cut short when he realized that the women's carriage was no longer behind them. Looking around he was irritated to see that they were not in front of his home. White's stood proudly before him.

Marc looked at the smiling men that surrounded him, his irritation quickly rising. Damn it, he had plans and they did not include whatever side trip this was.

"What is going on here, Father?"

"I thought you could use a little distraction. We told the women that we would meet them at the ball. We have seen the stress that you have been under and thought you could use a break. You haven't been to Whites in a while and thought a little gaming could relax you."

Gritting his teeth, Marc tried to remain calm. "Father, this will in no way relax me. I want to go home."

"Oh, it will do you no good. The women have been given instructions to take Alex to the shops to get her something nice. She can use a chance to relax as well."

Marc turned to look at his father. He could see the amusement seeded deeply in his face. "Father? We still need to prepare for the ball. I had hoped to…nap before I dressed."

Maxwell grinned. "Oh you shall have plenty of time to dress, the women are to head over early."

Marc stomped into Whites in front of the rest of the men. His shoulders were thrown back, and Maxwell could see the minute shaking in his hands as he reached for the inner door.

"So do you think this will work or did we just make things worse?" Thomas whispered close to Maxwell's ear.

"I do not know. If I would have seen that look on his face beforehand, I would not have arranged for all of this."

The men had gotten together about the two newlyweds the night before. They were stressed out and fighting nearly constantly, and when they were not fighting, they both were staring at the other.

Of course, they would only stare if they thought the other was not looking.

"They are a pain in the ass, my friend. They are very much in love. What the hell is wrong with them?" Thomas was not usually one for bad language and Maxwell swung his head to look at him. Thomas just shook his head. "I have never seen Alex like this, so remote and lost, and it is beginning to scare me. I just want my daughter back and, if a little time apart is what it takes to get them to realize they love each other and need to be together, then I am more than happy to stick my nose in."

Maxwell agreed with him. He had been relieved when they had appeared happy as they had left the theater, but it was still not Alex who had emerged from the theater box. It was this new woman. Maxwell didn't much care for her.

Something had to change.

დოდ

Alex had been annoyed to no end to step out of the carriage in front of the shops of London instead of at their home. She had wanted nothing more than to continue her torment of her stubborn husband. She had argued and fought with her mother to return home but was only told that the men were at White's. Alex had trudged around the shops for what seems like an eternity before they finally returned home to prepare for the party.

Chapter 22

Alexis, if you keep picking at your skirts, you will be unraveled and indecent by the time we arrive at the Grenville ball." Her mother reached over and gently pulled the material out of Alex's fingers.

"I will not be indecent, Mama." Though unraveled was a definite possibility, she thought. She laid her head on her mother's shoulder, careful not to muss either of their hair, and closed her eyes. She felt her mother's warm lips press a kiss against her forehead. The strings of worry loosened a bit, not a lot, but enough to allow her to breathe.

The carriage rocked to a stop, and Alex pulled her head reluctantly from her mother's shoulder. Catherine gave her hand a gentle pat and turned as the door swung open.

Catherine allowed Robert to assist her from the carriage and turned to await Alex, her hand held out. Alex smiled.

Alex looked past her to the Grenville Townhouse and cringed. Their affair was a social success every season, which meant it was a loud, hot, suffocating crush of people. Alex hated it last season and was dreading it even more so this one. At least last season she had only spent a total of half an hour in the mass of guests.

Alex took her mother's offered hand, gave it a gentle squeeze, and, together, they made their way to the ballroom followed closely by Alma, Amber, and Ashlee. Not one of them looking excited to be at this particular gathering.

At the sight of the nearly empty ballroom, Alex sighed in relief. They were among the first to arrive, and she would, at the very least, have a short chance to get her bearings before the crush arrived.

Alex left her mother talking to some old friends and made her way to the refreshment table, hoping they were serving something stronger than punch. She was disappointed.

Music swelled through the ballroom, and Alex turned to watch the dancers. She tried to picture the rest of her life as a domesticated wife, but found it was not a future that looked very promising. Where was the fun and the adventure?

She just wanted the life she used to have and the easy going relationship that she used to have with Marc before last summer when everything had gone dreadfully wrong.

"May I have this dance?" Alex cringed at Danton's voice. His moist words caressed her ear.

Alex pulled her head away. "No, thank you. I am not looking to dance with anyone until my husband arrives."

She turned her attention back to the dancers, but Danton remained, his breath on her neck and his legs brushing against the base of her skirt. "Let me rephrase that, my love. You want to dance with me."

Alex spun around to face him. She took a deep breath to control her temper and forced a smile. "I am not your love and why on earth would I want to dance with you?"

Danton held his hand out to her. "You want to protect your husband, do you not?"

Alex considered refusing, but after a moment slid her hand into his. After all, more harm could come from a scene than from a dance. She tightened when he pressed his hand against the small of her back, but allowed him to direct her onto the dance floor.

Danton led her past most of the dancers, but Alex only hesitated when it looked as though he were planning to take her off into the Grenville's small garden.

"Relax," he smiled widely, "I am just getting us to the back of the dancers where we will have a semblance of privacy."

She glared at him and pulled away. "Talk,"

He looked around carefully, and Alex began to get nervous. If he had something good enough he didn't want the ton to know, she might have an issue.

Finally, satisfied, he turned back to her and grinned. "You would not imagine the wonders you can see at the theater."

The music began, Danton kept to the steps, and, to her surprise, his movements were smooth and elegant.

She looked at him expectantly but did not prompt him.

As the dance brought them close he smiled. "I went to see Romeo and Juliet before I came here. It was a lovely afternoon showing and the actors did a magnificent job."

Alex stumbled, barely catching her balance. She had vivid images of fondling her husband in the box. She tried to calm herself. After all, the boxes were dark without the curtains open. It was unlikely that they were witnessed. "Yes, I know, I was there. Get to your point, Danton."

"I saw something interesting." Danton looked around the room at the other dancers.

"Either tell me what you want to tell me, or I will end the dance now. It would not be the first time your old *injury* acted up."

His smile faded. "I saw you there."

Well, she thought, it would be a scandal if anyone found out she had practically molested her husband, but she knew it was not the first time it had ever happened at the theater, and it was with her new husband. The talk would be short lived and not too detrimental. It would, she figured, keep the rumors of a forced marriage to a minimum. Alex just shrugged her shoulders and waited. "So you saw me in the theater? And…"

"No, I saw you outside the theater. You were speaking with Lady Ashlee, my love." He stressed the title as he pulled her closer.

Alex could feel her face heating up as she thought of the conversation. How could she have been so stupid? She took a deep breath and smiled. Keeping the tremors of concern contained, she forced herself to relax. "And?"

"And?" She could hear the confusion in his voice. "I heard that you are A.H."

"Oh, is that all? I thought it was something important."

Danton's face dropped at her cavalier attitude. She smiled.

"I would think that the end of your husband's reputation would be important." He looked around nervously.

She just laughed gently. "Oh, do not look so upset, Danton. It was a good plan. There is just one flaw. You cannot prove it. You obviously did not hear the whole conversation. I am no longer racing."

"Oh, I heard, and I do not have to prove it. There are already enough rumors going around that A.H. is a woman that all I have to do is point them in your direction. That will be enough to start the rumor mongers running away with the story. Plus, A.H. has his hands in enough stuff that it should not be hard to find someone to talk. Even if not, your reputation is such that it will not be hard to believe that you are the famous man. Alexis Hollister. A.H. Someone should have thought of it sooner."

Alex knew he was speaking the truth. The people of the ton would have a field day with it, but it didn't matter because she wasn't racing again. "What do you want?"

"You wound me." He tried to give a pitiful look, but his grin had found its way back and ruined the affect.

"Just tell me what it is you want, Danton."

"I want you to race, and I want you to lose. I plan to bet heavily on Reed, and you are the only one I believe can beat him."

"You want me to race against him so his point spread is higher. The odds of him winning will be reduced if I am in the race because I will be the odds on favorite. That will mean your payoff is greater."

"At least tenfold, more if I am lucky."

Alex allowed him to twirl her around the floor as she kept an eye on all the other guests. "Plus, with it being the last race of the season the stands will be packed and betting will be rampant. I suppose you want me to throw the last race. My rematch with him?"

"You are smart, my love. I knew you were. You should have married me, then I would have been able to help you race instead of you having to hide it. Who do you think will be the most upset when they learn the truth, the ton or your naive husband?" He laughed and pulled her into his arms much too tightly before releasing her into the next steps of the dance.

Ignoring his taunts, she shook her head. "I will not race again. Not for you and, if I did, I sure as Hell would not throw the race. I race fair, and that is the only way I race." She looked around her at the other dancers, relieved that none were close enough to hear.

"You would risk your husband's reputation. I am sure he will not take kindly to hearing that you are a racer. I have seen his reaction when you act independent and the way he is so overprotective when you ride."

Alex shuddered, not so much at the thought of Marc finding out, but at the idea that Danton had been watching her so closely. "I will not be risking anything, and I would suggest for your own safety that you do not push it."

Danton grinned. "You cannot do anything to me. You would not dare, not anymore. You are a respectable wife now."

She smiled sweetly at him. "I do not have to do anything. I have friends who will do it for me."

"If you think that Edward Barlow scares me, then you better think again."

"No? Well, how about Bellevue White? He would be glad to help me."

The breath hitched in his chest, and his perfect steps faltered. "He is dead."

"Look at that. He has helped me already." She tightened her grip on his hand as understanding drained the color from his face.

Bellevue White had been a powerful merchant, but he had also been an arrogant and violent man. Danton had raped his daughter on several occasions, and Danton knew as well as Alex that Lonnie's fear of her father was the only reason she had not spoken against him.

"She will not come forward. She may be from a rich family, but her brother is a sniveling coward. He will not help her. Are you going to stand up for her? That would be a scandal in itself." He gave a tight laugh.

Alex tilted her head and sighed. "You are correct. Lonnie does not want everyone to know what you did to her. There will be no scandal, though. If you push it, I will tell the right people, and no one will ever know what happened to her." She gave a small shrug. "Or to you."

The music ended as they reached the far side of the dance floor. Looking toward the open garden, Danton tightened his grip on her arm.

"Do not even think about it, Danton."

His panicked face worried her. Perhaps she had pushed it too far. Danton looked like a cornered animal. He bowed low to her. "Thank you for the dance, my lady."

He walked stiffly away and concern grew into worry as Janice Rutmeyer took his arm for the next dance.

❧❦❧

Marc scanned the quickly swelling mass of guests from his spot in the doorway as he waited for the guests in front of him to be introduced. He smiled when he caught sight of his wife standing next to her mother on the sidelines. His smile faded. She looked sad and lost.

Alex looked up as the butler announced him. She smiled. It was a forced smile at best. He had hoped she was going to be all right, that they were going to be all right, but this marriage wasn't working, and he didn't know how to make it work.

Heading straight for her, he took a deep breath and pasted a smile on his face. "Come and dance with me, baby."

She inclined her head to him and placed her hand properly on his arm. "Yes, my lord."

He had made it through three turns of the dance before realizing that this respectable ghost of a woman was pushing on his nerves beyond anything she had ever done before. He wanted the woman she had been in the theater box, but he couldn't just molest her in the middle of the dance floor.

If he could get her to the gardens though—he forced himself not to grin too lecherously. He could not convince her that his plans were acceptable if he looked about to devour her. "Would you like to walk in the gardens with me?"

"No, my lord. It would be unseemly of us to disappear this early. Later after dinner, we can. That is proper, my lord."

"You need to stop calling me that. I have a name, and you have always used it in the past, why are you not now? Are you trying to make me mad?"

Alex's bottom lip trembled, and Marc felt it to his core. "No, my lord. I am trying to make you happy. I am trying not to embarrass you."

Her voice cracked at the end, and looking into her shimmering eyes was more than he could stand.

"Look, we are married, and there is nothing wrong with us strolling in the gardens. Just come out there with me." Marc pulled against her waist, but she resisted.

He did not want to make a huge scene, but he was on the verge of throwing her over his shoulder and carrying her out. Perhaps, he thought, if he were to go out there, she might follow him. He might not get to molest her, but perhaps just some alone time would help cheer her up. Anything to be away from all these people.

Marc looked down at her withdrawn face and sighed. All he had wanted was for her to control her temper and not wander off by herself so much. Not too much to expect, in his opinion.

He had not expected this shell of a woman. Alex was calm, subdued, and looked as if she had never lost her temper or her wits.

Marc looked down quickly to hide his sudden grin. He thought he had a plan. All he had to do was make her mad and then go into the gardens and wait. Once she lost her temper, he would have her where he wanted her.

He knew it could backfire, but it was worth the risk, besides, it was the only thing he could think of to try. She had to follow him, she just had to.

Once he had her out in the darkness of the garden, he would take her against the back wall behind the shrubs where no one would see them. He would consummate the marriage and show her that he trusted her and that he believed her. That had to pull her out of her fog.

He wasn't sure what he needed to say, but he figured if he said ridiculous enough things she would have to defend herself eventually. He controlled his hopeful grin and scowled at her.

"So, you want to make me happy, do you? Well, you are not making me happy. You are not being the wife I want."

"How can I not be what you want when I am being exactly like you said to be? I have not interfered with the shipping contracts, I have not wandered off, and I have not even gone to see the orphanage since we have gotten married. I am doing exactly what you want, so why are you not happy?" Tears were brimming in her eyes and Marc was sure they would break forth, but somehow she managed to keep a hold on them.

"You have become a sniveling little girl and a spineless woman. All you do is whine all day. You cry and moan like you are a small insolent child instead of a grown woman." He was exaggerating—all right he was completely lying—but it was doing the trick. Her confused look faded, then the shininess disappeared from her eyes, and her lips no longer trembled. No, now they were set in a firm line.

He opened his mouth to continue, but as her nostrils flared and her nose wrinkled he realized he had better not push her any further. She was angry. Now, he could only hope that the rest of his plan went off so well.

People were beginning to gather around the edges of the dance floor casting glances at them. He knew he had kept his voice quiet enough they couldn't hear him, but it must be obvious they were having a disagreement about something.

"I do not need this embarrassment again," Marc snapped quietly and could only hope it was enough.

He turned on his heel and left her standing there alone. He made his way to the garden to await her.

He had no doubt that the outspoken girl still lived inside her. He grinned, looking forward to it.

In the garden, Marc leaned against a small tree and closed his eyes. It was not much more than a moment or so before he heard footsteps approaching him. They were small, dainty footsteps. She was walking quietly. His brow furrowed, he had expected her to come stomping out.

Marc had a moment's doubt. What if she believed him and was coming to apologize? He couldn't have that. He opened his eyes as the quiet footsteps stopped before him. His eyes narrowed. "What do you want, Lady Janice?"

Janice smiled. "I just want to talk to you. I know and everyone knows that the marriage has not been consummated. I know you do not want her. I have come to make sure you know that I still want you, and you deserve so much better than her." She swayed her hips closer to him.

He looked over her shoulder anxiously. Alex would be here any moment.

"I am very happy with my wife. I have no intention of leaving her for you, or for anyone."

Janice stepped closer until she could almost touch him. Her smile faltered, but she seemed determined. "You cannot want her. She has lovers, you know."

"No, she does not have a lover." Marc was shocked to realize that he believed his own words. He was not sure when he had decided it, but he didn't think that she was capable of having lovers. Yes, there was a lot of time he couldn't account for, but lovers? No.

Janice only smiled. "Perhaps, but I have it on good authority that she is to inherit the entire estate of one—" She paused, her smile becoming sly and unbecoming. "—Edward Barlow. His lands and his money all go to her." Marc sucked in a breath. "Now I ask you, why would a man leave everything to a woman who was not his lover?"

Marc shook his head in denial. "You are wrong. Whoever told you that lied."

"Oh, Marcus, I have seen the proof, a document that states it. I am not sure how they got their hands on it, but they have it nonetheless." She reached for his face and stepped closer to him.

He pulled away from her touch. "I am sure there is an explanation." Though he could not think of a reasonable one. A forgery perhaps, or maybe she was just lying about it altogether. "I do not have time for this now. I am—"

His jaw dropped as Janice threw herself on him. "Marc, take me now." She wrapped her arms around his neck and yanked his head down to her level. Janice rammed her mouth onto his nearly crushing his lips as she ground her head back and forth.

"Janice—Jan—Jan."

She pressed her kiss harder making it impossible for Marc to get any words out.

Finally, he had had enough. He grasped her arms, his fingers digging into her flesh, but before he could pry her away he heard a painful gasp. Janice pulled away with a satisfied smile and Marc turned. He looked into the hurt eyes of his wife.

"Baby, it is not what it looks like."

Alex could feel the pain swelling inside her chest and threatening to explode. She took a deep breath and smiled as calmly as she could. When she spoke she was surprised at how steady the words were. "No? Because it looks to me like a two-faced hypocrite. Heaven forbid if it should even be rumored that I have lovers, but you can do this...this trollop."

Her head was pounding, and her chest hurt. Tears burned at her eyes, but she managed to ignore them. "I am sorry for forcing you into this marriage. Obviously, you had your heart set on her the whole time."

Marc began to speak, but Alex could not hear what he was saying. All she could hear was the rushing sound of blood as it pounded in her ears. His lips were moving but she was certain he was blathering about how it was different for him to cheat because it was a man's right or some such nonsense, but she didn't hear and at the moment she didn't care.

Alex saw Marc push Janice out of his way and take a step toward her before her vision blurred. Her head spun wildly, and she feared she would pass out.

She turned and fled. She didn't look back nor did she hear anyone pursuing her, but she knew that didn't mean they weren't there. She was not going to risk getting caught.

Her first thought was of Edward, but she knew that would be the first place they would look. She tore through the doors. Everyone stopped to stare, but she kept running across the dance floor. She threw open the front door and kept running.

Alex ran until breath tore in and out of her lungs with a searing heat and her sides felt as though she had been kicked by a horse. She didn't know how long she had run, and she paid no attention to where she lay as she fell exhausted to the ground.

Her eyes closed against the pain as thousands of needles pricked her dry throat. Alex took slow gasping breaths and tried to force herself to relax. Pain shot through her arms and legs when she tried to move. Tears began to fall to the cold damp ground. The pain in her lungs subsided slowly, but the ache in her chest did not release its hold.

A warm hand gently caressed Alex's tear covered face. "Are you all right, my dear?"

Alex opened her eyes, wondering how long she had lain on the cold grass. She looked up into the caring eyes of Lady Pettlenoster.

"What are you doing out here this late, my lady?" Alex's voice cracked.

"You know me, I cannot sleep at night. I should have gone to the Grenville's tonight, but just was not up to that many people. Now, what, may I ask, are you doing laying in my grass this time of night, my dear child?" Lady Pettlenoster gently pulled her to her feet, wrapped an arm around her trembling shoulders, and led her into the house.

"I ran away." Alex laughed softly though she wasn't kidding. It was a strained laugh at best.

Rachel grunted at her. "From your husband, your family, or society?" She gave a gentle laugh. "I have felt like running away on many occasions, my dear."

"From everything, I suppose. I am lost."

Lady Pettlenoster led her into the warm library and sat her in an overstuffed chair by the fireplace. The crackling flames warmed her body, but could not touch her spirit.

"Why are you lost? Things looked like they were falling into place. Are you missing the shipping business?" Rachel poured two glasses of brandy and handed one to Alex who slouched in the chair and fought tears. She sat across from Alex in a high backed Chippendale seat and smiled encouragingly.

Alex took a long sip of the warming brandy and sighed. "A little, but it is the racing that I am missing most."

She took another long sip of the spiced liquor and slumped her head back against the seat. She closed her eyes and realized she could not have ended up in a better place than Rachel Pettlenoster's library. No one would look for her here, and Rachel had helped her out a lot over the years.

"Racing? What do you mean, you miss it?"

Alex could hear Rachel scoot forward in the high backed chair, but didn't open her eyes as she answered.

"I had decided that, in order to protect Marc's reputation and the family's, that I will not be racing anymore. Now? Well, now I do not know." Alex sighed deeply and finished the rest of her brandy in a long swallow.

"Why do you not know? I am not sure I would have given it up if I were you." Rachel's voice sounded confused. Alex didn't open her eyes as her glass was taken from her shaking hand.

"I do not know what the right thing to do is. I have given up so much to make Marc happy, and now I have given up my dream and he still does not seem to even care about me." Alex finally opened her eyes as a refilled glass was put into her hand. She took a small sip.

"He loves you a great deal. Everyone can see that."

Alex wished she was as sure as Rachel sounded.

"Everyone can see what he wants them to see. He yelled at me on the dance floor, left me standing there alone, and then when he thought I would slink off into a corner somewhere he went out to the garden." Alex jumped to her feet and paced before the crackling fireplace. She swirled the brandy as she trounced back and forth. "When I followed him, he was deep in the embrace of that wretch Janice."

"Janice Rutmeyer. That prude? Are you sure you saw what you think you saw?"

Alex stopped to face Lady Pettlenoster. The elderly lady looked dismayed by the very thought of it.

"Rachel, I know what I saw. He had her in his arms and was kissing her. Moaning her name over and over again. No wonder he does not want me if he is already getting—"

"Now, now. Do not allow those thoughts." Lady Pettlenoster stood and sat her own brandy on the small table beside her chair. "Listen to me. There are some things that are not as they appear, but there are some things that are. What you need to do is worry about yourself right now." She walked over to Alex and put her arm around her. Alex allowed her to lead her away from the fireplace, but instead of taking her to the chair as she had expected Lady Pettlenoster began to pace with her.

Rachel Pettlenoster took a deep breath and smiled. "I spent a long time worrying about my first husband and where he was and what, and who, he was doing. That changed when I took the new husband."

Alex walked alongside Rachel as she led her across the hardwood floor. Their footfalls fell silent as they crossed the massive Egyptian Rug Rachel had imported directly from Egypt. How she had gotten the connections there, Alex still didn't know, but A.H. had purchased several Egyptian silks from those contacts.

"So what am I supposed to do now?" Alex could hear the cracking in her voice. "I gave up my dream for him, and he does not even want me."

Rachel shook her head, turned them around, and headed back across the room. "You follow your dream. Nothing should have changed when you got married. I understand that compromises have to be made, but both parties have to compromise. He cannot expect you to give up your dreams. You have a lot of people counting on you. With the new home and the servants, what are you going to do?"

"I had thought to sell to Marc. He wanted it. I know he will keep the manor running, but I do not know what he will do with Tess or my horses. He is not into training and racing. He loves to watch, but he does not want to soil his hands by such menial labor as training." She smiled suddenly, "I am surprised he is getting into the shipping so much. He is doing a fine job of dealing with the clients." She laughed gently thinking of the men at Rose Hall. At first, they were unhappy with the change, but even they had admitted he was doing a good job.

Alex turned her attention back to Rachel. She was glad she had confided in the woman all those years ago. It had been in this very room that she had come to her for advice. She had barely taken over the shipping contracts that Taggard had been demolishing. Rachel Pettlenoster, through her husband's name, had been a client of Clifton Shipping for quite some time.

Alex had discovered problems with Lord Pettlenoster's shipments as she went through them, but when she had sent a messenger to speak with him about it, he had no idea what she was talking about. Rachel had stopped the confused young messenger on his way out and spoke with him about the shipment.

Later that week, Alex decided to take a risk. She had big hopes and dreams and wanted nothing more at the time than to become a successful business woman. Terrified as she was, she knew that no one but another business woman would be able to help her.

"Alex?" Alex jumped at the sound of Lady Pettlenoster's voice beside her.

Alex looked up with a smile and took the glass of brandy the Rachel held out to her. "I was just thinking about the first day I came to you for advice."

Rachel smiled as she took her seat again. She motioned Alex back to her seat as well. "You were so scared that day. It was so cold, I could not fathom why such a young girl was out in such ghastly weather, but I am glad you came."

"I am too. You have always been such a great help to me."

"Good. Then take my advice now. Race if you want to race. Do not give up on your dreams. You love him, so do not give up on him either. Take life for everything you can. Race the last race and do as you planned and go from there. See what he does then, do not just assume how he will react. He may yet surprise you and himself."

"I do not know about that. I can only hope." Alex sighed deeply and shifted in her chair. She didn't know what she was going to do, but she knew that she could not live like this for long. Straightening her shoulders, she emptied her glass. "You are right," she said. "I have worked my whole life for this, and I am not going to give it up for a man who does not have the decency to be faithful to me. I am not changing everything for a man who will not change anything for me."

Chapter 23

Marc sat in the library of the Clifton residence with the rest of the family and watched Alex sprawled on the floor with Blake Jr. and Darla. The room was slightly crowded with all ten members of both families sitting around watching the two young children playing with Alex. *The prim and proper wife act obviously didn't apply to rolling around on the floor like a hoyden,* Marc thought with irritation.

He scowled at her, but she didn't even notice. His mood was dark, and his irritation at his wife was growing with each unhappy look he caught in her eyes.

He had wanted to apologize to her. Wanted to explain what had happened in the garden and that it was not what it had looked like. He had wanted to explain to her that he did not want the prudish Janice, had not wanted her when he was still betrothed to her.

He had wanted to talk to Alex last night, but she had not even deigned to come home. She had left the party at a run and had not shown up until partway through breakfast this morning. She had told them she was with Lady Pettlenoster and he did not know if he should believe her or not. He also knew that asking Lady Pettlenoster would do no good, because he was certain she would say yes, no matter what the truth may be.

Marc was drawn from his miserable contemplations when Stuart Rodgers walked briskly into the room. He had a harried nervous look about him that set Marc's hair on end.

Alex looked up from her position on the floor, and Marc glanced back at her. Her excited look brought on a burst of lust and irritation at his sweet little bride. He wanted her, but that look was never a good sign.

It was mischievous and sly, and it meant she was up to something. She had looked like an angel sprawled on the floor with the kids until Stuart Rodgers had walked in looking ruffled. "Your grace," his voice trembled slightly.

"What is it?" Maxwell asked.

Marc looked from Alex to Stuart Rodgers. The nervous man took a deep breath and tried to regain his composure. "That large man, Tess, is here to see you all." He stood patiently waiting as the members of the families looked back and forth from one to another and then back to him.

Marc stood up and carefully stepped around the kids. "He wants to see who? All of us?"

"Everyone, my lord. He specifically asked to make sure that everyone was here, including the women."

"Send him in. This ought to be good." Maxwell said as Marc stopped at his side.

Within a few moments, Tess walked into the room with a stern look on his face. He glanced at Alex who still sprawled on the floor and seemed to relax. The corners of his mouth twitched as he seemed to struggle with a grin. "My ladies." He looked past the men and directly at the ladies, who were all now standing.

Thomas took his place beside Maxwell and Marc so that the three men stood protectively in between the big man and the women.

Marc was not concerned about it, though. He trusted Tess. At least as far as Alex was concerned.

Thomas smiled. "What can we do for you, my big man?"

Tess grinned. "I have been sent to you with an invitation. The infamous A.H. would like to invite all of you to watch the final race as his guests."

"What?" All the men seemed to say in unison, and the women behind them began to clamor loudly between themselves.

"After the races, A.H. would like to meet with all of you."

The women all started rattling off questions at the big man. Marc smiled as he looked over his shoulder at the ladies. They had lost the look of fear. It had been replaced by a look of excitement. They all stepped forward as if to break through the men who protected them and mob Tess for the answers they wanted.

"Easy, ladies, calm down. Do not scare the poor man," Maxwell said with a laugh.

Marc jerked his head back around to stare at his father. Scare Tess. That was ridiculous. He looked at Tess and was surprised to see a look of nervous fear on his face as he watched the women advance upon him. His eyes were wide, and he had taken a step back.

The women quieted, and Marc thought that they had seen the look on his face as well. Alex got to her feet, taking the hand of each child as she did so. She stepped forward into the group of now silent women.

Marc gazed at her with suspicion. She didn't look at all surprised by Tess's visit, nor did she look excited to see the races. Marc still wanted to know how Alex knew the big man, but he had not been able to get a straight answer from either of them.

Marc grunted and looked at his father.

Maxwell grinned widely and turned to Thomas. "In all the years of the races, these women have never shown any interest in going, with one exception." He glanced at Alex with a small wink. "I do not think they really want to go now, I think they just want to meet the jockey. They do not need to go just for that. They will be bored to tears."

Marc and Jeremy both threw their hands over their ears dramatically as the women began to loudly protest.

Maxwell laughed, waving both hands for silence. "Be still, women, and let the men folk talk."

He turned back to Tess, and several pillows hit him squarely in the back. He ignored them. "Let your man know that we will be there. All of us."

The women all began chattering at once on what they should wear and how exciting it was going to be. Alex followed along silently behind them as the women left the room.

Marc felt a jolt of concern at her satisfied smile. She didn't look excited like the others, but she was happy about the decision.

芝芝芝

Danton paced outside the stables waiting for Reed to show up. He knew the man liked to practice early, but he did not see him, and he was beginning to get nervous. His gaze bounced quickly from place to place as the nervous tension swam through him. He could not allow it to get out that he had raped that girl. He would be totally ruined or killed.

Reed stepped from the shadows of a stall. "You looking for me?"

Danton jumped and let out a small gasp. He spun toward the stable doors. He cursed himself for assuming the man had not shown up yet. He forced his breathing to slow and tried not to squeak when he spoke.

"I have a lucrative proposition for you if you are interested." Danton shifted his gaze back and forth, making sure they were alone.

"There is no one else here. I like to run alone," Reed snarled at him.

That did not relieve Danton's tension any, but he stepped forward. Leaning close to Reed he smiled. "I need there to be a little accident."

"And, what does that have to do with me?" he asked, stepping back into the darkness of the stables.

Danton hesitated only a moment before following him in. He watched Reed check his horse's saddle. He was quiet for a moment while he let his eyes adjust to the dark interior of the barn.

"I know that you hate A.H. as much or more than I do." Danton smiled when Reed's hands stilled.

He waited until Reed turned to him. His eyes gleamed in the dark shadows of the stables.

"And?" Reed asked, the snarl now gone from his voice. "How lucrative?"

Danton grinned, he knew he had him. Now it was just a matter of the details. "I plan to bet big on you to win the last race, the challenge match. I will give you twenty percent of my winnings."

Reed turned back to his saddle once more. "I am already watched closely. I will not jeopardize myself again for a measly twenty percent. Sixty perhaps."

Danton laughed. "I will find someone else." He turned to walk away, knowing full well that Reed would not let him go.

"I could perhaps do it for less," Reed's voice sounded with irritation behind him.

Danton turned. "And I could perhaps give you more. I would be generous with you and do it for thirty."

Reed looked as if he would complain, but he did not. He just looked at him blandly for a moment.

Danton knew the type of man Reed was. He was a bully and a braggart, but in the end, he was spineless and would have done it for the twenty, but Danton could be generous.

Finally, Reed smiled. "Do you want him hurt or—"

Danton smiled at him and shook his head. "No, not hurt. I cannot have him walk away from this accident."

Reed's brow shot up, but he nodded. A sly grin slipped over his face. "I have just the thing for that."

"You cannot get caught. If you do—" Danton started, but the look of anger on Reed's face stopped his words. He might just be a bully, but he was a big bully, and Danton had no desire for Reed to put him in the ground as well as Alexis Hollister.

"I know what I am doing. I will not get caught again," Reed said and clenched his fists.

Danton held up his hands in acquiescence. "Good. You do what is needed, but I want him dead." Danton did not wait for an answer. Instead, he turned and walked out into the bright sunlight.

Reed glared at his back as he disappeared into the glare of the rising sun, his body first shimmered and then faded completely from Reed's view.

He closed his eyes, dragging in the soft coolness of the stables with its pungent aromas of horse manure and hay. He opened them again and patted his stallion on the side. He shook his head as he considered what he could do.

He knew the reasons he had been caught before, when he had tried to cut A.H.'s girth. He had been too blatant about his tampering with the horse's saddle. What he needed was a more subtle diversion.

He looked around the stables and considered his options. He walked past his horse and back into the darkest portions of the stables.

A.H. would not arrive until after the first race and his horse and gear were well guarded especially after Reed had cut his girth.

He turned into the last stable. It was cool and dark and empty of all but saddles, bridles and assorted pieces of the two of them. There were damaged saddles, worn girths, and bridles of all conditions. These were left here, and the manager of the stables used the pieces and parts to assemble good used equipment and sold it to the lower classes.

Reed snarled and kicked at a tall pile of tack. "Ridiculous," he said angrily into the empty air. "The beggars can go without."

Even though he did, indeed, believe that the lower classes had no business getting anything from the better class, he knew that this was not his real anger. His real anger was that he believed he should be of the better class.

He had worked hard to get the horses he had, and he had money set aside, but, still, they considered him just a higher grade of low class. There was nothing he could do about it.

He let out a frustrated growl and reached down grasping a saddle and flinging it across the stable. It hit a tall pile of saddle blankets, and the stack fell in a flourish of swirling colors.

He shook his head.

That was not the only thorn in his side. A.H. was the biggest pain he had. A.H. beat him every time and, even though no one knew who the man was, he had higher status than Reed had ever had or could expect to have.

He turned toward the bright light shining through the open doors of the barn. He could barely see the track, but he didn't need to see it to know every bump and dip.

He scowled heavily and clenched his fists. He thumped his hand against the railing of the nearby stall and cursed. He rubbed his hand rapidly and began to shake with anger.

He wanted to see the man dead before he had a chance to reveal himself to the crowd. If he had a chance to expose himself, then A.H., whoever the man was, would be a legend while Reed was once again a loser.

A loser, he thought and shook his head. He closed his eyes in frustration. A loser, even though he won every race he was in as long as that meddling A.H. was not involved and, even at that, he usually came in second.

Second was not good enough for the ton, though. Like these second-hand saddles. A lot of them still in mostly good condition. Nothing wrong with them, but a few worn and rusty fasteners—

He stopped and cocked his head, trying to make the thought that had begun to form in his head come forward.

He turned toward the saddles once more, and a grin began to spread across his face.

He knelt down and began to sift through the girths and saddles. He dug for several moments before he found what he wanted.

An older saddle that had been well worn, but one with a new girth on it. Whoever had replaced the girth had used the old fasteners and they were rusty and worn through, but on the saddle they would not really be noticed. No they were on the underside of the girth and pressed against the horse.

He could just imagine the cursing the stable hand who had changed the girth had gotten. He was sure a lashing had been involved. Reed smiled joyfully.

He pulled the girth quickly from the saddle, careful of the fasteners.

He carried it to the stall that he used and dug into the fresh hay in the corner. He slid it under the hay and kicked a pile of it back over the top. He smiled.

There would be just one other thing to take care of. He needed a distraction that even A.H. and that big man Tess could not resist.

He began to laugh. Raymond was racing the last race, the race right before their big rematch. That would be the perfect time. A.H. would watch Raymond race. A small incident would suffice to keep him occupied.

With that decided, Reed pulled his stallion out into the bright morning air and laughed again as he mounted.

e⁄ɔe⁄ɔ

Marc watched all the women with a small smile on his lips. They rushed around the house, each of them dressed as if they were going to a ball with the Queen herself.

They had giggled when he had pointed this out saying they would probably never get the chance to meet someone so famous again and they were going to take full advantage of it.

He laughed and, when they stopped to look at him, he just waved them away. His laughed faded when he spotted Alex. She was dressed to the same extravagance that the rest of them were, but she looked ill. She was pale and shaky.

She fidgeted with her hair and her dress and then started to chew on one of her nails. She forced herself to stop, nearly throwing her hand to her sides in disgust.

Marc stepped toward her.

She smiled a small, timid smile that hit him hard. He felt the guilt swim through him. He was irritated that he felt guilty, because he had done nothing wrong, but it was still there. He thought that if she screamed at him, it would be better, but she would not. She was pleasant and acquiescent. She played the part of the docile wife more today than she ever had, and he thought he knew why.

He believed she was afraid to lose him. Afraid that if she did not act the part of the perfect wife and lady, that he would leave her again for the arms of another woman, and that, he realized, was what was making him feel so guilty. Whether or not he had been responsible for Janice's unwelcome advances, he was the reason for Alex's fear, for her surety that she had to act the malleable wife.

He reached out and slipped his hand through her arm. He hoped, in a way, she would push him away, but she did not. She allowed him to draw her away from the women.

"What is the matter with you?" he asked, more irritated with himself than with her, but when she cringed at his tone, he knew how it seemed.

"I do not think I should go." Her voice was small and timid, and she dropped her head.

He stared at her shocked. "Why? You have always said how much you like horse racing and now you are going to just walk away from an opportunity to see one live."

Her father and his were standing close, and both had jerked their heads up at his words. He cursed himself.

They walked toward them. Thomas wrapped his arm around her shoulders. He placed his hand under her chin and forced her head up. "Sweetheart, what is going on?"

She looked from man to man, but her gaze settled on Marc. Marc was surprised at the look of anger that adorned her beautiful eyes. It pulsated inside them, and he could only stare at her. She was angry with him, after all, but now he was not sure if that made him feel better or worse. Worse, he was sure, because he saw more than anger, he saw hatred and betrayal. Her voice, though, showed none of the anger and pain that swam in her ice-blue eyes. She stared at him as she spoke. "I do not think I should go."

"You do not want to go?" her father asked, pulling her close.

When she looked up at him, she smiled, and Marc noticed that the look she had given him was completely gone. She looked up at her father with a look of warmth and love, and Marc felt a pang of jealousy. He was too angry to even deny it. It was jealousy because he wanted her to look at him like that.

"It is not a matter of what I want or do not want, Papa." She laid her head on his shoulder and closed her eyes. "I just do not feel well."

"Thomas," Maxwell said gently.

When Marc looked up at him, he was startled to see his father staring deeply at him.

"I think we should leave them alone for a moment." Maxwell reached across and pulled gently on Thomas's arm.

Alex opened her eyes and looked up at her father. She stood on tip toe and kissed his cheek gently. "I am sorry for everything, Papa." Her voice was so sincere and pained that Marc felt tears lump up in his throat.

When Thomas spoke, Marc knew he was not the only one touched. "I love you, my girl." Thomas's voice was tight and thick. He hugged her tightly and allowed Maxwell to lead him away.

Marc took a deep breath and swallowed hard. "Talk to me."

She looked at him, the look of pain still there, but the anger and hatred seemed to be controlled. Now that he had seen it, he was surprised he had not noticed it before. Once it was seen, it seemed impossible not to see.

"I have not known how to tell Mother and the others. They are so excited." She took a deep breath, and Marc forced himself to wait. "I sent a message for Lady Pettlenoster, and she should be sending a carriage for me soon. I will take tea with her this afternoon. It will keep me occupied while all of you are at the races."

"Alex," he started, but she held up her hand.

"My mind is made up on this, and I will not be swayed." She shook her head, the anger in her eyes growing again.

He opened his mouth to dissuade her again, but Stuart stepped into the room and cleared his throat. Marc's heart sank.

"My lady," Stuart said looking directly at Alex. "Lady Pettlenoster has sent her carriage for you. He awaits you out front."

The murmuring roar sweeping through the women made him cringe. Alex rushed toward them and made some explanation that Marc could not hear, and then she rushed from the room without a glance in his direction.

The women all stood, shaking their heads at her pitifully but, within moments, Stuart Rodgers was back in the room. He smiled. "Your carriages await."

Chapter 24

Alex sat silently beside Rachel Pettlenoster feeling every jolt as the carriage rocked across the rough cobblestones of Piccadilly Street. She could see the crowded streets out the window of the as they rocked their way toward Hyde Park.

They made their way through the streams of horses and carriages, the streets packed with people on their way to watch the last race of the season. Her big race.

The crowds thinned as they made their way down Rotten Row and disappeared completely as they entered the circle of old elms at the rear of the park.

In the thick trees would be a dark black carriage and, in its driver's seat, would be an impatient Tess. Alex could almost see him tapping his fingers against the seat beside him.

A soft touch to the hand drew her away from her musings. She turned toward Rachel with a weak and trembling smile.

"You sure about this?" The look of sympathy on Rachel's face hit Alex hard.

The worry that had been poking at her all day suddenly jabbed deep into her heart. Tears clogged in her throat and she did not trust herself to speak, all she could do was shake her head.

Rachel Pettlenoster patted her hand and smiled widely, but a little shakily. "It is not too late to change your mind."

Alex almost laughed. It was Rachel who had talked her into it, and now she looked as nervous as Alex felt inside.

Well, she told herself, *she did not actually talk me into anything. She just gave me advice, and it was my decision to take it or not.* She shook her head once again. The carriage pulled to a stop, and Alex held her breath. They were close to her carriage and the awaiting Tess. If the driver saw anyone taking notice of them, or anyone who might, then he would drive on.

The carriage started rolling again, but slowly and Alex was sure the coast was clear. Within moments her thoughts were confirmed as the carriage stopped again. It rocked to the side and then jolted back when the driver dropped to the ground.

Alex began to tremble and held her breath. A slight sweat broke out on the small of her back, and a thin rivulet tickled her as it slid down beneath her tight jockey pants. The changing of the carriages was always nerve wracking for her, at any point, any one could come around the bend or through the trees and spot the two carriages together.

She gave a short bark of laughter.

Rachel looked at her with wide eyes. "What is so funny, my dear?"

"I am concerned about someone seeing your carriage next to A.H.'s, but I suppose here in a little bit it will no longer matter." She shook her head and gripped Rachel's hand. "I am not sure about this, and I am scared as Hell, but I do know one thing." She released her hand and slid toward the door.

It opened and the door across from it opened to making a small hall in between two. She slid out and dropped onto the ground, her shiny black boots thumping into the grass. She turned back and smiled at her longtime friend.

"I know," Alex said calmly, "that I cannot go on with the lie, and I do not want to be anyone but me."

Rachel smiled. "Win big tonight."

Alex had invited Rachel to watch as well, but she had declined, saying she would be a nervous wreck the whole time, but she had kissed her gently on the cheek and wished her luck.

Luck, that she needed. Not in winning, but in not cowering out.

Alex found it easier to go to the races, knowing when it was all over she would still be anonymous. Now with the looming knowledge that everyone would know who she was pushed at her nerves. She was more nervous now than she ever had been before, with perhaps the exception of her first race. Before that one, she had thrown up.

She closed her eyes as the carriage began to roll forward. Her stomach rolled with it and she hoped she would hold down what little Lady Pettlenoster had forced upon her at the lunch table.

Alex rode with her eyes closed and tried to force all thoughts from her head. She must have dozed because it seemed like only moments had passed before the sounds of the crowd broke into the peaceful silence she had made for herself. She could hear the roar for several minutes before Tess finally pulled the conveyance to a stop.

Alex took several deep cleansing breaths while she waited for the door to open.

The first thing she saw was Tess's smiling face and she relaxed. She knew that, no matter what happened, she had friends around her who would love her.

When he stepped back, she jumped to the ground with her head held high. She looked over to the crowd and caught sight of her families. She smiled. Her mother looked excited to see the carriage pull up and all the ladies were pointing at her.

She waved.

She glanced around and saw many faces gazing curiously between her and the family, but she ignored them. She glanced back at the stands and caught sight of Marc staring intently at her.

His gaze was like a touch. It made her shiver. It was almost as if he could see right through her and already knew her secret.

She looked quietly toward the race track.

Reed was first, but Raymond was holding a close second and seemed to be gaining. She scowled, the excitement of the race not touching her as it normally did.

Robert shook her arm. She turned and was surprised to see the concern on his face. He raised his brow questioningly and opened his mouth, but she just shook her head.

"I am fine, just a little rattled today," she said and took a deep breath. She looked toward the horses of the first race. Raymond was edging his way to the front.

"Nervous about the big unveiling?" he asked.

"No," she said, looking at him with a grin. "I am terrified, but I guess I better get on a horse and get to it."

He nodded and patted her shoulder. "Nyssa is saddled and ready."

She looked toward the stands again and sighed. Her gaze was drawn by Edward as he made his way through the stands and took his seat.

He nodded to her and she returned the nod.

She saw Marc turn and look at Edward with a deadly scowl and she shuddered. Her chest tightened and guilt swirled through her. She was going to hurt Marc—she took a deep breath and shook her head.

Images of him in the arms of Janice Rutmeyer raced through her mind and steeled her heart.

She straightened her shoulders and tightened her resolve. She waited until Marc turned back to her and then she calmly and deliberately turned her back to him.

She watched Reeves Dalton lead Becca, Alex's long-legged gray mare from the stables. He turned and gave her a wide smile.

This was his first race, but Becca was a good enough racer that she could almost run the race herself.

Alex took steadying breaths and made her way to her mount. She gave her a sugar cube and ran her fingers through her long mane, pulling small tangles out and running her hand along her graceful neck.

Nyssa was one of her best mares and Alex planned on winning big. She had considered losing the first races on purpose to drop her odds, but she was not going to throw a race just to rile Danton. If she was going to make herself known to the world it had better be after some spectacular wins. She had picked her best horses for these races and prayed that all went smooth.

She closed her eyes and took several deep breaths. She was wound too tight, there was too much riding on these wins. She was trembling with nerves and could not focus on this ride, all she could picture was turning to the crowd and pulling off her helmet as she walked toward her family. Toward Marc.

Nyssa, feeling the tension in her rider, fidgeted nervously and pawed at the ground. She tossed her head with wide eyes and skittered. Alex could feel the muscles bunching in her long neck and her low nicker penetrated Alex's troubled thoughts.

The thick smells of horse and leather, the crisp wind that ran across them and the thrumming excitement of the crowd were finally seeping in. All of Alex's troubles seemed to fade from her mind like the morning wisps of fog dissipating with the warmth of the sun.

Her body relaxed, she smiled and opened her eyes. She wrapped her arm around the horse's trembling neck and leaned her helmeted head against her temple. She could feel the horse begin to relax.

She turned her attentions back to the race in time to see Raymond nose toward first, but Reed spurred his horse forward and kept his lead. Reed crossed the finish line with barely a necks lead.

Pride swelled within her. Second was something to be proud of, especially since Raymond was new to jockeying.

She turned toward Nyssa and patted her companionably. Robert moved beside her and held his hands out for her booted foot. She allowed him to boost her onto the slick saddle and her heart began to race.

She didn't even look at him as he guided her feet into the high stirrup. Adrenaline thrummed through her veins, and she could feel Nyssa begin to fidget beneath her, but this was not nervousness, this was excitement.

Raymond rode toward her with an ecstatic expression and she could feel her face smile back at him, but her mind barely registered it. It pushed at her, rushing her. *Hurry, hurry, hurry*, it said.

With nothing in her mind, but a steady and all-encompassing buzz of exhilaration, she leaned against Nyssa's neck and urged her forward. The soft dusty smell of her mane tickled at Alex's nose and the power between her thighs filled her. She had a fleeting question run through her mind—how could she ever have thought of giving it up?—and then that too was gone.

Reed watched A.H. as he rode past him. He tried to peer under his helmet to get a good look at his face but as usual A.H. kept his head down. He gave a soft snort, he supposed it was pointless now to try and guess who the man was, for by the end of the rematch all would know the small man's identity.

Reed watched as the racers took their places on the line and awaited the sound of the gun that would signal the beginning of the race. He waited impatiently and the secretive jockey took his place in line. A.H. was too easy on his horses in Reed's opinion. He was weak. Reed hated to lose to him for that very reason. He snarled at the racers. In almost every past race, he had been pitted against A.H. because it had encouraged higher betting. He had been momentarily surprised when he had seen the score card and found that they had no races together.

Then he had realized why. He was sure that the officials had purposefully put him and A.H. in separate races to build up the suspense of the rematch race at the end. He could just imagine the betting amounts this night.

If all went well after tonight, he would be a very rich man. He sighed. If all went well. If not, he would end up in Newgate or dangling from the end of a rope.

He groaned, shut his eyes, and leaned against the stables. He could hear the cheers of the crowd and the rustling of the horses and men around him. The sun warmed his upturned face and he took several deep breaths and let his mind wander. It seemed like only moments before he heard the horn blare at the end of the race. He opened his eyes to see A.H. in first place, and he had won by at least two horse lengths. Reed snorted in disgust. Reed mounted his horse and kicked it forcibly in the sides. It jerked forward. He wrenched on the reins yanking the horse around and took his place.

His mind whirled with plans and his heart raced. He knew what would happen if he were caught again, and he had no intention of being caught.

He grinned as the gun shot rang out and the horses burst forward.

The races went smoothly, and the crowd, while excited for each race, seemed to be thrumming with cords of anticipation and each race brought them to a more fevered pitch. The betting for the last race got more extravagant with each win of either A.H. or Reed.

Excitement gripped Alex as the announcer's words echoed across the field to announce the final race before the rematch of Reed and AH. "Get your final bets in now," his voice boomed.

Alex started to glance toward Marc and stopped herself. She took a deep breath and fought the urge. It was almost time, and she needed nothing to distract her. She allowed her gaze to drift around the other racers, but was cut short when she came across the hateful eyes of Reed staring straight at her. She shivered and looked away.

Reed took a deep breath and looked back to the line of horses waiting for the signal to start the race. Jonas Brecken, a short dark-haired man who had worked with Reed in his past criminal activities, caught his eye and gave a slight nod. Good, Reed thought with a widening grin, all was going as planned. The small amount of money promised for a small distraction was well worth it, and Jonas would not disappoint him.

The loud report of the pistol startled the horses and they were off. Jonas kicked the sides of his small dun mare and lashed across her flanks with his riding crop. She tossed her head and screamed, but was soon side by side with Raymond's leggy palfrey.

Jonas lashed out with the riding crop once more, this time catching the small palfrey in his wide swing.

Raymond's horse jerked to the side with a stumble, losing her pacing and falling behind. Raymond leaned closer to her neck and urged her forward. She passed Jonas, who had slowed his horse imperceptibly to wait for Raymond to catch up.

Raymond gave wide berth to the small dun, but Jonas pushed her into Raymond's mare.

Jonas leaned over, nearly off his saddle, and threw his elbow toward Raymond's face. Raymond jerked back barely avoiding the blow. Both horses stumbled, other horses colliding into them.

Raymond and Jonas slammed into the ground.

Jonas swung his crop at Raymond. Raymond threw his fist.

A.H., Robert, and Tess all rushed forward. Reed grinned and turned toward the now empty stable.

In the cool dark room, Reed went to his stable. From beneath the hay, he pulled the hidden girth, the new one with the old fastener. Rushing to the large black stallion, already saddled for the next race, he reached for the girth. The horse sidestepped and snapped at him. Reed ignored him and quickly unfastened the girth. He replaced it with the new one, was on his horse, and out into the bright sun, as the two fighting men were broken up.

Reed nudged his horse into the waiting area and looked toward the stable. Tess was just disappearing into the darkness. Reed gritted his teeth and waited.

Tess returned with A.H.'s mount and Reed tensed. Tess stopped and tugged on the girth. Reed held his breath. Tess gave the horse a light pat and helped A.H. mount. The jockey reined the horse toward the starting line and Reed relaxed.

ↄ⁊ↄ

"Bloody Hell, is it always like that?" Amber asked in a rush.

Marc turned to her in surprise. She stood with her hands over her chest, as though trying to keep her heart contained. He smiled. "Not usually."

"If that does not push the betting, nothing will," Jeremy said, a large grin spreading across his face as he looked out across the now calming jockeys and trainers.

Marc watched Reed sneer at A.H. as they took their places at the starting line and shook his head. "The runners are working hard keeping up with the bets." He turned his attention back to the by-standers and watched the young men in white coats run from person to person as, one after another, hands from all different sections of the stands began to wave them down. "This will be a big race, no matter who wins."

Ashlee suddenly wrapped her arms around his and laid her head against him. "Is…A.H. going to be all right? I did not think the races were this violent."

Marc smiled down at her and kissed the top of her head. "He will be fine. That is something that almost never happens. I am sure it is because there is so much stress swirling around this rematch. Tensions are high."

"Raven Blood, not the mount I would have chosen," Maxwell said.

Marc looked back to the racers and realized for the first time that it was indeed the stallion that Alex had won in the back room of Rose Hall. "He is a good racer, he has made well on his other races." He turned back to his father. "I think I might place my money on him."

Thomas shook his head. "Normally, I would agree, but A.H. himself seems jumpy. I think on this one I agree with Maxwell. He is a good racer, but he is inexperienced. I would have chosen one with a known track record."

"Does it make a big difference with the racers?" Amber asked, leaning heavily against Blake to get a better look at the starting line.

The horses snickered and blew, tossing their heads with nervous anticipation, and Jeremy turned to his sister with a gleeful smile. "It makes a huge difference. Look closely at the horses." He pointed from one to the other. "See Reed's mount..." He consulted the schedule. "...Ashby. See how Ashby stands mostly calm, his ears perked forward and his eyes black all the way around. A few snorts, but that is all."

"Yes, he looks excited to run," Amber said.

"Indeed, now look at A.H.'s mount," Blake said. "What do you see?"

She peered closely at the other horse, her brow furrowed in concentration. "His ears are laid back," she finally said, "and there is a lot of white showing around his eyes," Amber said.

"Good, and?" Thomas asked.

"He is stamping the ground and throwing his head," Catherine added. "Not remaining in one spot."

"He is also all shiny," Amber said. "At least I think he is?" She looked to her husband for confirmation.

He smiled and nodded. "He is. Raven glistens because he is nervous, he is starting to sweat. He is excited, but he is also scared. He is a good racer, but with the excitement of the spectators, the other horses, and all the noise, it is hard for a horse who is not accustomed to it. It is easier to get distracted and lose his rhythm."

"Just like in a dance?" Amber asked, looking up at her husband with a warm glow in her eyes.

He leaned down and kissed the tip of her nose. "Correct, if a dancer loses the rhythm, then the dance is lost."

"My lords, may I take your bets." All attention was momentarily drawn to the tall, gangly red-headed boy as one by one they placed their bets on A.H.

Marc turned back to the starting line. A.H. was looking around but seemed to be purposely looking everywhere but at Marc. It was disconcerting. It was the first race that A.H. had not looked at him at all. Marc shook his head at his own silliness. He had been irritated that the way the little man had searched him out in the beginning, and now he missed it.

A.H. tugged the reins and took his position. The announcer's voice boomed across the sea of people calling an end to the betting, and all eyes were on the racers.

Reed took his spot, twisting the horse at the last moment so that he slammed into Raven. A.H. didn't even look at him. The horses snorted and dug at the ground, and both riders worked the reins to keep the excited horses in place.

Marc could almost feel the tension coiling through the jockey, the horse jittering beneath him in response. A.H. glanced toward Marc, but his gaze did not linger. Marc wondered why his attitude toward him seemed to have changed. It was silly, Marc knew, but it seemed as though the man was displeased with him. He had never even spoken to the man, not officially anyway. He could not fathom why he would be angry, but it was obvious he was.

The horses tossed their heads, snorting and pawing at the ground, gathering beneath the riders, impatient to be off. The shot rang out, the horses leapt forward, and the screams of the crowd drowned out the rest of Marc's thoughts. Beside him the women were jumping up and down and yelling, the men were cheering with an enthusiasm to rival anything Marc had ever heard.

A.H. shook the reins, Raven lengthened his stride, and A.H. leaned low over the long neck of the massive black stallion. The jockey was stiff, his movements jerky. It was so different from his usually fluid grace that Marc was surprised.

Reed drove the riding whip hard across his horse's flank and kicked him in the side. Ashby laid his ears back but put on a burst of speed coming alongside Raven and, for a moment, passing him. The crowd screamed.

The horses pounded along the track, tearing great gouges of dirt and grass from the earth and leaving a swirling cloud of dust and grit trailing behind them.

Raven pulled ahead, but Ashby, with a sharp blow to his flank as encouragement, retook the lead. The horses strained at the reins and pulled at bits, blowing and snorting as the riders pushed them hard.

Glistening muscles bunched and quivered as the horses thundered across the track. Tension swirled through the crowd, weaving around them, whispering to them and driving them to an even greater frenzy.

The horses nipped at each other, both stretching their necks to overtake the other. A.H. urged Raven Blood toward the rail, hugging it in a tight turn to gain the advantage. He leaned low, his head nearly at the horse's shoulder.

Reed swung his crop once again and yanked the reins hard as the horse leapt forward. Ashby slammed into the side of Raven, and both horses stumbled. They scrambled to keep their balance and managed to keep their feet beneath them.

Raven Blood kicked out at the offending horse and lost ground. Reed, instead of taking advantage of the moment seemed to slow. Once again the horses collided and Raven gave a short jump and tried to buck. They slid across the railing, but A.H. had been prepared.

A.H. had swung his leg over the horses back and balanced precariously on one leg allowed the saddle to take the brunt of the force from the railing. There was a rending sound, and the girth of A.H.'s saddle tore, unfortunately not completely. It held on by a small fraying section of leather. The jockey fell as the horses were coming into the home stretch.

The crowd surged forward screaming. Many had pushed their way past the rail and were almost onto the track.

A.H. screamed as he hit the ground, but to Marc's horror, he did not fall free. His foot caught in the stirrup, and he bounced on the ground fighting to get free. The girth slipped farther, the saddle askew. The stallion bucked and twisted, racing across the grass trying desperately to get away from the pursuing havoc. A strong hoof caught the dangling rider several times, his struggles ceased, and he was dragged like a child's plaything behind the terrified horse.

The girth, with one final rip, fell free. The stallion gave a sharp kick, freeing himself from the saddle and catching A.H. in the side, before racing on down the track. The limp jockey rolled several times before coming to a stop, facedown, before the biggest part of the bystanders.

Marc suddenly felt hard hands shove him from behind. He turned to see the horrified look on Edward's face. Flanked by the men from Rose Hall, Edward gave him another shove, this time adding his forceful assault to Thomas.

"Go now. We have to get there before the crowd does. This is not how it is supposed to happen." Another hard shove got the shocked men moving. "Go."

Marc and Thomas raced to the fallen jockey, followed closely by Blake, Maxwell, Jeremy, Edward, Gideon, and Spencer. Tess was to him first pulling the saddle from him and covering his small body from the swarming crowd.

Marc, concerned for the safety of the ladies they had just abandoned, turned in time to see Michael Cranston, Porter Farthing, and Edward's two body guards Finch and Brandon circle the women and start leading them away from the melee. He relaxed and turned his attention to the mob before them.

Tess had been joined by Robert and Raymond and they were doing well to keep the jockey hidden, but they were losing ground. Marc rushed to his side along with Thomas and Edward.

Edward gave the Tess a push. "Get these people back. We can do this."

Tess's concerned look turned to a scowl, and Marc sent a quick prayer up for the safety of the offending people who were now crowding close.

Edward then turned to Robert. "Get the carriage. Bring it right into the middle of them."

Without hesitation, Robert was off.

Marc moved to pull the helmet free, but Edward stayed his hand. "Not yet. Wait until you are in the carriage."

Marc scowled, but it was only a few moments before the rattle of the carriage drove the people away.

Encircled by the men of Rose Hall, Marc and Thomas lifted the slight frame into the carriage. Marc climbed in, and Edward held out his hand assisting Thomas into the carriage as well. Thomas looked at him questioningly.

"Go. I will come as soon as I can." Then he slammed the door, and Marc heard him call to the driver, "Take them to Hollister House as quickly as possible."

The carriage jerked and the outraged protests of the crowd faded into nothing.

Thomas unstrapped the helmet and pulled it off. Wiping mud and grass away, he gasped.

"Alex," Marc cried. He dropped to his knees on the bottom of the carriage and shook her gently. No response. "Alex...baby." Still nothing. He looked over his shoulder at her father. "I do not understand."

"We will get her home and go from there. It is all we can do."

They both looked down at the small girl they were both so protective of and wondered how they had missed who she had really become.

Chapter 25

Alex awoke in the soft, comforting warmth of her own bed. She could hear voices in the room and, unwilling to face them, she kept her eyes closed. The voices were blurred into an unintelligible rumble that was lost in the whirring buzz of pain that filled her head. The pain, thankfully, was not sharp, it was dull and muted. She assumed someone had given her something, which was good, but it was affecting her thoughts.

She struggled to remember what had happened. She could see herself falling from the horse, but could not remember anything after that. She wondered who had brought her here, what had happened at the racetrack, and if everyone now knew. This was not how she had wanted to come out to the ton, not in a crumpled heap at the bottom of a horse. That would be great for her reputation as a horsewoman. With a sinking feeling of horror, she groaned.

"Alex?" She could hear the concern in Marc's voice and clinched her eyes shut. "Alex, are you awake?"

"No." Her voice was tight, and a burst of fire filled her throat. She coughed, felt herself lifted by the shoulders and then the cool relief of water was pressed to her lips. She opened her eyes and drank the small sips Marc allowed her. She smiled.

Looking around the room, she saw her father standing close to the bed, with a look of worry and concern, but not anger. She wondered again who had brought her here. She wanted to know, but she was afraid to ask. If they didn't know, she did not want this to be how they found out.

"Are you all right?" Marc ran his hand across her face. "You have been out for over an hour. The doctor just left, but we can get him back in here now if you need him."

She smiled at him. "I think I am fine. Sore, but fine." Alex wiggled her fingers, toes, arms, and legs to test the honesty of her statement. She realized that she was indeed alive and in one piece and she relaxed. "I am good. Although, a little confused."

"Do you know where you are?" Her father asked taking her hand

and kissing it gently as he knelt beside the bed.

"Do you know who you are?" Marc asked with a nervous smile. She thought it was supposed to be a joke, but she also thought he was truly concerned about it.

Alex smiled and shook her head. "Yes, I know who I am, I also know where I am." She turned her attention to her father. "I am just not sure what happened or how I got here."

Marc sat on the bed beside her. Pain warmed her from her hips to her neck, and the right side of her body felt as though it had been rubbed raw. She had a flash of being dragged and was grateful that short image was all she could remember.

"Well, I can explain that, my dear." He smiled, but it was an angry smile that did not match the softness of his tone. "Your girth broke, and you were dragged halfway down the track behind a massive bucking stallion." His eyes were hard.

She sighed. "So everyone knows."

"No one knows." Her gaze swung to her father, and he smiled. "Well, some of us know, but as for the ton—your secret is still safe."

"Thanks to your lover." Marc pushed himself off the bed and crossed the room. "He literally shoved us down there so we could save you." He kept his back to her and peered out the window. She could see his shoulders shaking. His hands trembled as he pushed the thin curtains aside, throwing light across the room to pierce into Alex's brain with a sharpness that made her cringe.

"I have told you, I do not have any lovers." She struggled to get to a sitting position. Her father was quick to help her. He placed an extra pillow behind her head and back. She sank into the softness with a sigh of relief. "Marc, I do not know why you refuse to believe me, but I am telling you the truth." She glanced up at her father, looking uncomfortable and refusing to make eye contact with her. "This is not the time or the place to discuss this."

"When is a good time to discuss it?" Marc spun on her, keeping his fingers clinched to the drape. "When is a good time for you to explain why it is that that man knew about who you were and what you were doing? Why is it that that man seems to be so close to you?"

"Because he actually listens to me and supports me." Her throat was raw and her shout felt as though it was ripped from her. She began to cough.

"Marc, now is not the time," Thomas said. He waited until Marc had returned to staring out the window before he turned back to Alex. He offered the water once again. This time she was allowed a larger drink. "Right now, all you need to concentrate on is getting well. We will figure all the rest of it out then."

Alex laid her head back on the soft pillow. A small twinge in her neck was all the protest her body gave.

She closed her eyes and tried to relax as he began to explain exactly what had happened. "I can tell you I was surprised, once we had you in the carriage, to find your face beneath all the mud and grass."

Alex opened her eyes and frowned. "I am sorry, Papa. I have tried to tell you many times."

He waved off her apology. "There is no need for sorry, I know you have tried. I have not listened, and I am the one who needs to apologize." He took the spot on the bed that Marc had vacated and pulled her hands into his lap. "I should have listened. You are a strong and determined woman, and you are obviously capable of accomplishing your dreams, even without my help. I should have had more faith in you." He suddenly clutched her hands to his lips and kissed them. "I have just been so scared that something would happen and I would lose you. You are my world, and I do not know what I would do without you."

Alex wrapped her arms around his neck. "Papa, you will never lose me."

He kissed the top of her head. "I hope not, but there are things that you might learn that will make you hate me."

She tried to pull away, to look at his face, but he did not release her. "I could never." Her words were muffled into his chest. He relaxed his grip, and she pulled away. She smiled at him. "Never."

She looked across the room to Marc, still looking out the window.

"He is terrified of losing you as well," her father whispered and glanced behind him. "He is not as angry as he is worried."

"Worried he might be, but he is still angry. He—" Alex's words slipped away as the door opened and Edward stepped into the room.

Marc turned and froze, and her father's grip tightened on her shoulders. Finally, he released her and stood. "Barlow." He gave a small nod of welcome, it was not warm, but Alex was grateful that it was there.

"Hollister." Edward returned the nod, but his smile was warm. "I waited until I knew the doctor was through with his exams, but I could not wait any longer." He turned his attention to Alex. "Are you all right?"

"I am sore but fine. Thank you for keeping me a secret. I know I wanted to do the big reveal today, but this was not how I wanted to do it."

Edward glanced at Thomas and took a hesitant step. Thomas relinquished his spot and nodded once again. Alex could feel the strings of tension swirling throughout the room as Edward stopped beside her bed. He grasped her hand and kissed it gently. "I am happy to hear you are well."

"That is enough," Marc said. He dropped the curtain, and the room was cascaded in muted shadows. He stepped toward them. Thomas caught hold of his arm, but Marc shook him off. "How dare you come here?"

"I needed to make sure she was well." Edward deliberately laid her hand on the bed and gave it a soft pat before he turned to face Marc.

Alex reached for him, too late. He took two steps toward Marc. "I thought we were through with this jealousy. I am only here to check on her, not to cause problems."

"Not to cause problems? You have done nothing but cause problems." Marc's fist clenched, and he took a step closer to him.

"Stop this," Alex said, trying to rise. "Marc, you are being ridiculous."

Thomas moved to her side, pressing her back to the bed. "Stay." He turned back to the men. "Marc, you are overwrought, and now is not the time for this conversation."

"*Now* is never the time. I am tired of the whispers and the rumors. I am tired of being the butt of the jokes." He took another step. "I am tired of so many men sharing the bed of my wife, and I am tired of you, rubbing her infidelity in my face." He shoved his finger into Edward's chest.

Edward scowled and glanced down at the spot Marc had touched. "I am not rubbing anything in your face. I am not her lover, for she has none." He stepped forward, the two men now nearly nose to nose. "I will not stand for you speaking of her in such a way."

Alex tried to rise, but Thomas pressed her back without even turning toward her. "Marc, stop. Now."

"If you are not her lover, explain to me why you are so close to her?" Marc's voice shook.

"She is my friend. It is as simple as that."

"Please stop." Tears stung at her eyes and she could hear them in her voice. All three men ignored her.

"Friend? People do not leave their estates and fortunes to *friends*." Marc shoved him again.

Edward shoved back. Marc threw a punch and then both men hit the ground, throwing punches, kicking and rolling. A small table crashed to the carpet, the white pitcher of water shattered on the floor beside them, soaking them.

Thomas rushed to them, grasping Edward around the shoulders and pulling on him. Edward kept a firm grip on the front of Marc's jacket with one hand and threw a punch with the other. Blood trickled from the corner of Marc's mouth.

"Stop." Thomas pressed his foot into Marc's chest and pulled hard. Marc's fist connected with the side of Edward's face, and Edward lost his grip. Thomas stumbled backward but managed to keep hold of Edward.

Marc jumped to his feet. Thomas shoved Edward behind him, trying to hold him and put his hand on Marc's chest to stop his charge. Marc reached past him from the front and Edward from the back. Thomas ignored the random hits that made their way to him. "Stop, this is—not getting—us anywhere." His words came in heaving gasps.

Alex pushed herself to her feet and teetered. She grasped the smooth posts of her bed to still the spinning nausea that overwhelmed her.

"Just admit you are her lover." Marc's voice was nearly lost in breathless anger. "That is why you are leaving her your estate."

"He is not my lover—he is my father." Her voice, shaking with pain, cut through the chaos.

All three men froze, slowly turning to her.

Thomas was the first to recover from the shock of her words. He rushed to her. "Get back into bed." She shook her head, but he ignored her and pushed her onto the mattress. "Lay."

She did as she was told.

Marc walked to the bed, side by side with Edward. "I do not understand."

He looked from her to the man he thought was her father to Edward and back to her.

Thomas ignored him. She sat back against the pillows, now askew. He fixed them but now seemed to be avoiding touching her or even looking at her.

"Papa." His face nearly fell at the word. Tears glistened, and she was suddenly scared that he would cry. If he did, she would fall apart. She grasped his hand and kissed it. "Sit."

He tried to pull his hand away, but she refused to let him. Finally, he sat, still not looking at her.

"Papa, I am sorry to say it like that. I had hoped you would never find out."

Thomas finally looked at her. "You did not want me to know?"

She shook her head, tears sliding down her cheek.

He reached across and wiped her tear away. "I have been terrified that you would find out."

Marc looked back and forth between them but refrained from interrupting.

Thomas sighed. "How long have you known?"

"You already know?" she asked. Her brow furrowed as she looked at Edward. "Did you know he knew?"

He nodded.

"Why did you not tell me?" she asked.

Edward shrugged. "For the same reason that I did not tell you that you were my daughter. It was not my place."

Thomas glanced at him, and Alex thought she caught gratitude in his look.

"How long have you known?" he asked her again.

She lowered her head and spoke to the bed coverings. "For as long as I can remember. Nurse took me there when I was a baby."

"You told me that before, but I still do not understand why she would—" He scowled at Edward. "Michael Cranston. Alex's nurse had great references from the Cranston family. I did not make the connection even after I knew Michael was spending so much time at Rose Hall. Does every patron of that gaming hell know?" His voice took on a barbed edge.

"No one knows. I asked Michael to speak to his parents about a friend who needed a great nurse, that was all. Over the years, I am sure that the regular patrons of Rose Hall have guessed—Michael, Gideon, Spencer, and Porter. They may have their theories, but they have never asked. "I chose Rhona because she was a good nurse and because I had a relationship with her. She came to see me every day, anyway, and she had brought the children with her sometimes. When she started working with Alex, she began to bring her when she came."

"A good nurse? I do not think a responsible caretaker takes a child to a gaming house," Marc said. All anger seemed to have evaporated.

"Never to the house itself, to my home. It was not until Alex was older that she crept into the backroom, and that was after Rhona was no longer in the picture. Rhona may have put it together and guessed that she was my daughter, though she never outright asked, and I would never have told her."

"Is she the one who told you?" Thomas asked.

Alex shook head. "No, but I had always wondered. I did ask her, but she would not tell me. The only reason I guessed was because I overheard an argument between you and Mama one day that put it all together."

"What argument?"

"You were angry about Edward. Something about her seeing him alone."

Thomas glanced at Edward. "The night I found the two of you at the Roquemore Ball, hidden away in the gardens. She refused to tell me why you two were alone."

Edward seemed to consider the question and then finally nodded. "I suppose she will not be too angry for me telling you in light of everything. She had discovered that Rhona was bringing Alex to me, and she was concerned that it would get out, and someone would discover the truth. She sent me a message, and that was the only reason I had gone to the ball." Edward sat heavily in the seat beside the bed.

"I wondered why you had made an appearance at one of the ton's little fiascoes. Though that does explain why she had decided that Alex was now too big for a nurse, even though she was still young to be without one."

"It made her more comfortable," Edward said.

"It made it more difficult for me, though," Alex said with a nervous chuckle. "It was much harder to get there."

"I was surprised when you showed up after I found out she was let go." Edward smiled. "Happy, but surprised."

Marc wrapped his hand around her foot, running his finger up the arch and smiled at her, but when he spoke it was directed at Edward. "Is that where Robert came in?"

"That made me feel more comfortable. I needed someone I could trust to make sure she was safe, since she refused to not come to the house, even when I told her it was too dangerous."

Thomas laughed. "That probably just made her do it more."

"Of course it did," Marc added.

"I am sitting right here," she protested.

The men looked at her as if they had forgotten she had been there. Thomas took her hands and kissed them. "I have always been terrified that you would find out I was not your true father, and you would no longer love me. That I would lose you."

She shook her head. "I did not want you to find out for two reasons. One, I did not want you to be hurt, or Mama, and two, because I thought that you would not love me anymore if you knew I was not really your daughter." Tears swelled and slipped down her cheeks. "You may not be my father, but you will always be my papa. I love you. I never realized how much you really loved me until now. You knew I was not really yours, but you always treated me like I was."

Thomas pulled her into his arms and hugged her tight. "You have always been my daughter, and I could not love you any more if things had been different."

Edward looked at Marc and could see the pain etched in his features. He reached over and placed his hand on Thomas's shoulder. Thomas looked up. "Perhaps, we should go tell the others that she is doing well." Edward shot a quick glance at Marc.

Thomas glanced behind him and nodded. "Yes, they will be worried." He gave Alex another quick hug and stood. "We will be back up to check on you later."

Edward leaned down and kissed the top of her head. "I love you, my girl, and I am so happy you are all right."

Marc waited until Thomas pulled the door closed behind them before making his way around the bed. Unsure of what to do or say, he only stood there.

Alex took his hand. "Sit." He hesitated and then did as she asked. She ran her finger across his lip, the blood drying in the corner, and frowned. "Are you all right?"

"Yes. It is fine." He closed his eyes and let the sensual smell of lavender and lilac wash over him. He could still smell the faint odors of horse and leather, but he found that only added to her appeal.

"Good, in that case—are you stupid?"

His eyes flew open. "Excuse me?"

"Well, that is the only explanation that I can come up with as to why you would roll around on the floor like a child throwing a tantrum. I cannot even get water to wash your injuries because you broke my pitcher and you are wearing most of the water." She stared at him, awaiting an answer.

He didn't answer. Instead, he smiled. "I was temporarily insane due to an overwhelming concern and the shock of my life." He ran his fingers up her arm and traced the path back down to her wrist. "I am stupid. I know you do not have a lover. I have for a long time, and the night of the ball, where I was rude and definitely stupid, I was trying to get a reaction out of you."

"You were what?"

"I thought I could pull you out of your depression if I made you mad. Then I went to the garden to wait for you. I, unfortunately, got Janice instead. I do not want her, have not wanted her, ever. You are the only irritating woman I want."

She laughed, but it was gone quickly. With a serious tone that, to her disappointment, caused the spark in his eyes to fade, she decided to put it all on the line. "We have to decide now. We either have to start fresh, with trust and openness, or we have to admit defeat."

"I vote for a fresh start." He wrapped his arms around her shoulders and pulled her close. "Hello, my name is Marc." He kissed her softly on the corner of her mouth.

The breath ran from her and she leaned into him. Pressing a kiss against his cheek and then his neck, she spoke in a soft whisper. "Nice to meet you, Marc. My name is Alex."

He traced her lips with his and pressed her tight against him. "No, your name is baby."

Epilogue

The heavy aroma of pine filled the manor. Alex took a long breath and smiled. She looked across the massive ballroom of her parent's country manor, decorated from floor to ceiling with boughs of holly and pine, long silvery stands of tinsel, painted glass balls, and flickering candles, just as it had been every Christmas for as long as she could remember.

She glanced up at the mistletoe hanging from the doorway and started across the glittering room. The floor was cold to her bare feet. She shivered and rushed straight to the tall pine tree that stood in the center of the room like a sentinel. She threw a quick glance over her shoulder and, seeing only the empty room, slipped a large package from beneath her robe.

She sat the package, wrapped carefully in shiny silver paper and covered in golden ribbons and bows, upon the large pile of presents that sat safely beneath the protective watch of the towering pine.

She gave the bow a loving adjustment and grinned in anticipation.

Wishing she had taken a moment to grab her slippers she walked toward the heavy winter drapes. The thick green drapes had replaced the thin blue ones when the weather had turned cold, and the winds had begun to invade the manor through the tall expanse of windows that surrounded the ballroom. That had been right before Alex had moved to Linden Manor with Marc.

She grinned when she thought back to the day she had reminded Marc that A.H. had purchased Linden Manor, and Malacinda was the housekeeper. Alex snorted in her effort not to laugh at the image of his shocked face.

While it had been awkward at first, Marc and Malacinda had been friends much longer than she had been his mistress, and they had quickly fallen into a comfortable and happy household.

Her family had taken longer to get used to the idea. Alex shook her head and admitted that they were still not used to it. Jeremy and her father would come around, Marc's family would as well, but Alex was sure her mother never would.

Alex sent up a small prayer that her mother would not be angry with her for long. Alex had considered giving Malacinda a great reference and sending her to live somewhere else, but she could not bear to do so.

Well, Alex thought, her mother would not have to worry about it much longer. Malacinda was getting ready to leave her anyway. Not long after Alex's accident at the track, she had gone with Marc, with Malacinda in tow, to March's office to discuss the shipping contracts. March had agreed to take control of them, and Malacinda had fallen hard for his young dark-eyed assistant, Randall Breckman. Alex had only met the man on two occasions, and that had always been in the office, but now, every time March came to the house Randall was with him.

Two weeks ago he had asked Malacinda to marry him.

Alex would miss her, but she was very happy for her. She reached for the drapes, wondering if the sun was waking for the day yet.

"Stop." The sharp command stilled her hand. it paused just a whisper away from her goal.

She turned with surprise to see her husband, in his robe as well, heading toward her with her slippers dangling from his fingers and two large throw pillows under his arm.

"What?" she asked without dropping her arm.

He smiled widely. "You are not allowed to look out there."

"We always have the drapes open. It is all shadowy in here, and I cannot see if we got the snow that Rock was predicting. She grinned and touched the curtain.

"Not yet. We will open them soon."

With a slight movement, she gave the curtain a gentle push. The soft reddish light of the waking sun spilled across her bare toes. She grinned but did not look out the crack.

"Hoyden, get over here." He dropped the pillows on the floor and dropped heavily onto one of them. He pulled the other close to him and wiggled her slippers at them. "You can either release the drape and come get you little toes covered or peek out there and risk losing your present."

With a squeal, she dropped it and raced mockingly across the room. "Oh, no, please," she whined, but her smile widened as she dropped on the pillow beside him.

Marc pulled her feet into his lap and rubbed them gently to warm them before sliding her slippers onto them, but did not release them.

She leaned forward, her lips nearly touching his—

"What are you two doing up so early?" Thomas said, laughter in his voice.

Marc cursed softly under his voice and placed a quick kiss on the corner of her lips before she could pull away. Alex smiled at her father and mother as they made their way into the room, large pillows under their arms.

"I had come looking for my wayward wife. I caught her trying to look out the windows." He gestured toward the curtain she had just relinquished.

Jeremy, just having walked in behind his father, shook his head. "Just like her. She has always been bad at trying to peek at things she has no business peeking at."

"I was not peeking at anything…well, the sunrise, but if that is my present, you should have let me look at it, because it will be gone by the time I get to it. And I do not know what you are talking about. I am very patient when it comes to presents."

Blake snorted with laughter. "You are not patient with anything."

Alex looked behind Jeremy to see Blake and Amber, each carrying two pillows. She opened her mouth to argue, but two squealing children pelted around their parents and flung themselves into her lap, cutting of her denials.

Ashlee made her way into the room followed closely by Marc's parents. Everyone began dropping their cushions to the floor and taking their spots.

Everyone was talking at once. It was loud and cheery and infused with laughter. Alex leaned into Marc and kissed the top of Darla's head. Blake Jr. squirmed his way free and began to poke around through the presents.

"I think that means it is time," Jeremy said. "Impatient as his aunt."

Alex glared at him. "Funny."

Thomas and Maxwell, as they did every year, began to rummage through the presents and one by one made a stack beside each person.

Marc wrapped an arm around Alex's shoulders and was in lively conversation with Jeremy when suddenly his voice died. Alex turned to him in surprise.

He had picked up the large silver package with the golden bows.

"Is everything all right?"

He nodded, opened his mouth, but nothing came out. His chest had clinched the moment he had seen Thomas heading toward him with the package. His heart raced, and he turned it in his hands. It was heavy, it was wrapped with expensive paper, and it was very familiar.

Alex repeated her question, but he still could not answer. This was the package he had discovered in the carriage the day they had followed her to the docks. This was the package that had infuriated him into a rage because he had stupidly thought it was for one of her lovers. This was the package he had had to restrain himself from smashing. A package that was obviously for him.

He felt stupid and could feel his face warming up in embarrassment. He could only hope that it did not show. With the concern on Alex's face, he was afraid that it was as red as it felt. He glanced at the others, who held the same look as Alex, and shook his head. "I am fine."

It was custom to wait until everyone had their presents before anyone opened theirs. Blake Jr. and Darla sat in their parent's arms and stared longingly at the ever-growing stack of presents before them. They looked like they were ready to wiggle out of their skin and Marc felt the same. He fingered the ribbon and bow, ran his hand across the cool paper, and found he could not concentrate on the conversations that were going on around him.

Alex pressed herself into him and whispered close to his cheek, "Are you sure you are fine?"

He turned his head and kissed her nose, her cheek, and then her neck.

His breath warmed her neck, sending shivers across her skin as he spoke. His words were quiet, and she leaned closer to catch what he was saying.

"I am stupid. You remember the day we followed you and Pierre to the docks?" A blush touched her cheeks, and she felt his lips brush against her ear when she nodded. "I saw this present and thought it was for one of your..." His words faltered.

She turned so her check lay against his and her lips were close to his ear. "One of my lovers?"

"I wanted to kick it and break whatever was in it." He laughed. "Guess it would have served me right to get a broken present."

She kissed his ear and leaned back to look in his eyes. "I am just glad we figured it out."

He kissed her. "It took us forever, but it was sure fun when I finally got to find out just how wrong I was."

She blushed at his reference to her loss of virginity and shushed him.

"Are you two going to be mushy all night or can we start opening our presents?" Blake asked. Alex ducked her head, but could see Blake Jr. squirming in his arms and reaching for a present.

"Sorry." She turned to Marc and smiled. "Open it."

He ripped the wrapping paper with no regard to the time and effort that had gone into making it perfect. Opening the box, he paused.

"What is it?" Maxwell asked his son.

Marc reached inside and carefully brought out a large glass bottle that lay on its side attached to a balsa wood base. It was a long bottle, round and tall in the middle with a short wide neck. Filling the inside was a Spanish Galleon. The large multi-decked ship was made of dark wood, ornately carved, and showing minute details of ports and cannons.

Marc turned it slowly admiring the craftsmanship and dedicated time that had obviously gone into it. The three tall masts, including a lateen-rigged mizzenmast, stood tall, nearly brushing the top of the bottle. The large curved sails billowed out as if a never-ending wind blew the ship ever onward toward the horizon.

Marc turned with a large smile to his wife. He kissed her soundly and whispered as he pulled away. "Glad I did not kick it." He lay it over to the side and turned back to her.

She laughed and reached for a present of her own.

"Oh, no," Marc said and pushed it out of her reach. "Those can wait."

He jumped to his feet and pulled her along with him. Jeremy and Blake had already risen and were rushing to the spot on the curtains where she had tried to greet the morning.

"What are you up to?" From behind her, she heard footsteps of many people following her.

"You will see," Marc said.

He stopped her a few steps from the hidden windows and nodded. Jeremy and Blake yanked the curtains open, and light flooded the room. Sunlight gleamed on the soft white landscape, glittering off the new snow that had fallen sometime during the night.

She stepped forward, and they pulled the drapes open fully. She stopped, her breath catching in her throat. Tied to the tall oak that decorated the entrance into the garden was the massive chestnut she had been so drawn to at Tattersall's.

He jerked his head at the end of his lead and snorted. He pawed at the snow and blew heavily, steam billowing around his muzzle. He dropped his head to the uncovered grass and began to tear chunks from the frozen ground.

Tears stung Alex's eyes and clogged her throat. She opened her mouth to ask how he had gotten here, but all that came forth was a soft choking sound.

"Well, that was worth all the effort of getting that high-strung creature out to the garden," Jeremy said.

"What was?" Blake asked.

"Something had to finally shut her up," Jeremy said.

That was enough to help Alex get control of her shock. She scowled at him, but could not find any anger within her. She decided to let it go and, instead, turned her full attention to her sneaky husband.

"Where has he been hidden?" Alex asked, glancing back at the feeding horse.

"You brought the horses from Edward's stables and left a lot of empty stalls." He wrapped an arm around her shoulders and pulled her tight against his side. "I saw the way you were looking at him at Tattersall's. I could not resist. I had him hiding in our stables, but I was afraid you would find him. I know how you like to go wandering around the horses, so when I had the chance to move him, I was grateful."

She leaned against him, struggling to keep control of grateful tears. "Thank you."

A deep clearing of a throat drew their attention to the doorway. Rock stood stoically. "I was walking past the door, my lord, and there is a large party here to see you." He bowed low to Catherine, smiled one of his rare smiles, turned, and walked away without giving any indication of who had arrived this early in the morning on Christmas morning.

Thomas turned and started to the door, but before he made it a few feet a loud and laughing parade of people came into the ballroom all bearing armloads of gifts.

Alex glanced at her mother's smiling unsurprised face and realized they were here by invitation. She glanced at her father, and he smiled in wide welcome at the group.

"I am very glad you could make it," Thomas said. "Come in."

Edward bowed low and led the procession. Close behind him came his two bodyguards, Brandon and Finch, their arms fuller than any of the others with presents piled high above their heads.

Next through the door were the men from Rose Hall's back

room; Michael, Porter, Gideon, and Craig Connelly. Malacinda, on the arm of Randall Breckman, her newly betrothed, gave a nervous smile, but to Alex's surprise, Catherine took her arm and led her into the room with a comfortable smile.

Alex grinned. Victoria and Vanessa led in a rambunctious troop of children from the orphanage into the warm ballroom. In the middle of the children, to everyone's surprise, with a child clinging to each hand was Bradley Hamilton. He grinned widely at Ashlee and blushed. "I was in the neighborhood."

Ashlee's face reddened in return. She walked into the group and, picking up one of the children, walked back into the ballroom by his side. The family had been told of their betrothal, and they would announce it formally at the beginning of the season.

The last ones in were Robert, Raymond, and the large Tess. Tess carrying what appeared to be a carriage full of presents. He quickly began handing them out to the children.

Edward grinned at her, handed her a small blue package, and kissed her cheek. "Merry Christmas, my dear girl."

She frowned slightly. "Merry Christmas, but I sent your present on to Rose Hall."

He gestured to the two body guards who were putting presents under the tree. "I brought them. I also brought news." He gestured to Gideon. "Well, I have brought the news bearer."

Gideon kissed her on the cheek in welcome and shook Marc's hand before he spoke to the assembly. "Reed, who has been being held for suspicion in A.H.'s accident during the last race, finally broke down and admitted to his part in the wrongdoing. The surprise came, when he blurted out that Lord Oliver Danton had offered him a healthy payday if A.H. did not survive the race. Danton was arrested and has implicated Janice Rutmeyer in the scheme, as well as at least one other accomplice."

Edward gave a small chuckle. "The Rutmeyer family has disappeared, so it seems his gaming debts will not be paid, and Janice will not be questioned. It is worth it, though, to be rid of them."

Edward glanced across the mass of people and shook his head. "I wanted to ask you something else, but there are more people here than I thought there would be," he said as more of the guests began handing presents to the children.

Alex looked at him and smiled. "Ask away."

He looked considering for a moment and then shrugged and spoke carefully. "You had a surprise for the ton at the end of the season. Is that going to come out next year—since you missed your chance?"

"I would like to know that as well," Marc asked.

She was surprised that he did not seem angry. They had not discussed her plans for racing the next year, but she knew he did not want her to.

"I will support you either way, though it terrifies me, especially after what happened," Marc said.

Alex nearly cried. His support meant more to her than she would ever be able to tell him. She looked around the room at all the curious looks.

"That surprise will not happen. I have another surprise, though," she said. Marc raised a questioning brow. With a glance down, she cradled her stomach. "It would not be safe in my condition."

Edward whooped. Thomas, who had been close to the tree with the children, looked over to the huddled group. Edward looked at him with a wide grin. "You are going to be a grandfather."

Thomas picked up Catherine, spun her around, and kissed her.

Marc beamed, wrapped his arm around Alex, and enveloped her in a tight hug. "I love you."

Alex looked over his shoulder around the ballroom, filled with more people than it had ever seen for Christmas, crumpled and torn wrapping paper was piling up, and the laughing excitement of children echoed off the tall ceilings.

She had dreamed of how great her life would be, how happy she would end up when she came out to the ton, and everyone admired her for her bravery and talent as a business woman. She had dreamed of being rich and famous, of being envied and desired.

Her life had not turned out that way. No one, outside the family, knew who the jockey was. No one envied her, she was not famous, the ton was not vying for her knowledge in horseflesh, and no one was talking about her courage for standing up to society rules.

She looked at the people she loved and smiled, tears stung at her eyes. For all she had lost, she had gained so much more. She was happier than she had ever imagined was possible, and she would not change a thing.

About the Author

Dawn Chandler was born in Coffeyville, Kansas, but doesn't remember much about it. Though she recently had the opportunity to visit there with her husband, and she very much enjoyed the Dalton Museum, she always thought she should have been born in the Wild West. She moved to Idaho when she was six and grew up on Murtaugh Lake, where her father was the dam keeper and the ditch rider. She spent her days in the lake, swimming, catching fish and tadpoles, from sunup to sundown most days. Not hard to imagine that her first full length novel was about a mermaid.

At night, she would spend her time watching football with her dad or cooking with her mom. In eighth grade, she had a teacher, Mrs. Smith, who wanted her to publish one of her short stories. Looking back on it, she says she should have done so. If she had, she would have been an author before now, but she was not ready to be published back then. When she first started writing in school, she hated it. She had to write their way and only their way—in the correct process, outline, rough draft, and so on. Chandler has learned in the progressing years that she is a seat-of-the-pants author, but in the beginning, she just thought that writing was not for her. She could not, no matter how she tried, get the outline done. She could not sit and sketch out a whole story from beginning to end. She found quickly that, if she just sat and wrote, she could get the first draft out without a problem, but the teachers didn't want her to do it that way. She really began to love writing when she met Mrs. Smith, and she told Chandler that she could write it in whichever order she wanted. She understood her as a writer and didn't push her to be something she wasn't. Chandler has been writing ever since.

She is grateful to have the support of her husband and children. Together they have seven, Charles, Cynthia, Kara, Mary, Tina, Pam, and Richie. She loves them all dearly and is happy to have them in her life. Now that her kids are all grown up, she likes to spend time on the semi-truck with my husband, Rod, seeing the country. She loves visiting all the small towns and is grateful to all the nice people she has met. She enjoys swimming, camping, four wheeling with her 4 X 4 group, spending time with family and friends, hiking, writing (of course), drawing, painting, reading—a vastly wide list of authors, her favorite, though, is Stephen King—and she loves taking pictures as she travels the countryside (if she is lucky and they are not in a big hurry and can even stop to take them). Today she is busily writing her novels, *The Dark Lady, The Infamous A.H.*, and about fifty more started in the computer that will be released as time and her muse allows (fingers crossed).